P9-EKC-456

JERICHO

JERICHO

A NOVEL

ALEX GORDON

HARPER Voyager
An Imprint of HarperCollins*Publishers*

JERICHO. Copyright © 2016 by Alex Gordon. All rights reserved. Printed in the United States of America. No part of this book may be used or reproduced in any manner whatsoever without written permission except in the case of brief quotations embodied in critical articles and reviews. For information, address HarperCollins Publishers, 195 Broadway, New York, NY 10007.

HarperCollins books may be purchased for educational, business, or sales promotional use. For information, please e-mail the Special Markets Department at SPsales@harpercollins.com.

FIRST EDITION

Harper Voyager is a federally registered trademark of HarperCollins Publishers.

Designed by Paula Russell Szafranski

Library of Congress Cataloging-in-Publication Data has been applied for.

ISBN 978-0-06-168738-9

16 17 18 19 20   OV/RRD   10 9 8 7 6 5 4 3 2 1

JERICHO

CHAPTER 1

Carmody Peak, Northern Coast Range Oregon

Dead silence.

The words drifted through Dave Garvin's head, a whisper as faint as the breeze. In all his years of roaming the Pacific Northwest, he had never hiked through woods this still, this quiet. No birds flitting overhead. No squirrels or chipmunks darting across his path. No distant rustlings. Just the crunch of his footsteps, and the flicker of his shadow across the narrow trail whenever the late spring sun managed to work its way through the trees.

He stopped and adjusted the straps of his backpack, then untied the bandanna from around his neck and wiped his face. Heat had come early to northwest Oregon, settling over the Northern Coast Range like a wool blanket, thick and smothering. Unfortunately, no rain had hitched along for the ride.

Garvin plucked a browned leaf from an overhanging bigleaf maple branch and crumpled it to powder. *Drought.* It was hard to associate that word with what most folks still thought of as the PacNorWet. But the last few years had been dry, the threat of forest fires rising with the temperature. If he spent the night on the mountain, he would keep his flints and tinder in his backpack. He already risked getting arrested for trespassing. No way did he want to add a charge of arson as well.

He unhooked the water bottle from his belt and drained it, shaking out the last few drops. *I have two more liters in my pack.* But according to the route he'd worked out, he still had at least a ninety-minute hike ahead. At this rate, he would run out of water before he reached Jericho.

Slow down. Nerves—he always drank more when he felt nervous. He dragged off his backpack and stuffed the empty bottle inside, then pulled out a full one and clipped it to his belt. Looked back over his shoulder at the trail, a tunnel of low-hanging branches and hazy air that angled downward so steeply that if he threw a stone, it would fall straight to the base of the mountain.

Garvin removed his GPS unit from the side pocket of his pack. He always checked his location every so often, like most hikers did when they roamed the backcountry. The signal served as your lifeline.

He reached for the power button, then stopped. *Just because there's no fence doesn't mean there's no guards.* That meant no GPS. No phones or tablets, either. Aging golden boy Andrew Carmody seldom visited the family compound on the other side of the mountain, but he kept it staffed year-round with the sort of humorless bastards who handled security for high-profile multimillionaires. That meant scanners, jammers, tracers, and every other sort of electronic tracking device known to man.

Carmody's got his own little kingdom up here. NSA-type stuff. *The best money can buy.*

Then other voices ran through his head. The warnings from friends. That strange things happened at Jericho. That he shouldn't go. But if he did, he shouldn't go alone.

So of course, Garvin had done both.

He once again looked back the way he had come. *Get out of here.* He flinched as his own voice sounded in his head. *No photo's worth it.*

He stuffed the GPS unit back into his pack. "Wanna bet?" After a moment's thought, he pulled out his camera and hung it around his neck, readied it in case he spotted something interesting on the trail. Then he shouldered his gear and continued his climb.

MISPLACES . . . NOPLACES . . . Garvin pondered names for his new website as he trudged. *Abandoned* had already been done to death. *Lost.* He wanted something different, a single word that unsettled, that told the visitor that this wasn't just another display site filled with creepy photographs of unexplored woods and decrepit houses. No, this site would offer things that no one else had, images as disquieting as the name. After so many failures, this site would finally make him some money.

Nowheres . . . Neverwheres . . . Nehalem.

He stopped. *Nehalem.* He knew it was the name of a river, a town, a Native American people indigenous to the region. But it always flipped into *Nephilim* in his head. Something he picked up as a kid, at the Bible study classes his parents had sent him to.

Funny, the things you remembered.

Nephilim. The name cropped up in horror movies and television shows whenever they needed some biblical reference to make it all seem real. "Nephilim." Garvin said the word aloud, then shook his head. Too obscure. Besides, the Nephilim were people—well, sort of, at least—not places.

He took a swig of water, then looked up through the trees to see if he could get a glimpse of the sun. But the sky had hazed over as cooler Pacific air mingled with the mountain heat, dropping the temperature and causing fog to form. He imagined chill mist brushing his sweaty face, sighed, and glanced at his watch. It felt as though only minutes had passed, but he had walked for well over an hour.

I shouldn't have come by myself. His mind wandered when he hiked alone. He should have paid attention to his surroundings instead of thinking about business. If he had, he would have noticed the point at which the woods around him changed, the hemlock and bigleaf maple giving way to towering spruce and fir, the moss now thick beneath his feet. Old growth. Forest primeval.

Gorgeous. Garvin brushed his hand over a spruce bough, then jerked back as something sharp jabbed beneath his fingernail. It felt like an insect sting but proved to be a dried needle, jammed in deep enough to penetrate.

"Dammit." He tried to brush the thing out, but it failed to budge. He had no choice but to take hold of it and pull it out, as blood welled around his cuticle and dripped to the ground. *Fucking needles.* They didn't have to be made of metal to get you.

Garvin licked the wound clean. Then he dug a chocolate bar out of his pack and ate a few squares to get rid of the taste of blood. Took a few deep breaths to settle himself, then wiped his brow with his sleeve. Even with the mist and shade, it felt no cooler, as though the trees trapped the heat and blocked any breeze. His head ached—he blew his nose to try to ease the pounding, then paused as he caught the faint whiff of vanilla.

He checked his camera settings as he hurried up the trail, tweaking and adjusting to compensate for the half-light. Rounded a steep bend, and stopped.

The trail overlooked a small clearing shaded to dusk by low-hanging boughs. Against the darkness, strange plants shimmered, tapered stalks studded along their lengths with inch-long blooms. White as candle wax from top to bottom, from the leafless stems to the small, curled petals. Only the centers of the flowers held any color, tiny daubs of butter-yellow bright as brass against the pale.

Phantom orchids. Garvin had never seen more than a small cluster in one place before, but here they carpeted the ground, hundreds of plants, upright as ghostly tin soldiers, filling the air with a scent like holiday cookies. *Chlorophyll.* They contained none. *Saprophytes.* That meant they lived off decaying matter. But how much rot did it take to feed so many?

Garvin snapped photo after photo as all the old gossip flitted through his head. Fernanda di Montaldo Carmody, wife of Andrew, mother of his teenage daughter. Ex-supermodel, sometime actress, full-time party girl. *Forever corpse?* Last seen arguing with her husband outside a Portland restaurant. Then she drove off in an Italian sports car that cost more than the average house, out of the Pearl District and into oblivion.

Ten years ago this month. Garvin pondered the eerie orchids.

Is this where you buried her, Andy? But even if Carmody had murdered his wife and stuck her here, would enough of her still be around after a decade to feed the flowers?

"Way to get morbid, Dave-O." Garvin took one last shot, then resumed his hike. "Fernanda." The name flowed off the tongue like honey from a spoon. Brazilian by birth, she had been in her mid-twenties at the time of her disappearance, with a face that was the near occasion of sin. Tits like melons. Legs that went on forever, and hip-length hair like an ebony waterfall.

Some guys have all the luck. Garvin looked back at the orchids, and wondered if there were times when that wasn't enough.

HE SAW MORE phantom orchids as he continued his climb, small clusters that marked his way like beacons in the shaded gloom. Sweat runneled into his eyes, stinging, blurring his vision. His wounded finger throbbed, and his feet ached. Just when he thought he had somehow taken the wrong trail and needed to turn back, he spotted the first stumps at the top of a rise, the remains of the trees used in Jericho's construction. Old, they were, grayed and split, the bark long since fallen away.

Garvin stepped off the trail into the knee-high grass and snapped image after image. Then he stopped, sniffed, swallowed hard. A different smell here, one that set the back of his neck to prickling. The tang of meat just gone to rot.

He bent close to one of the stumps and hunted until he found the source. Shelf fungus, jutting from the dead wood, silvery-white as a fish's belly. He ran a finger along the edge of one of the outgrowths, then jerked his hand away, rubbed his fingers over and over on his pants leg to erase the sensation. Spongey slickness, like raw liver, and cool to the touch despite the heat.

He held his breath as he took more pictures. Orange—all the shelf fungus he had ever seen had been orange. *Chicken-of-the-woods.* He had eaten some once on a dare, hacked it up and stewed it. As the name implied, it tasted just like chicken.

This wouldn't. Garvin choked back the acid that rose in his throat and tried not to think how this moist, stinking mess might taste.

He took one last photo, then paused. The camera's soft shutter hiss seemed to echo, as though he stood in a bare-walled room instead of a forest. Then a fly buzzed past, circling his head before zipping away. A beat later, he heard rustlings in the shrubbery.

Garvin looked around, and spotted ferns shuddering some distance down the trail. *Just a critter.* Something small, a squirrel or fox. *Finally.* He felt his shoulders loosen, and realized how much the silence had disturbed him.

He continued his trudge, his new escort following at a distance.

THE SECOND SIGN of Jericho appeared around the next bend, a tumble of old logs and rusty hinges that had once been a gate. A few yards past that, in a clearing at the top of another rise, were the remains of a small shed or guard shack, jutting upward like a broken tooth.

Garvin entered the shack, took a few pictures, then hunted through the weeds that poked up through the floorboards. People often left behind the damnedest things when they abandoned a place—photographs, books, bits of clothing. Not much would have survived the years and the elements and animal predation given that Jericho had been abandoned in the early 1900s. But maybe he would get lucky.

He took it for a shadow at first, the darkness in a far corner of the ruin. Only as he drew closer did the detail emerge. *Feathers.* The remains of a small bird, tufts of white and gray fluff settled in a circle around a pile of bones.

Garvin bent closer, driving away a few flies that had settled. *No, not a pile.* Someone had arranged the bones with care, setting the longest, the wing bones and spine, to form a square. They had then layered the rest according to size from largest to smallest, rib and leg, scapulae and breastbone, then capped the tiny pyramid with the bird's skull. Those empty eye sockets— they stared at him now. The tiny beak gaped wide, like a nestling begging to be fed.

What. The fuck. He touched the feathery circle, then flinched as it tumbled apart and scattered in all directions. The bones still showed pink and red in spots, remnants of ligaments glistening—whatever it was, it sure as hell hadn't been there since the early 1900s. Someone had assembled it more recently.

Garvin brushed the down back into place, then photographed the . . . whatever it was. A shrine? A sacrifice? He then tried to resume his search, but the mound of bones kept drawing him in. He debated burying it, giving the poor bird a proper send-off. But every time he bent down to pick it up, the voice in his head stopped him. And so he backed off, even as he wondered what in hell he had to be afraid of. He had encountered death before during his explorations, stumbled over human remains more than once. There was no earthly reason why something small enough to fit in his hand should bother him like this.

He edged into the doorway of the shack, and once more thought about turning around and taking the long, sweltering hike back to his truck. If he started now, he could make it back to Portland before dark, maybe drag the gang out to dinner.

And pay for it how? Garvin felt the all-too-familiar clench in his gut. That was what this little jaunt was about, after all. A couple of the cable crime shows had scheduled updates about Fernanda Carmody's disappearance over the next several weeks—he could ride the wave, sell weird photos of Jericho to them, or to one of the tabloids.

But timing was everything. He needed to start hawking photos as soon as possible or he would miss the window of opportunity. But if he hit it right? With a little luck, he might even get competing bids. But for that he needed more than photos of a dead bird, no matter how creepy.

Garvin looked everywhere but at the pile of bones. Rechecked the camera settings, made sure the battery still held enough charge. Then, for the first time since childhood, he made the sign of the cross, and resumed his hike up the rise.

Ten paces, and the remains of a half-dozen cabins and a scatter of smaller outbuildings came into view. They formed a rough circle around a large rectangular structure. A meeting-house of some sort, or a dormitory for lumberjacks.

Garvin stared. The other buildings were half-collapsed tumbles of rotted wood but the dormitory still stood intact, the roof in one piece, sunlight shining off window glass. No way had it stood empty for more than a hundred years. *It's been repaired.*

He started down the hill toward it then stopped and reminded himself to use the damn camera. He took shot after shot, adjusting the settings when the windows flashed reflected sun in his face. His headache had vanished. And soon his unpaid bills would do the same. *I've got it now.* Almost all the pieces. The Carmodys' history of scandal and secrecy. The bird shrine. *And now this place.* All he needed was to find one spooky thing inside, a scratched date on a wall or a water stain in the shape of a cross or, oh if it were possible, another bird pyramid.

And if he didn't find one, well, maybe he could make it himself.

In the middle of a shot, Garvin stopped. Lowered his camera. Listened. It sounded louder than it had at any time during his climb, the rustling. But there was something new this time. Clicking, like the rolling of dice or the tap of a keyboard. He turned, saw the shuddering in the bushes at the foot of the rise. His unseen escort.

"Don't worry, little buddy. I'm not interested in you." He smiled. "It's the guy who owns this place who'll have to worry." He hesitated as he considered what steps, legal or otherwise, Andrew Carmody might take after the photos leaked, then shook his head. The guy was a public figure with a sordid past—hell, his daughter had just been released from rehab for what, the third time this year? Whatever happened, Carmody had no one to blame but himself.

Garvin headed down toward the building, then slowed when he saw the steel door, the shiny new knob. *It's probably locked.* He would be lucky if that's all it was. *NSA-type stuff.* As soon as he opened it, some hidden device would transmit a signal back to the house. They would know he was there.

He scanned the clearing. No sign of a road, but Carmody's goons might not need one—a Land Rover or a Jeep would make short work of the underbrush. He hiked through knee-high grass to the far edge of the site, searched for any sign of old tire tracks. Instead he found the rotted remains of railroad ties, a few yards of rusted track. No surprise there—a lot of the old logging sites installed their own railways to transport timber. The important thing was that it couldn't be used now.

He turned and headed back toward the dormitory. Stopped at the door, counted to three, then braced his shoulder against the panel. Grabbed the knob and twisted and pushed—

—and stumbled forward as the door swung open. He held out his arms to break his fall, but his backpack shifted and he tumbled sideways onto his left shoulder, cried out as the pain shot up his arm and across his upper back.

"Fuck fuck fuck." Garvin undid the backpack straps and eased out of the harness, then worked into a sitting position as stars glimmered before his eyes. He gagged, turned his head just as he vomited, missed his camera but nailed his pants leg instead. He shuddered through a bout of dry heaves, then sat slumped and cradled his injured arm to his chest.

Time passed. The pain got no better, but it didn't get worse, either. He maneuvered to his knees, then ever so slowly to his feet. *Dislocation? Separation?* He twitched the arm an inch or so. *Maybe just a sprain?* Except it didn't matter what it was, did it? His mobility had just been shot to hell. Nothing for it but to bind his arm as best he could and head back down the mountain. *Can't afford the ER.* Not that he would go, anyway. *All white coats and needles and blood—* He pushed that thought from his mind.

Garvin waited until the pain settled down to a manageable throb, then rummaged through his pack for the extra bandannas he always carried, tied them together with his good hand and his teeth, then looped them around his neck to form a makeshift sling. He found that if he moved slowly, he could still use the arm. If he lifted the camera just right, he could snap photos one-handed.

He took deep, slow breaths to steady himself as he scanned the room for something, anything, that would make this disaster worthwhile. It looked a large space, maybe ten feet by thirty, with a low, beamed ceiling and plank floor and windows on three sides. Walls of rough tongue-in-groove. No furniture, no sinister altars or statues. No lighting of any sort. Just a shell.

He edged along the wall to the far end, which was windowless and cast in shadow, saw nothing until he stood in the darkness himself. Only then did he spot the small pile in the near corner.

"Bingo." Garvin adjusted his camera and headed toward the arrangement of bones. Then he stopped, straightening so quickly that his shoulder cramped. Took a step back, and studied the floor. One section appeared lighter than the rest, faded by sun and age.

But that fade line is pretty damn straight. Garvin bent as low as he dared, brushed his hand across the floor until he felt it. A narrow groove, almost invisible to the eye, engineered to blend with the edges of the boards.

It's a fucking trapdoor. He brought up the camera with a shaking hand. One photo, another, the light of the flash bringing the difference between the color of the door and the rest of the flooring into sharper relief.

Garvin's heart stuttered, then pounded, as adrenaline kicked in. The pain in his shoulder eased. His mind raced. He had to get that door open. He hoped like hell that there were steps or a ladder leading down to whatever lay beneath, but he knew that he would leap into the darkness if he had to.

What's down there? He swallowed hard. *Who's down there?* An image flashed in his mind. A heartbreaking face, half-hidden behind a wave of ebony hair.

Garvin stepped around the trapdoor, searched for a latch or handle. Then he paused. Raised his head and sniffed. His senses were on the alert now—he picked up smells that he had missed before. The herbal sharpness of incense. The rank saltiness of sweat.

Then he heard it. The clicking, growing louder, getting closer.

You should have run when you had the chance, Dave-O.

Garvin tensed. It was the voice in his head again, yes.

You should have paid attention to your surroundings.

Except that it wasn't his own voice.

He turned toward the door just as it swung closed. Heard the dead bolt slide into place.

You never pay attention.

Shadows flitted across the floorboards, converging in the middle of the room. Like steam escaping through cracks in a pipe, darkness streamed out from between the planks, tumbling into round shapes that massed around Garvin.

Then the shapes formed hands that scrabbled at his clothes and pinched his skin. Nails scratched, leaving bloody, burning tracks in their wake, like wasps stinging over and over.

13

Garvin tried to run, but pain knifed through him and he stumbled. He swung his backpack at the things, but the weight knocked him off-balance and he careened into them instead. Arms wrapped around him, squeezing the air from his lungs, crushing and twisting his injured shoulder. Faces pressed close, black and bristly with eyes like a thousand mirrors and round mouths rimmed with teeth.

Then came the buzzing. It filled his ears and rattled his bones until his whole body vibrated.

Blackness closed in. The roar in his ears drowned out his cries. The stench enveloped him, filled his nose and flowed into his mouth and down his throat, thick as syrup, as the room spun faster and faster and the walls curved and the floor opened and narrowed into a tunnel that led down, down, down into the dark.

A white-clad arm reached out to him.

"Don't fight it, Mr. Garvin. It will all be over soon." A beat of silence. "Blood, is it?"

And that last word, that clawed his ears, and drew one last, silent scream.

"Needles?"

CHAPTER 2

Gideon, Illinois

L auren Reardon loaded the last box onto the flatbed of the pickup truck, then closed the tailgate, shaking it to make sure that the latch caught. Kept her eyes fixed on the gray plastic trim, the spots of rust that marred the white-painted metal, the gouges and the dents.

But no matter how she tried to distract herself, she still heard it. A distant gibber, like radio station interference, a program in some unknown language. She tried to block the sounds by thinking of something pleasant, a memory from her youth. Lying in the backseat of the old Forester, her father driving and her mother wrestling with a paper map. Late at night, returning home from a day trip to Portland or Vancouver, British Columbia, her father scanning stations in search of his favorite classic rock. That AM-radio crackle and wobble.

It worked, for a little while. Then the muttering worked its way back, as it always did.

"Mistress Mullin?" A few seconds, then a hesitant throat-clearing. "Mistress?"

Lauren turned. "Sorry, Fred." She forced a smile. "You'd think that after six months, I'd be used to the Mullin part." But she doubted she ever would. Reardon was still her legal name, and so it would remain. To change it would open the door to questions about her father's past, about what drove him to leave behind his life as Matthew Mullin of Gideon, Illinois, to become John Reardon of Seattle, Washington. No. That can of worms needed to remain well-sealed.

She looked up to find Fred Parkinson nodding as though he read her thoughts.

"You didn't need to help us pack." He stood head and shoulders above her, a bear of a man in a faded Harley-Davidson T-shirt and cargo shorts. "I know you must have more important things to do now."

"I'm glad to help." Lauren rubbed a dirt smudge from her hand. *Not as if I have any other job.* She thought of the thick envelope from Billings-Abernathy waiting for her in her room back at the Waycross place, the release she still needed to sign, the forms for where to send the balance of her retirement account and her personal effects. The myriad pieces of paper that marked the end of a career.

"I wanted to talk to you before we left." Parkinson stood up straighter. "I just wanted to say—"

"It's all right."

"—that we wouldn't be going if we didn't have to." He pointed at the other houses on the dead-end street, half of which stood vacant, FOR SALE signs fading in the sun. "But there ain't nothing here. I mean, there's the hardware store, and the diner, and Rocky's taken over Lolly's garage and wants to start fixing tractors and stuff." He shook his head. "But it ain't enough."

Lauren nodded. She had heard the same thing from others these past months. *How many does it make?* Fourteen families? *Fifteen, now.* At this rate, Gideon would be a ghost town by the end of the year. In every sense of the word. "You're headed down to Bloomington."

"Yes, Mistress." Parkinson jerked his chin toward his house, a yellow split-level, now with its own FOR SALE sign centered on the lawn. "Rayanne's folks are from there. Her uncle owns a machine shop, had an opening for a setup man."

Lauren turned to see Rayanne Parkinson in the front window, watching them, a lanky former biker chick with a toddler in her arms and two older children pressed close, one on either side. "Well, I want you to know that there's a place for you here if you ever decide to come back."

"Yes, Mistress. Thank you, Mistress." Parkinson started to back away. Then he stopped, and stuck out his hand. "Never thanked you for all you've done for us, this past winter and everything since."

"You're welcome." Lauren hesitated, then held out her hand. Felt the man's rough, calloused grip and through it the static electric shocks of his embarrassment and nerves and anger—

—*keeping the kids inside—it's an insult—Mistress Mullin saved our lives but Rayanne thinks the magic will rub off on them and then we'll have to stay*—

—and slowly extricated herself, biting her tongue to keep from blurting out that she understood, that it was all right. Everyone in Gideon knew that she could sense strong emotion with a touch, that she could hear thoughts and memories that were most definitely none of her business. So she simply nodded and watched Parkinson's shoulders sag in relief, and let him think he had escaped with his privacy intact.

Then she waited out on the sidewalk as Parkinson locked up the house and he and Rayanne and the children got into the truck, and asked the Lady to keep them safe as they pulled out of the driveway and headed down the street. Parkinson honked the horn and waved. Even the two eldest kids twisted around in the jump seat and looked. But Rayanne kept her hands inside the truck and her eyes fixed on the road ahead.

Lauren waited until the truck turned onto Main Street and disappeared from view. Then she walked down the cracked asphalt, eyeing each vacant house in turn, on the lookout for signs of squatters or vandals, human or animal. Knew even as she checked that she needn't have bothered. Her wards protected them and besides, nobody came to Gideon anymore, for reasons fair or foul.

Gideon, Illinois—population . . . ? Less than a hundred, now that the Parkinsons had gone. Add to that the half of the town that had been lost that past winter. A freak storm, according to the outside world. Temperatures dropped so quickly that those caught outdoors succumbed to shock, hypothermia. Then came the snows, the loss of power, the fires caused by heaters and wood flames and asphyxiation due to gas leaks. A litany of accident and misfortune, all spelled out in the official report.

So many lost. So much death.

Lauren turned onto Main Street, following it as it looped around Gideon's town square. There had once been a gazebo in the center, a memorial to those lost in another disaster, the Fire of 1871. Dismantled during the blizzard, the news reports said, for use as firewood.

She shaded her eyes against the noonday sun and surveyed the area, instead of hurrying past like she usually did. A ring of hydrangeas now stood in place of the gazebo, softball-size pink and white blooms bobbing in the light breeze. There had been rosebushes once, but they had been destroyed along with the gazebo.

The laughter and shouts as they built the pyre, the half-dead of Gideon. Those gray faces, all humanity stripped away.

And in their midst, Nicholas Blaine, astride a mortal horse driven mad by pain and dark magic, urging them on.

Yes, a storm had struck Gideon that past December, just not the sort that most folks were familiar with.

But we're over that now. Nicholas Blaine had been defeated, sent back into the wilderness to suffer whatever punishment awaited him. The evil he had inflicted upon Gideon, the weight of his influence, had been lifted.

So now, half a year later, why did it feel as though he had won?

Lauren headed toward the small cluster of buildings that constituted Gideon's business district. A few vehicles lined the street, customers of the hardware store, the new bookkeeper. The diner's parking lot was half-full thanks to the workmen Rocky had hired to upgrade the garage. Anyone passing through would think Gideon a typical small town, busy enough, if not bustling.

But it was a lie. Simple economics, the need for jobs, schools, a chance at a better life, hurt them more than Blaine ever did.

So people are leaving. And Gideon needed people. More specifically, the town needed certain types of people. People who
could keep away the dark.

Gideon needs witches. And as Mistress of Gideon, Lauren
knew it was her responsibility to keep the ones who still lived
there from leaving. *Not doing a very good job of that, am I?*

She kept walking, through the town and up the short hill,
where the road turned rough and Main Street changed into Old
Main Road. A half-mile farther she stepped off onto a footpath
that led into the woods. She concentrated on who she was going
to visit and what she wanted to say, because thinking drowned
out the voices in her head.

THE RIVER CONSTANCE flowed gently beneath its leafy canopy, the
water bright and sparkling, clean and cold as the snowmelt that
had fed her months before. She had been called the Ann once,
after Ann Cateman, Gideon's first Mistress. But after it came
to light how the Catemans had conspired with Blaine over the
years, well, no one wanted to be reminded of them anymore.

But folks remembered Connie Petersbury kindly, and it com-
forted them to know that a woman who had been through so
much, who had lost everything that awful winter—including
her life—could be memorialized. That, in a way, she would
always be part of Gideon.

Little do they know. Lauren smiled as she rounded the river's
widest bend and sat at her usual place, a broad, flat rock that
jutted out over the water. She pulled off her running shoes and
socks and immersed her feet up past her ankles, shivering as the
chilly water lapped over her skin. Dug through the pockets of

her shorts for peanuts, which she tossed into the nearby shrubbery; a few moments later, a pair of crows wheeled overhead
and cawed, then swooped in after them.

Lauren kicked water into the air, watched the drops flash
back rainbows. Eventually she felt the change in the air, the
softest of breezes.

"Heard you comin'." Connie Petersbury sat on the rock next
to hers. Temperature and weather no longer affected her, so
she could change her clothes to suit her mood. Today she wore
denim shorts and a sleeveless red blouse, and had managed to
work her short salt-and-pepper bob into two stubby pigtails.
She pointed to the crows, still squabbling in the brush. "No way
you can sneak up on anyone, the way your friends follow you
around."

"They follow me for the peanuts."

"They follow you 'cause you're you."

Lauren shrugged. Then she looked up at the sun through
the trees, savored the warmth on her face. "Just saw the Parkinsons off."

Connie tsked. "Surprised Fred lasted here as long as he did.
Rayanne started crabbing at him about leaving five minutes
after they met." She wrinkled her nose. "He's no loss. Stuff they
flushed down the toilet while they packed shocked me, and you
would think I'd be past shocking by this point." She met Lauren's gaze with a slow headshake. "Folks have no secrets from
their septic tank. Something I've come to learn over the last few
months. Unfortunately."

"I didn't know you could sense things like that."

"Anywhere that water goes, I can go. You know that."

Lauren felt her face heat, only this time the sun had nothing to do with it. She sensed Connie's pointed stare, and kept her eyes fixed on the river.

After a time, Connie sighed. "It's been . . . odd, lately. I feel other things, too, you know? Things that aren't me. Places. Like when you go outside on a windy day and catch a whiff of someone else's fire, or cookout. Except I ain't smelling. It's feeling, like I said." She made a vague motion toward the trees. "Something's wrong out there, somewhere. I don't know what it is. But it's wrong." She tapped Lauren's hand with her finger, her touch like drops of water, cool and light. "You feel it, too. That's why you're here."

Lauren started to speak, then stopped. She had come to see Connie because she could tell her things that she could tell no one else, but now that she was here, the words stuck in her throat. "I'm Mistress of Gideon," she said, eventually.

"Yes. You are."

"Virginia told me yesterday she's been enjoying the break."

"That's what she told you, huh?"

"You think she's lying?"

"I think you're both still adjusting. Ginny Waycross can't accept that there's anyone knows more than her. You can't accept that you know anything." The sunlight flickered across Connie's face, like tiny prisms. "I think it's worse for you than it was for any of us. We were born in it, but you came into it so late. First thirty-some years of your life, nothing. And now?" She waited. Eventually, one eyebrow arched.

"I'm hearing things, people, beings." Lauren forced the words, and they tumbled like rocks down a mountainside. "I think it's talking. It's like a recording in my head. It never stops."

"What do they say?"

"I can't understand it. I don't even know if they're real words."

"When did it start?"

"A few weeks ago."

"Have you told Ginny?"

"No. I don't know what I'm hearing. I don't know where it comes from."

"But there's a reason you're hearing it. You have to figure it out."

Lauren nodded. She had come here for respite, but she should have known she would find none. She pulled her feet out of the water, shook off the drops, put her socks and shoes back on. Stood up on the rock and leapt to the opposite bank. "I don't even know where to start."

"Start by walking around here, like you been doing for the last few weeks." Connie stood, and you would have had to look carefully to see that she hovered just above the river's surface. "Do you want me to walk with you? I can, as long as we stay close to the river."

"No. I'll be okay."

"I wish I could help. But I can only do so much. It's not my world anymore."

"I know."

"You've started down the path. You're going to have to follow it through to the end. That's what we do."

"I know." Lauren picked out a trail through the knee-high grass and resumed her hike.

The crows escorted her for a time, keeping one step ahead of her as they swooped from branch to branch. But soon even they vanished, leaving her alone.

She trudged past maple, oak, and ash, heavy with the lush foliage of early summer, a thousand shades of green. She had first walked these narrow trails in winter, when all was brown and bare and the barrier between this world and the next so thin that time and space lost all meaning.

But everything's back to normal now. At least, as normal as a place like Gideon could be. She paused to rub her ears, then listened. The mutterings sounded softer now, lower in pitch. She took one step forward, another.

Silence.

She held out her hands, fingers spread, and turned in a slow circle—anyone who saw her would think she walked in her sleep. When she turned to face the way she had come, the voices in her head resumed. When she turned in the direction she had been walking, they stopped once more.

Is this a sign, Lady? Lauren asked the question even though she expected no answer. She wondered sometimes whether the tales of the Lady of Endor, who had wandered the world so long ago and gathered followers to guard the "thin places" between the worlds of human and demon, were nothing more than hope-filled fiction, an attempt to explain the inexplicable. A delusion that she herself had come to share.

She looked overhead. *Sky's still blue.* Good news there, at any rate. In her limited experience with the nether realms, blue sky had never been a feature. Nothing bright existed there, nothing welcoming or beautiful or sane. "Great time to pull the rug out from under me." She announced her challenge to whoever, or whatever, might be listening. Heard nothing in reply but silence, and kept walking.

She couldn't pinpoint when her surroundings changed—she knew only that they had. She sensed it in the air first, the smell, the taste of it. Salt and storm and vast depths. *Ocean.* But green smells, too, old and rich and mossy.

Lauren looked down at the ground and spotted clusters of ferns. *They grow in Illinois, too.* But not these trees. Sitka spruce. Hemlock. Bigleaf maple.

Her breath caught. She had become accustomed to the temporal tricks that the woods played on anyone who ventured too deeply, but something other than time had flipped here. *I don't think this is Gideon anymore.*

The air in front of her shimmered, and the trail grew steeper. She walked until she arrived at a gap in the trees, and pushed through until she came to a rocky outcropping. Her heart pounded as she scrambled to the top, then slowly stood up straight and looked around.

She stood on one mountain among many, some bare green, others covered partially or totally with trees. Old-growth in some places, the same hemlock and spruce. Younger trees in others, which had been planted by logging companies.

Home. Lauren bit her tongue to keep from saying the word aloud, fought the desire to believe what her senses swore to be true. She squinted into the distance, spotted a jutting, snow-covered peak, then checked the location of the sun. *Mount Hood.* Okay, so not home, exactly. Oregon. She tried to see if she could catch a glimpse of the Pacific, but the mountains blocked her view. Still, she had a pretty good idea where she stood. *The Coast Range.*

She breathed deep as much to calm herself as to savor the scents. Her heart slowed, eventually. *So who do I thank?* Who among those who dwelt in the wilderness had sent her this gift? Were they friend or foe? "Why are you showing me this?" She waited for the answer she knew would never come, as the breeze touched her face, and the tears sprang.

After a while, she wiped her face with her sleeve. Spotted a Steller's jay watching her from a nearby branch, and tossed it a peanut from her crow cache. "That's a Gideon peanut. Lady knows what will happen to you if you eat it," she said as it swooped down and collected its prize, then returned to its perch.

She listened to the *tap-tap* as the bird cracked open the nut, the whisper of the air through leaf and needle. Then she sat on the edge of the rock and toyed with a scatter of stones, stacking them into a pile, then knocking them down. "If your point was to make me feel homesick, whoever you are, you're doing a great job." She waited . . . for what? An answer? A sign?

She remained seated, drank in the views. Every so often she checked the sun—when it had moved almost overhead, she stood, brushed the dirt from her hands.

Then she stilled as bushes rustled at the spot where she had stepped off the trail. Too much noise and movement for a fox or a squirrel. *Something tall.* A bear? No, a different sort of animal. The worst sort.

"Who's there?" The movement ceased as soon as Lauren spoke. "I heard you—you may as well come out." She struggled to get a sense of whatever it was, but felt nothing. Blankness.

Nothing good would hide itself. She wondered who would have lured her all the way across the country just to attack her. "The last demon that challenged me, I left a smoking husk in the snow." Her voice echoed as the air around her changed, grew heavy and thick with the stink of rotted things.

Then it lightened again, green mountain freshness erasing the stench of decay.

Lauren waited, until she felt sure that whatever had followed her had gone. Knew that its voice was one of the ones she heard, that its presence was what Connie had sensed.

Months before, she had been sent back from the realm of the dead with a warning that other dangers existed, and that she would need to face them. Now it looked as though that time had come.

Lauren allowed herself one last, long look at the mountains. Then she turned and walked through the gap to the trail, the scenery wavering like the air above a hot road.

She started her descent. Soon, too soon, the ground leveled, the trees changed back to oak and ash and elm.

And the voices returned.

CHAPTER 3

Lauren stepped out of the woods and onto the road that led to Virginia Waycross's ranch, and spotted the woman standing on the front step of her old farmhouse. She waved when she saw Lauren, then folded her arms and waited, a lean, tall figure in her work-hardened fifties. She wore jeans and a long-sleeve shirt despite the heat, gray curls hidden under a wide-brimmed straw hat.

"Wondered if I'd ever see you again, or if this time you'd just keep walking." The remnants of a summer cold added a rasp to Virginia's mellow voice. "Rocky called a couple of hours ago to say he saw you head through town and up the hill. Lost sight of you after that."

Lauren struggled to hide her irritation. One of the less enjoyable aspects of living with Virginia Waycross. Nowhere to run, nowhere to hide. "You've got folks watching me?"

"Always. Zeke thinks we should stick one of those GPS units on you while you're sleeping."

"I like to walk. Gives me a chance to think."

"About what?"

"Whether we'll be the only two people left in Gideon by the end of the year."

Virginia didn't reply. She waited for Lauren to mount the steps, then opened the door for her and followed her inside. "Parkinsons weren't one of the first families." She took off her hat and set it on the entry hall table, then fluffed out her hair with one veiny hand. "They arrived after the Civil War. Council recruited them—that was one of the things they did back then. Looked for folks with potential, who could be trained. Brought them into the fold." She passed through the living room and dining room and into the kitchen.

"What does Council do now?" Lauren fell in behind her. The interior of the old house felt cool and close, scented with the mustiness of old furniture and a hint of the morning's coffee.

"Lady knows." Virginia snorted. "I sure don't." She took a pitcher of iced tea from the refrigerator, then collected a couple of glasses from the cupboard. "Back when I was Mistress, I used to get letters from them every few months, asking me to submit reports about skill levels and training programs." She sat at the kitchen table and poured. "I used to file them in the compost pile." She hesitated, jaw working. "Of course, now that you're Mistress, you might wish to do things differently." She spoke slowly, haltingly, as though every word had been extracted with pliers.

"A little help from an outside source wouldn't hurt right now." Lauren sat down and concentrated on slicing a lemon into wedges. "Maybe we should get in touch with them." She sensed Virginia watching her, and kept her eyes on her task. "It couldn't hurt." She waited for the protest she felt sure would come, heard nothing but the muttering in her head, and looked up to find the older woman stalled in mid-pour.

Virginia set down pitcher and glass with a sigh. "You going to tell me what's going on?"

Lauren shrugged. "You know that as well as I do."

Virginia nodded. Then she walked out of the kitchen to the dining room and opened the sideboard in which she kept her small stash of liquor.

Shit. Lauren turned away just as Virginia returned, refused to look at the whiskey and vodka bottles that the woman set on the table until she picked them up and set them back down hard.

"Three inches out of each, give or take." Virginia pointed to the pair of black lines drawn in marker along the side of each bottle. "That's about two days' worth, I'm guessing, though I didn't start to measure until I hunted for that raspberry liqueur last week to use in Zeke's birthday cake and couldn't find it. Or the rum." She set the bottles on the counter behind her chair, then finished filling a glass with tea and placed it in front of Lauren. "Anytime you're ready."

Lauren set down the knife and arranged the lemon wedges on a plate. "I thought it would help me sleep." She forced herself to look Virginia in the eye, saw fatigue and concern and the barest hint of fear, and focused on her glass instead. "Did you know that Connie can sense what you put down the drain?" She nodded toward the liquor bottles. "No secret is safe, I guess."

"I will file that away for future reference. Now could we

please stick to the matter at hand?" Virginia sat, then took a wedge of lemon and squeezed it into her tea, twisting it until it tore in half. "Why do you need help sleeping?"

Lauren thought about denying it, even as she knew it would do no good. Difficult, lying to another witch, especially one as perceptive as Virginia. "Voices. I hear . . . voices."

Virginia pinched the bridge of her nose, then shook her head. "What kind of voices?"

"I can't tell what they are. I don't understand what they say."

"But it's more than one?"

Lauren thought back to her forest encounter. Did more than one thing follow her? *No.* But the voices? They were a jumble, layers of sound she could never sort out. "Yes. I think so."

Virginia scraped the dregs out of the sugar bowl and added them to her tea. "Your daddy saw things. That's rare. Hearing them's bad enough." She got up and carried the bowl into the pantry to fill it. As usual, she grew restless when she talked about Matthew Mullin. "It started after he lost his folks. I think whatever it was tried to use his grief as a way in." She paused, sugar bag in hand, eyes soft with memory of the man she never stopped loving. "He used to draw them. The things he saw. He'd buy special notebooks. Then he'd tear the pictures up and burn them. He said it was like erasing them. He said it helped."

Lauren sat back. Her father had taken such pains to hide his past from her. How many times a day did she wish she could talk to him now, about the things he knew, the things he had seen? "What did they look like?"

"He never let me see."

"How long did it last, for him?"

"About four months." Virginia added sugar to the bowl, tapping the spoon on the edge with each scoop. "When did yours start?"

Lauren counted on her fingers. "Eighteen days ago." She tapped the side of her head. "At first I thought I was going nuts, or that it was a brain tumor."

Virginia put away the sugar and returned to the table, cradling the bowl like an offering. "You've been through so much since you came here, you must feel ready to explode. You've held it all back and you won't let anyone try to help you." She set the bowl on the table and sat down, brow furrowing as she struggled for the words. "What I'm trying to say is that it can go away like that"—she snapped her fingers—"and you have to wait it out. Because the drinking will just make things worse, inside your head and out. They want you to destroy yourself, you know. Saves them the trouble."

"I didn't have anything to drink last night." Lauren hoped she kept the edge out of her voice. She knew that Virginia was only trying to help, but still. "I dumped it down the drain."

"Lauren, you can't keep these things to yourself. Being Mistress of Gideon means—"

"I know what it means."

"I'm not sure you do." Virginia leaned forward, hands clasped like a child at prayer. "I can guess what you think. That I'm meddling. That I can't let go. But I can see what this is doing to you. You can't keep it bottled up until there's nothing for the rest of us to do but bury what's left."

"That's why I went to see Connie. I thought she might have gotten a sense of whatever it was."

"And did she?"

Lauren nodded.

"All right—what does that mean for us?" Virginia sighed. "You see, that's what I'm trying to tell you. We're not disinterested bystanders here. We each have our own skills, our own talents. We can help." She reached out until her hand brushed Lauren's. "Yes, you're Mistress. What you're not, is alone."

Lauren took a sip of tea, which proved strong and a touch harsh, like the woman who had brewed it. "When I was in the Cateman house, with Blaine, when I fought him—"

"When you destroyed him." Virginia sniffed.

"Yeah." Lauren paused, searched for the words to describe what she still couldn't believe had happened. How she had released the memory of fire from wood once used to burn a witch. How that fire had almost consumed her as well. "The flames engulfed Leaf's office, and the smoke . . . I died, I think, for a little while. Dad came to get me—I saw him as clearly as I see you now. He led me into the borderland."

Virginia sat back, arms folded, one hand pressed to her lips.

"I met Eliza Mullin—she was waiting for me. She told me that it wasn't my time to go, that I had more work to do. She said that there were other thin places that needed to be dealt with, and that this was my job. To deal with those places."

"You think those voices you hear—" Virginia stopped, coughed. "You think they're from another thin place?"

Lauren nodded, then hesitated as she considered what to say and how to say it. "I had a vision, today. A little while ago. I saw it. The place. In the woods here, except that it wasn't here. It was back home. I'm pretty sure it was in Oregon."

Virginia slumped back and stared up at the ceiling. "Oh, Lady love us all, but you terrify me." She drummed her fingers on the table, quickly at first, then more and more slowly, until eventually she stilled. "It could be a trick. A trap."

"I'm sure it is. Baited with homesickness, concern for those I left behind." Lauren rose, paced. "Still, I need to go there."

"They could be trying to lure you away from here to split us up, make us weaker." Virginia held up her hand, index finger extended. "During all the years I served as Mistress of Gideon, I took one overnight trip. To Chicago. I was gone two days." Her hand dropped. "Some folks never let me forget it. They felt I had abandoned them."

"The difference this time is that you'd be here." Lauren boosted herself atop the counter. "I think Zeke and the others still consider you their Mistress."

"You'd be wrong."

"No, I don't think so. For some of them, you're the only Mistress they've ever known. I'm still the outsider. They acknowledge me, yes. But they don't come to me when they're troubled or need to discuss a personal matter." Lauren caught the distant look that filled Virginia's eyes and softened the hard lines of her face. Connie had been right, as usual. Her friend did miss her old job. "Funny how this works out. We both get back something we've lost, at least for a little while."

"That's not what I want. That's not—" Virginia quieted. Then came a long, slow smile. "Oh, they play dirty, don't they?"

"Like we didn't know that?" Lauren could barely keep from knocking her heels against the cupboard doors. *Home. Home.* The word sparkled in her mind like some inner star, and it occurred to her that she had fallen under a spell, that she could no more reject this invitation than she could stop breathing. "Something has contacted us. I think what happened here last winter got their attention." She pushed off the counter and headed out of the kitchen toward the back stairs.

"What do you think they want?" Virginia stood, her voice soft and touched with worry. "Whoever—or whatever—they are?"

"Same thing they always want." Lauren paused in the doorway. "They want in."

SHE STARTED TO pack, then sat on the narrow bed in her tiny bedroom and pulled together thoughts that had scattered like dried leaves in the wind. But every time she tried to concentrate, the memories flooded back of the mountain views, the smell of the air.

I've been bewitched. Damn. *I'm not even scared.* With that realization, she felt the first loosening of the spell's hold. Fear snaked in to take its place, touched with the anger that drove her to walk her days away and try to drown her nights in liquor. Anger over all she had lost—her parents, her career, her friends. Her life before Gideon.

Anger with herself. For letting her weakness show. For letting *it* in.

She imagined taking that seed of rage and planting it in the ground, watering it and nursing it until it burst forth, a tangle of red and black that filled her mind with sharpened fury that staked her false happiness like the foul lie it was. One thing she had learned about this new life of hers—lies meant death. They stripped her ability to reason, left her unprepared to face all those things that now defined her.

You're a witch of Gideon, Reardon, for now and for always. Get used to it.

Another tremor of fear. Nicholas Blaine, the thing that had first called her to Gideon, had gone to Seattle for her, shattered her world like glass and dragged her into his. He had been strong, but this thing that had shown her visions of home felt stronger, knew enough to mask its strength in sweetness and beauty.

Remember the smell. Funny how that always seemed to slip her mind. Like something crawled under the house and died. Something foul, desecrating her home.

Her fury chilled now, to something gray and weighty and coated in frost. Something that would fight to protect its own.

Something that, if necessary, would kill.

And now that she had come to the place where she needed to be, Lauren veiled the fury, drew a curtain around it. Let whatever it was think that it had her. Let it think it had won.

Until it was too late.

BY THE TIME Lauren packed and returned downstairs, the others had arrived, those with whom she had weathered the battle against Blaine in the old Pyne house just off the town square. Zeke Pyne, who owned the place. Phil Beech, from the hardware store. Rocky Barton and Brittany Watt, who managed the diner and the garage and had just moved in together, finally admitting to themselves what everyone else in Gideon had known for months.

They stood chatting around the dining room table, munching cookies and drinking iced tea, like any impromptu neighborhood gathering. When Lauren entered they fell silent, looking first at her, then at the suitcase.

"Poker night won't be the same without you." Zeke shook a stubby finger at her. "I hope you're not thinking of driving. It'll lie in wait for you at every rest stop, whatever it is that called to you." He shuffled his feet and frowned. "Not sure that flying's any better, but at least it's quicker."

"Too bad that was just a hallucination and not a real doorway—you could just walk through it and be there in a flash. Save a ton o' money." Rocky raised his glass to her. "You'd have folks falling over themselves to learn that trick." He dodged Brittany's warning punch. "Well, it's true."

Lauren met Virginia's eye—the woman glared sidelong at Rocky, then nodded. "I see Mistress Waycross filled you in. I know I don't have to tell you to keep it to yourselves for now. Let me find out what's going on first." She took note of the downcast expressions. "I don't want you to think I'm abandoning you."

Phil straightened with a jerk, like he had been called on in class. "We know that, Mistress. I figured something was up when I seen you walking all over town all the time. My pops used to do that, when he had things on his mind. Said that getting the blood flowing helped him think. Hope it helped you."

"Yes. Yes, it has." Lauren felt their collective gaze, expectant, like dogs awaiting that guiding word. "Lady keep you until I return." As they bowed their heads, she inscribed the X-centered circle in the air, the symbol of the Lady of Endor. Struggled to find words of reassurance that didn't sound like greeting card pap. "Maybe you should all stay out of the woods for a while."

She waited as they came to her one by one to shake her hand and wish her well. Then she hefted her suitcase and headed out to her car, a silver Outback that glimmered bright as a fish in the summer sunshine.

"Lauren?"

Lauren slowed until Virginia drew alongside.

"You will keep me informed." Virginia had already resumed her long-accustomed role, her voice taking on that measured cadence that brooked no argument.

"Of course."

"I hope I didn't make a mistake telling them why you felt you needed to leave."

"We went through a lot together. They have the right to know."

"Rocky's the one I'm concerned about—he does tend to blurt things out in front of, well, civilians." Virginia popped the car's hatch so Lauren could load her suitcase, then slammed it shut. "I will impress upon him the need to keep his own counsel, but I fear it'll be hard. We never tried to hide before. We never had to."

"That's going to change." Lauren looked across the road to the woods beyond, but the mutterings in her head told her that they were still Gideon woods. "Someone will talk, someday. For the money. Because someone they loved vanished last winter. The more I think about it, the more I'm amazed that you managed to keep this place under wraps for this long."

"Well." Virginia sighed, pressed a hand to the back of her neck. Then she walked around the car and opened the driver's-side door. "The important thing is keeping out whatever it is that wants in."

Virginia wasn't the hugging type, so Lauren didn't even try. She just got into her car and started it as the woman slammed the door.

"Lady keep you." Virginia inscribed an X-centered circle on the hood of the car. A blessing for the journey ahead.

"And you." Lauren backed out of the long driveway, and watched Virginia in the rearview mirror until she rounded a corner and the woman disappeared from sight.

CHAPTER 4

Lauren spent part of the flight to Seattle staring out the window, watching the terrain grow more and more wrinkled, like a cotton sheet just pulled from the washer. The rest of the time, she alternated between pondering her rapidly worsening financial situation and worrying over what awaited her in Oregon. She had debated flying directly to Portland but realized that she had no idea where to begin her search for that particular mountain. She also knew that she wouldn't be able to concentrate unless she took some time to sort out the mess that had become her life.

Savings. Enough to last a year, maybe two. Longer, if she continued to live with Virginia. *Assuming she wants me around.* Their relationship had seen some rough patches since the winter, a victim of their different personalities and ways of working, and Virginia's chafing, despite her protests to the contrary, over her loss of position. *She can have the job back—I don't want to be Mistress of Gideon.* But the title, and the responsibility, went to the most skilled practitioner, and Lauren had been the one to slay Nicholas Blaine.

New job. No luck in that regard. Her barrage of résumés to Chicago-area companies had met with canned responses, and the phone calls she had placed to local contacts had been funneled straight to voicemail and gone unanswered. *Expand the search.* St. Louis. Kansas City. Maybe they could work out a compromise where Virginia could serve as weekday Mistress of Gideon and Lauren could return on weekends.

A dull ache had settled behind Lauren's eyes. She dug some ibuprofen out of her handbag and asked the flight attendant for water.

Sell something. Her condo or her parents' home, both of which had been infested by Blaine. *Not until I know they're safe.* The last thing she wanted to do was inflict any residual evil on the new occupants.

Lauren looked around the cabin at the other passengers, sensed the overlapping currents of scores of lives, their thoughts and emotions. And beneath it all, the incessant yammering, like the bass line in a recording, the beat around which all else revolved. She had hoped the aircraft rumble would drown it out. No such luck.

It won't go away until I'm where I need to be. She looked out the window as the Cascades came into view.

LAUREN MANEUVERED THROUGH the sprawl of Seattle-Tacoma International Airport on autopilot, rehearsing her answers to the questions she knew she would hear. *What happened? Why did you leave? Why were you gone so long?* Her answers weren't great, but they were simple. *Relatives of Dad's . . . I wanted to meet them . . . got stuck in the blizzard . . . stayed to help out.*

She soaked in the windshield-filling expanse of Mount Rain-
ier as she merged her rental car with the incessant I-5 traffic.
Tried to ignore the voices. They seemed different now—she
could pick out variations in pitch and timbre, knew now that
some were female and others, male. She turned on the radio,
hunted for a dance station, music with a beat heavy enough to
cancel them out.

Lauren knew she needed to attend to business. Assess. Make
decisions. Depart for Portland as quickly as possible. Instead she
bypassed her parents' house in Wallingford and her condo in the
University District for the sylvan quiet of Montlake, and drove
along the wooded streets until she came to a two-story cream-
and-white contemporary trimmed with pink and peach rosebushes, housewarming gifts from her late mother. She pulled
into the driveway, and sat for a moment to gather her thoughts.
Then she got out and walked up the short sidewalk to the front
door, soft rose scents wafting round her. Rang the bell.

The light step. The click of the lock. Then the door swung
open to reveal a tall, slender woman in a camel shirt and trousers, high-heeled pumps in hand, copper-penny hair twisted
into a loose nape knot.

"Hi, Katie." Lauren met her best friend's wide brown eyes.
Heard the clatter of shoes hitting the tile floor, and felt the
warm wrap of summer-weight wool, the wash of soft floral per-
fume, and the wetness of tears and a hug so tight it squeezed
the breath out of her.

KATIE WESTBROOK STEPPED out onto the sunny flagstone patio, a
steaming mug in hand. "I wish you had told us you were com-

ing. I could have picked you up." She handed the mug to Lauren, then sat across the glass-topped table from her.

"It was a spur-of-the-moment trip." Lauren inhaled the bracing aromas of weighty dark roast laced with cinnamon, then drank deep.

"Well, that's consistent with recent performance." Katie pulled a hand mirror and packet of wipes from her handbag and set about repairing her tear-smeared makeup. Then she paused and fixed on Lauren over the top of the mirror, like a mother assessing her child. "Oh hon, you look . . ."

"Tired." Lauren forced a smile. "I know."

"I'd say it was more than that." Katie shook her head. "What the hell is going on?"

Lauren hesitated. She had told Katie more than anyone else about Gideon, even as she had struggled to keep things as vague as possible. No mention of anything otherworldly, of course. "The town was devastated. I thought I could help, so I stayed. The recovery just took longer than I thought it would."

"But was it worth—" Katie sighed, uncapped a tube of mascara, and dabbed her eyelashes. "You lost your job, hon."

Lauren twitched her shoulders. "I'll find another one."

"Okay, fine. So. Are you here for good, or do you have to go back?"

"I will have to get back. First, I have to go to Portland."

"Portland."

Lauren nodded. Stared into her coffee for a few long moments, then looked up to find her friend regarding her with narrowed eyes.

"Paul thinks you got a job with the government. Something

with a top-level security clearance, where you can't tell anyone what you really do." Katie sniffed, as if to say that was no excuse for Lauren to remain so closemouthed. "I mean, first you just take off, and then you get stuck in this blizzard. Then we don't hear from you for weeks at a time other than texts. It's like you're some deep-cover operative or something. I won't find out the truth until you write your memoir and they make a movie about your exploits."

Lauren laughed. "'Oh Hell Forty,' where whoever plays me wonders what happened to her life."

"Jessica Chastain plays me, or I won't sign the release." Katie sat back, arms folded, one corner of her mouth upturned in a sly smile. "Well, Jane Bond, you're not the only one who keeps secrets."

Lauren felt a tremor in the air, like the shock of a slammed door. "Is everything okay?"

"Yes." Katie leaned forward, hands clasped under her chin, eyes bright as a child's. "I'm pregnant."

Lauren's stomach clenched as the voices in her head intensified. "How far along?" She could hear laughter now. The buzz of excited whispers.

"Three months." The light in Katie's eyes flickered. "Paul and I kept it quiet until we were pretty sure that things were going to be, you know, okay this time." She looked up at the sky, that blazing blue that reassured Seattleites that yes, they had summer just like everybody else. "So far, it's been a nice, boring pregnancy."

"How do you feel?" Lauren struggled to keep her voice steady.

"Great, now that I've stopped throwing up every morning." Katie jerked her chin toward Lauren's mug. "I can't stand the taste of coffee anymore—who thought that would ever happen? And I've developed an insane appetite for butter pecan ice cream. Paul wants to buy an ice cream maker, before we have to take out a second mortgage to support my habit." She patted her stomach, which showed the barest hint of rounding. "We've put plans for the second store on hold. And I'm having lunch with Chelsea tomorrow. She's helping us design the nursery."

Lauren took Katie's hand. She tried to speak, but her voice faltered as the din in her head ramped up.

"Oh, please don't say anything serious. I'll get all weepy and then I'll have to fix this crap all over again." Katie pulled her hand away and waved toward her eyes, then stuffed her makeup back in her handbag. "I'm sorry—I need to get to the store."

Lauren looked out over the landscaped backyard. "I have some things I have to do, too."

"But we are having dinner here tonight. Don't you dare try to slip out from under."

"I wouldn't dream of it." Lauren waited until Katie returned to the house. Then she walked out into the backyard. First she surveyed the shrubbery, the stands of spruce and maple. Then she followed the property line, past the birdbath and the rock garden and the overflow rosebushes that hadn't fit in the front yard.

"I know you're here." She turned a slow circle as the voices in her head rose and fell. "You know I can hear you." She sketched symbols and sigils in the air. The Eye of the Lady. Shapes taught to her by Connie that bothered demons, caused them pain and anxiety. "Leave my friends alone, or I will come after you. You know I can. You know what I'm capable of."

For a few moments, the voices quieted to wonderful, wonderful silence. Then they flooded back, louder, more raucous, a demonic New Year's Eve.

You asked for it. Lauren rooted through the foliage until she found a short length of dead, dried branch studded with thorns. She raked the largest across the base of her left thumb and massaged the wound until the blood welled.

"You will not cross this line." She walked clockwise along the edge of the property, leaving a drop every few feet until she had encircled the house. As she did, the voices receded once more, their tone altering from strong and deep to whiny and complaining.

Lauren dug a tissue from her pocket and wrapped it around the wound. Blood magic had so far proved her strongest ward, and if anyone merited the heavy artillery, it was her closest friends. She had tried to find herbs or objects that could serve as substitute, but nothing she tried worked as well. *Unfortunately.* Virginia had once told her that if witches used blood to set wards, they soon wouldn't have any left. *So what's the next-best thing? Animal sacrifice?* No—that was where she drew a line. Taking an innocent life to save life struck her as the worst sort of bargain, hypocritical at best, evil at worst. So, her searches would continue, and, as needed, she would bleed.

She reentered the house and spotted Katie's handbag on the entryway table. She yanked away the tissue from her thumb, caught the drop of blood before it fell, and dabbed it in one of the bag's deep folds where it wouldn't be seen.

Then she went back outside to the driveway, where Katie's Audi was parked. White car, tan upholstery—Lauren smeared blood underneath the driver's seat, a place she hoped even the most anal-retentive detailer would miss.

"Anyplace you smell my blood. Anyplace you smell my scent. That which is mine is mine forever. Where I've been, invade it never." Not her best spell, but it served. The flow of words focused the mind, the power. She could have spouted gibberish and it would've had the same effect, but she preferred using words. They reminded her of what she was.

She shut the car door, wrapped her finger with a clean tissue. Looked toward the street, and spotted a man standing a few houses away, watching her. He wore a dark business suit and stood with his hands clasped in front of him, like an usher hanging fire at the back of a church. Even from that distance, his was a riveting face, angular and high-boned.

"Lauren? Do you have your bag?" Katie stuck her head out the front door. "I'm going to be locking up."

"Be right there." Lauren shoved her bandaged hand in her pocket. Turned back to look at the man, but he had gone.

LAUREN FOLLOWED KATIE to her store, using the excuse that she wanted to grab lunch at her favorite downtown place. She parked across the street and waited until her friend went inside, then hurried to the entrance, rose thorns in hand, and shed a few more drops of blood in front of the doorway.

How much is enough? Five drops? Ten? A pint? A gallon? She thought back to that horrible time two years before, Katie's miscarriage and what came after. *They told her the odds were that she would never have children.* For a moment, Lauren's anger boiled into something that tinged her field of vision as red as the blood she had spilled and silenced the din in her head.

Then, slowly, something else crept in, and brought the voices back with it. Guilt, because the only reason Katie would be hurt was that she was friends with the wrong person.

Lauren returned to her car, then sat quietly, hands resting lightly on the wheel. She closed her eyes until her mind settled as much as it ever did these days. Then she started the car and pulled out into the midday traffic.

The U-District proved as crowded as always, everyone out soaking up the summer sun. The familiar scenery relaxed Lauren a little, but her heart thudded as she entered her complex for the first time since the winter. She parked in the space in front of her condo instead of in the attached one-car garage, then got out of her car and paced up and down the short sidewalk, front door key in hand.

She crept to the front window and peered inside, picked out the dark shapes of furniture, the dots of standby light from the cable box. *Blaine is dead.* That meant she should be able to enter without fear. She unlocked the door, slipped inside, and disabled the alarm.

The stench hit her as soon as she entered, the sour stink of rotten food. "Next time we flee the scene, let's remember to put out the garbage." She opened the front door and the living room windows. Hesitated, then turned, and stared at the scant pile of dust in a far corner, all that remained of the large rolltop desk that had stood there. Her father had built it for her, larding it with protective wards. But they faded after he died, and dark powers had done the rest. Her first magic lesson, learned before she had uncovered what her father was, and what he had passed on to her.

She stood over the dust pile and had another of the many one-sided conversations she'd had with her father since his death. *How are things where you are? It's still a laugh a minute here.* Then she hurried to the kitchen and shoved the stinking trash bin out the back door into the garage, stopping first to empty the refrigerator of solidified milk and fuzzy green things in jars and bowls. She unearthed a can of deodorizer and sprayed it throughout the place. Finally, when she could breathe through her nose again, she scooped the ashy remains of the desk into a plastic bag and tucked them in her handbag, because consigning them to the vacuum cleaner seemed the height of disrespect.

Then she surveyed the place. *Sell it.* She had loved it once, but now it held too many bad memories. She would clean it, both physically and magically, ask Virginia for help with the latter if necessary.

"Or maybe someone from the Council. Might be a good way to introduce myself." Lauren trooped off to the bedroom and packed additional clothing for Portland. Then she turned off the lights, activated the alarm, exited the front door, and met the piercing gaze of the man she had seen outside Katie's house. He stood on the edge of the lawn in front of her condo in the same pose he had assumed then, hands clasped in front of him, back straight.

Lauren looked him over, ticked off all the signs and markers, the comparisons with past executive encounters. He appeared older upon closer inspection, a well-tended fifty, clean-shaven, dark brown hair touched with just the right amount of gray. Conservative charcoal suit—no skinny legs or trendy cuts. White shirt. The only hint of color she could see was the maroon striping in his dark silver tie. Not a flunky, this one. He came from the toothier end of the food chain.

Even the ever-present voices had quieted. She could sense them waiting, expectant.

"Mistress Mullin." The man held out his hands, palms facing out, and bowed his head. "My name is Gene Kaster. Might I beg a few moments of your time?"

CHAPTER 5

Lauren entered the retro-style diner and asked to be seated at a booth overlooking the parking lot. The place was located a few blocks from the condo complex, on a busy street lined with popular shops and restaurants, and was currently half-filled with the late lunch crowd. It wasn't that she feared Kaster physically—she didn't sense that sort of menace from him. But he had called her "Mistress Mullin." He had apparently followed her from Katie's house to her condo, and likely had followed her from the airport as well. He had her at a distinct disadvantage. She just wanted to even things up.

After a few minutes, an older-model Mercedes-Benz Maybach swung into the parking lot. A sleek shark of a sedan, black and shiny as a pearl. Not as showy as a Rolls or a Bentley, but just as expensive. Other diners turned to watch it pull in, then to see who got out. As Kaster crossed the lot and entered the place, men looked him up and down and shifted in their seats while women just watched him until he took a seat across from Lauren. Then they turned their attention to her, the old compare-and-contrast. *Why her why him why why . . . ?*

The young server checked her reflection in the espresso machine before bustling over, menus in hand.

Lauren shook her head. "Just coffee, please."

"Are you sure?" Kaster unbuttoned his jacket, then rested his elbows on the table and rubbed his hands together. "My treat."

"That's not necessary."

"Of course it is." Kaster beamed up at the server. "Do you have apple pie?"

The young woman took a half step back, her hand fluttering to her throat. "B-best in Seattle."

"I will have to have some then, won't I? Coffee as well, please." Kaster gave the server's rear a quick once-over as she hurried away, then scanned the diner's chrome and red vinyl decor. "Well, this is charming." He looked around a bit more, then settled on Lauren. "And I am remiss." He reached inside his jacket and removed a flat silver case. Took out a card, and slid it across the table.

Lauren picked it up, felt the stiff smoothness of highest quality paper stock. Not laser printed, no, but embossed in soft black, a few simple lines of print. "Eugene Kaster, Chief Operating Officer, Carmody Incorporated." She studied the address—Carmody was an international conglomerate, but the main headquarters were still located in Portland. "Are you offering me a job, Mr. Kaster?" She set the card back down on the table.

Kaster's good humored expression never changed. Only the light in his blue eyes altered, from the dappled reflection off water to the sharp refraction through glass. "Are you in need of one, Mistress Mullin?"

You bastard—you know about that, too. Lauren bought time as the server returned with their orders; added cream to her coffee, stirred, sipped.

Then she put down her cup. "Let's get to the point, all right?"

"You're so abrupt, Mistress." Kaster seemed focused on his pie, pulling out the slices of apple and eating them one by one.

"You've apparently been monitoring me in a manner that I have no doubt is illegal. What did you expect?"

Kaster pointed his fork at her. "I couldn't believe what I saw when you warded your friend's car. Blood magic." His brow arched. "You have gone primal. Don't think I've seen that in years."

Lauren studied the man's manicured hands. Long-fingered. Ringless. A musician's hands. "You're a witch?"

A side-to-side nod. "I'm familiar with some of the practices." Kaster speared the last slice of apple, then picked at the pie crust, breaking it into little pieces with his fork. "So, are you looking for a new position?"

Lauren shook her head. "No, not at all."

Kaster smiled. "You're a skilled liar. Did you learn that from your father?"

Lauren's chest tightened. Tears sprang. She grabbed her handbag and slid out of the booth. "We're done." She stopped when Kaster grabbed her wrist, stared at him until he released his hold.

"I mean you no harm. You've already done enough to yourself to last a lifetime." Kaster glanced at the other diners, a few of whom had turned to check out the commotion. Then he pushed his plate aside and sat back. "Look at what you've become these last months. Rootless. Fearful of the future. Think where you could be now if he had leveled with you from the start. Trained you as you should have been trained."

Lauren forced words through an aching throat. "You don't know a damn thing."

"Anyone with an ounce of sense could piece together what happened in Gideon, what came before." Kaster looked out the window for a few moments, then back at Lauren. "Answer me this: what good did it do for him to shield you?"

Lauren lowered to the edge of the seat as the memories flashed and faded. Those last days in the hospice. Her father, cheeks sunken, skin waxen, dead in every way that mattered. "He thought he was protecting me."

"Little good that did either of you." Kaster held out a hand. "And despite that, here you are. That's why I'm here, Mistress Mullin. That's why we've been, as you say, monitoring you. Because of who and what you are." He sketched a figure in the air that might have been a sigil or a simple case of nerves. Then he drew an X-centered circle on the table top.

Lauren stared at the spot. "You're a follower of the Lady?"

"I follow no specific practice. I am aware of her."

"So you're not from the Council?"

"The Council of the Children of Endor is not unknown to me. But I don't speak for them." Kaster waved off their server as she approached with a coffee carafe, and she returned crestfallen to the counter. "Mr. Carmody has a particular interest in matters—what is the proper term these days—alternative spiritual? He wants to meet you. More than that, he wants to help you. He can offer you support. Peace of mind. Advice. For instance, I am certain he would recommend that you keep your condominium, at least until the new term at UW begins. Students with resources are always looking for attractive housing off-campus."

Lauren said nothing. She felt naked before this man. Humiliated. Angry, because he had learned all there was to know about her and threw it in her face. She looked across the table to find him smiling a winner's smile, but the expression wavered when she met his eye. "And might I be correct in assuming that he is aware of one or two such students?"

"You might indeed." For the first time, Kaster acted as though he realized that he had pushed too hard. He smoothed his tie. Clenched and unclenched his hands. "He would prefer to discuss this with you personally. If you are not otherwise engaged, he would be delighted if you would join him and some other like-minded souls for a few days. At the family compound, in the mountains outside Portland."

"Like-minded? You mean other witches?"

"Yes."

Lauren nodded. Now was the time to play things very close to the vest. "I have to think about it."

Kaster frowned. "Of course." He nodded toward his card. "I will be returning to Portland this evening. We depart for the compound the day after tomorrow. Just call that number between now and then, anytime, day or night. I may not answer directly, but my assistants are available around the clock." He slid out of the seat and buttoned his jacket in a single smooth motion. "Thank you for providing me the opportunity to enjoy some excellent pie. I look forward to seeing you again." He started to hold out his hand, then stopped, as though he knew Lauren would refuse to take it. "I realize I've given you reason to dislike me, Mistress. I do hope you will give me the chance to change your mind."

Don't bet on it, Eugene. Lauren watched him walk away. He bent close to their server as he paid the check, and whispered in her ear. Whatever he said, it made the young woman giggle. Then he departed the diner, and drove off without a backward glance.

The mountains outside Portland. Once again, Lauren smelled the clean, woody air of the forest, tinged with the sweet sickness of rot.

LAUREN RETURNED TO her condo and spent the next several hours on mindless chores that allowed her mental space to think. By the time she headed back to Katie's house, she had almost convinced herself to refuse Kaster's invitation. Better that she search for the mountain on her own. She would drive throughout the Northern and Central Coast Ranges, use the voices in her head as her guide. Maybe it was a fool's quest, but it would be better than dealing with Kaster's suspicious helpfulness.

She arrived at Katie's to find the driveway filled with cars and her friend standing in the doorway, a bottle of wine in one hand and a corkscrew in the other.

"I'm sorry, hon—I hope you don't mind a crowd." Katie ushered Lauren inside. "I told Chelsea you were here. I should have known she'd inform the universe." She handed Lauren the wine and corkscrew. "Take care of this, could you? The smell is killing me."

Lauren cut through the living room on the way to the kitchen and soon found herself surrounded by friends and colleagues, hugged and kissed and shoulder-rubbed and peppered with questions, which she fielded as best she could. After a few minutes, she felt like a greeter at a convention, rotating the same stock answers over and over. She eventually worked her way through the crowd to the quiet of the kitchen. She leaned against the counter and hugged the wine bottle like a comforting toy. Then she fiddled the corkscrew into position and set about opening the bottle.

"Lauren?"

Lauren turned, then stared at the twenty-something man in horn rims and business casual, straight black hair trimmed into a spiky crew cut. "Ken?" She hoped her surprise didn't show. Ken Masako had been a coworker, yes, but even though they worked in the same group, they had never exchanged more than a few words. She would never have expected him to attend an impromptu gathering in her honor.

"Word whipped 'round the floor that you were back in town." Ken tugged at the snaps of his leather jacket. "So what happened?"

Lauren watched him. In any sitcom, he would have played the jokey, unflappable roommate, but now he looked edgy, shifting from one foot to the other, gaze darting around the room. "Pretty much what I said out there. My father died, and—"

"I don't mean that. I mean after." Ken glanced back over his shoulder, then took a step closer. "I have a reason for asking. Please."

Lauren waited until a chattering couple moved away from the kitchen entry. "I applied for personal leave. They refused to give it to me, so I had no choice but to resign."

"When did you apply?"

"When my vacation and sick time ran out, mid-February."

Ken looked back once more over his shoulder, then bent close and dropped his voice to a whisper. "You didn't hear this from me, okay?" He waited for her nod. "It started way before then. Right after New Year's. We came in that first Monday, and your office is all cleaned out. Name plate gone. We asked Stellan 'what the hell,' and he told us that was privileged info. You know how he is."

"Yeah, I know how he is." Lauren thought back to the stack of paperwork still sitting on atop her dresser back in Gideon, the terms of her separation from Billings-Abernathy set forth in the vague language of lawsuit-leery HR-ese. "I did go out of town without informing him."

"Who the hell is he, a cop? You had enough banked vacay and comp time left to see you through the end of August. Melinda checked." Ken hung his head. "Yeah, sorry. I know that wasn't any of our business."

Lauren twisted the corkscrew, tried not to see it as indicative of her situation. "I was on the news a few times. Maybe they didn't like the publicity."

"What publicity? I mean, yeah, we saw your face, but you never said anything. We were all waiting for the big interview, but they talked to everyone but you."

That was on purpose. Lauren took a wineglass from the cupboard and filled it to the rim, and thought back to that awful time, when they were still counting the missing and aiding the survivors and she feared she would blurt out some damned thing about witches or assaults from the netherworld that would have brought the news media down on them like a second blizzard. "Thanks for telling me."

"You should talk to a lawyer. Something about this stinks." Ken raised his glass to her, then drained it and set it on the counter. "Take care."

"You, too." Lauren stood for a time, drink in hand. When Katie and her husband, Paul, bustled in with deli bags and six-packs of soda, she excused herself and bolted outside. Dodged friends and well-wishers until she found a private corner of the backyard, hidden from view of the house by a curved stretch of retaining wall. Sat on the ground, and hugged her knees to her chin.

They forced me out. Maybe she had always suspected it, but hearing it from Ken drove the point home that much harder. It also cast her recent spate of job rejections in a different light. They would never admit it on the record but managers from different companies talked, and when it came to rankings as the good little corporate soldier, well, given her recent behavior she doubted that she would have made the top of any of their lists.

That being the case, there were worse people to have begging her time and attention than the witch-tolerant COO of Carmody Inc., however much she distrusted him. *Managers talk.* She guessed that Council members did, too. They would have known what happened in Gideon, and before long the facts of her joblessness would have made the rounds. *I inhabit a very small world now.* Maybe her private affairs were no longer as private as she would have wished.

Lauren downed a few gulps of wine. Then she took out her phone and Kaster's card, and punched in his number. Hated herself a little, even as she realized that, like Fred Parkinson, she might have had a foot in the next world, but she still had to live in this one.

She listened to the ring. Once. Twice. Then came a soft, honeyed "Hello?"

"Mr. Kaster, it's—"

"Mistress Mullin." Kaster's voice brightened. "I was so hoping to hear from you this evening. I assume you haven't called to turn us down?"

Lauren stuck out her tongue at the phone. "You assume correctly."

"Splendid. One of my assistants will messenger you the itinerary."

"I have a rental car I need to drop off first—"

"That will be handled. Just leave it parked in front of your condominium with the keys inside."

"Oh. Okay. Thank you, Mr. Kaster."

"Please, call me Gene."

"Thank you. Gene."

"Until we meet again."

Lauren disconnected, then rose and paced back and forth to settle her racing mind. *It will be good for me.* A chance to meet others like her, to talk openly about spells and demons and what lay beyond the pale, just as she did back in Gideon.

I'm doing the right thing. Yet even the gabbling in her head had quieted, as though the owners of those voices felt as uncertain as she did.

Then she heard Katie call her name, and returned to the house to enjoy her party.

CHAPTER 6

Lauren spent the night at her condo and awoke the next morning to find the promised messenger waiting for her in the parking lot. The young man asked for identification, scanned it, had her sign for the packet, then immediately transmitted the receipt to Carmody headquarters. Somebody wanted to make very sure that she received her travel instructions.

Lauren perused the itinerary over coffee. She would be picked up at the condo and taken to Boeing Field. Private jet to the Carmody field outside Portland, then helicopter to the compound. A list of suggested clothing was included. Business casual for day. Hiking and swimming attire recommended.

I'm going to Witch Camp. Well, she had a day to prepare, despite the fact that she had no idea what she was letting herself in for. She doubted they would be making s'mores around the campfire. But she might be expected to give the magical version of a presentation. Show what she was capable of.

Lauren's stomach gave a nervous flip. Virginia had done

her best to instruct her in formal spellcraft, but the lessons had trouble sticking. No matter how hard Lauren tried to concentrate, her mind wandered. When she needed to do something like ward a place, she did as she had in Katie's backyard—she used whatever was at hand and made things up as she went along. It either felt right or it didn't.

In a few cases, yes, the right plants and herbs mattered. Elder, for example. To a human, it smelled like cat piss. To a demon, it smelled much worse. But even so, it was a speed bump only, a warning to the entity that something even worse awaited if it kept pushing. And that "worse" was the will of the practitioner. The power she possessed to bend the space between this world and the next to her will, and the demon along with it.

Dark space. Lauren's name for it. Like dark energy, you couldn't see it, but its properties affected everything else. *I have an affinity for dark space.* That was her explanation for her ability to see and talk with Connie when no one else in Gideon could, for how she could pass back and forth with relative ease between this world and the next when for so many others, it had proved a one-way trip.

She tucked her itinerary back into its burgundy leather portfolio and set it to one side. Then she sat still, hands spread before her on the table, and closed her eyes. The ever-present voices, now so much a part of her that they didn't register unless she stopped and listened, chattered merrily in her ear. Sometimes she wondered if maybe they weren't inside her head after all, but outside, that the reason she could hear them was that they were part of the space between, too. A case of hypersensitive hearing instead of a glitch in her head. *Maybe*

I'm just an eavesdropper. The thought made the prattle easier to deal with.

Lauren imagined the individual voices as threads, brass and silver and copper tarnished black and green, the gaps between the words like the space between her world and theirs. In between the words, there was silence, and she reached for that, shrank herself to a pinpoint so she could burrow into it. As she did, the voices receded, dopplering to a distant whine and then, finally, to nothing.

She opened her eyes and looked around her dining room, the living room beyond. The air shimmered in places, opalescent waves separated by clear air. She grabbed her handbag and the car keys, and entered the nearest swirl. When it ended, she stepped into open air, and then into the next stream—as she did, the voices rose, then died again.

Outside, the situation wasn't as clear-cut. Other people, birds and dogs and vehicles speeding through the parking lot, all combined to disturb the streams so that they thinned, dissipated, vanished. She managed to insert herself into the scraps, zigzagging down the sidewalk like a child playing hopscotch until she stood next to her rental car. The air still eddied around her, and she wondered what a passerby would see if they looked at her at that moment.

"Lauren, is that you?"

Lauren looked around and spotted one of her neighbors hurrying toward her. Elena, a nurse at one of the local clinics.

"My God—it's been ages. Are you—" Elena looked directly at her for a few moments. Then she closed her eyes, shook her head, mumbled something under her breath. "There's nobody—I could've sworn I saw—" She turned and headed back to an Explorer parked nearby. Stopped, and looked back once more toward the place where Lauren stood, puzzlement flashing across her face. Then she got into her vehicle and drove off.

Lauren remained beside her car, and watched Elena leave. Eventually, she smiled.

LAUREN'S FORAY IN invisibility proved brief. She needed to reset herself firmly in this reality in order to drive—the few times a shred of darkness passed through the cabin, the car slowed, as though it no longer felt her foot on the gas. The kiosk in the parking garage balked a few times and spit out the cash she tried to insert, unable to sense her touch on the keypad.

Once she walked out onto the street, city noise washed everything magical away and the voices streamed back. Cities, it seemed, weren't the best places to attempt to vanish into the spaces between. Too many people and buildings, too much machinery and activity, disrupted the dark space. Lauren imagined it blending with her reality, the diluted remnants altering it just enough so that something as common as a brick could look strange and out of place, or making it so that a face you had never seen before looked familiar. A touch of weirdness, just enough to remind someone sensitive that the world wasn't always as it seemed.

That was why so many thin places turned up in woods, or sparsely populated areas like Gideon. Lauren imagined the Carmody compound, a mountain hideaway surrounded by miles of wilderness. *It's going to be odd.* Just how odd, she wouldn't know until she got there.

Her wardrobe needed updating, so she spent some time shopping for clothing suitable for a warm weather business retreat. Then she found a quiet table at one of her favorite sandwich places, dug out her phone, and placed a long-delayed call.

"Hello?" Virginia sounded harried, as though she'd been interrupted.

Lauren figured in the two-hour time difference. *Ah.* She had phoned just as the woman prepared for her late morning horseback ride. "You were headed out to the barn—I can call back."

"Bert can wait." The sound of squeaking springs as Virginia settled into her old office chair. "I wondered when you'd call."

Lauren gave her a rundown of the encounter with Kaster and the upcoming trip to the Carmody compound. Listened to the sound of papers rustling as Virginia straightened her desk.

"Are you sure you should go?"

"No, but I'm going anyway. Have you heard Kaster's name before?"

"No. Should I have?"

"I'm wondering if he's involved with the Council."

"Why would you think that?"

"Because he knew I didn't have a job anymore, and I figured that someone on the Council might have told him."

Silence for a few long moments. When Virginia finally spoke, it was in the slow, deliberate tone she used when she struggled to keep the sharpness in check. "They didn't hear it from me, if that's what you're not asking." Then came a snort.

"That's the sort of thing they're good at. Finding out those bits of personal business that don't matter. The Catemans kept them off-balance for almost two hundred years, telling them everything they wanted to hear. They don't like being upset. They like order. And they like money—is this Carmody fellow rich?"

"Oh, yes."

"It figures."

"You don't trust them."

"It's not that. It's because the things we have to do, the guarding, the vigilance—they've gotten away from that. I used to speak to one of them on the phone, and hang up wondering whether they had ever set a ward or read the sky."

"I'll remember that, in case any of them are there. But I have to go. Connie told me that I've been called and I need to see it through to the end."

"Fat lot of good that ever did her." Virginia sighed. "You will be careful?"

"As careful as I have to be." Lauren looked out at the street scene, the so-familiar Seattle traffic. "Can you . . . protect someone you don't know? From a distance?"

"It's not easy, but I can try."

"I have a friend. Her name's Katie Westbrook. She's pregnant. I've warded her house and car and some of her possessions, but I just want to make sure. I have photos in my room, on the dresser, if those would help. She's the one with long red hair. Her husband is the one with black hair and wire-rimmed glasses. His name is Paul."

"Yes—the photos would give me something to focus on. I can ask Zeke to help boost the signal if I have to. But they'll be fine, and so will you. Rocky says you have to give him a chance to win back all the money you took off him last week."

Lauren managed a smile. "Tell him to save his nickels, because I'm coming back for them."

"I will." Virginia cleared her throat. "Lady keep you."

The blessing caught Lauren off guard, hit her harder than she would have expected. She blinked as tears welled and her eyes stung. "Thanks." She disconnected, then sat back and stared at nothing for so long that her server came to her table and asked if she was all right.

"I'm fine." Everything was fine. "It's going to be okay," she continued under her breath, the sandwich shop's background music just loud enough to cancel out the babel in her head.

FOR THE FIRST time since Lauren's arrival in Seattle, the restlessness that had dogged her in Gideon returned. She drove through Downtown for a while, then headed east through Capitol Hill and Broadmoor before finally winding up in Madison Park, where she cruised along the tree-lined streets until she came to a formidable wrought-iron gate.

Abernathy College had been founded in the early 1900s by the same family that owned Lauren's former employer. It was a blink-and-you'll-miss-it liberal arts institution, a few spacious converted homes surrounding a main building tastefully rendered in old red brick and stone, all hidden behind towering stands of oak and maple. Lauren had never met anyone who graduated from there; they were the sort who journeyed to Europe or Asia for their advanced degrees before vanishing into university libraries, museums, or positions curating private collections. She only knew of the place because of her father. He had made his living repairing old furniture, and had taken night classes there in design and restoration. Every so often she had met him after class and driven him home, on the days her mother used their car.

She drove through the gate and parked in a small lot near the library. No one questioned her when she entered the building and wended her way past the front desk and through the stacks to the computer lab. There she checked the kiosks for the next available terminal and added her name to the waiting list.

So quiet, this place. Like a forest, which in a way, it still was. She killed time paging through books and edging in and out of the dark space that revealed itself in the afternoon light that streamed through the windows. Her voices griped in complaint when she did so, and she wondered why. Did they lose track of her? Did it hurt them?

Finally, her turn came. Because there was a waiting list, she had only an hour to accomplish her task. She settled into a kiosk, signed in with the guest password that someone had helpfully taped to the desktop monitor, and set to work.

Andrew Carmody. She plugged his name into the search engine, then scrolled through the results. The official website of the Carmody Foundation, the philanthropic organization started by his father, Steven. Gossip sites, years-old stories about the disappearance of Andrew's wife and the part, if any, that he played in it, interspersed with more recent tales of his daughter's brushes with rehab, the law, and Portland-area hospitals. The man himself was forty or so, a graduate of Stanford Business School, the shaggy-haired idol of men like her former bosses. One photograph in particular seemed to define Carmody, a shot taken at an awards banquet. There he stood, amid older men in staid business suits, dressed in jeans and an oxford shirt with half-rolled sleeves, sporting a three-day growth of stubble and a surfer dude grin. The PacNorWest casual look of a man who had no one left to impress and nothing to prove.

Except . . . Lauren clicked another link.

Nyssa Carmody. Photographs of Andrew's daughter revealed a colt of a young woman, crop-haired and taller than most men, her mother's model angularity combined with her father's sandy-haired fairness. Her beauty shone regardless of the circumstances, whether she had just been pulled from a wrecked car or caught exiting an after-hours club on the arm of a man three times her age. If the columnist felt charitable, they blamed her problems on the loss of her mother, the continued rumors of her father's involvement in the disappearance. If they didn't, they called her every printable variation on a spoiled little bitch theme, yet another clickbait cautionary tale.

She's only fifteen. Lauren thought back to her own teen years, the comparative calm of cigarettes, the odd toke or raid on the liquor cabinet, and backseat tussles with boys as inept and clueless as she was. A different world. A different universe.

The next link. *Fernanda Carmody.* Lauren studied her face, its flawless lines and curves frozen in time. It had stared out from the covers of numerous magazines until she married and vanished into motherhood. *Stuck in Portland before it was Portland.* A woman born in Rio de Janeiro, who had called New York, Paris, and Milan home.

Lauren found herself feeling sorry for Fernanda. *Mired in*

a world she didn't expect. Surrounded by strangers. *I know how that goes.* She contemplated one photo in particular, a rare unretouched image of Fernanda without makeup, the goddess come down to earth. Frizzy hair, a crooked smile, and a tiny scar on the tip of her chin. The photo of a human being, a missing wife and mother.

Lauren closed the image with a sense of relief, and moved on. *Eugene Kaster.* A family business, apparently, the care and counsel of Carmody men. Kaster's father, Frederick, had served both grandfather Elias and father Steven, but had passed away before Andrew took over the company reins. Stockier, balding, a gnome of a man, the sharp bones that made the son appear so distinctive giving the father the look of a grinning skull.

Lauren continued to click links and skim articles, unsure of what exactly she searched for. *Something that explains all this.* Some indication of why Carmody wanted to adjourn to the wilderness and surround himself with witches. *Maybe he's searching for his wife.* Assuming he hadn't killed her in the first place.

Lauren stared at the screen, mind churning. She had never formed an interest in gossip, the reams of idle speculation about famous people she would never meet. *But now I'm going to meet one of those people.* She squelched further thought by opening another link, and squinted as red calligraphy filled the display.

The Curse of Carmody Peak!!

Lauren groaned. It was the sort of website she usually blew past on reflex, white text against a black background, throbbing headlines and illegible captions. The first stories were a mishmash of legends from northwest Oregon, everything from haunted movie houses to the "Bandage Man" of Cannon

Beach and sightings of Sasquatch-like creatures. Only one story mentioned Carmody Peak specifically, a series of recollections from campers and loggers who spent the night on the mountain. Talk of weird sounds and sightings. Noises in the undergrowth, as though they were being followed. A sensation of being watched.

Because weird sounds in the woods at night are so unusual. Lauren moved on to the meat of the article. Several Fernanda Carmody photos, along with a rehash of the details of her disappearance liberally peppered with exclamation marks.

She paged down. When attempts to alter the display failed, she tweaked the brightness and squinted when necessary in order to read the vibrating verbiage.

Carmody employee missing!

An article cut and pasted from a small-town Oregon newspaper, date June 1978. Dr. Elliott Rickard, forty-six, a scientist in the basic research division, vanished during an employee picnic at the Carmody compound outside Portland.

Lauren studied the photograph that accompanied the story. A half-dozen men crowded together, including Steven Carmody and Frederick Kaster, who between them held a pair of the overlarge scissors used in ceremonial ribbon-cuttings. Next to them stood Rickard grinning broadly, hands shoved in the pockets of his lab coat.

Finally, at the bottom of the page, a flashing banner.

Another victim?!?

A short article from the Portland paper followed. David Garvin, age thirty-four, a Portland photographer, had told friends he would be spending a few days hiking the Northern

Coast Range. His truck was found in a clearing near the base of the peak, but Garvin had yet to turn up.

That was two weeks ago. A photo showed Garvin standing beside his truck, a camera hung around his neck. He was broad-shouldered, stocky, and dark-haired, his face obscured by a beard.

Lauren flinched as a soft *ping* sounded from the desktop, an indication that her time was almost up. She printed out the section of the website concerning Rickard and Garvin. Just as the last page emerged, someone knocked on the kiosk door. She had just enough time to shove the pages in her bag and clear her search history.

She hurried out of the library through a side exit and down a corridor lined with offices. She walked in one direction, rounded one corner, then another and another, and found herself in the same place at which she started. A few of the doors had windows—she spotted movement in one, the dark shape of someone looking out at her, and waved. "Excuse me. I just left the library, and I'm all turned around." She stepped closer and found herself staring at her own reflection.

Great. Lauren hurried down the corridor in the reverse direction, and again wound up in the same place. Tried the library door and found it locked. Knocked, softly at first, then harder, in an effort to draw someone's attention. But no one answered.

Overhead, the fluorescent lights stuttered and hummed, then dimmed, casting the corridor in shadow. She heard one of the doors open, and turned just as a woman emerged from an office at the far end. "Excuse me? Could you tell me if there's another way out of here?" She pointed to the library door. "It locked behind me and I can't find another exit."

73

The woman said nothing. She watched Lauren for a few moments, then started toward her.

"I don't want to be any trouble. I just need an exit." Lauren backed away as the woman drew closer. She came to end of the corridor, looked both ways, and found the other hallways had vanished, replaced by walls. She was trapped.

As the woman continued to approach, the overhead lights winked out one by one.

Lauren stilled. Even her voices had gone quiet.

She traced the Eye of the Lady in the air.

The woman quickened her step. Just as she came within arm's reach, another office door opened and a man stuck out his head. "Is something wrong?" As soon as he spoke, the lights blazed. The voices blared in Lauren's head.

The woman vanished.

"I'm sorry." Lauren looked in both directions, found that the hallways had returned to normal. "I left the library by a side door and wound up here."

The man stared at her. "The library's on the other side of campus." He pointed to the door through which Lauren had entered. "Go out that way, follow the path, it's the first building on your right."

Lauren walked to the door that a short time before had been locked. She could open it now. Of course she could. "Thanks. I'm sorry if I disturbed you."

"These are all faculty offices." The man stepped out into the corridor. He held papers in one hand and a red pen in the other, and looked irritated enough to call security. "Were you looking for someone in particular?"

"No, I just came in through the wrong door—"

"Are you a student?"

"I'm sorry." Lauren slipped outside and hurried down the walkway. When she didn't hear the door close behind her, she turned, and found the man standing in the open entry, watching her.

She smiled an apology, then continued to the library, entered, and walked straight through to the doorway that opened out to the parking lot. Got into her car, and sat still. Breathed slowly. It took her some time to come to grips with what had just happened, and to realize that yes, she definitely had to go to Portland.

When the lights had flashed on in the hallway, she caught a glimpse of the woman's face.

It was Fernanda Carmody.

CHAPTER 7

Lauren returned to her condo and spent the rest of the day cleaning, packing, and arguing with herself. That she had only imagined seeing Fernanda Carmody. Or that even if she had seen *something*, it had been a trick played by whatever had summoned her to Oregon, and had nothing to do with the missing woman.

But she knew better. If her adversary had wanted to taunt her, it would have shown her an image of her father, her mother, or one of Gideon's lost souls. She had never known Fernanda Carmody. Beyond a vague sense of regret and disquiet over the unexplained loss of another human being, she felt nothing concerning her disappearance.

She came to me. But why? Lauren pondered the question as she finished packing. She set her suitcase by the front door, then went to the window, pushed aside the curtain, and looked outside. It was a clear night, and she counted a handful of stars that managed to shine through the light pollution. *It will be different tomorrow.* Even with the lighting around the compound, she expected that the mountain night sky would be amazing.

That's one thing to look forward to. Lauren brushed the curtain back into place and returned to the living room. There would be no more playing with dark space that evening. No skeins of otherworldliness winding through the air. She settled on the couch, turned on the television, and tried to concentrate on a reality show.

Instead she pondered her hallway encounter. More and more details surfaced in her memory, like a figure emerging from fog. Fernanda had been about twenty-five when she vanished, but the face Lauren had seen had not been that of a young woman. *She looked much older.* Worn and battered, her face drawn, heavily lined.

Lauren had never heard of ghosts aging. They remained frozen in time, bound to the event that had rendered them thus. *So she could be alive.* Possibly hiding. *Or being held captive.* That sort of stress, the assumed lack of care, would age a person prematurely.

She closed her eyes and once more saw that ashen face framed by long, black hair, eyes wide, hands reaching out.

"She wants something." Not exactly a stretch. The question was what. Freedom? Justice? Her husband's head on a plate? Lauren folded her arms and nestled against the cushions. Eventually she fell asleep, and dreamed of being chased by a shadowed woman, down winding corridors that led nowhere.

THE DAY DAWNED brilliant and the flight to Portland offered a taste of a different life, awe-inspiring mountain vistas viewed over a made-to-order breakfast of an omelet and fruit so fresh it still held warmth from the sun.

Lauren proved the only passenger for that leg of the trip, and she worried that Kaster had lied to her about the other guests. But those fears abated when she disembarked and spotted the group milling outside the entrance to Carmody Field's small terminal. Two men and three women, all dressed in summery garb, the men in khakis and short-sleeve shirts, the women in sundresses.

Lauren looked down at her white linen pants and yellow T-shirt. First test passed.

"Ah, the special snowflake." One of the men, round face shiny pink with sunburn, bowed to her with a hand-waving flourish. "Some of us had to find our own way here."

A sun-bleached blonde in green batik clucked her tongue. "Quiet, Heath. We drove all of twenty minutes, including a stop for coffee." She held out her hand. "I'm Samantha Dane. But everybody calls me Sam." She had adorned her fingers with henna, whorls and rings that traced from bases to tips, and sported multiple piercing in her ears and nose and an overlarge shoulder bag of whipstitched leather. "You must be Lauren— I'm sorry, is it Mullin or Reardon?"

"Reardon's my legal name." Lauren tensed as the woman took hold of her elbow and steered her toward the rest of the group. "Mullin is a family name." Not the clearest of explanations, but she hoped it would suffice for the time being.

"How interesting." Samantha positioned Lauren in front of the others, then gestured that she should remain still. "Okay, everyone, one at a time."

The second man stuck out his hand. "Peter Augustin." Tall,

but slightly bent, his short black hair tipped with gray, his skin the same deep brown as his eyes.

"Stef Warburg." That from the eldest woman. A slight figure, face obscured by the round black frames of her eyeglasses, brown hair wound into a tight bun.

"Heath Jameson." Pink Face looked Lauren up and down, then arched his eyebrows and turned away.

The youngest woman stood leaning against the terminal wall, attention fixed on her phone. She wore a crisp red linen blazer over her tan dress; a thin leather briefcase rested on the ground next to her. "Jenny Porter." She raised a hand, then resumed reading.

Okay. Lauren smiled, muttered a greeting. Tried to ease out of Sam's grip without appearing rude, but the woman seemed bound and determined to hang on to her.

"So, what's your specialty?" Sam smiled broadly, but her eyes held that certain glint that indicated points would be awarded or deducted depending on the answer. "Spells? Herbs? Prognostication?"

Lauren thought for a moment. "I'm afraid I'm more a GP." She fielded the woman's puzzled look. "General practitioner. Whatever's needed?" She glanced at the others and caught Stef frowning. "I can get a sense of things sometimes, when I handle them. Their history."

"Well, that sounds very . . . useful." Sam pressed a hand to her chest. "I myself am a trained herbalist, and I have brought a veritable cornucopia with me. If any of you feel the least bit ill or out of sorts, physically or spiritually, just come see me and I will fix you right up."

"Don't worry—it's all legal." Heath jerked his thumb at Jenny, who had yet to look up from her phone. "The steely eye of Carmody's legal department, here to make sure we do nothing to embarrass our host."

"I would never—" Sam colored, then walked up to the man and swatted his arm.

Peter stepped around the pair and bent close to Lauren. "Don't mind Heath. Nerves bring out his edges."

"He's nervous?" Lauren looked past him to Heath, who had just laughed and shaken his head at something that Sam said to him.

"Aren't you?" Peter twitched one shoulder. "I am."

"I don't—" Lauren fell silent. *Nervous?* Yes, maybe a little. *Maybe a lot.* "I was told this was a chance to, I don't know, relax?" She caught a flicker in Peter's eyes. "It isn't?"

"Do you mind if I ask how you acquired your invitation?" Peter's expression remained friendly, but his voice held an edge.

Lauren hesitated. She could see Stef hovering nearby, doing a poor impersonation of a disinterested bystander. "Gene Kaster."

"Really? He . . . contacted you?"

"Yes."

"In Gideon?"

Lauren forced a smile. "No. I first met him in Seattle." She could see the questions form in Peter's eyes. He obviously knew something about her. *But he didn't hear it from Kaster, or he'd have known I was coming.* So how did he know about her? A feeling returned from her corporate days, a sense that she had stepped into the middle of a territorial squabble. "Sam mentioned that she was an herbalist. Do the rest of you specialize as well?"

Before Peter could reply, Stef joined them. "Heath is a well-regarded dealer in antiquities." A corner of her mouth twitched. "I believe his current snit is because he thought he'd been invited for a solo visit. He's been dying to get a look at the sculptures for years now."

"The house has a pretty well-regarded sculpture garden," Peter said to Lauren, "though not many folks have seen it. The architectural magazines have been trying to get up to the place for decades, but—"

"But?" Lauren guessed what was coming and decided against filling in the blanks. She had participated in retreats before. Anything said always got back to the hosts, and gossiping about the man who had invited her to his home seemed rude. Given all the poking around she intended to do, she didn't want to risk whatever goodwill might be out there for her to tap. Who knew when she would need it?

"The Carmodys were always very private. Until the last several years, of course." Stef shook her head. "The curse of—"

"Hey, Pete!"

Peter rolled his eyes. "Yes, Heath?" He turned to the man, who had retired to the air-conditioned waiting room inside the terminal and now leaned out the door.

"Come in here a minute. I need to ask you about that book that Fraley's is auctioning next week."

As Peter grumbled his way out of earshot, Lauren followed Stef to the shade of the building awning. "Were you going to say the curse of Carmody Peak?"

"Don't tell me you visited that horrid website." Stef took an embroidered hankie from her shoulder bag and dabbed sweat from her brow. "The pet project of a former acquaintance, emphasis on former. Friends shouldn't let friends post in sixteen-point Gothic, but one can only do so much." She motioned for Lauren to accompany her and headed around to the side of the building. "No, I was going to say the curse of too much money, though I'm sure we would all love the opportunity to prove our ability to cope." As soon as they were out of sight of the others, she raised her hand and drew an X in the air, then enclosed it with a circle.

Lauren stared, unsure whether she had just seen what she thought she saw. "You're a Child of Endor?"

"A bit more than that." As the seconds ticked by, Stef's brow arched. "Please tell me that Virginia told you."

Lauren waited for assistance, but none proved forthcoming. Then the penny dropped. "You're from the Council."

"You've heard of us?" Stef sighed. "That's reassuring, I suppose." She leaned against the building, folded her arms. "You seem puzzled."

"Gene Kaster led me to believe that the Council wasn't involved in this."

"Gene would prefer if we weren't involved in this. Gene doesn't always get what he wants." Stef cocked her head and studied Lauren. "So, you're the woman who saved Gideon." Her voice held a bit of wonder and a lot of question. "How is Virginia? We haven't heard from her since January, when she sent us a rather terse account of your ordeal."

Lauren looked toward the helipad located alongside the airfield's single runway and wondered when the helicopter would arrive to bail her out of this conversation. *You never told me you filed a report, Virginia.* The woman had made it sound as though she ignored the Council as a matter of course. "She's fine."

"Forgive me for being blunt, but I find it concerning that she sent you here without consulting us."

She didn't send me. The decision was mine. Lauren met Stef's eyes, narrowed behind her owl glasses. *She thinks Virginia is still Mistress of Gideon. Best to let her keep thinking that, at least for now.* "Maybe she felt the decision was hers to make."

"Well, we'll have to see about that." Stef looked up as the *whop-whop* of an approaching helicopter rattled the air. "This isn't the time or the place, but rest assured, we will address this." She turned on her heel and headed toward the runway.

Lauren hurried after her. "This is what you choose to get upset about? Seriously? When it served you to leave Gideon in the charge of a family that had a long-standing relationship with the demon who tried to destroy it?"

Stef stopped and turned. "If you're talking about the Catemans—"

"I am. From the very beginning, they ruled Gideon, and every Council since the founding of the town was content to stand aside and let it go on. So don't try to tell me that you know what's best for us, or that we're not capable of taking care—"

"You lost half your population to the blizzard, and you're losing the rest to economic realities. Virginia is the Mistress of a town in crisis, and yet she has seen fit to send you here. Why?"

"Yes, Gideon is in crisis. That being the case, how could she not send someone to talk to you directly?"

Stef stared at her. Then her eyes slowly widened. "You're her emissary?" She snorted softly, but before she could say more, Heath poked his head around the corner. "Heads up, ladies. Our bladed chariot has arrived." He pulled Sam after him toward the helipad. "Took them bloody long enough."

"As I said, this is neither the time nor place." Stef turned and followed the others to the helicopter.

Lauren waited until the others had boarded and the pilot had stowed the luggage and she had no choice but to follow.

CHAPTER 8

Lauren spent the forty-five-minute flight staring out the window, and pretended not to hear when Peter made an attempt to talk to her. When he wasn't trying to get her attention, he and Stef sat close together, heads bent, deep in conversation.

She sneaked glances at them, took note of the hand motions and half smiles, the hundred tiny gestures that marked them as close friends. *Very close.* She wondered what they intended to do after they arrived at the Carmody compound. *They know something is going on.* They had to. Surely she couldn't be the only witch in the United States who sensed that something was rotten in Oregon.

She took some comfort from the views of the mountains, the ribbon of the Pacific Ocean visible on the horizon. No danger to be seen or smelled from this height, and no voices thanks to the chopper noise.

But the respite didn't last long. A few minutes later, the Carmody compound came into view. The helipad, jutting out from the mountainside like a giant shelf fungus. Assorted support structures and outbuildings artfully obscured by landscaping. And through the trees, the light veining of roads and trails, bits of roof and flashes of skylight and window glass that drew closer and closer until before Lauren could draw her next breath the spruce and hemlock loomed overhead and all motion had ceased and the sounds of rotors and motors slowly died.

Lauren and the others disembarked and walked away from the helicopter, eyes fixed on the scene before them like explorers taking their first steps on a new world. The Carmody house hugged the summit of the peak, an arrangement in wood, stone, and glass that blended with the trees and reflected passing clouds, that seemed to have emerged from the side of the mountain rather than been built on it.

"Welcome to tonight's episode of how the other hundredth of a percent lives." Heath tried for flippant but missed, the wonder in his voice all too apparent.

"The main part of the house was built in the late sixties." Peter pointed to the lower levels of redwood-stained beams and balconies. "Steven Carmody, our host's late father, wanted it to look as though it had always been part of the mountain."

"Places like this always have names." Sam held on to Heath's arm and gasped as a hawk flew overhead, its mirror image coursing along the side of the house. "Did he give it a name?"

Jenny spoke for the first time. "The house on our mountain? The little cabin in the woods?"

They all continued to marvel until a strange sound filled the air, like steam escaping from a teakettle. Then came a metal-on-metal whine, at which point a small train emerged from a gap in some shrubbery and chugged toward them. It ran along a narrow track, a trio of open cars attached to a miniature loco-motive complete with cowcatcher.

"Mornin', folks." The driver doffed his cap as the train rounded a curve until it faced the direction of the house. "All aboard." He smiled at the stares. "A lot of the logging outfits installed their own rail lines to transport cut timber. You'll see the old track if you visit the Jericho camp. Mr. Carmody's father had this installed for guest use. Kinda like a tribute."

Sam stroked the side of the locomotive. "Could we ride this train to Jericho?"

"No, ma'am. This is like a miniature version. Track's too narrow."

As staff appeared out of nowhere to unload the luggage from the helicopter onto a flatbed for transport to the house, Lau-ren and the others boarded the train. Lauren looked over the driver's shoulder at the array of electronic gear and paperwork spread across the dashboard. Amid the clutter, she spotted what looked like a WANTED poster poking out from beneath a clipboard. "Who's that?

"Picked it up down at the truck stop off the main road." The driver pulled out the sheet of paper and handed it to her. "He went missing around here two–three weeks ago." He hit the starter and the train jerked into motion. "Hikers go missing all the time. The woods are pretty. Folks forget that pretty can hide bad things."

Lauren studied the image, a copy of which was currently stashed in her messenger bag. "David Garvin."

"Do you know him?" Peter asked.

"No." Lauren handed the poster back to the driver. "I figure that if we went hiking, we could keep an eye out."

The driver shook his head. "It's been almost three weeks, like I said. Anyone who's been missing that long doesn't want to be found. Or they're dead." He glanced back at his passengers. "Poor fellow could be a ghost by now."

Sam clucked her tongue. "What an awful thing to say."

"Fact o' life around here, ma'am, much as I regret to say it. Respect the woods, because they sure as hell ain't got no respect for you." Sensing an audience, the driver sat up straighter and cleared his throat. "Even if, God willing, that Mr. Garvin is still alive somewhere, we've got more than our share of spirits. There's Bandage Man—they see him mostly near Cannon Beach, but he's been known to turn up in these parts. A lumberjack, he was, injured in a horrible sawmill accident. They tried to treat his wounds—wrapped him in bandages from head to toe like a mummy—but he died anyway. Now he haunts the woods and roadways around here—"

"—especially lovers' lanes." Heath snickered. "Where naughty teenagers park 'n' fark."

"The woods and roadways." The driver raised his voice to drown out Heath's commentary. "Most folks smell him before they see him, and that's a good thing because the sight of him is terrible to behold."

Lauren thought back to that last afternoon in Gideon, the evil that permeated the air along with the stench. "He smells?"

"The stink of his rotting, infected flesh." Heath poked Lauren's arm once, then again when she ignored him.

Lauren leaned forward beyond his reach. "Has he ever been seen around this mountain?"

The driver turned and frowned at Heath. "You hear things." He shrugged, his storytelling mood squelched.

The train rumbled through a wooded stretch and up a steep incline, then came to a stop beside a flagstone walkway. "Okay, folks, just follow the path." The driver pointed toward the house. "It'll take you to the doorway that leads into the parking garage. There's an elevator at the far end that will take you up to the ground floor."

"Of course there is," Heath muttered.

LAUREN'S ROOM WAS located on the top floor of the four-level house, overlooking what was technically the backyard. She caught glimpses of the helipad when the breeze fluttered through the trees, and she could just see the bright blue thread of the Pacific in the distance.

Her suite proved spacious, but the layout and decor allowed for little privacy, with floor-to-ceiling glass in the bedroom and sitting area. Even the bathroom left her feeling exposed. The open-air shower was located out on the balcony, sheltered from view by strategically placed evergreen shrubbery.

Lauren stepped outside, and savored the warm breeze as she worked out the controls for hot and cold water. But attractive as the setting was, something about it gave her the creeps. She looked over the railing to the sheer drop below, and took comfort from the fact that a Peeping Tom would have needed climbing gear to get a decent view.

She scanned the trees. Her voices had lowered to whispers,

so she could hear clearly the chitter of squirrels, the trill of birds. *But there's something else.* She stilled, held her breath, and listened. Caught the barest hint of a hum. Or was it a buzz?

Then an insect zipped past within inches of her face, a fly or a bee.

That answers that question. Lauren went back inside and toured the rest of the suite. Well, if modesty got the better of her, she could always get dressed in the closet, which came complete with three chests of drawers, a dressing table and a floor mirror, and had more square footage than the living room of her condo. She sat at the table and surveyed her few articles of clothing, which had been unpacked and hung up in the few minutes between the housekeeper telling her the location of her room and her ascent of the winding staircase.

What am I doing here? Lauren spun in one direction in the dressing table chair, then the other, as that question warred for her attention with her voices, images of shambling, stinking ghosts following her through the woods, and a wide-eyed, beseeching Fernanda Carmody reaching out to her in a dead-end hallway.

Then a familiar warble joined the chorus. Lauren dug her phone out of her bag and checked the incoming number. Counted to three. "Hello, Virginia—"

"Is this my emissary? Never had one of those before. So fancy."

"Stef Warburg called you already?"

"Oh, yes. We just hung up. My ears are still ringing, and I have a headache from trying to back up whatever it is you told her without knowing what in Lady's name that was."

"She wanted to know why I was here given the state of things in Gideon."

"Yes, I got that."

"That's when I told her that you sent me."

"Could you tell me why exactly I sent you? That way we'll both know."

"I think we should ask the Council for help."

"What kind of help?"

"Financial. Manpower."

"You won't get it."

"Did you ever ask?"

"No. Because I knew I wouldn't get it." A man's voice rumbled in the background and Virginia swore under her breath. "In a minute, Zeke, dammit, I'm on the phone with Lauren." She sighed. "Zeke says hello."

"Back at him." Lauren winced as animal screeches of wood sliding over wood grated her ear—she envisioned Virginia opening and closing desk drawers and pushing her chair under the desk. "Did Warburg say anything else?"

"She asked if we've been bothered by any recurrences, any new visitations." Virginia paused. "She asked if you had been experiencing anything out of the ordinary. I said no, Lady help me. I am pretty sure she suspects we're holding back." Again, the sounds of her rooting through drawers. "Walked through any strange woods lately?"

Speaking of holding back. Lauren decided against mentioning Fernanda Carmody. She had already shoveled enough onto the woman's plate. No sense giving her even more to worry about. "Not since I got here." She revisited her balcony, looked both ways, then reentered the suite and closed and locked the glass doors. She doubted anyone else staying on the floor could hear her, but she still couldn't shake the sensation of being monitored. "You filed a report about me. About what happened last winter."

"I had no choice. We were on the news every damn day for two weeks." Virginia's voice softened. "That was the best report I ever submitted. It had footnotes and everything."

"That means the Council knows a lot about me."

"Given what you might be facing, that's a good thing, don't you think?"

"Maybe. Were you able to set the protection spell I asked about?"

"Yes. Me and Zeke."

Lauren looked out at the nearby trees, the birds flitting from branch to branch. "Thank you."

Virginia grumbled an acknowledgment. "So we have our story straight now? I sent you to beg. Any trouble you get into from here on out, I can say that I have no knowledge and it's all your fault."

Lauren smiled. "Sounds good."

"So if Stef calls me again to complain about you, I will tell her to go to blazes."

"No, you won't. You'll be your usual charming self." Lauren stilled at the sound of approaching footsteps. Then came a knock on the door, and someone announcing that drinks were being served in the downstairs lounge. "I have to go." When she disconnected, Virginia was still laughing.

CHAPTER 9

Lauren braved the shower, then donned a black silk T-shirt and beige linen pants. Fixed her short brown hair as best she could given its innate unruliness and the humidity. Gave herself as much of a pep talk as she could manage given the circumstances.

She exited her suite and peeked over the railing of the open corridor, and listened to the laughter that drifted up from the lounge. Skipped the elevator for the spiral staircase, descended past the original paintings and sculptures, the museum-quality wall hangings, and stopped on the landing to study one piece, a netlike construction in black and silver that reminded her of a web. She looked around to see if anyone could see her, then touched one of the cords. It felt rough, gritty, as though it had been newly excavated from some den or cave and hung on the wall.

Welcome to my parlor, said the spider to the fly. Lauren shivered, rubbed her arms, and hurried downstairs.

The lounge was an open, multistory space that over-looked a steep descent into a forested ravine. Views of nighttime skies through the glass-paneled roof would no doubt prove extraordinary, but now the midday sun blasted through, making the room look floodlit and feel uncomfortably warm despite the air-conditioning. Stef, Peter, Sam, and Heath sat on a circular couch at the far end while near the entrance, a lone server stood polishing glasses and lining them up on the bar.

Lauren opted for local pinot noir and downed half the glass on the way to the couch. Peter waved to her as she approached, then scooted over to give her room to sit.

"We were just talking about the showers." He cocked an eyebrow and shook his head. "I guess on a rainy day, you don't need to bother running the water."

"Forget rainy days—what about winter?" Sam wore a sweater over her wrap shirt and trousers despite the warmth, and cradled a cup of hot tea. "The snow falling on you while you're naked—gah!"

Heath nudged her with his elbow. "I don't know. Sounds kinda hot to me." He tossed back his whiskey, then looked back over his shoulder at the server and raised his empty glass.

Stilted silence fell. Lauren looked toward the darkened corners to see if Jenny Porter had opted to sit by herself. But the woman was nowhere to be seen.

"I hope you don't mind my asking, Ms. Mullin, is it?" Heath waited until the barman departed. "Where did you study?"

"I went to school at the University of Washington." Lauren

glanced at Peter, who nodded for her to keep going. "Bachelor's in business admin, then an MBA, emphasis on project management." She felt the stares, caught the not-so-fleeting frowns.

Heath snorted. "Well, that sounds very . . . I don't know, Stef—what's the best word you can think of? Mundane?"

"You don't think witches need to understand business?" Lauren sat back, felt the warmth of the alcohol suffuse her limbs. *Be careful.* Her tact filter tended to malfunction when under the influence.

"I believe we as creatives lose something vital when we allow ourselves to be consumed by everyday concerns." Heath sat with his legs crossed ankle on knee, one arm draped along the back of the couch. "The bean counters of the world have sucked enough out of life. Why should they suck the magic out of it as well?" He ran a finger up and down the back of Sam's neck as he spoke, pausing every so often to stroke a tendril of hair.

"I feel magic in my life every day now." *Sometimes I wish I felt a little less.* Lauren sensed everyone's eyes on her, looked out toward the woods to avoid meeting them. "My education didn't have anything to do with it. My everyday concerns don't dull my senses."

"As with any faith, the day-to-day worries occupy minds best focused elsewhere." Heath pointed to her with the hand that held his glass—the glass tipped, sending watered whiskey splashing across the leather upholstery. "The village wise man didn't also keep shop or run the local pub. He lived to counsel, to instruct."

"And let others do the cleaning up," Sam muttered as she dried the cushions with the hem of her skirt.

Lauren held back a wisecrack about counseling bartenders, as one of her last Gideon memories replayed in her mind. The Parkinsons' loaded pickup truck, headed out of town. "That might have been true back in the day when a village supported their witch and paid for her services. But those days are gone and they're not coming back." She tried to choose her words carefully, even as she felt the frustration rise. "Unless you have a money-printing spell up your sleeve, I don't see how you can function without paying attention to the bottom line."

Heath's face reddened. "My bottom line gets sufficient attention from those paid to do so." He finished his drink, then stood. "If I need your advice, I'll ask for it." He rounded the couch and headed toward the bar.

"I better go see—" Sam struggled to her feet. "I better go." She hurried after Heath, who had grabbed a bottle of whiskey, and followed him out of the lounge.

Lauren waited until the clatter of Sam's sandals on the wood floor died away. "I put my foot in it, didn't I?"

"Maybe a little. But how were you to know?" Peter rocked his head from side to side. "Let's just say that Heath could use a little counsel in what he considers more mundane concerns, and leave it at that."

"Do I need to apologize?"

"He started it. But if you feel compelled, it might make the next few days go a little more smoothly. It's your call."

Lauren nodded. Stared out at the trees. Checked her watch. Less than a half hour gone by, and she already had someone pissed at her. "What the hell am I doing here?"

She meant to speak under her breath, but Peter's chuckle informed her that she had come through loud and clear.

"We've all been wondering that very same thing." Stef had kicked off her pumps and tucked her feet under her.

"Well." Lauren rose and moved to the couch across from the woman. "You told me you're on the Council." She nodded to Peter. "I assume that you are, as well?"

Peter nodded, eventually. "Stef is Mistress of the Council, in fact. She leads it."

I wish Virginia had told me that. Lauren imagined the amount of chair-squeaking and drawer-slamming that must have accompanied that phone call. "And Heath and Sam?"

"Heath advises us on purchases of rare documents and artifacts. Sam? Lady forbid. She's just along for the ride." Stef swirled something caramel brown in a small snifter, but seemed more intent on inhaling than drinking. "I spoke with your Mistress a little while ago. She said she sent you here on a mission that you will explain in good time."

Lauren nodded. "I—*we*—wanted to discuss some issues related to Gideon, and felt it better done in person. And since Mistress Waycross couldn't leave—"

"But you went to Seattle first before coming to Portland."

"Seattle's my hometown. I had some personal business that I needed to see to."

"And you just happened to meet Gene Kaster while you were there?" Stef smiled, but the warmth stopped there—her brown eyes glittered like ice in coffee. "Forgive me, but it just seems more than coincidental."

"He tracked me down and extended the invitation." Lauren

looked up through the glass ceiling to find a vulture circling lazily overhead. Was it a verdict or a prediction? "I had never even heard of him up to that point."

"But you'd heard of Andrew Carmody?" Peter's turn. His voice came softer, more conversational.

Stef's the fist. You're the velvet glove. Together they made quite a team. "Everyone in the Pacific Northwest has heard of Carmody." Lauren held up a pleading hand, then let it fall. "How many times do I have to say it? The first time I met Kaster was the day before yesterday, when he invited me here."

"But he didn't tell you the purpose of this get-together?"

"He made it sound like Witch Camp. A break. A chance to meet with like minds."

"Witch Camp." Stef shook her head. "That sounds like Gene." She sipped her drink, then set the snifter on the table. "If you'll excuse me, I'm going to try to nap before dinner. Doctor's orders." She brushed her hand over Peter's, then stood. "We'll continue this later."

Lauren watched her leave. "Is she all right?"

Peter pressed his hand over his heart. "They want her to take it easy."

"And I'm not helping?" If Gene Kaster and his shit-eating grin had appeared before Lauren at that moment, she'd have slapped him. "He didn't say 'Witch Camp.' He just made it sound like a retreat."

"Gene is good at making everything sound like a party. Until you sit across the negotiating table from him." Peter passed a hand over his face. "You understand our difficulty? We came here for our own reasons."

"Which are?"

"Council concerns."

"Carmody's a member of the Council?" Lauren waited, even though she knew Peter would never tell her. "So what if Kaster sought me out for whatever reason. He works for Carmody. He's acting for his boss, right?" She caught Peter's eyes narrow, and the realization hit her like a slap. *It's about more than my appearing out of nowhere. They're worried about something.* All wasn't well in Council-land. "You know, there are ways that you could determine whether or not I speak the truth."

Peter broke eye contact, which probably indicated that he had been thinking along those same lines. "That would be intrusive."

"Not if I gave my permission." Leather crackled as Lauren shifted in her seat. She had mined truth from so many others, both by accident and on purpose. Saw the fear, anger, and yes, sometimes the hatred in their eyes when they realized what she did, and that their innermost thoughts were no longer their own. *Payback's a bitch.* "Consider it given."

Peter nodded. Then he finished his beer, and stood. "You are acknowledged to be a talented practitioner, Lauren." He looked down at her for a few moments, lips pressed into a thin line. "Later."

Lauren watched him leave. *He thinks I'd beat his test. He'll never believe me.* Stef wouldn't, either. *Good luck asking them for help.* Or for anything else. *I'm on my own here.*

She sat for a time. Then she recalled Peter's mention of the sculpture garden and decided to give it a look even though sculpture wasn't her thing. *If I were back in Gideon, I'd be headed for a walk in the woods about now.* She needed to move, think, figure out what to do next.

As she left the lounge, she realized that her voices had quieted almost to nothing. The only sign of their presence was the occasional buzzing in her ears, like the pressure change signaling a storm.

THE FIRST HINT of cooler ocean air had drifted in as the sun sank into the west. Lauren walked down to the ground floor of the house and out onto an immense flagstone patio. Beyond that were terraces that reached a third of the way down the peak. They were connected by wide stairways of hewn rock, and filled with flowering plants, shrubs, and small trees. Here and there she could see stone benches and planters, steps and walkways that wound through it all.

She walked down to the first level and was enveloped by rose scent seasoned with evergreen bite. Clusters of herbs and medicinal plants served as ground cover—Lauren's lack of diligence with respect to her herbology lessons had driven Virginia to despair, but she recognized mandrake, vervain, rosemary, and wood betony. Near a bushel-basket-size spray of lemon thyme, she spotted the first sculpture, an attenuated figure the size of a kitten, which looked like a running rabbit. She poked through the thyme until she found a small placard. *Fleeing hare, Etruscan, 700–600 B.C.*

Lauren wandered throughout the level, spotted a few more animal sculptures of the same stylized appearance as the hare. Most were Etruscan, of the same general period. Others were labeled Upper Paleolithic, Dark Ages, Renaissance.

On the next level stood a grouping of shoulder-high shrubs with sweet-smelling white flowers. *Downy thorn apple.* Around them grew clusters of plants with curly kale-like leaves and pale yellow flowers. *Horned poppy.* She walked around the beds, spotted a few more plants with poisonous seeds, leaves, or fruit, and a few that were bad news no matter which part you dealt with. *So this is the poison level.* She looked for warnings not to touch, but couldn't find any. Apparently the Carmodys knew better, and assumed their guests would, too.

Lauren missed the statue at first, then found it during her search for placards. It appeared like nothing more than a free-form lump of clay. But when she looked more closely, she could pick out the outline of bulbous eyes, a narrow jaw and rounded mouth, hands with fingers so short they might have been claws.

She hunted for some type of identification, something about the sculptor or the name and age of the piece. Slapped away a few insects that she flushed from the undergrowth. Dug a tissue out of her pocket and brushed away the dirt and dried leaves from around the base.

At first she found nothing. Then, on closer inspection, she found the etching on the surface of the pedestal on which the statue rested. Messy, indistinct letters, as though someone had scratched them with the edge of a stone or piece of glass.

WE ARE THE FOREST

She polished the inscription, then cleaned the stone, on the lookout in case she had missed something. But the ragged carving was all she found.

She hunted until she came to another statue. A deer, this time, a fawn or doe. It stood about knee-high, a spindly-legged creation with a featureless face. She thought it another Etruscan figure but could find no identification of any kind.

She examined the piece more closely and found it bore a large mark that almost encircled its neck. *A scratch?* No, an actual slice through the metal—she could see the hairline space between the deer's head and its neck. It reminded her of a gash, as though the beast's throat had been cut.

Then, around the corner, another mound creature. On the ground, this time, half-hidden behind the bloom-laden branch of a rosebush. Lauren crouched down and cleaned the area around it to find it rested upon a small slab of stone. She expected to find another scratched phrase. She wasn't disappointed.

WE ARE THE DARKNESS THAT HIDES

She searched that level for more mound creatures but found none. Moved down to the next, hunched low, and poked through the comfrey, parsley, and other ground cover. Was about to round the corner into the central section but stopped when she heard sounds of arguing. Not her voices. Somebody else's.

"Keep it down."

"Let them all hear me. I don't fucking care!"

"Dammit, she's here to help you. Five minutes of your time—that's all I'm asking."

Lauren crept to the end of a planter, peeked around the

corner, and spotted a middle-aged man in jeans and a denim shirt and a teenage girl in cutoffs and a tank top. They stood in the center of a circle of flowering dogwoods, which were tall enough to hide them from view from the house. Her host and his daughter, having an afternoon meltdown.

"Nyssa." Andrew Carmody pointed toward the house. "We can get through this."

"Just stop, okay?" Nyssa covered her ears with her hands. "Nothing she or any of them can do will help. They came here because you paid them, and they'll tell you what you want to hear." She turned and headed up the steps toward the house, bare feet padding softly on the stone.

"You're not leaving," Carmody called after her.

Nyssa didn't bother to turn around. "You can't stop me."

"As a matter of fact, I can. I've locked up your phones, so you can't contact any of your usual accomplices. All the car keys have been secured. Anyone who provides you a set will be fired."

"I'll just walk down the mountain and hitch. I've done it before."

"And I've talked to the sheriff and Greg and Millie at the truck stop. Anyone who sees you calls me. Anyone who picks you up will be stopped. If you make it as far as Portland, all your usual bolt holes are being watched. All the places you go, and a few you haven't thought of yet."

Nyssa slowed, stopped. Then she turned and stared at her father. Her look held no heated emotion, no anger or hatred. Resignation, maybe. Weariness with an argument that they'd had too many times before.

"Why do you bother?" Her voice came low and quiet and devoid of feeling. "Who are you really trying to protect?" She studied him for a moment longer, then continued back up the steps.

Carmody had been standing shoulders back, arms folded across his chest. But as soon as Nyssa vanished from sight, he crumpled—his head hung, and his hands fell to his sides. He paced a ragged circle, kicked a stone into the shrubbery.

Then he stilled, straightened, and looked toward the spot where Lauren stood hidden. "I know you're there." His voice could have been chipped and used to chill drinks. "You may as well come out."

"I—" Lauren stepped out from behind the planter and held up her hands in surrender. "I'm sorry. I was just walking through the—and I'm going now." She turned tail and fled, almost falling on her face when she tripped on the edge of a step. She scurried into the house and down the first hallway she came to, all the while checking over her shoulder to see if Carmody followed. She ducked through the first open doorway into what looked like a media room and almost tripped over a dark shape in the middle of the floor.

The room lights blazed, triggered by her movement.

"Uh—hello?" Jenny Porter stared up at her. She sat cross-legged, a bottle of wine cradled in her lap.

CHAPTER 10

Jenny had changed out of her business wear into cream linen slacks and a blue tank top over which she'd thrown a raggedy denim jacket, and had loosened her dark brown hair so that it formed an aureole of tight curls around her face. She fixed on Lauren, eyes wide, the startled expression of someone who hadn't expected to be found.

"I'm sorry." Lauren backed away and started to leave. "I didn't mean—"

"It's okay." Jenny beckoned for her to come back in. "I was just . . . hiding." Her phone rested on the floor next to her—she picked it up and checked the time. "Is it dinnertime yet? I'm trying to decide whether to blow it off or not."

"I think they said it's at six." Lauren walked to the window, which allowed a view of the edge of the garden, and caught sight of Carmody entering the house.

"Sorry about being such a bitch this morning." Jenny freed a jackknife from the recesses of her jacket, then held it up so Lauren could see. "Girl's best friend." She fiddled with it until she flipped open the corkscrew, then set about opening the bottle. "Jameson introduced himself by asking if I rode a broomstick when I chased ambulances, and that just—" She gave the corkscrew a hard twist. "Is he always such a dick?"

"I don't know. I just met him today." Lauren lowered to the floor. "But I think the answer's yes."

"Hmm." Jenny extracted the cork, then took a swig from the bottle. "I didn't bring any glasses. They were all hanging around the bar when I went into the lounge and Jameson was sitting under the overhead rack thing and I couldn't bring myself to get that close to him. I just swiped the first alcoholic whatever I could reach and hid in here." She wiped the mouth of the bottle with her sleeve and handed it to Lauren.

"That's okay. It's turned into a drink-straight-from-the-bottle kind of day." Lauren read the label. "Syrah. Isn't it a crime to drink red in Oregon if it's not pinot?"

"I think you get special dispensation if you don't use a glass."

"I totally knew that." Lauren took a long pull. Then she dug in her pocket for a clean tissue to wipe the bottle, but came up empty. "I don't have a sleeve."

"I don't have a cold—do you?"

"Nope."

"Then the hell with it." Jenny held out her hand for the bottle.

They drank in companionable silence. Lauren replayed the scene in the garden, alternated between wondering whether Nyssa had attempted her escape and thinking about the strange mound figures. Eventually she stood and returned to the window, looked out in time to watch an owl glide through the trees. "It's beautiful out here. I wish this was an actual vacation and not—whatever the hell it is."

Jenny rose a little unsteadily, put a hand on a nearby couch for support. "What do you think you'll have to do?"

"I don't know. Kaster made it sound like a retreat."

"Kaster's good at making things sound the way they have to in order to get you to do what he wants." Jenny shrugged. "I know him. I mean, I know of him. How he operates."

Lauren held back her questions. She had already experienced enough of what Kaster was capable to figure out the rest. "Are you here in case someone gets hurt?"

Jenny laughed. "I wish. I'm in patents and trademarks."

"What's Carmody going to do, patent magic?"

"Be nice. At least I'd have something to do." Jenny leaned against the window. "I think they just wanted somebody with 'Legal' in their title here in case some bullshit thing happens, and I drew the short straw." She studied Lauren with bleary-eyed bemusement. "After what I heard this morning, I thought it might be you. But you don't seem the type."

"What did you expect?"

"I'm just thinking about the way they talked about you before you showed up. Like you were, I don't know, some kind of intruder. 'Who is she? Is her name Mullin or Reardon? What's her pedigree?'"

"My pedigree?"

"That's the word Jameson used. I guess there are certain people that you can train with to get good at what you do, and none of them knew you, so no one here knows you. They just know about you."

"Sounds like grad school." The wine urged Lauren to say more, but she refrained. All she did know was that the new-kid-in-class feeling had overstayed its welcome.

"So you're some superstar magic queen." Jenny waved her hand in a woo-hoo gesture. "I heard them talk about what happened in Gideon. What you did. I think that's what got their backs up. They've all got advanced degrees, and they've all studied this stuff for years, and you apparently did all what you did without any training and they're like, whoa."

Lauren's smile wavered. Jenny seemed friendly enough. More than friendly. Very understanding of things that would have sent civilians screaming for the exits. "You seem to be taking all this in stride. Do you practice?"

"Practice? Is that the term?" Jenny grinned. "No. But I keep an open mind."

Apparently. Lauren nodded, and took another swallow of wine.

JENNY DECIDED TO skip dinner, so Lauren begged directions to the dining room from one of the house staff and entered to find the others already well into the first course. The table was an odd kidney shape that left her with no good choices when it came to seating. The open chair next to Sam would leave her sitting across from Heath, while the spot next to Peter would stick her right next to Andrew Carmody.

She opted for the seat next to Carmody as the lesser evil and settled in. Heard Heath mutter something to Sam, then caught his poisonous look.

"Glad you could make it." Peter offered a halfhearted smile, then turned back to Stef.

Lauren focused on her appetizer, a deconstructed crab salad sandwich that proved complicated enough to claim the better part of everyone's attention. Conversation remained sporadic until staff arrived to clear plates and set out the main course of grilled salmon.

Simple as you can get. Dammit. Lauren pretended to be engrossed in her food, then made the mistake of glancing up to find Carmody watching her.

"Did you find anything of interest in the sculpture garden?" He took a sip of his wine, then regarded her over the top of his glass.

Lauren started to speak. Stopped. Carmody looked as he had in every photograph she had ever seen, an unmade bed of a man in perpetual need of a haircut. He wore the same clothes he had in the garden, battered jeans and a denim shirt faded to silvery blue.

It matches his eyes. Except that his eyes were more than a single color. Light blue centers, yes, but darker blue around the outside of the irises, circles sharp and clean as pencil lines. *And there's gold.* Rings around the pupils, soft and smudged, the color of banked fires.

"Hello?" Carmody pressed his lips together as though struggling not to smile.

Lauren blinked. "I'm—I'm sorry." She felt the blush rise, her face heat. Sensed the stares of the others and sat back, bought time by taking a sip of water. "I tried to apologize before. I didn't mean—"

"That's not what I asked." Carmody rested one elbow on the table and propped his chin in his hand. "I watched you rummaging through the shrubbery earlier. You seemed pretty intent. I thought perhaps you'd lost something."

Lauren tried to read Carmody's expression but could sense nothing other than simple curiosity. If he still felt irritated that she had blundered into his argument with his daughter, he hid it well. "I saw the—" She drew an oval in the air with her fork. "'We are the forest.'"

"I've heard about those." Ice cubes clattered as Heath shook his glass. "I look forward to examining them."

Carmody said nothing. As the silence continued, Stef nudged Peter, who arched his brow. Sam sat in stiff politeness while Heath shifted in his seat.

Finally, Carmody looked up, eyes widening, as though he just realized they were there. He took a large gulp of wine and cleared his throat. "I doubt they'd be of any interest to you. The Etruscan and Bronze Age works, however—"

Heath pushed on, despite Sam's not-so-veiled gesture that he shut up. "But Celia Carmody is so well regarded. Her exhibit in London last year . . ." His voice fizzled under his host's fixed gaze.

"Her name is Celia Westin. She resumed her maiden name after the divorce, something of which I'm sure you're aware, given that you know her work." Carmody glanced at Lauren. "My mother."

Lauren nodded, struggled to think of something she could say that wouldn't make the tense moment worse, and finally settled on "I'm sorry."

Carmody shrugged. "It happened almost thirty years ago. I'm well over it."

Sure you are. Lauren looked down the table at the others. "Are there local legends of forest creatures?" She caught Sam's eye, as well as her mouthed *thank you.*

"Every culture has its tales of nature gods and demigods." Sam gave Heath a last warning glower, then picked up the conversational ball and ran with it. "The Japanese *kodama,* or tree spirits." Her expression softened as she warmed to her subject. "Dryads, the Greek forest nymphs. They guard the woods, inhabit certain trees. They also protect those who live there, if they're so disposed."

"But do the creatures here have a name? I'm a little familiar with stories of the Coast Range, but I have never heard of anything like them." Lauren almost added that they were just the sort of thing the engine driver would have enjoyed telling them about. But given his boss's mood, she didn't want to be responsible for getting the poor man fired.

"I always found them hideous, but they're part of the collection and according to the terms of my father's will, they have to remain." Carmody sat up straight at the sound of approaching footsteps, then slumped when they proved to belong to a staffer who had come to check on the progress of the meal. "Nothing magical about them. They were a product of my mother's artistic imagination. They're what you invent when your marriage is falling apart."

Everyone quieted as plates were cleared, drinks replenished, the next course set out. A palate cleanser, tiny dishes containing golf-ball-size scoops of sorbet garnished with mint. Lauren took note of the empty chair opposite her, the unused plates and silverware, and realized that Carmody had been on the lookout for his daughter. That was confirmed when one of the servers hesitated in front of the place setting, then glanced at Carmody, who shook his head.

Stef caught the exchange as well. "I saw Nyssa as I was on my way downstairs. I believe she was headed for her room."

"Kids these days!" Heath's voice boomed. "They have everything they want in their rooms—TV, computer, phone." He watched Sam as he spoke, as if daring her to stop him. "Stick a fridge in there, they'd never leave." He raised his glass in a toast to himself or kids or room refrigerators, then drank.

"I could strip that room to the bare walls and she'd still . . ." Carmody started to say more, then picked up his spoon and shoved it into his sorbet with such force that it almost spilled out of the dish.

Oh Jenny—what art thou up to? Lauren wondered if the woman had retired to her room with the last of the wine, or found a quiet corner of the house in which to curl up, and wished to hell that she had joined her.

I should tell them.

Soft as a whisper, a quiet voice sounded in the back of her mind.

I should tell them who I saw.

As minutes passed, it grew louder, more insistent. Like a child demanding a toy, it urged her on.

Well, why shouldn't I? A sighting of a woman thought dead, however strange the circumstances, was important, wasn't it? And if any crowd could appreciate strange circumstances, it was this one. *I might piss off Carmody even more than he is already.* Of course she could, but was that her problem? *Maybe I should wait.*

Poke around a little first. She found herself watching Carmody's hands, the broad palms and blunt fingers, and wondered if the rumors were true, if he had indeed murdered his wife. *Then why did she appear so old?*

"You look so deep in thought."

Lauren turned to Peter to find him eyeing her. "Trying to think of something to say. I'm guessing that the conversation would be different if I weren't here."

"Oh, I don't know." Peter stirred the remains of his sorbet into mush. "More of the same ol' same ol'. Sometimes I think we could use a little shake-up."

Okay. You asked for it. Lauren set down her spoon. "I don't know how to couch this, so I'm just going to say it. Yesterday. In Seattle. I saw a woman who—"

"Let me help." Carmody pulled a wine bottle from a nearby ice bucket and refilled his glass, then Lauren's. "You saw a shade of my missing wife."

Lauren looked from Carmody to Peter, to the others. She expected pushback, argument. What she didn't expect were the slow nods and matter-of-fact gazes, as though she had told them she had spotted a Steller's jay or heard a western meadowlark singing in the garden.

"We've all seen Fernanda." Peter pointed his spoon to the others. "I've seen her in New York. Chicago. Andrew? I recall you saying you encountered her in Paris."

"Late last year, while crossing Le Pont Neuf." Carmody massaged his ring finger at the spot where a wedding band would have been. "Her first photos were taken there. It was one of her favorite places."

"I saw her in my apartment, in Seattle. She came to me a crone. She pointed to her face, then to mine." Stef shrugged. "Perhaps she sought to insult me in the only way she had left to her."

"So you assume she's dead?" From the corner of her eye, Lauren saw Carmody set down his spoon and sit back, hands braced on the edge of the table.

"We have assumed that for quite some time." Stef's voice sounded soft, but careful, the tone of a doctor explaining a tricky diagnosis. "Fernanda was wild before she and Andrew married. It's reasonable to suppose that she resumed her old ways after she left."

"But wild ways are usually pretty public, and no one has seen her since . . . ten years ago." Lauren paused as something she had read during her library search finally clicked. "Ten years ago this week." She sensed the stillness, the held breath, as though the mood of the room were a stone that teetered on the edge of a cliff and needed just one more push to send it tumbling.

"No one has seen her alive, no. There have been rumors, but aren't there always?" Stef studied Lauren with a lighter expression, as though they had just met. "You seem surprised. You of all people should appreciate that the netherworld is all around us all the time."

"I am. I do." Lauren struggled to think what to say next. *They don't want to talk about this.* Well, could she blame them? "I expected you to tell me I was full of it."

"We still might." Heath sniffed. "But we'll give you the night off."

Lauren tipped her glass toward him, which was as much of a toast as she could muster.

"Strange she should appear to you, though. She never knew you." Peter hid his bite better than did Carmody, but it was still detectable. "Or did she?" Feathers of frost, sharp outlines in winter sun, earlier warmth a memory.

"No. I never met her." Lauren stretched out her foot under the table, then kicked the air. Shook things up. Sent a stone tumbling. "So where do you see Fernanda around here?"

"We don't." Carmody smiled, a social curve of lip that indicated that the subject was now closed.

Silence for a few moments. Then Sam cleared her throat.

"Can I ask a question?" She raised her hand, like a child in class. "I know it's a silly thing, but . . . those showers. In the winter? Really?"

Carmody's brow furrowed. Then the famous smile bloomed and he laughed while Heath groaned and Peter and Stef eyed one another and shook their heads. "All the glass walls can be disassembled and moved. When it starts getting chilly, we enclose the showers. It's still a little cold, but you can't beat the views."

With that, the conversation revived, starting with talk of the history of the Carmody house, then moving on to houses in general, and awful bathrooms they all had encountered while traveling. Lauren said little, all the while pledging that she would have a very long talk with Gene Kaster when he finally made his appearance. *Misrepresentation.* A nice way of saying that he lied to her about what she was getting herself into. *Friendly gathering of like minds.* Like minds? Maybe. Friendly? Not so much.

And then there was her host. In Seattle, the things she had read about Andrew Carmody had seemed like so much baseless gossip, but now that she had met the man, she wasn't so sure. *Intense.* Oh yes. *With bonus mood swings.* Even better.

And I came here hoping for a job. Lauren laughed softly, which drew an odd look from Carmody. She waited until the staffers arrived with dessert and coffee, mumbled an apology, and made her escape amid the bustle. Paused outside the door to get her bearings, and heard the raised voices as soon as the servers had departed.

"—coached her. Of course, he coached her. He's not an idiot." Stef, as heated now as she was all coolness before.

"If she saw Fernanda, I'm the Queen of Sheba." That from Heath, whose voice cut through wood and wall like an ax.

"It's a matter of trust, Andrew." Peter, words soft and measured, the eye of the building storm. "We've known you since you were a boy. If you had questions, you should've asked us directly."

Then Carmody, words softer still, because men in his position never needed to yell in order to be heard.

Lauren pressed her ear to the door and held her breath, but could catch only the occasional word or phrase.

"... Gene ... business ... trust, as you said ... questions—"

"They really don't like you."

Lauren spun around. The voice had come from the beneath the central staircase, an elfin whisper that rattled her skull.

Then Nyssa Carmody emerged from the shadows. She still wore the same cutoffs and tank top as she had in the garden, over which she had thrown a faded green zippered hoodie that skimmed her knees. "They think you work for Gene." She walked toward Lauren, bare feet silent on the hardwood, and looked her up and down. "You're not the type Gene usually hires, but maybe that's the point."

Lauren found herself backing away from the girl, and stopped. *It's the eyes.* Nyssa had inherited her father's eyes. Hypnotic. Disarming. "But if I work for Gene, that would mean I work for your father, wouldn't it?"

"No." Nyssa twitched one shoulder. "Gene handles all the grubby stuff so Dad doesn't have to get his hands dirty."

"But why would they think Gene hired me?" Lauren shook her head. She felt turned around, confused, as assaulted by noise and color as if she had entered a crowded football stadium or a casino. "I mean, he didn't. To tell the truth, I don't know what I'm doing here."

"Well, maybe you'll find out." Nyssa stuffed her hands into the pockets of her jacket. "Gene'll be here in the morning. He likes to skip the first-night dinners because Stef and the others don't like him." She stopped just beyond arm's reach. "He set you up to take his heat. He's good at that."

Lauren leaned against the wall and pressed her hands to her temples. Amid the color and the noise, the intermittent sounds of argument from the dining room leached through, waxing and waning likes cries in the wind. "You need to back off."

Nyssa took a step closer, her voice a quiet touch amid the battering. "Why?"

Lauren lowered her hands and dug deep, mined the place in her core where Virginia had shown her that her own power rested, a place where she didn't like to go. Dark. Cold. She imagined plunging into frigid, black water, felt the chill envelop her, numb her limbs, work its way through skin and muscle to bone. "Because it's not nice." Her head cleared, and when she met Nyssa's eyes again, the girl took two steps back. "With strangers, you ask permission."

Nyssa's jaw worked. "I'm—I'm sorry."

Lauren looked around. She could still see with her inner eye, still detect the dark space. Saw the girl's power coloring the air like smoke. "You're still doing it."

"I don't know how to stop."

"Imagine closing a door, and being in a quiet room." Lauren sighed. "Sometimes that helps me."

Nyssa squinched her eyes shut, bundled her fists in the sleeves of her jacket, and pulled them close to her chest. "I don't know what quiet is."

Lauren stepped closer to the girl and lowered her voice. "Sun on your face. And your favorite song playing in your head."

"That's not quiet."

"Then think of something that relaxes you. Something you like."

Nyssa nodded. A minute passed. Two. Then her breathing slowed, and the white-knuckle grip she'd had on the cuffs of her jacket loosened. She opened her eyes. "Is that okay now?"

"It's better. You need to practice." Lauren passed her hand through a remnant wisp, felt its tingle. "You really need to practice." She broke the connection with her own inner self, a nasty sensation like hooks tugging under her skin. The air cleared, the only sound once again the occasional snatch of dining room discussion.

Nyssa jerked her chin in that direction. "The others don't sense me like you do. Does that mean you're stronger?"

"No. It's like people who can't stand cilantro because they're supertasters. I'm like that, only with respect to sensing the magical." Lauren took a step back so she could look Nyssa in the face. *She's taller than Katie. Five ten, at least.* With flawless skin and corn-silk hair and eyes wide and glittery as those of a child just awakened from a nightmare. "We all have different talents, different affinities."

Nyssa studied her, then managed a smile. "They find out everything about you, they're really not going to like you."

"Not my problem." Lauren looked back at the dining room door. The voices had quieted, which probably meant that some sort of agreement had been reached, and the breach healed, at least for the time being. "Nyssa, can I ask you a question? It's about your mother—" But when she turned back, the girl had gone.

CHAPTER 11

Lauren hunted for Nyssa throughout the main floor of the house, then hesitated at the foot of the stairs leading to the private suites. *Does she know about her mother?* Anyone as powerful as she seemed to be must have seen Fernanda. The first person a mother would seek out would be her child.

Nyssa, we can get through this. What else could Carmody have been referring to?

Any number of things, really. Nyssa faced legal problems, possibly another date with rehab. She was a troubled teenager saddled with a power she could barely control. The list of things she and her father needed to get through had to be formidable.

I need to talk with Carmody first. Lauren didn't particularly care for the man, but he was Nyssa's parent. If nothing else, she hoped he would tell her how much training Nyssa had received to that point, if any. *Then I can call Virginia*—Lauren checked her watch and calculated the time difference—*tomorrow.* Ask the woman how best to go about helping an untrained witch who possessed more power than she knew what to do with, and ignore the muffled laughter that she felt sure would be forthcoming.

Every parent's curse—that their child would grow up and have a child just like them.

Lauren drummed her hands on the railing, then headed for the rear of the house. *Nyssa Carmody is not my problem.* At least, not yet.

She checked to see that the dining room door was still closed. She had kept an eye on the place all during her search, and saw that no one other than staff had entered or left since her departure. Either Carmody and the others were in the midst of the longest dessert course in history, or talks were still ongoing. *I wonder what happened.* Why were Stef and the others so concerned about the possibility of Kaster planting a mole in their midst? Peter's words replayed. *It's a matter of trust.* Then, Nyssa's. *Gene handles all the grubby stuff so Dad doesn't have to get his hands dirty.* So what grubbiness had Stef and company done to merit Kaster's subterfuge?

So much to think about, on what was supposed to have been a restful getaway.

Oh Gene, we need to talk. Lauren walked out onto the patio that led to the first level of the sculpture garden, stopped to give her eyes time to adjust the dark, then passed through the levels she had already explored. The house itself emitted enough ambient illumination to navigate by. In addition, pinlights had been installed in the stone steps, and electric torches placed throughout the shrubbery. Not quite enough light to read a newspaper, but sufficient to pick out the flowers, the shapes of the sculptures, and help prevent inebriated guests from tumbling into the poisonous herbs. Enough to swamp out the stars.

She continued to descend, past the planter behind which she had hidden after coming upon Carmody and Nyssa, then lower still. At that point, the lighting ended, and she had moved far enough away from the house that the spillover no longer reached her. These were the areas of the garden where visitors seldom wandered, apparently, where the soft scent of roses gave way to earthier odors of damp and dirt. Now she felt the signals of unease from the primitive depths of her brain, but ignored them because she felt more herself in places like this than any other. She had come to think of the night as truth, as a time that revealed the world as it actually was, a fact so easy to forget when surrounded by streetlights and neon and the 24/7 life. Here were sounds that sent the heart hammering, snapping branches and soft growls and the silken slice of wings through the air. There were the shadows where none should've been, the red reflections of watchful eyes that would hide its identity as predator or prey until too late to evade one or capture the other. The night of the wilderness, where Man was just another animal who needed to watch where he walked.

Lauren lowered to a step, then lay back, shivering as the chill of the stone seeped through her clothes. The air still held on to the day's warmth, and the skies were clear—she looked overhead at the stars, too many to count, like sprays of white powder across black cloth. The skies of Gideon were sometimes the same. Cloud cover permitting, she would spend hours hunting for the few stars she knew amid the thousands whose names existed only in astronomers' databases. Occasionally, Virginia would join her, sitting downwind so she could smoke her single cigarette of the day. Sometimes they talked, about lessons past, present, or future, or some bit of Gideon history or current gossip. Other times they sat in silence, teacher and pupil, fellow guardians of the borderland, the unlikeliest of friends.

"I am not homesick," Lauren whispered to the stars. *Gideon is not my home.* But aspects of it offered her as much comfort as she ever felt these days, and she longed for that now. Her voices, so insistent for weeks, had gone quiet. *Here you are, witch,* their silence seemed to say. *Get on with it.*

"Shut up." Lauren followed the blinking trail of a plane across the sky, then closed her eyes and listened to the whisper of leaves in the light breeze. The movements of small animals. The distant hooting of an owl.

Then she heard a splash. The musical giggle of a small child.

Lauren sat up. "Who's out there?" The sounds of splashing and laughter continued unabated, as though whoever it was hadn't heard her, or didn't care to respond. She got up and crept down the steps, cracked flagstones crunching beneath her feet, as the scenarios tumbled through her head. A lost child. Trespassing campers.

The steps ended and she walked out onto a stretch of well-tended lawn centered by a pond. It was small, no bigger than a large wading pool, and shallow, with flat stones jutting up along the diameter to form a walkway. She shouldn't have been able to see anything clearly—the moon had yet to rise above the trees. But she could see the rocky bottom of the pond through the few inches of clear water, the tiny fish that darted through the cracks and crevices. And, here and there, a submerged toy, colors vivid against the dull stone. A red ball. A dark-haired doll dressed in a yellow bathing suit. A tiny blue car.

Then came flashes of light that swirled together to form a reflected scene. Fernanda, barefoot in shorts and a tank top, hair bound in a messy ponytail. And toddler Nyssa, tow-headed and rosy-cheeked, one strap of her white bathing suit slipped down her arm. They played tag around the edge of the pool, first mother giving chase, then daughter, amid squealing and splashing.

Then Fernanda paused, and looked up. When her gaze settled on Lauren, she smiled, the relaxed expression of a woman content with the world and her place in it. Then she looked away, gathered up a towel, and dried off Nyssa, speaking in either Spanish or her native Brazilian Portuguese while Nyssa stared up in gape-mouthed rapture, every so often struggling to repeat one of the words.

Then, in a heartbeat, it all vanished. Lauren looked down and found she stood in knee-high scrub, a few short strides from the woods. She walked to the spot where the pond had been, kicked through the weeds in search of the stones, but found only soil, hard and cracked from lack of rain.

She listened, and heard nothing but forest sounds. "What are you trying to tell me, Fernanda?" She waited. "That you miss your daughter?" Another beat. "That you were happy once?" She heard silken rustling at the edge of the woods, as if someone had grabbed the branches and shook them. Then that stilled. "So what happened? You need to give me a little more than this." She reached out her hands, and felt for the opening that Fernanda had used to gain passage into this reality. She should have been able to retrace the woman's path, but she could sense nothing, either good or bad. Only muffled blankness.

Lauren backed up, eyes fixed on the woods. As soon as she felt a step beneath her feet, she turned and ran. She reached the patio in time to see Peter, Sam, and Heath depart the dining room and stroll toward the stairs, and was about to go after them when she heard a heavy footfall behind her. She stopped and looked toward a darkened corner just as Carmody stepped out into the light.

"It's a little late for a walk." He jerked his head toward the garden. "You can't see much now. We set the lighting to a minimum; otherwise it shines into the bedrooms and keeps folks up all night."

"I just saw Fernanda." Lauren struggled to keep her voice down. "At the bottom of the garden."

Carmody stared at her for several moments before speaking. "That's not possible." Before he could say more, there came the sound of the French door that led out to the patio opening, then slamming closed.

"No, it isn't possible." Stef strode toward Lauren, hands bunched into fists. "This house, this property—both are protected in ways you cannot begin to imagine."

Lauren kept talking. She had to say what she saw, whether anyone believed her or not. "I saw a younger version, the way she looked before she disappeared. Nyssa was a toddler. They played in a small pond at the bottom of the garden—"

"There has never been a small pond at the bottom of the garden. Has there, Andrew?" Stef glared at Carmody. When he said nothing, she fixed back on Lauren with shining eyes, chin raised in triumph. "You are a liar. A dirty spy. You tested us during dinner with information that Gene fed you. You saw how accepting we were of your story about seeing Fernanda in Seattle, and decided to push. Well you can tell your scummy little master—"

"*Stef.*" Carmody's voice bit.

Stef closed her eyes. "Think of him as you will, Andrew. Believe him if you think you must." She shot Lauren one last hard look, then turned on her heel and headed back to the house. "He will bring you nothing but heartache in the end." This time she opened the door gently, closed it softly, and walked slowly in the direction of the stairs.

"I should go with her. Make sure she takes the elevator. Pete will kill me for letting her get upset." Carmody hurried after the woman. "Stef? Stef? Wait for me!"

Lauren watched him go. For a time she leaned against the patio railing and imagined bailing out of the whole damned business, stealing one of the staff vehicles and driving back to Portland. Then she paced, from one end of the patio to the other, and tried to figure out what in hell Fernanda Carmody was trying to tell her. *In Seattle, I saw her older, panicked.* Now she had gotten a glimpse of the younger woman, in happier times. *What do you want?* She worked the question over and over in her mind, hugged herself against the growing chill, and almost collided with Carmody when he bulleted back outside.

"Let's go." He handed her one of the pair of flashlights he held, then started down the garden steps. "Don't turn it on until we reach the bottom. I don't want Stef to see us."

Lauren hesitated. "How is she?"

"Settled. Resting. Pete's looking after her." Carmody stepped to one side, then gestured for Lauren to move up beside him. "She really should retire. But the Council is her life. Poor Pete's been relegated to second place for years."

Lauren's heart quickened as she stared down into the dark. "You believe me."

"Yes." Carmody watched her. Waited. Then he gave a bare hint of a smile and his shoulders drooped just enough. "Does being alone with me concern you?"

Lauren shrugged. "Should it?"

Carmody lowered his gaze. The half smile faded. Then he reached into his pocket and pulled out a phone. Pressed a single key. "Michael? Send a few men. I want them to check out the lower garden. Have them meet me at the top of the walkway." He paused. "One of our guests saw something suspicious. Probably just animals, but we can't be too sure given the current situation." Another pause. "I know the area is monitored, but sometimes you can't beat several pairs of eyes." He disconnected, then leaned against a planter and looked out over the garden. "Lovely evening. A bit warm for the time of year, though." Before he had a chance to say more, three fit-looking men in black polo shirts and khakis approached from the far end of the patio. They nodded to Carmody as they passed, then continued down the walkway, Tasers on their belts, wires in their ears, and industrial-size lanterns in hand.

Carmody straightened, then looked up at Lauren. The faint smile returned, this time colored with a *fuck you* edge.

Touché. Lauren joined him and they started down the steps. "What's the current situation?"

"The . . . anniversary of her disappearance. One of the logging companies is being picketed. Twenty-seven more emailed death threats arrived with the sun." He sighed. "It wouldn't do me any good to tell you I didn't murder my wife, would it?"

Lauren considered her answer. "I used to try to assume the best about people. Then it almost got me killed. Call me gun-shy."

Carmody nodded. "Believe me or not, I understand." Then his step slowed. "As for what you saw. Nyssa had just turned three. She had seen some tropical fish at a pet shop and wanted one. Fernanda, as usual, went overboard."

Lauren thought back to the scene she had witnessed, the happiness she sensed. How strong must that emotion have been to work its way through whatever protections Stef had put in place? "You mean she built Nyssa a very big fish bowl?"

"Who the hell installs something like that with a small child around? I ordered it filled in the second I found out about it. Then I had nightmares for weeks afterward, about walking down there and finding Nyssa—" Carmody stopped, his breathing ragged. "She said she would watch her, that she would never let her out of her sight." He stared straight ahead, transfixed by memory. "You would have to have known her to realize that she was incapable of that level of discipline." He resumed his descent, one long, slow step at a time. "You can turn on your flashlight now."

Lauren hit the button. Somehow the beams of light bouncing over the broken flagstones unsettled her more than the prospect of what they might find. "What are we looking for?" She waited. "Mr. Carmody?"

"Oh, please, call me Andrew." Carmody walked out into the weeds. "Just not 'Andy.' That's a child's name." He joined his security men at the edge of the woods, where they poked through bushes and scanned the trees overhead.

Lauren searched the ground where the pool had been located. "So could I have learned about this pond from Gene?"

"No one else saw it but Fernanda and me. And whoever built it. Gene did not know, and I never told him because—"

"Because?"

Carmody moved closer and lowered his voice. "Because I forgot. Because we were in the middle of the European expansion and so much was going on and it—" He shook his head. "And it was handled. There's no reason to keep discussing something after it's been handled." He turned his back to her and went to rejoin the guards.

"Did Fernanda want to discuss it?" Lauren waited, until it became obvious that Carmody considered the subject closed. She kicked at the ground as she had before, but this time she struck something hard jutting up through the soil. She crouched down and worked her hand through the weeds, felt something small and rounded, took hold of it and wiggled it back and forth until she freed it, then held it under the light. It proved to be a tiny toy car that had once been blue, now rusted, tires broken. The car she had seen in the reflection, resting at the bottom of the pool.

One of the guards approached her. "Did you find something?"

"Just a rock." Lauren pretended to drop the car back on the ground. As soon as the guard turned his back, she slipped it into her pants pocket, then stood and examined the rest of the area.

Carmody rejoined her. "I don't see signs that anyone was here."

Lauren turned slowly, lowering her voice so that only her host could hear. "I can usually sense a ward. I don't sense anything like that here." She waited. "You aren't going to tell me what's going on, are you?"

"No." Carmody turned to face her. "You're the type who would go off and do something on your own, and this needs to be handled a certain way."

You mean your way. Lauren felt the weight of the toy car in her pocket. "At least Stef and the others tolerated me before. I doubt they'll want anything to do with me now."

"From what Gene told me, being the outsider is something you're comfortable with."

"Do you believe everything Gene tells you?"

Carmody looked at her as if she had sprouted a second head. "Of course." He gave an overgrown yew one last prod, then dismissed the guards. "Let's head back before someone misses us."

They walked back up the steps in silence, shutting off their flashlights when they reached the lighted part of the garden. There, Lauren stopped. Held her breath, and listened. Reached out a hand, and felt.

"What?" Carmody backed up and stood next to her.

Lauren felt his chest press against her shoulder, then picked up the faintest hint of sandalwood cologne. She edged away from him and drew back her hand. "Nothing."

"And that's a good thing, right?"

"I mean, nothing. I can usually sense some sort of life about a place, but it's too quiet out there."

"That means Stef's wards are still working."

"Why don't you want Fernanda to come here?" Lauren waited, heard nothing but Carmody's breathing, looked to find him regarding her with eyes gone ice cold.

"Grow to hate someone you once loved, then ask me that question." He looked down at the flashlight in his hands, rapped it against his thigh, then resumed his climb.

Lauren took her time following in the hope that Carmody would have gone inside before she arrived. But when she reached the patio, she found him leaning on the railing, looking out over the garden. As she approached, he straightened, then turned to face the house.

"This place. It has a better memory than most. There are days when I swear I hear my father pace in his office. Mine is on the ground floor, just off the family wing, and his was on the second, directly above. I left it untouched after he died. I sometimes wonder if that was a good idea." He chuckled. "Most of my senior staff visit it every so often. They say they need to dig through the old files, but I think they look on it as a shrine. Longing for the good old days. I'm pretty sure that some of them light candles."

Lauren set her flashlight on the railing, just beyond Carmody's reach. Kept her distance. *Arm's length at all times.* Because of propriety. Because every time he drew near, she felt as she had with his daughter. Off-balance. Drawn in. "Don't they like you?"

"They wish I had kept the company small. They miss—whatever the hell they miss. I've made them all millionaires fifty times over, but there you go. No good deed ever goes unpunished." Carmody fell silent. Then he folded his arms, lowered his head, studied Lauren through his lashes. "Gene said you could prove useful. Is that why you came, because of him? I ask because, I don't know, he seems to like you. Despite the impression he gives that he loves the world and everyone in it, he doesn't like many people."

"To be honest, I don't know why he would like me. He barely knows me."

"Then why did you come here?"

Lauren looked out toward the garden. "I was called."

"I hear that a lot, in these circles. Working with the Council. From you it sounds—"

"Phony?"

Carmody rolled his eyes. "I was going to say, like you know what the word means." He nodded to himself, as though he'd made a decision. "I want you to meet my daughter."

"I ran into her after I left the dining room." Lauren recalled the girl's soft voice. *I don't know what quiet is.* "She's powerful."

"Good—I'm glad she met you on her own. Makes things a little simpler." Carmody pushed away from the railing and walked toward Lauren. "No pressure. No expectations. Just talk with her, and we'll go from there." He extended his hand. "Let's shake on it."

Shit. Lauren tried to get away with a limp fish touch of the fingers, but Carmody enclosed her hand in his and held on and she felt the rough, dry skin and the muscle and bone beneath and in the space of a breath she could read it all, like the biggest block letters on an eye chart.

Hello Lauren I'm Andrew and I'm really not the sonofabitch that everyone says I am—

She yanked her hand away. "If you pull shit like this on purpose, yeah, I think you are."

Carmody's eyes widened. "Damn."

Lauren tucked her hands as she folded her arms, as if that could make any difference at this point. "Why did you do that?"

"Just—testing."

"Please don't do it again."

"I won't." Carmody backed away until he hit the railing. "It gets so messy so quickly, this thing we all share. You're unsure of me—I can accept that. But I believe that we can reach a mutually beneficial arrangement separate from personal feelings." His tone had grown formal, more businesslike. "You need a job. Your town needs help." His voice wavered. "I need help."

Lauren pressed her fingers to her cheekbones, then above her eyes. This was new. Nothing like this had ever happened before when she touched a person, no matter how strong the emotion she had sensed. Her head ached, and she felt a weird trickle down the back of her throat that made her think *nosebleed*. "I will talk to your daughter, if she wants to talk." She walked toward the house. "Good night."

Carmody called after her. "Thank you."

"I'm not doing it for you, or for what you think you can offer me." Lauren placed her hand on the door handle, then looked back at her host. "Andrew."

Carmody nodded. "Lauren."

Lauren tried to think of something else to say, pithy last words that would inform Andrew Carmody once and for all that her mind and talents were her own, and that she couldn't be bought. But her headache had grown worse, and she felt nauseated to boot. All in all, it had been a crap of a day, and she decided the best way to end it would be to say nothing at all.

LAUREN KEPT AN eye out for the others as she trudged up the stairs to her suite. She wouldn't have minded running into Nyssa, even though she would have had a difficult time coping with the girl's intensity. Jenny seemed all right. Even Sam seemed likable, if high-strung. She wouldn't win any popularity contests with Stef and Peter, but they had probably turned in for the night. *Please, Lady, not Heath.*

But all proved quiet, the soft echo of her footsteps on the bare wood floors the only sound. Once inside her room, she cleaned off the toy car in the bathroom sink, dried it, and set it on the nightstand. She showered quickly, all the while fighting the sense that something watched her through the shrubbery.

She fled to the walled confines of the walk-in closet to dry off and put on her pajamas, and wondered if Sam did the same. Mined a bottle of lime-flavored seltzer from the well-stocked room refrigerator and climbed into bed, dimmed the lights, and took hold of the car.

It fit easily inside her palm, two inches of plastic and cast metal that had once been glittery electric blue with bright white striping if the flecks of paint that survived over a decade in the dirt were any indication. She tried to race it along her forearm but the remains of the tires had rusted in place, and she had to content herself with zooming it through the air like a spaceship.

Then she enclosed it in her hands, held it close, and waited to see if it had anything to tell her.

Lauren sensed nothing at first. She laid her head back, closed her eyes, breathed slowly, all the steps one was supposed to take to slip into a meditative state. But she couldn't get comfortable. The edges of the broken wheels cut into her hands no matter how lightly she held the car.

Then she flinched as something jabbed her finger. Pain followed, sharp at first, then hot and radiating, spreading under the skin. She dropped the car and tumbled out of bed, looked back to find the wheels moving, the car shaking as though trying to flip itself over.

Then she looked closer, and saw twitching bodies, and wings. Wasps—no, flies, large, shiny black things that took to the air above the car, hovering over it as though guarding it.

Lauren grabbed a towel from the bathroom, then dug a newspaper out of a stack of reading materials that had been left in the sitting area and rolled it tight. She returned to the bed to find the flies settled on the car and the surrounding bedding, a half dozen or more.

"By the Lady." Lauren flipped the towel over them. "In her name." Then she leapt atop the towel, holding down the edges with her knees and free hand as she brought down the newspaper again and again, all the while uttering prayers and pleas to the Lady because the car wasn't hollow and it was so small that there would have been no place for the flies to hide and yet here they were. As she struck, a foul odor seeped through the towel, the salty tang of sewage mixed with the sickly sweetness of rotting flowers. Then came the staining, soaking through the thick terry, black and viscous, too much to have come from a handful of insects.

Lauren gave the towel a final whack, then pulled it back. The stench hit her full force, and she gagged. She flicked the car off the bed to the floor, made sure all the flies were dead, then stripped off the ruined coverlet and sheets and thanked whoever had made the decision to cover the mattress with a waterproof pad, which kept the mess from seeping through. The sheets had the texture of shredded silk, and she tried not to think about how much they cost as she bundled them along with the towel into the pillowcases, which she knotted closed and tossed out onto her balcony. Then she threw open all the doors and windows and let the suite air out as she showered off the stink that had attached to her skin and hair.

After donning fresh pajamas and cleaning and bandaging the bites, Lauren returned to the bedroom. She stood over the car and used a clothes hanger to nudge it back and forth. When additional wildlife failed to emerge, she picked it up and examined it. It looked as it had after she cleaned it, as spotless as a rusty old toy could be, a smidgen of soap still stuck to one door. No staining. No horrid stench.

"You know, whoever you are, if you meant to warn me off, this was the last thing you should have done." She returned to the sitting area and stretched out on the couch, and tried once again to get a sense of the little toy. Inhaled the clean mountain air. Listened to the night sounds. Let her mind drift.

The car didn't give up its secrets readily. But scenes appeared eventually, like images through fogged glass. Pleasant, at first, green grass and the jewel faceting of sunlight on water. Sounds of laughter. A woman's. A child's. The sensation of rolling back and forth. The pressure of a small hand.

Then came quiet, followed by what might have been a scream. But it held a single note for far too long. A whistle, maybe, or a siren.

Then the daylight altered, turned harsher, colder. Room light. Fluorescent bulb light. Clicks of locks. Doors opening and closing.

No more laughter. Different voices. Men's mostly, but, every so often, a woman's. Words ran together, layer upon layer, like conversations at a party, so loud that even the language spoken remained a mystery.

Time passed. Same voices, but now an added undercurrent. Restlessness. Anxiety. Fear. Flashes of jerky movement, arms and legs kicking. Eyeless faces, mouths gaped wide. Tumbles of black clouded the scenes. Whatever it was, it moved as though sentient, surrounding figures, hiding them, revealing them, forming them.

Lauren heard buzzing, barely detectible through the gabble.

Then smells rushed in, the sort that triggered fear like a cold finger touching a heart. Sweat. Shit. Urine. Vomit.

Blood.

Finally, a new sound. It began low, ramped high, then higher still. Another whistle?

No. Not this time.

A scream. It knifed the air, sliced the soul. Held every pain there had ever been. Then it cut off, as though the volume had been turned down or a door slammed or a throat cut.

Lauren's eyes snapped open. Her heart pounded and she listened for voices in the hallway or a knock on her door, because the scream had rattled so loudly that others must have heard it, too. But seconds ticked by, and no one came, and she realized that it had all been in her head.

She felt wetness on her face. Dabbed it with her finger, then tasted it. Too familiar, the salt of tears.

She set the car on the floor next to the couch, then went to the bathroom to wash her face. After she finished, she stood over the sink, hands gripping the sides, and stared down at the white porcelain. Eventually she lifted her gaze and looked in the mirror. Minutes passed before she recognized herself. The eyes that stared back belonged to someone else. Someone who never awoke from the nightmare. Who dreamed it still.

Where are you? Lauren thought the words, then said them aloud, her throat raw from cries of others that were never voiced. "Where?" She coughed, drank some water, mulled over the images.

She paced, her bare feet as cold as the floor tile. *First came Nyssa and Fernanda.* The light, the happiness. *Then the whistle, the siren, the what the hell ever.* It was like some sort of signal. Everything went downhill after that.

"We're out in the middle of nowhere—there's nothing like that out here." Lauren thought of the truck stop, the air horns of semis, but that didn't make sense. *Have I heard anything like that on the mountain?* Something settled in the back of her mind, bugged her like a stone in her shoe. Her step slowed. Then she stopped.

"The train from the helipad." Similar, maybe, but a mouse squeal in comparison.

But there had been another train. According to their driver, it had been abandoned long ago.

Lauren walked about the suite, adjusting the doors and windows, grabbing a pillow and blanket from the closet. She needed to get some sleep, because tomorrow would be a busy day.

Tomorrow, she would go to Jericho.

CHAPTER 12

Lauren awoke to a blazing sunrise. The first thing she did was stretch her back, which had stiffened up after the night spent on the soft couch. Then she checked the fly bites and found they had gone from hot welts to itchy, hard bumps. No weird colors. No red lines of infection tracing up her arm. *Maybe they were just plain old flies.* If she didn't think about it too long, she could just about convince herself that this was the case.

She dressed in shorts, a long-sleeve shirt, and battered hiking shoes. Tucked the toy car in her pocket. Then she gathered up her discarded bed linens, sought out the housekeeper, and handed off the bundles along with the tale of an invading forest critter and a chase around the room that led to torn and soiled sheets. She received assurances that such things happened all the time, and almost asked for details. But Carmody's staff had no doubt signed formidable nondisclosure agreements as a condition of employment, so she knew that no further information would be forthcoming. *Too bad.* She would have liked to have heard more about strange happenings from an inside source.

She encountered no one on the way downstairs. The breakfast buffet had been set up in the bar, which allowed access to an adjacent deck and the incredible views. She filled a plate with fruit and eggs, snagged a carafe of coffee, headed outside, and was relieved to find the deck deserted. She found a table in the shade, and ate to the accompaniment of birdsong and the chatter of squirrels in the trees.

Then she heard footsteps coming from behind, and her appetite fizzled.

"Mind if I join you?" Peter sat down before Lauren could respond. "I didn't think I'd run into another early riser." He spread his napkin across his lap and dug into a daunting pile of scrambled eggs. "I'm particularly glad it turned out to be you. We all got off on the wrong foot yesterday. I think it's past time for a reboot, don't you?"

Lauren wondered how much of that comment was directed at her. "I didn't mean to upset Mistress Warburg last night. I hope she's feeling better."

"She is." Peter grabbed the carafe and filled his cup. "She and I—we've known the Carmodys a long time. Stef was like a mother to Andrew after Celia left, and she adores Nyssa. She takes all that happens here very personally."

I got that impression, thanks. Lauren pushed a chunk of melon back and forth across her plate. "I did see Fernanda last night."

"I have no doubt that you saw something." Peter offered a quick smile. "We will be discussing it later this morning, after Gene gets here."

We *being everyone but me*. Sure, Carmody had told Lauren that he believed her, but that was before she drop-kicked his spell back in his face. How long would his professed belief withstand an emotional assault by his substitute mother? "I know it's none of my business, but why did Fernanda leave?"

Peter shrugged. "Why does any marriage fall apart?" He paused in the middle of buttering toast. "Steven and Andrew—in some ways they couldn't have been more different. But like his father, Andrew is a workaholic who was attracted to a glittering woman whose life to that point had not included living for extended periods in the middle of nowhere. At least Celia had her sculpting, an artist's need for occasional solitude. Fernanda needed an audience. She settled down for a time after Nyssa was born, but the calm didn't last. Obviously." He broke off a piece of waffle and flicked it toward a squirrel that watched them from the railing. "Stef's worried that Nyssa inherited her mother's tendency toward self-destruction."

Lauren watched the man fuss over the squirrel, and wondered if he had volunteered to be the one to blow the smoke screen in her direction, or if Stef had put him up to it. *Poor Nyssa.* She wondered if the girl's ears were burning right now. "Was Nyssa always a problem?"

"No. She was the perfect child until just after her fifteenth birthday." Peter sat back. "Andrew threw a party for her at the house in Portland. I blame some of the kids he invited, children of business associates who had grown up much too wild. They say that all some people need is a tiny taste to get them hooked. Unfortunately, Nyssa seems to be one of those unlucky ones. The drinking started at the party. Soon after, the drugs. The . . .

men." He pushed back his chair and looked out over the woods. "Would you mind if we changed the subject? I talk about this all the time with Stef, and it just gets—difficult to deal with."

"No worries." Lauren refilled her coffee cup, just to have something to do with her hands. After a while, she realized the silence had lasted a bit too long, and looked to find Peter studying her.

"I have a confession to make." He rocked his head back and forth. Wrinkled his nose. A man of many tics. "I knew your father."

Lauren's heart skipped, and she wondered if she would ever learn all of the late Matthew Mullin's secrets. "Did he repair furniture for you?" She knew the answer even before Peter shook his head.

"He took a couple of my classes. World Religions One and Two. At Abernathy. I taught there until last year, when I moved down here to Corbin. I saw you a few times, when you came to pick him up."

Lauren met the man's level gaze, caught the sharpness buried like a sliver of ice amid the warmth. "That was over three years ago. Do you remember all your students?"

"I remember the interesting ones." Peter smiled. "He was an interesting man." He nodded toward her. "More so than I realized, as it turns out." His expression softened in memory. "He had this effect on people. He kept pretty much to himself, but everyone noticed him. Some folks went out of their way to sit close to him, while others didn't seem to care. But then there were some who couldn't sit far enough away. After a couple of weeks, I learned that they were the ones I needed to keep tabs on. A few I caught cheating. The rest flunked. He was like a, I don't know, 'human lie detector' is too strong a term. He just made certain types of people uncomfortably aware of what they were." He hung his head. "I was sorry to hear of his death. I would have attended the funeral, but I didn't find out until sometime later." His smile returned, this time friendlier, warmer. "I see him in you. I daresay that if you ever sat in my class, you would have the same effect."

Lauren cradled her coffee, inhaled the steam. "It seems so strange. A city the size of Seattle, and you and he just happened to cross paths."

"It's a small world we inhabit. And those of us with the talent, well, I believe we're drawn to one another. Like attracting like." Peter glanced toward the door and lowered his voice. "Although sometimes, it's more like opposites attract."

Lauren turned just as Heath and Sam entered with their plates. She felt a touch of relief when they merely waved and headed for a table at the other end of the deck.

Then the door opened again. Peter swore under his breath and sat up straighter.

"Good morning, everyone." Gene Kaster surveyed the assembled, waved to Heath and Sam, then headed toward Lauren's table. He had opted for the more formal end of the business casual spectrum. Gray summer-weight wool slacks, perfectly pressed. Pale blue oxford shirt, cuffs neatly rolled to mid-forearm. Black leather belt and loafers.

"Gene?" Peter stood. "I didn't hear the chopper. What did you do, fly here under your own power?"

"I spent the night down the coast, so I just drove in." Kaster thumped Peter lightly on the shoulder. "Good to see you. How is Stefania?"

"She's fine." Peter looked from Kaster to Lauren, then back again. "I'll tell her that you asked."

"Please do." Kaster turned his personal spotlight on Lauren. "Mistress Mullin. Your face is as bright as the morning." He looked her up and down, brow arching as he settled on her hiking shoes. "And what do you have planned for the day?"

"A walk." Lauren tried to figure out a way to indicate to Kaster that she needed to talk to him, but before she could, Peter picked up his half-filled plate.

"I just need to—" He jerked his chin in the direction of the buffet. "Time for a refill." He hurried away, glancing back at them just before entering the house.

"I believe we've scared him away." Kaster frowned. "And Peter doesn't scare easily."

"He thinks I'm your mole. They all do." Lauren took a deep breath and let loose. "I saw Fernanda in Seattle. I saw her here last night. I informed Stef and your boss. Stef doesn't believe me. Carmody does, I think. Then he tried the Vulcan mind meld, and we both got a shock."

Kaster lowered to Peter's chair, then covered his mouth with one hand. "You did have an eventful day," he said through his fingers.

"Yeah." Lauren stuffed her hands in her pockets, her fingers closing over the toy car. "What about the flies around here?"

"What about them?"

"Are they particularly vicious?" Lauren waited for an answer, but the man just shook his head in puzzlement. "Carmody told me that you both would like me to help Nyssa. That it was your idea. I really wish you'd told me that in the first place."

Kaster lowered his hand. Absent the force of his persona, his age showed, the lines around his mouth, the dull skin. "I thought you'd say no."

"This background info is proving kind of important."

"I'm sorry. But you will talk to her?"

"She doesn't know me from a doorknob. If she wants to talk, fine, but I am not going to force myself on her."

"I will smooth the way. Today. This morning." Kaster leaned toward Lauren as he spoke, eyes a little too wide.

He's genuinely worried. Lauren's stomach grumbled in nervous sympathy. *This can't be good.* "Has something happened recently?"

Kaster hesitated. "Just that she's been through so much. The sooner you can help her, the better." He frowned. "As for what Andrew did—tried to do—I'm afraid that's my fault. I told him you were very good. I knew he would take that as a challenge and try to test you, but I didn't expect him to be quite so direct."

Lauren stared at the man until the light in his eyes flickered. "What's your game?"

Kaster shook his head, eventually. "No games. Not about this."

"But there are things you aren't telling me."

"As I am sure there are things you haven't told me." Before Kaster could say more, the sound of the door opening snagged his attention, and he stood. "Ah, ladies." His persona reasserted itself, and all signs of care fell away, along with about twenty years. "Until later."

"Yeah." Lauren watched him usher two blondes to a secluded table, sylphlike twenty-somethings in pastel shifts and nothing sandals, with smiles that did more to describe the previous night than any film or book of erotica ever could. *And twins to boot.* She didn't know whether to condemn Kaster's lack of imagination or admire his stamina.

Peter returned sans plate. Instead, he carried a coffee travel mug, which he filled from the carafe. "Well, looks like Gene has his weekend planned." He shook his head.

"Part of me thinks he doesn't look the type, but then again . . . ?" Lauren shrugged, then waited for Peter to look at her. "I know you won't believe me, but I'll say it again for the record. He invited me here under false pretenses. He said this was a retreat. What he really wanted was for me to meet Nyssa. He thought if I knew he wanted me to counsel a troubled teenager, I would decline." She sagged against her chair back and wondered if Katie was still at home, and if she could risk a call just to hear a friendly voice. "He wasn't wrong." She decided against it. She had no clue whether a phone call from this place could disturb Virginia's protective wards, but now wasn't the time to experiment. "Take that any way you want, but it's the truth."

Peter concentrated on his coffee, sugaring and stirring with an overabundance of care. "It took me some years to figure out exactly what Andrew wanted out of life." He set aside the spoon, snapped on the lid. "Then one day, it hit me. It was so simple, really. Almost cliché. But it explained everything from his business dealings to his personal issues. Andrew has to win."

What does that have to do with what I just told you? Lauren

glanced back at Kaster, now happily holding court, and decided
to play along because what else could she do? "So what's Gene's
stake in all this?"

"Gene wants Andrew to win. They're very well suited."

"Stef doesn't like him. You don't, either."

"I find him unsettling. Too intense. Smile's always a little
too bright. But deep down, I think he's just a happy hedonist.
Stef thinks his behavior puts Andrew at risk, but he's more disciplined than she gives him credit for." Peter tested his coffee,
then nodded.

Lauren twitched her head in the direction of Kaster and his
twins. "Are those Carmody employees?"

"I said, disciplined." Peter sniffed. "If past performance is
any indication of present results, he met them in a coffee shop.
The grocery store produce aisle. While crossing the street. He's
like a magnet. It should piss me off, but all one can do it marvel." He raised the mug in a toast. "Well, this has been—let's
call it educational." Another sip. "I need to get back upstairs."

"And prepare for your meeting." Lauren waited for Peter to
say something, and knew she could have waited all day. He had
ignored her explanation. He and Stef had made up their minds
about her, and nothing she said would change them. "I better
get going before the sun gets too high in the sky."

"Have a nice walk." Peter waved without turning around
and disappeared into the house.

"You're going for a walk?"

Damn. Lauren turned to find Sam waving to her from her
table. Broad sweeps, as though she hailed a ship far out at sea.

"I'd like to come along." Sam stood, grabbed coffee with

one hand and a sweet roll with the other. "I'm not included in the morning confab, and I can't just sit around while this guy bathes in Carmody's shadow."

"Love you too, honey." Heath poked her lightly in the rear with his fork.

"Sure." Lauren headed for the house, then paused and waited for Sam to join her. "Why not?"

"Oh, you're all serious." Sam pointed to Lauren's hiking shoes, then frowned down at her flip-flops. "I need to change— it'll only be a minute." She shuffle-ran through the bar in the direction of the stairs, trailing crumbs.

Lauren killed time wandering through the public parts of the house, the main living room furnished with a massive round sofa built around a specially ventilated fire pit, and small sitting areas designed to take full advantage of the views. Eventually she came to the vestibule, a four-story, metal-spined glass tower overlooking the sweeping pavered driveway, and decided that this must be what a goldfish felt like when it got dumped into an aquarium.

Photographs lined the vestibule on two sides, framed in clear acrylic and hung so that they seemed to float above the glass walls. Sepia-tinged, most of them, whether by age or the restorer's art. They spanned well over a century, starting with the wild, early days of Portland, corruption and bordellos, shanghaied sailors and murder in the streets. Lauren stopped before one of the first images, a Gold Rush–era shot of rough-clad men standing by a stream. She thought she could pick out the Carmody in the group. Something about the smile spanned the generations.

Then she noticed one of the faces in the background. Framed by dark curly hair and obscured by a ragged beard though it was—yes, she'd have bet the rent. *Wherever you find a Carmody, there's a Kaster close behind.* This time, both men shared the same smile, a bright expression that claimed ownership of the world.

Lauren moved on through the history of Carmody Incorporated. From the Gilded Age, through the world wars. Korea. Vietnam to present day. Most had the same general theme—a Carmody, a Kaster, assorted executives, and larger and larger buildings in various stages of construction.

But one photograph stood out from the rest. Steven Carmody and another man, standing in front of a wooden pole gate. Carmody wore jeans and a white T-shirt and supported a small boy who sat on the top railing. Young Andrew, wearing a western-style shirt, shorts, and a cowboy hat, his feet bare, face scrunched in a smile.

But it was the man standing next to Carmody who captured Lauren's attention. No lab coat this time. Instead, Elliott Rickard dressed like his boss, and topped the ensemble with a Los Angeles Dodgers baseball cap. He stood so that the gate hinges, ornate diamond shapes painted black, pointed to him, like arrows indicating the person of interest in a crime scene photo.

She hunted for a date, found one etched in a corner of the frame. *April 1978.* A couple of months before Rickard disappeared. *He and Carmody were close.* This wasn't a staged photo, a memento for an underling—it wouldn't have been hanging in this place if it were. *They were friends.* She studied the photograph until she heard the loud *clump* of footsteps, then left it reluctantly.

"Sorry I took so long." Sam stood waiting at the foot of the stairs. "First I couldn't find my shoes. Then I couldn't find my socks. That's the last time I let Heath pack the bags."

They circled behind the staircase to the elevator that would take them down to the rear exit of the house. That route led them past the sweeping windows that ran along the patio. Outside, Carmody stood with Kaster at the same railing he and Lauren had stood by the previous night. The two men weren't arguing, exactly. Kaster did all the talking, his face inches from Carmody's. Judging from their expressions, Kaster wouldn't have taken kindly to an interruption, but Carmody might have welcomed it.

If Sam sensed the undercurrent of drama in the scene outside, she kept it to herself. "God, Andrew's so gorgeous, isn't he?" She pressed her hand over her heart. "If Heath wasn't here, I would probably be doing my damnedest to be a very bad girl." She gave a theatrical sigh. "Then again, maybe I wouldn't. One hears stories."

Lauren just nodded. She didn't have to ask which stories one heard.

They rode the elevator down to the lower level, where a staffer provided them maps of the trails and day packs complete with water bottles, snacks, and other assorted necessities, including bug spray, which Lauren dug out and applied generously.

"It's just like being at a state park." Sam looped her pack over her shoulder, bounced on ahead for a few strides, then stopped and turned around. "I wanted to thank you for what you did last night. Changing the subject when Heath seemed bound and determined to put his foot in it."

"Not a problem." Lauren answered automatically as she struggled to recall that part of the dinner. Only twelve hours before, yet it seemed like years.

"Heath and Andrew grew up together. Well, to a point. Heath's parents worked for one of the Carmody companies. They didn't exactly run in the same circles." Sam waited for Lauren to draw alongside, then resumed walking. "Men always have to compete, you know. Even when they know there's no chance of winning."

They continued side by side. Then Lauren lagged behind, stopping every so often to wander down a side trail or sniff the air, in search of the place she had passed into back in Gideon. *How hard could it be to find one little ledge on a mountain?* It didn't help that Sam took a ballistic approach to hiking; she seemed more interested in covering as much distance as possible rather than stopping occasionally to look at the scenery. It wasn't until they arrived at a small clearing a mile or so from the house that she stopped.

"This is weird." She pointed to the ground near the base of the tree nearest the trail.

Lauren looked over Sam's shoulder and saw two short sticks a foot or so from the tree's base, laid one atop the other to form an X. "They could've fallen that way."

"I know what it is—it's some kind of—oh my God." Sam ran back and forth across the clearing. "They're by every tree. They form a circle, almost. Something's been going on around here."

"I think I know what this is." Lauren broke off a dead branch and stuck it into the ground under the nearest set of crossed sticks.

Sam ran up to her. "What the hell are you doing? You don't want to disturb it. You don't know what it is."

"I'm not disturbing anything." Lauren worked the branch up and down. "Have you ever gone camping? Backwoods camping, where there are no facilities?" She pulled the branch out of the ground, then held it out for Sam to examine. "What's that on the end?"

"Is that what I think it is?" Sam sniffed, then took a step back. "That is what I think it is."

"You dig a toilet hole, you do what you have to, you bury it." Lauren shoved the branch back in the ground. "Then you mark the spot so that no one else hits it when they're digging their own hole. Camping manners."

"You've done that? Oh my God, that's just—" Sam pretended to gag. Then she gave the scene a final disgusted look and leapt back onto the trail. "You know, when you said that you could get the sense of an object, feel its history, I knew we were kindred souls. I feel that way about plants. I can touch them, and know whether they're safe or not, whether they'll make me feel happy or calm." She walked backward so she could talk to Lauren face-to-face. "The fact that you can touch something and know all about it—that's some gift."

"It's not that simple." Lauren kicked herself for letting slip her talent in front of the others, since it gave them that much more of a reason not to trust her. "It has a mind of its own. It doesn't always work."

"Really? I lose my touch sometimes, too." Sam turned to face forward. "Nice to know it happens to the best of us." She grinned like a kid let out early from school, then bounded ahead, jumping up every few strides to slap at overhanging branches.

Then, just before a bend in the trail, she stopped. "Phantom orchids." She pointed to a cluster of the eerie flowers growing in the shade of a dying spruce. "I've heard folks say that they live on decay, but they get their food from the fungus that lives on decay. Of course, that's just one step removed from the rot. Splitting hairs, don't you think?" She took a deep breath. "But they smell good, don't they? Like cookies."

"Just like." Lauren pulled out her phone and checked the time, wondered if Kaster had yet talked to Nyssa, and what Stef's reaction would be when she learned of his plan.

"Did you want to go back?" Sam's voice sounded small, a field-trip-cut-short tone. "It is almost lunchtime."

"We've got granola bars in the packs." Lauren dug her trail map out of her pack. "Besides, I want to see Jericho."

"Oh, good. So do I." Sam pulled out her own map. "I love old places like that. They give you a real sense of history."

"History." Lauren folded her map and stuffed it back in her pack, then reached into her pocket and massaged the toy car like a lucky charm. Nothing she had seen so far looked or felt like the trail she saw in Gideon, and the rooms she had seen in her sensing of the car weren't the types you would find in a long-deserted logging camp. *Lauren's power lets her down, example the first.* She debated turning back and letting Sam go on alone, but ingrained outdoors etiquette stopped her. *Ideally, there should be three of us.* If one person got hurt, one would stay with them and the third person would go for help. *We're one short.* But they weren't in danger, were they? She had yet to see any flies or sense anything even remotely threatening, and they walked a path so nicely groomed it might as well have been paved.

"We've about a mile to go. If we hustle, we can be there in fifteen–twenty minutes." Sam went into speed-walk mode, elbows flying and heels kicking up dust.

"Right behind you." Lauren picked up her pace, even as she wondered what in hell she would find at the end of the trail.

CHAPTER 13

A brisk twenty-minute walk later, Lauren and Sam came upon a short stretch of old railroad track almost hidden by heavy undergrowth. At that point the trail curved uphill, out of the woods and into the open.

"This is so exciting. Just like the driver said." Sam broke into a run.

Lauren trotted after her to the top of the hill, then stopped. *So this is Jericho.* It was smaller than she expected, the tumbled gate and guard shack, the skeletons of smaller cabins surrounding the main building.

"It's disappointing, isn't it?" Sam walked down the narrow path through the gate to the ruined shack. "They should restore it, like Colonial Williamsburg. Get the train working again. Hire guys to impersonate lumberjacks."

"I don't think Carmody would go for that, do you? All those people driving around his mountain." Lauren followed her inside the shack and immediately felt the currents in the air. *A quiet place*. Well removed from the noise and bustle of civilization, a location where the dark space would remain stable. She walked around the small room, felt the old wood flooring flex and squeak beneath her feet.

Then she caught a flash of white in one corner, and headed toward it. Slowed, then stopped before a small pile of bones surrounded by a ragged ring of feathers.

Sam pressed alongside. "Is that what I think it is?"

"I think it's a ward of some kind." Lauren crouched in front of it, passed her hands over it, felt the rippling in the air.

"Oh! That's horrible. Some poor little creature gave its life." Sam clucked in disgust. "I hate sacrificial spells, don't you?"

"I don't know much about them." Lauren ran a finger over the still-scabbed wound on her hand, the source of the blood she'd used to ward Katie's house and car. "But anything made from something that lived is supposed to be pretty powerful." The order of sacrifice rattled through her head. Self-sacrifice unto death. Partial sacrifice of self. Sacrifice of the other. Sacrifice of something inanimate. After that, it was a matter of degree. How valuable the offering. How close to death one came. Entire books had been written about the rankings. Discussions over interpretation dissolved into feuds between witches that spanned generations.

"What little I know about these bone mounds, which isn't much." Sam crouched in front of the pile. "The skull is positioned so that it can see all that happens in the protected area. If it sees something bad, it contacts the person who cast it."

"So you would expect to see one of these in each of the buildings." Lauren worked to her feet.

"I guess, if they wanted to keep an eye on the whole entire place. Personally, I think cameras and motion detectors would work better."

"Depends what they want to keep an eye on, doesn't it?"

"I suppose." Sam bent close to the mound. "That's weird."

Lauren saw one of the feathers tremble, the black shape emerge from beneath. "Sam, get back."

Sam waved her off. "I just want to see—"

In a burst like a flare, the flies erupted, swarming over Sam's hands, her face. She screamed and fell backward, then rolled to and fro as through trying to smother a fire, arms waving and legs kicking. "Get them off me—*get them off!*"

Lauren tried to bat away the flies with her hands, but they darted past her and resumed their attack on Sam. She pulled off her shorts and swept them back and forth, whipping the flies away, then grinding them into the floorboards with her boots. "Get up! Get outside."

"*Ow. Owowow!*" Sam scrambled to her hands and knees and crawled out the door.

A few flies tried to follow, but Lauren snapped them in midair, then smashed them when they fell to the floor. Their stink filled the shed, and after she killed the last of them, she tried to scrape their remains off her shorts before they soaked into the cloth. But their foul guts stuck like glue and spread like oil, leaving one leg and the backside blackened and reeking. She carefully extracted the toy car from the now-soiled pocket and stuck it in her pack, weighed modesty against the idea of wearing innards against her skin for the duration of the hike, and decided that if anyone got off on seeing her purple boy-leg briefs, they could go nuts because no way in hell was she putting those shorts back on.

She checked the condition of the ward, and found the feathers swept about the room and the bones scattered. *Damn.* She would have to inform Carmody or Kaster and hope that whatever the ward was supposed to contain remained trapped by the other protections that were in place. She pulled out her phone, realized she didn't have the house number, swore softly, then searched her outgoing calls until she found Kaster's. She called it and was immediately switched to voicemail. "Gee, what could you be up to, Gene?" She tried not to visualize the possibilities as she left her message.

She walked outside to find Sam still slapping at her ears and the back of her neck. The woman's bites had bloomed into red welts on her cheeks and forehead. She also sported a gash under her knee that she must have gotten during her crawl out the door.

"They sting like hell." Sam sniffled, then wiped her eyes with the heel of her hand. "I'm sorry for going off like that, but damn. One second I'm fine, and the next I feel like somebody's jamming needles in my face."

"A few got in my room last night and attacked me the same way." Lauren showed Sam her bandaged fingers. "I'm sorry. I should've warned you about them. They're vicious little bastards."

"I've never seen anything like them before and oh God they stink so bad. Why do they stink so bad?" Sam looked down at Lauren's underwear and bare legs, and her eyes goggled. "And your shorts are ruined." She started to scratch her face, then jammed her hands in her pockets. "I guess we should start back. Dammit." She turned and headed back up the hill toward the trail. "So much for Jericho."

Lauren went back inside the shed and made one last circuit of the space, sniffing the air all the while. The stink of the flies had weakened, letting the other forest scents seep through, the aroma of old wood and the musty undercurrent of small animals. She started to leave, then paused in the doorway, pressed her hand to the dry wood, and felt . . . nothing.

"Are you coming?" Sam paced at the top of the hill and rubbed the backs of her hands. Her neck. "I don't mean to be a pain, but if I don't get a shower soon I'm going to scratch the skin off my face."

"In a second." Lauren dug through her day pack, extracted a ballpoint pen, and drew an Eye of the Lady on the jamb. The ink skipped several times, so she pressed harder, sacrificing the pen tip as she inscribed the X-centered circle into the wood. Then she left to join Sam.

As she approached the tumbled gate, she stopped. Stared. The backdrop of trees had changed over nearly forty years and the gate itself had fallen into disrepair. But the hinges remained. The blackened metal had rusted over the decades, and in a couple of places the bolts that held them in place had fallen out, leaving the plates hanging. But nothing had altered the distinctive diamond shape, and she imagined Elliott Rickard standing there as she approached, his smile as wide as the one he wore in the photograph hanging in the vestibule back at the house.

It was taken here. At Jericho.

"*Lauren.*" Sam started down the incline toward her. "Please?"

"Be right there." Lauren resumed her hike up the hill, as the feelings settled that the breached ward needed to be healed as quickly as possible, and that as they departed Jericho, something watched them leave.

LAUREN AND SAM spoke little during the return trip, and finally broke into a run in their haste to return to the house. When the first outbuildings came into view, Lauren slowed her pace and let Sam jet ahead. The woman disappeared into the lower level, then returned a few minutes later, a bath towel in hand.

"That's all they had, sorry." Sam tossed her the towel, then resumed patting her face with the palms of her hands, her alternative to scratching.

Lauren checked the condition of Sam's welts as she wrapped the towel around her waist. "They look better. A few are almost gone."

Sam pretended to shiver. "I never want to go through anything like that ever again. I swear I'm going to spend the rest of the weekend out on the patio."

"I'd go with the Jacuzzi myself."

Lauren and Sam turned to find Jenny Porter ambling down the path toward them. She wore a bright orange one-piece bathing suit over which she had tied a multi-hued pareu, and had bound her hair in a tight topknot.

"It's in this hidden grotto-like place just off the garden. I found it last night while the rest of you were at dinner. It's wonderful." She sidestepped onto the lawn as Sam hurried past, her hands over her ears. "Was it something I said?"

"We hiked to Jericho and ran into some insect trouble. Sam got stung a few times." Lauren looked past Jenny toward the house. "Have you seen Carmody or Kaster?"

"I saw Kaster with his twins at breakfast." Jenny arched one eyebrow. "Then maybe an hour or so ago, I saw him head out into the garden with Nyssa." Her eyes widened. "You don't think he'd try something with her, do you?"

"No, I think he'd rather chop off his hand. You haven't seen Carmody?"

"No, I haven't seen Carmody." Jenny folded her arms. "What the hell is going on?" She stared down at Lauren's makeshift skirt. "And what on God's green earth did you do to your pants?"

Lauren gave her a quick rundown of what happened at Jericho, taking care to leave out the part about the ward. "You're a Carmody employee?"

Jenny's eyes narrowed. "Yes?"

"And you're a lawyer."

"Uh-huh."

"Carmody's father—his old office is in this house. Nothing's been moved or changed since he died. Execs go up there all the time to hunt through the old files."

"And I know what you're going to ask, but I'm not executive level. And whether I was or not, if I tried to use my ID to gain access, I'd ping security, and you know damn well that they would inform Carmody and I would have to explain why I needed access and what would I say? It's not the most exciting job in the world, but I'm fond of it." Jenny looked down at the path, scuffed her sandal along the edge of a flagstone. "What do you want to know?"

Lauren sensed a change in Jenny. How her voice quieted. How she edged closer, as if to keep from missing anything. *She could go straight to Carmody with this.* But Lauren planned on confronting Carmody anyway. Whether he became angry now or sometime later didn't make much of a difference. "Elliott Rickard. What sorts of steps Carmody's dad took to search for him after he disappeared."

"You think they would keep that here?"

"Where else would they keep it?"

"You remember I said I was in the Jacuzzi while you guys were at dinner?" Jenny slowly raised her eyes to meet Lauren's. "I was still there after dinner, too."

Lauren felt her face heat. "How much did you overhear?"

"Everything, pretty much." Jenny shook her head. "The ghost stuff—I don't know what to say to that. You thinking Carmody's a killer and then whatever the hell else you guys did? And then that stuff about his daughter?" She sighed. "Which is why I want to know what you're looking for."

"I'm not looking for dirt."

"Are you sure?"

"Yes." Lauren massaged her forehead, tried to press away the growing ache behind her eyes. "I'm sorry I asked."

"It's not that. It's just—"

"It's just that as a lawyer for Carmody, you can't consciously take steps to injure him."

"Or his company. I'm not his personal attorney, but I am an employee and all that other crap. I signed forms. So many forms." Jenny stared down the trail that led into the woods. "You think there was something funny about Rickard's disappearance?"

"He was a close friend of Carmody's father. There's a photo of them in the vestibule. It was taken at Jericho."

"So?"

"All I have are feelings." Lauren sniffed, and caught a whiff of her shorts, which she had shoved into the waterproof pocket of her pack. She sidestepped Jenny until she stood downwind. "You don't believe in any of this."

"No. But I'm surrounded by people who do, and when they do things, they do them for reasons, just like normal folks. They're not reasons that make sense to me, but they are reasons." Jenny paused to chew on her lip. "And I like to know what those reasons are, because I am nosy by nature and then I decided to get a license for it." Then her mouth twisted, as though she had bitten something sour. "You're the only person who's seen Fernanda here." She twitched her thumb toward the house. "I heard Pete and Stef talking on their balcony after breakfast. Their voices carry when they're upset."

"You overhear a lot in that pool, don't you?"

"Beats the hell out of morning cable." Jenny paced, once again chewing on her lip. Then she stopped. "There's another library here. It's open to guests—it has DVDs and audio books and stuff like that. But it also has some company archives. I'm guessing it's mostly promotional material, but I'll see what they have."

Lauren shrugged. "It won't be anything sensitive."

"I'll see what they have." Jenny looked down at Lauren's towel, and frowned. "Let's go. You need to put on some pants."

They walked up the path to the lower-level garage and from there hopped the elevator for the upper floors. Lauren pressed her hand to the wall of the car as it glided upward. Felt the same thing she always felt when she touched a surface that had nothing to offer. The soft shimmer of blankness. The static buzz of a white noise generator.

In other words, nothing. It had taken her a while to acquaint herself with the ins and outs of her power, and she knew it probable that she still had things to learn. Even so, she couldn't help but think that the reason the Jericho guard shack had felt like magic-free dead space was that someone, or something, had thrown up a shield that made it seem so. *Except for around the ward.* That power, she felt. *But that's gone now.*

She and Jenny disembarked on the guest floor, then headed in opposite directions to their respective suites. Lauren stashed the pack containing her ruined shorts out on her balcony, then showered, changed, and returned downstairs. Checked out the dining room, and found the staff setting up the lunch buffet. Grabbed a bunch of grapes from the fruit tray and walked out to the garden to see if she could find Kaster and Nyssa. Wandered from level to level, past the medicines and the poisons, the herbs and flavorings. Walked around a sheltered corner and found Heath kneeling on the stone examining one of the statues.

"Oh, Lauren." He struggled to his feet. "I was so engrossed, I didn't hear—" He stopped, swallowed hard, then pointed to the statue. "I noticed you perusing the collection last night. What did you think?"

Lauren bent close to the object, which proved to be one of the Etruscan works. A stylized boar, from the same time period as the hare she had seen the previous evening. "I'm no expert.

I like it well enough, but I like animal figures in general." She waited for Heath to make some smart-ass comment about her depth of knowledge or lack thereof, but instead he nodded and stroked his chin as though she had said something profound. "I could have lived without the other ones, though."

"The little bubble people?" Heath snorted. "That's what I call them. Crude copies of Paleolithic figures. Not Celia's best work by any means." He clapped his hands, then rubbed them together. "Well, must get back. Time for lunch."

Lauren looked down toward the lower levels. "You didn't happen to see Gene out here, did you?"

Heath's leather-soled shoes scraped on the flagstones. He turned. "Gene's here?" His eyes rounded. "I mean, I knew he was here—I saw him this morning—but I didn't know—" He stopped, blew out a breath. "No, I haven't seen him." He nodded curtly, then continued on his way.

Lauren watched Heath walk back to the house. Sam stood waiting for him at the top of the steps and started talking as soon as he reached her. They both turned back to look at Lauren once, then again, before going inside.

Lauren pondered for a few moments. Then she walked back to the boar and knelt close to it. *It should be in a museum, not out in the open like this.* She jostled it, found that there were no bolts or fittings that held it in place, and pushed it farther beneath an overhanging branch.

We're all on edge. She straightened, returned to the walkway, listened for voices. But she heard nothing but the breeze through the trees, the odd chirp or trill, and returned to the house.

CHAPTER 14

Sam freed herself from Heath's embrace and slid out of bed, then gathered up the clothes that had been strewn across the floor and lay them at the foot. Daytime sex wasn't her favorite thing in the world, but Heath had been so jumpy after encountering Lauren in the garden that she had no choice but to settle him down.

She knows—the way she looked at me.

She looks at everybody like that, baby. She's a weirdo.

Sam showered in record time because how could anyone in their right mind dawdle with their ass hanging out for all to see? Scooted into the closet to dry off and dress and checked the welts in the mirror. *Lauren was right. They're almost gone.* She'd had visions of her face puffed out like an aging movie star's lips, but all in all, she looked okay.

She studied herself for a few minutes more. Touched the places where the welts had been. Recalled their sting, how the pain had radiated along her skin. How it had spread beneath the surface, hot as boiling liquid, and how for one terrifying moment she had yearned to tear her flesh with her fingernails and peel it off. Anything to stop the pain.

But now she felt fine. Perfect. Never better.

It was time.

She rooted through the drawers for clean clothes—shorts, a T-shirt—and dressed. Tied her damp hair in a ponytail. Put on her hiking shoes. Listened for the grumbling roar of Heath's snoring, a sure sign that he would sleep for at least another hour. Tiptoed across the room to the door, opened it just wide enough to slip out into the corridor.

The elevator proved to be stuck on another floor, so Sam opted for the stairs. She heard footsteps coming up in the other direction and forced a smile when Pete Augustin came into view.

"Sam? How are you?" Pete stopped and leaned against the bannister. "I heard you had a rough time out in the woods."

"Yes." Sam tried to remember why Pete had to lean. Heath had told her. His hip . . . his knee? She couldn't remember. "It was scary, but I'm fine now."

"You went to Jericho?"

"Yes."

Pete frowned. He had one of those brows that wrinkled, and a high hairline as well. So many furrows, as though someone had removed the skin and replaced it with dark brown ruching. "Heath told you to stay away from there, didn't he? It was a Council decision."

Sam nodded from reflex, and to let Pete think she paid attention. Yes, she recalled Heath telling her something, but when she tried to remember exactly what it was, it slid out of reach. Like the reason Pete leaned, and like all those things you struggled to recall but couldn't quite put your finger on. "Lauren wanted to go."

"Yes, well. We're going to have a talk with her." Pete ran his hand up and down the bannister. "Once we figure out what story to tell her."

Sam nodded, even as she wondered what was the problem. Stories were easy. She was living one now. "I'm sorry."

"As long as you're okay."

"I am. Thank you for asking." Sam resumed walking. To the end of the stairs, then across the vast central room and through the bar, then outside to the deck. At one end was a narrow stairway used by the staff, which allowed her to circle around to the back of the house without being seen. She had never known about it before, and wondered how she knew about it now. But she didn't ponder for long. She had more important things to do.

As she crossed the lawn, a fly landed on her left arm. Large, glossy black, a beautiful onyx marble. It twitch-stepped down to her hand and bit her on the web between her left thumb and forefinger. The pain spread like an oil fire beneath her skin— tears streamed and she bit her lip to keep from crying out. Then as she watched, a blister raised, flesh blackening and thickening until it mirrored the creature that had made it.

Then she heard the buzzing, the soft, sweet sound. It filled her head, made all that had been there before seem weak and foolish by comparison.

She had become part of something greater now.

A voice wended its way through the velvet of her mind. *You know where I am.*

Yes. Yes, she did.

SAM NO LONGER needed the trail map to find her way back to Jericho. She could have found it in the dark. In her sleep. She paused atop the hill overlooking the encampment and gazed at the tumbled ruins.

"Hello, miss."

Sam turned and stared at the man who stood down the trail. Not dressed for hiking—no, far from it. He wore a white shirt and dark tie, gray trousers. A lab coat. "Hello?" She waited for him to say something else, but he watched her in silence, his weird little smile coming and going like a facial tic. "Did you follow me?" Still, silence. "Did you follow me from the house?"

The man pointed to the name sewn above the breast pocket of his coat. "Dr. Elliott Rickard, miss. I've been expecting you."

"You have?"

"Yes. They told me you would be coming." Rickard took a step toward her.

"They." Sam held up her left hand, then turned it so that Rickard could see the raised, blackened blister.

"They." Rickard held up his own left hand, then turned it as she had, showed her that he bore the same mark, in the same place. Then he reached out to her.

Sam walked to him and took his hand. It felt cold. Damp. And there was a smell about him, like the flies Lauren killed. *My little friends.* She would have to do something to make it up to the rest for the loss of their siblings.

"But first you must come with me." Rickard spoke as though he could read her thoughts, which no doubt he could. They were family now. He led her away from Jericho and down a trail she had not yet walked. "There is something you need to do first." He held her hand as a father would, gently but firmly. "The restorative properties of forest flora are vastly underrated, don't you believe?" He nodded. "Yes, I know you do. I can sense that in you. You are a student of plants yourself, are you not?"

"Yes." Cold though Rickard's hand was, Sam felt warmth move up her arm, as though he had injected something into her vein.

"We should be willing to experiment, don't you agree? How can we evaluate the effect that a plant has on others without a basis for comparison?"

"Yes."

Rickard steered Sam off the trail toward a tumble of dead stumps, logs, and large branches, all covered with shelf fungus that held the same gray sheen as his skin, as though it sweated a substance that spread and coated it like wax. "Take this humble entity." He bent down and tore off a piece from one of the semicircular growths. "You would not think it edible, like some of its cousins. But it is more nourishing than any of them." He held the piece out to her. "Here."

For the first time, Sam felt a shiver of doubt. Her eyes watered as the stink of the man and the fungus filled her nose, and acid bubbled to the base of her throat. "Are you sure?"

"Please. It isn't often I find myself in the company of a fellow experimentalist." Rickard stepped closer, a strange light in his eyes turning them as silvery and clouded as the fungus. "I look forward to your assessment."

Sam blinked back tears and held out her hand. The fungus felt slick and soft as raw meat.

Rickard smiled, skin twitching as though something moved beneath the surface. "Trust me."

Sam closed her eyes, lifted the fungus to her mouth. Pulled back her lips and bared her teeth, bit down fast and swallowed, tasted bitterness and salt and felt the odd slickness. *Oyster.* It reminded her of a raw oyster.

"Now." Rickard's voice held an odd harmonic, like a distant echo. "Isn't that better?"

Sam breathed in slowly, then out. Hugged her stomach, and felt the warmth that suffused her skin now grow to fill her belly. She had expected the fungus to make her feel sick, but instead it calmed her, like a soft touch. She no longer felt any doubt. "Yes." She smiled. "I do feel better."

Rickard took her hand again. "Come with me, please."

Sam closed her fingers around his, and wondered when her skin would hold the same cool smoothness. When that time came she would truly be of the woods, as one with the ground and the places beneath.

They walked up the trail to the top of the hill, then down into Jericho.

"We've been waiting for you for some time now." Rickard led her through the gate to the largest building and opened the door. "The little ones do so like company."

Creatures swarmed along the walls, the ceiling. Small ones, like the flies. Larger ones, like the figures in the Carmody garden that Heath didn't think were worth a damn. Their buzzing swept over Sam, so loud that she felt the pressure of the sound like a breeze from all directions at once. They leapt to the floor and clustered around her, round mouths opening and closing, like fish. They tugged at her clothes, pressed their mouths to her skin as though tasting her.

"They're adorable." Sam placed her hand atop the head of the closest, felt its shock of black hair stiff as wire.

"They are, aren't they?" Rickard smiled. "They take after their father."

CHAPTER 15

Lauren sat on the floor of the balcony outside her room and peered between the safety rails at the scene on the main patio three floors below. Kaster was seated at a table as Nyssa Carmody paced back and forth in front of him, arms folded, head down. Kaster had done most of the talking to that point, his voice a soft rise and fall, his characteristic expansiveness nowhere to be seen. What little Nyssa had said had been limited to pushback commentary and the odd expletive. *Bullshit . . . Dad paid her . . . what difference. . .*

But as the minutes wore on, the occasional question popped up in the mix. The pacing slowed. Then Nyssa sat down across from Kaster and leaned forward, elbows on the table, her voice now as low as his. They had reached the negotiating stage.

He almost has her convinced to at least give it a try. Lauren's stomach rumbled with nerves. *Why am I letting myself get pulled into this?* She knew the answer before she finished asking the question. *Because I've been where she is now.* At sea, battered by powers that encroached upon every aspect of her life, isolating, terrifying and, yes, occasionally thrilling her. *Hell, I'm still paddling.* Why Kaster and Carmody felt her competent to counsel another, especially someone as brittle as Nyssa, worried her as much as the counseling itself.

Lauren watched as Kaster reached across the table, placed his hands on Nyssa's shoulders, and gently shook her. Then he released her, sat back, crossed his legs at the knee, and flung his arms wide as Nyssa watched him, chin cupped in her hands. *Deal sealed.* Achievement unlocked. *We are good to go.*

Lauren stared up at the milky blue sky. *Shit.* She watched birds flit from tree to tree. Listened to squirrel squawk. Scratched her fly bites, which had pretty much healed but still bothered her. Debated the wisdom of phoning Virginia for moral support if nothing else, and fell so deeply into thought that when she finally did hear the knock on her door, she had the impression that it had been going on for quite some time.

"You have got to see this." Jenny had switched her bathing suit for cutoffs and a yellow tank top, and carried her flip-flops in one hand. "I have no more words." She waited for Lauren to put on sandals, then led her down two flights and a narrow hallway to a more utilitarian section of the house.

"I'm guessing that this is the section that gets the business use write-off." Jenny took her ID card out of her pocket and waved it in front of the reader located next to a plain panel door. "Unless they've figured out a way to declare the whole damn place." When the indicator turned green and the door clicked, she opened it and held it for Lauren. "I really can't believe some of the stuff I'm finding in here."

Lauren followed her inside, then paused and looked around. "Are we alone?"

"Yeah. Judging from the dust on some of the furniture, I don't think this place sees much traffic." Jenny motioned for her to follow and led her down a narrow aisle lined on both sides with utilitarian metal shelving. "Just around this corner." She stopped in front of a glass-topped display case set against the wall. "Please tell me that isn't what I think it is."

Lauren studied the closed book nestled beside several others beneath the glass. A grimoire, judging by the magical symbols embossed in gold on the binding.

Then she looked closer and saw that the binding, a medium brown that lightened to cream at the corners and edges, had a certain familiar look to it. The tiny pores. A scatter of fine hairs. "You think it's human skin?" She tried to open the case, but it proved to be locked and, judging from the blinking red light she spotted near the underside of the lid, alarmed as well. "I can't tell just by looking. I do know that some books of magic are bound in that way. Sometimes it is the skin of the author, and occasionally the binding is at the request of the author himself."

"That's—" Jenny winced. "How could anyone even touch that thing?"

"For some folks, it was just a way to remember dear ol' granddad."

"You're hilarious."

"I'm practicing."

"Practice more. Only not with me." Jenny led Lauren back the way they had come into the middle of the room. "There

I was, bopping along the stacks, skimming the odd annual report, and bam, it's serial killer time." She stood hands on hips and turned slowly. "This place is half *Wall Street Journal*, half Harry Potter. Anybody comes through that door in a robe and a pointy hat, I'm leaving."

Lauren scanned the contents of some of the shelves. *The Book of Enoch, The Testament of Solomon*. Histories of the OSS, the CIA. Not the titles one expected to see in a business library. "Can any Carmody employee come here?"

"No." Jenny flopped into a leather armchair. "You have to be invited to one of the off-site conferences. Or, like lucky me, seconded for a long weekend of who the hell knows."

"So they screen?"

"Yeah. Like I just said."

"I'm willing to bet that, somehow, Carmody screens for talent." Lauren pointed at Jenny. "Is it possible that something about you indicated to them that it would be safe for you to come into this room and see things like that book?"

Jenny shook her head. "Nope. Not buyin' it. Everybody knows that Carmody's a little weird. They put up with it because he makes them money." She jerked her head in the direction of the grimoire. "He could stick pickled puppies in there and the financial analysts would start tracking corgi futures."

"Now who's the sicko?"

"Just tryin' to fit in." Jenny rose and walked to the other side of the room, and a table spread with several open binders. "Do you want to see what else I found?"

Lauren joined her at the table and soon found herself immersed in Carmody history, both personal and professional.

Photos. Plats of sites worldwide. Self-congratulatory annual reports, bound in gold-embossed leather. But she also found information about Jericho, including albums of photographs from when it was a working settlement.

"It was never really a logging camp." Jenny leafed through one of the old photo albums. "Mostly it served as home away from home for crews who worked at other Carmody sites in the area."

Lauren studied the photos, comparing them with the mental picture she had retained of the ruins, their size and location. *They're not the same.* Early 1900s Jericho had covered a goodly portion of the southern sweep of the mountain. It had been a self-sufficient settlement, complete with a post office, general store, quarters for families, and a school for the children.

As the twentieth century rolled on, other Carmody businesses grew in importance while timber receded. It made sense that they would tear down structures as families moved away. There was a minor boom when Steven Carmody began construction of the house in the late 1960s. Workers lived in some of the loggers' cabins, while the area around Jericho was used as a staging and storage area for building materials. That was when the small railroad was built. It was used to transport workers and materials to the building site.

Then it all stops. Lauren closed the album. "According to this, work on the house was completed in the early seventies."

Jenny pointed to the stack of photo albums piled at the end of the table. "No more mention of Jericho after this house was built. I looked." She turned, then tapped the window to draw the attention of a squirrel. "So Andrew's dad decides the family peak should serve as a retreat. Nothing wrong with that."

"So why leave the remnants of Jericho in place to rot? Either fix it up or tear it down."

"Why bother? It's what, a mile and a half, two miles away?"

"And it's warded."

"Which means what?"

"Either they can't tear it down, or they don't want to."

"Like I said."

Jenny had picked up some of the albums and started putting them away when the door opened and Peter stuck his head in.

"We've been looking all over for you two." He shouted down the corridor, "She's up here!"

Lauren exited the library with Jenny. When she looked over the rail to the main floor below she saw Carmody and Kaster talking to a T-shirted man wired with multiple communications devices. "What's wrong?"

"Heath's losing his shit. Sam's missing." Peter motioned for them to follow and then hurried to the stairs. "You and she took a walk this morning?"

"Yes. We hiked to Jericho."

"When did you get back?"

"Around lunchtime."

They descended to the ground floor to find Stef waiting for them.

"Did you see anything unusual?" The woman took hold of Peter's hand. "Andrew says that they often have to evict people who camp without permission."

"We did find something." Lauren described the toilet hole ring. "It may have been fairly recent, judging from the condition of the waste." She paused as Heath approached from the direction of the bar, glass in hand and Sam's handbag slung over his shoulder. "We checked out one of the buildings. The guard shack by the gate. We found a mound of bones inside. The remains of a small bird." From the corner of her eye, she saw Carmody draw closer. "It looked like a ward. Flies swarmed out of it and bit her. When we tried to sweep the flies off her, we scattered the ward all over the place."

"Flies?" Carmody stood hands on hips, eyes fixed on the floor at his feet.

"Yes, flies, Andrew, the same flies we discussed earlier, when I replayed Lauren's extended phone message for you all to hear." Kaster focused on her. "Mistress Mullin, is there anything else that you would like to tell the class?"

Lauren felt the man's stare like a burn. "Some of the same flies came in my room last night. I did mention it to you."

"Did they bite you?" That, from Carmody.

When Lauren nodded, Stef gestured toward her.

"And she's fine." The woman clucked her tongue. "You're being dramatic, Gene. As usual."

"If Sam feared being bitten again, she wouldn't have gone back there." Peter looked to Carmody, who took a phone from his pocket.

"I'll notify my people. They'll find her." He punched in a speed dial code and was just about to speak when Lauren raised a hand.

"We're the ones who need to look. Not civilians. Not yet."

Peter nodded. "She's right." He turned to Stef, whose skirt and heeled pumps didn't lend themselves to a tramp through the woods. "Stay here for now. If I need you to bring anything

to me, I'll call." He bent closer to the woman as one of the security team strode past. "A safety invocation might help."

"I'll go get one of the trucks and meet you around front."
Carmody ran to the elevator.

"Can we do a locator spell?" Lauren flared out her fingers.
"We've done them in Gideon. You form a ring and invoke the
Lady's light and it sends out streamers . . ." She quieted as they
all stared, and wished like hell that she could have transported
someone from Gideon for just five minutes. "Did someone try
to call her? Did she have a phone?" She motioned to Heath and
fielded a blank look already unfocused from drink. "Did she
take her phone?"

"They already asked me that." Heath shook his head. "Why
would she? Just going for a walk. Why would she need a phone?"

Because common-bloody-sense. Lauren looked out to the driveway just as Carmody pulled up to the door behind the wheel
of a battered Range Rover. She fell in behind the others, then
slowed when she felt the pressure of a stare. She turned and saw
Nyssa Carmody standing in the shadows beneath the stairs,
watching them.

THE ROVER BUMPED and jostled along the trail, shaking them like
beans in a can. Carmody stopped once so that Heath could get
out and vomit, then hammered a rough beat on the steering
wheel as the man slipped back inside and buckled himself in.

"You done?" Before Heath could nod, he hit the gas, sending
stones shrapneling into the trees.

Lauren sat in the rear bench seat. More than once she caught
Carmody watching her in the rearview mirror. She looked out

the back window and caught sight of Kaster's Jeep not too far behind. Not enough room, he had said. But she had sensed anger, at her for not telling everyone about the flies sooner, and at everyone else for brushing off his concerns. *He wants to be alone.* Given how on-edge everyone was, this was probably wise.

After a few minutes, Carmody slowed, then stopped atop the hill leading down to Jericho. Peter grabbed a first aid kit from beneath the seat and hit the ground running, followed by Jenny and Heath, who still lugged Sam's shoulder bag like some sort of oversize lucky charm. As they hurried up the trail, Carmody caught Lauren's eye again. "Come with me."

Lauren followed him down the hill to the guard shack. As they drew near, she slowed, spread her fingers, and reached out her hands. Felt the change in the currents, like a chill riptide pulling her toward the ruins. "Oh, shit."

Carmody entered the shack, and swore when he saw the scattered bones and feathers, the smashed flies. "Can we put something else in place?"

"Now?" Lauren followed him inside. "If something got out, we wouldn't be able to shut it back in. We'd have to reopen the circle, and we don't know what else is in here that could escape." She hugged herself as the current widened and enveloped her and the temperature plummeted, shivered as though she stood in front of an open freezer. Turned to check the Lady's Eye that she had etched into the doorway, and found it gone, the wood returned to its original state. "What the hell happened here?"

"We found her!"

Lauren turned to find Peter waving from the top of the hill. She waited for Carmody to answer her question but he just shook his head, then brushed past her and pelted up toward the trail.

She turned back to the bare spot on the floor. Then she looked out the rear of the ruin toward the circle of buildings, and sensed the shimmer in the air. The view altered each time she blinked, scenes flipping as though she paged through one of the Carmody albums. Immense piles of lumber. Cement trucks. A crane. Then came voices. Only men's voices at first, barking commands, yelling, arguing.

Then, quieter voices and new scenes, which didn't match any photograph she had seen. Men and women in office clothes, coveralls, lab coats, walking from building to building and vanishing inside. The same buildings as stood there now, but newly constructed, with steel doors secured with combination locks and bars on the windows.

She looked toward the far side of the shack and saw the translucent figure of a young man in khaki and denim, high-powered rifle slung over his shoulder, holding a clipboard and flipping through the pages. Then he tossed the clipboard atop a nearby desk and walked right through her on his way to the door. *No one here by that name, Dr. Rick.*

"Lauren!"

She turned to find Jenny halfway down the hill, waving to her.

"Do you know first aid? Pete could use some help."

Lauren remained in the shack and beckoned for Jenny to come close. Waited until the other woman was within arm's reach of the door, then held up her hand for her to stop. "Do you have your knife?"

"Yeah." Jenny hesitated, then dug into the pocket of her shorts and pulled it out. "Why?"

Lauren took the knife from her, then opened and closed blades until she found the smallest, sharpest one. "I really need to figure out another way to do this." She gashed the inside of her arm, then ran the blade along the welling cut and flicked the drops of blood along the floor. "The Lady's Eye couldn't stop you, but maybe this will. Whatever's left here, stay here, and whatever's out there, stay close. You come to the house, I'll be waiting for you." She looked back out toward the ruins just as another figure formed, then faded. A woman with long, dark hair, dressed in a short dress or slip, watching her from a door-way. Fernanda Carmody didn't appear so pleading this time. Lauren could sense her anger like a needle through her skin.

A hard shot in the arm brought her back to the here and now.

"What the hell did you just do?" Jenny grabbed her shoulder and spun her around. "What the actual hell?"

"Just a warning to whatever is here that it should stay put." Lauren wiped the blade on her shorts, then closed the knife and gave it back.

They ran up the hill. Then Jenny led Lauren down a leg of the trail in the direction opposite the way they had come. "They found her in a clearing near a pile of dead wood. Pete thinks she ate something."

They pushed between two spruce, and found Peter kneeling on the ground beside Sam. He had donned nitrile gloves and begun on a physical exam, working his hands down her legs in search of injuries, while Carmody talked on the phone and Heath paced nearby.

Lauren knelt on Sam's other side, opposite Peter. "You think she ate something."

"That." Peter jerked his thumb over his shoulder in the direction of a dead stump.

"The shelf fungus?" Lauren took the phone that Peter handed her. "Would it have had an effect already?" He had opened a first aid app and started recording Sam's vitals. She scanned his notes—pulse rate, respiration, appearance—then turned her attention to the woman. *Shit.* Sam's skin was red, as though she's been running, and felt hot and dry. Her pulse was rapid and thready, her breathing, shallow. Peter had propped up her head, loosened her clothing, and applied a cooling pack to the back of her neck. Lauren continued to record her vitals, and tried to keep her still and calm, gently drawing her hands away when she tried to pull at her clothes or the pack.

"That's what I took out of her mouth." Peter pointed to the plastic bag on the ground next to him, the gray mucus like wad resting within. "Unless she swallowed something else beforehand. She hasn't vomited and I'm afraid to give her ipecac to make her because I don't know what else she ate out here." He wrote in the air. "Add that she has a sore on her left hand."

Lauren checked Sam's hand, then made a note about the large black blister.

"Do any of your bites look like that?" Peter asked.

Lauren held out her hands, which were normal but for the odd pink splotch. Then she motioned to Heath. "Did she have any insect allergies? Did she carry an inhaler or an EpiPen?"

"What? Allergies?" Heath started toward Lauren. "Look at

her—does that look like an allergy to you?" He stared at Sam and backed away, then returned to pacing at the clearing's edge.

"The paramedics are on their way." Carmody crouched at Sam's feet. "The chopper's almost here. It can take her to OHSU. My doctor will be waiting for her."

"That was fast." Peter pulled off the gloves, then rooted through the first aid kit, picking up the small bottle of syrup of ipecac, then setting it aside.

"The chopper's always ready to go." Carmody stood as the first rumbles of helicopter noise sounded from overhead. "And the paramedics were already here."

Lauren looked up. "You keep paramedics on staff?"

"Yes." Carmody's face reddened, and he motioned to Sam. "You never know."

"They're coming!" Jenny stood out on the trail and waved to the approaching vehicle.

Lauren recorded another set of vitals. She pressed her fingers to Sam's wrist to check her pulse and felt her fingers slide. She bent close, then scraped a patch of skin with her fingernail. Examined what turned out to be tiny globules of white and gray, which looked like fat gone rancid. She sniffed it and winced. "Did you put something on her wrist?"

Peter shook his head. "I didn't put anything on her."

"Does that fungus have a smell?"

"Yeah, it smells like crap. Why?"

"So do the flies after you smash them." Lauren showed him the gunk. "This is on her skin. It wasn't there a few minutes ago. I think it's exuding from her pores."

"It's on her face, too." Peter touched a shiny patch on Sam's forehead, sniffed it, and shuddered. "Damn."

"Damn? Why are you saying 'damn'?" Heath knelt on the ground beside Sam just as the paramedics barreled through with a stretcher and their gear. "It's all right, baby. It's going to be all right. I've got everything"—he patted her shoulder bag—"all under control. It'll be all right."

As the paramedics set to work, Peter gave them what information he and Lauren had compiled, and turned over the piece of fungus he had removed from Sam's mouth. Meanwhile, Sam grew more and more restless, pushing away their hands and trying to sit up. "I have to go. He needs me. The babies need me. I have to go. I have to go with him."

"I'm right here, baby. We're going to the doctor together." Heath tried to push close, but Peter took hold of his shoulders and steered him away. "I'm not going anywhere. I'm staying right here with you, and we'll go together."

"I have to go." Sam pushed one paramedic away and hit the other in the face when he tried to grab her. "He needs me. The children need me." She continued to struggle as they moved her onto the stretcher and strapped her in. They conferred for a few moments, then one of them gave Sam an injection. As the drug kicked in, her flailing slowed, and she quieted.

Carmody beckoned to Heath. "Come on. You'll go with the paramedics. The chopper's waiting at the house. It will take you to Portland." He repeated himself twice, then finally grabbed the shaky Heath by the elbow and pulled him along.

Lauren traced an Eye of the Lady on the foot of the stretcher as the paramedics hoisted it, then stood aside so they could pass.

ALEX GORDON

She checked the clearing for anything that had been left behind or looked unusual, then went to the wood pile and examined the shelf fungus.

Peter had been right about the smell. The air near the wood was thick with septic tank stink. *Just like the flies.* She stared at the weird silvery masses and tried to recall whether she had ever seen anything like them before. She reached out to touch one shining earlike protuberance, then changed her mind. Gave them one last look, then trudged back up to the trail to find Peter waiting for her.

"Thanks." He put his arm around her and gave her a quick hug. In the short time since they had arrived, his skin had grayed, and his eyes held that slightly wild look that spoke of the need for a quiet corner and a chance to breathe.

"I don't feel like I did anything." Lauren watched the paramedics pull away. "I read about mushrooms and fungi when I took backwoods first aid—they don't usually work this fast. When they do, it's GI upset. Vomiting. This looked like alkaloid poisoning."

"I don't know what else she ate." Peter worked his shoulders, rubbed the back of his neck. "Heath said that she would try things just to see what they'd do. Well, this might just have done her one too many." He jerked his chin in the direction of Jericho. "What happened back at the shack?"

"The ward is blown. I set something in place that I hope tides us over until we figure out what's going on." Lauren showed Peter the slash on her arm, then described a little of what she had seen. What she had felt. "That place has some strong memories. I don't know what happened there, but it was profound and for some reason, it's resurfacing."

Peter's jaw worked before he spoke. "We'll figure it out."

"I saw Fernanda again."

Peter said nothing. He just patted her shoulder, then walked slowly back up the trail.

Lauren leaned against a tree. Watched Peter slump against the Rover while Jenny paced and wiped her eyes. Off to the side, Carmody and Kaster sat in the Jeep, deep in conversation.

She yawned, the first sign that her adrenaline surge was wearing off, then listened to the sounds of the woods, the breeze through the leaves, and chirps of birds. Then she straightened and looked down the trail, in the direction she had not previously walked.

Except that she had, just a few short days before. She remembered it all, the trees and clusters of ferns and the steep grade of the path and the smells. The hint of rot, barely detectable amid the moss and the green scents and the distant touch of the ocean.

She looked up and spotted a Steller's jay watching her from the branch of a Sitka spruce, as if it expected something from her. Could it possibly be the same bird that she had fed a few days before?

"I left all my peanuts back in Gideon. Sorry." She took a deep breath, exhaled, and finally moved. Walked slowly, on the lookout for the gap in the shrubbery. When she spotted it, part of her wanted to turn and run, join Peter and Jenny and drive back to the house. But the rest of her knew that she couldn't do that, because running away wasn't what she did.

Follow the trail to the end . . . that's what we do.

She stepped through the gap and onto the outcropping, and

looked out over the mountains. She could see Mount Hood in the distance, glittery white with its ever-present cape of snow.

Lauren looked down and saw the stones, still in the pile where she had left them. A few had tumbled out of place, picked at by a bird or squirrel. But there was no doubt in her mind that they were the same stones. This was the place she had seen while in Gideon. *But not just a vision.* She had somehow actually, physically passed through some doorway and wound up here. For a short time, she had sat on this ledge, fed a bird, piled stones.

Then she remembered the sounds she had heard behind her. The stink. Someone, or something, had seen her. Did it know that she had returned?

Lauren stilled when she heard footsteps, and turned to find Kaster standing in the opening. But the charm, the glee, the quiet satisfaction with himself and everything around him—all that had been set aside.

"Is there something you're not telling me?" Even his voice sounded different. Too precise. Monotonal. Like the English in a recorded language lesson.

At any other time, Lauren would have denied. But watching what happened to Sam had stretched something inside her to the breaking point. "There's a lot I'm not telling you."

"And just think—if you had told me some of it, this might not have happened."

"Point the first, I did, at breakfast. I asked about the flies, and you shrugged. Point the second, I phoned you about the busted ward immediately. Point the third, don't give me that shit. You haven't played it straight with me since we met." Lauren took one step toward Kaster, then another, and as with Nyssa, something about the look on her face compelled him to back up. "Something is going on here. It's been going on for a while. It involves Jericho, and Fernanda, and you're scared."

"Just talk to Nyssa, and stay at the house. Keep out of everything else." Kaster made as if to say more, but before he could, the pounding of running feet stopped him.

Then Jenny appeared, panting from exertion, eyes wide. "Carmody just peeled out of here. Someone called him—from the house." She sagged against a tree, gasped for breath. "Nyssa's locked herself in her bathroom. They're afraid she'll try to kill herself."

CHAPTER 16

They piled into Kaster's Jeep for the ride back to the house, Peter in the passenger seat, Jenny and Lauren crammed into the rear jump seats. Lauren sat behind Kaster, close enough to catch the occasional whiff of his cologne, one of those indefinable blends that smelled like half the spice cabinet. Peter warned her and Jenny *not to walk alone in the woods for the foreseeable future, dammit.* Then he dug a couple of aspirin out of the first aid kit, swallowed them dry, and closed his eyes.

When they reached the house, Kaster drove straight into the lower-level garage. Tires squealed as he swung into a parking space near the elevator. Then he got out, pulled his seat forward, and held out his hand to Lauren. "You're coming with me."

Peter had been halfway out of his seat. Now he slid back in and reached out to Kaster. "Gene, no."

"Not now, Peter."

"Stef thinks—"

"I know what Stef thinks, and what you think. You've both

been quite generous with your thoughts." Kaster took hold of Lauren's arm and pulled her out of the vehicle. "We need to hurry."

Lauren let Kaster drag her into the elevator, then extracted herself from his grasp. "Has she done this before?"

"Not in this house."

"But Carmody keeps paramedics here, on staff."

"As a safety precaution." Kaster punched the floor buttons three times before hitting the one for the right floor. "He's had them at all the houses this past year." He stamped his foot once, then again, as though kicking the car to make it go faster. "You have no idea what it's been like."

The door opened and Lauren broke into a run to keep up with Kaster, who sprinted down the carpeted corridor. This was the third floor of the family wing, the rugs worn in places, the furniture old and battered. She passed tables stacked with books, chairs hung with jackets and sweaters, and smelled the faint buttery aroma of popcorn.

She followed Kaster around another corner and found a crowd had gathered near a door at the end of the hall, including Stef, a pair of security guards, and a trio of paramedics complete with equipment bags and a gurney.

Stef closed her eyes and shook her head when she saw Lauren. "Gene, please."

Kaster ignored her, taking Lauren's elbow again and steering her through the doorway of what proved to be Nyssa's bedroom. The gentle color scheme of grays and lilacs appeared fresh, the walls newly painted, and Lauren wondered if Nyssa had picked it herself or if Carmody had in an effort to provide a calming environment.

Carmody stood at the far end of the room, near the bathroom door. "Don't touch it. She said that if anyone tries to break it down, she'll cut herself so she bleeds out before we get it open."

"Did she say anything to you?" Kaster tried to put his ear to the wall near the door, but Carmody pulled him back. "Did she say why?"

Carmody shook his head, then started to pace. "Something happened while we were gone. She was fine at breakfast. We even discussed the possibility of her going back to school—" His voice broke. "I shouldn't have left her." He wiped his eyes with the back of his hand, then turned to Lauren. "Please. Whatever you can do." He walked toward the bathroom door, then stopped when he came within arm's reach. "Nyssa? Lauren Mullin is here. I really wish you would talk to her." He started to say more, then shook his head and walked out to the hall, where Stef waited for him. She took hold of his arm and started talking, her voice a low, level rise-and-fall like the murmur of a distant crowd.

"We'll be right here." Kaster touched Lauren's arm, then moved away to a place just outside the doorway.

Lauren remained still for a few moments. Then she sidestepped toward the bathroom door, as if she approached the edge of a cliff. "Nyssa?" She closed her eyes, focused her attention, strained for any sound, any sense of the girl. *She could be dead already.* Her eyes stung. *Please, no.*

Then she heard a noise, like a shaky sigh.

"My father paid you to talk to me. You've now officially talked to me." Nyssa's voice, flat, drained of life. "Pick up your paycheck on the way out."

"He hasn't paid me a dime."

"He will. Gene told him you're broke."

"'Broke' is a relative term. Compared to Gene and your father, most of the world is broke." Lauren shot a glare at Kaster, who shrugged sheepishly and turned away. Then she lowered to the floor as close to the door as she dared and rested her head against the wall. She drew her knees to her chest and tried to make herself so small. Wished she could be anyplace else in the world but this bedroom. "I don't know if I can help you. Sometimes I can't help myself." She spread her hands and felt the air. "Do you even want help?" Yes, it was quiet here, but she also felt tension, spent emotion. This was the silence that followed the rage, and if there was strength left for anger, there was still hope. "The thing I miss most about my life then, as opposed to my life now, is the not knowing. That there was this world out there that knew about me, and that there were parts of it that didn't want me to exist. It's like, I never did anything to you. I don't care about you. Why can't you just let me be?"

From the other side of the door came the clink of glass, the opening and closing of a drawer. The soft rush of water from a faucet, and the faintest of footsteps. "Gene said that you died." A grudging voice, curious in spite of itself.

"Yes, I did. Technically, I guess. For a few minutes."

"How did you do it?"

"Smoke inhalation."

A soft gasp. "You burned yourself?"

"I drew the memory of fire from some wood, and torched a demon."

"You did that?"

Lauren thought back. Seven months had passed since then, but it seemed so much longer. *And I'm still just as lost now as I was then.* "Yeah." She felt the pressure of stares, and looked toward the bedroom entry to find Peter and Jenny had joined the others. As she watched, Jenny clasped her hands together, raised them to her mouth, gave them a little shake. A gesture of prayer, of good luck. No one else moved.

"The place you went, was it quiet?"

Lauren edged around so that her back faced the audience. "I honestly don't remember. It wasn't loud. The people there—the spirits, I guess—they talked. I don't know if there was music or anything like that. I didn't get that far." She waited, every beat of silence stretching longer and longer.

Then she heard the soft creak of wood, as Nyssa leaned against the bathroom door.

"Why did you come back?"

Sometimes I wonder. "They told me I had a job to do."

"Like what, more demon torching?"

Lauren smiled. "Yeah."

"I've never had a job."

"You want mine?" Lauren rubbed her hands together and examined the fly bites, checking for any sign of a black blister like Sam's. "It's a different world. Sometimes I feel like I can see the universe in a wisp of cloud. Other times I walk somewhere, and the next thing I know, I've passed through to another place."

Nyssa's tone sharpened. "You can do that?"

"If conditions are right." Lauren thought back to her trip across the Abernathy campus, from the library to the office corridor where she saw Fernanda. "Thing is, I'm not sure what those conditions are."

"Can you do it now?"

"I can try." Lauren almost added *if I do, will you come out*, but stopped herself. This was no time to put pressure on Nyssa. *It's all on me.* She unwound and slowly stood, heard the questioning noises from Carmody and the others, and ignored them. "Tap on the wall where you want me to come through." She listened, and after a few moments heard the light rapping a foot or so to her left. Moved into position. Listened to the silence, then reached out and felt it.

It was easier, this time, to find the spaces between, work her fingers into them, and make them larger. The wall faded—she saw the shadowy outlines of the studs, the wiring. Then came the inside of the bathroom wall, the outline of the tile.

Soon the inside of the bathroom appeared. Fuzzy at first, then sharp and clear. The rubber goldfish on the rim of the bathtub. The objects scattered atop the vanity, the jars and tubes and the broken water glass, shards glinting in the sunbeam that shone through the skylight. The red lipstick smeared across the mirror.

No, not lipstick. Lauren took a step forward. Another. Reached though the wall that was no longer there, felt the warmth of the sunlight touch her hand. Saw Nyssa standing with her back pressed against the wall opposite, mouth hanging open, blood dripping down her forearms.

Lauren heard the sound that the drops made when they struck the floor. *Pat—pat—pat.* The soft squeak of Nyssa'a bare feet as she pushed along the wall, her whimper as she trod upon a piece of glass.

Her scream.

Lauren staggered back as the sound sliced through her and the air, once so calm, buffeted her like a gale. The wall shimmered back into view, overlaying the bathroom like a double exposure, then growing more and more solid. She felt the cold scrape of the tile down her left arm as she tried to pull away, the silkiness of wood and the gravelly crumble of wallboard as they formed around her hand. In place of it.

Through it.

Lauren struggled to focus as the pain engulfed her hand and spread up her arm, like hammers pounding again and again, as she shifted back into the world where the bathroom wall existed and wood and stone and metal pushed into flesh that had no business being there. She fought to ignore the blood that threaded down the clean, smooth, lilac paint and the way the wall shook when Nyssa flung open the bathroom door.

"I saw your hand come through the wall. *I saw your hand*."

Focus. Lauren forced herself to concentrate, to shift into the space between for one vital instant. Heard footsteps behind her. Voices that changed to cries. Commanded herself calm.

The air stilled. The wall faded. She yanked out her hand, then sagged against the wall and slid down to the floor. Cradled her arm close and choked back vomit as the pain washed over her.

"Ohmigod ohmigod." Nyssa knelt on the floor beside her, eyes wide and shadowed by circles dark as smeared mascara. "You're hurt. Dad, she's hurt." She placed her bloody hand over Lauren's.

"Don't." Lauren jerked away as the pressure of the girl's touch sent knives coursing up her arm.

"Honey, we'll take good care of her." Carmody met Lauren's eye as he bent to pull Nyssa to her feet, and gave her a small nod. "But you have to come with me now. The doctor's waiting."

"She needs one more than I do."

"We'll take care of her. I promise." Carmody lifted Nyssa to her feet, then paused so Kaster could wrap a towel around the girl's bloody forearms. He then tried to steer her toward the bedroom door, but when she balked he picked her up and carried her.

"But did you see what she did?" Nyssa twisted until she could watch Lauren around Carmody's shoulder.

"Yes, honey, I know. We all did. But you have to be quiet now because—" Carmody's voice trailed as he carried his daughter into the hallway and the waiting arms of his medical staff. Peter and Stef followed, muttered discussion alternating with backward glances at Lauren.

"You okay?" Jenny stood just inside the bedroom door, arms folded, her face gray.

She looks ready to pass out. Lauren nodded slowly. "I'm fine."

"I'll save you a seat at the bar." Jenny sidestepped out the door.

Lauren listened to the receding bustle of voices, the squeak and beep of medical equipment. Then she looked up to find Kaster regarding her. "Who saw?"

Kaster crouched beside her. "Only those of us who could cope with the sight of a woman passing through a solid wall."

Events of the last few hours had left him looking rumpled, his hair mussed and his shirt stained with dirt and sweat. One pant leg torn. "Not the paramedics or the guards. If they ask—which they won't, because they know better—we'll tell them you punched the wall to distract Nyssa." He looked down at her hand and winced. "Or something."

Lauren steeled herself, then assessed the damage. Her hand looked as though it had been mauled by a particularly pissed-off cat, the back crosshatched with deep scratches that seeped blood and a multitude of icepick-like wounds. Two fingers appeared swollen, and her wrist ached. But she could move everything, although her range of motion was definitely limited. "I don't think anything's broken."

"You should see the doctor after she's finished treating Nyssa." Kaster slid his hand beneath hers and examined the wounds. "You look a little shaky."

"Only a little?" Lauren shivered as Kaster brushed his fingers over hers, then traced one fingertip over the back of her hand, the self-inflicted gash on her forearm. "What are you doing?"

"Evaluating your wounds."

"So we can count medical expert among your many talents?"

"One makes oneself useful however one can." Kaster continued his tactile assessment. "According to circumstances."

Lauren felt warmth suffuse her hand and move up her arm. Her wounds tingled as though touched with antiseptic. "Actually, it doesn't feel that bad." She eased out of his grasp and worked to her feet, then turned to the wall and saw the streaks of dried blood marring the paint.

Kaster stood and moved closer until he hovered at her shoulder. "Thank you."

"It just kicks the can down the road until we figure out what's going on, doesn't it?" Lauren slipped past him toward the bathroom door. "Add to that the fact that I don't know what I'm doing. I could have scared Nyssa into hurting herself. Into killing herself."

"But you didn't. You caught her interest, which might keep her from trying this again. Seat of the pants your ploy might have been, but it worked."

"This time." Lauren stepped into the bathroom. The sun through the skylight felt just as warm as it had a few minutes before, and she held her injured hand in the beam as though it could soothe and heal. Inhaled clean, bright soapy scents, then stilled as she picked up the faint hint of metal.

She walked to the mirror. Nyssa's blood had long since dried, the coating so thick that Lauren could see no hint of her own reflection. She looked closer, spotted a ring of white surrounding the red, scraped it with her thumbnail and sniffed it. *Soap.* It looked as though Nyssa had tried other means to cover the mirror before resorting to cutting herself. "Has she ever done this before?"

"Self-harm? Yes. Many times." Kaster touched the edge of the mirror. "But not this." He sighed through his teeth, then looked down at his soiled shirt and frowned. "I'm going to go change, then go downstairs to the clinic."

Lauren nodded.

"It's at ground level. The blue door at the rear of the garage."

"Right." Lauren kept her back turned, felt Kaster's stare burn two neat holes between her shoulder blades, and waited until she heard him make a muttering exit. Then she pressed her uninjured hand against the mirror. Felt nothing at first but the chill of the glass, the slight roughness of the dried blood like a badly applied layer of paint.

She waited. Minutes passed, and she was about to give up when she felt prickling through the tips of her fingers.

Damp warmth followed, as though the blood had yet to dry. Then an instant later came the searing heat, the pain, as though she had pressed her hand to an electric burner. Screaming filled her head, the wail of a desperate, terrified soul. *Leave me alone.*

Lauren jerked away from the mirror and stood bent over the sink as the nausea once again washed over her. After she steadied, she examined her palm, half-expecting to see blisters and reddened flesh. But the skin proved pale, and cool to the touch.

What's going on, Nyssa? She wondered if she would be able to talk to the girl about what happened without making matters worse. She had no experience speaking to someone in such a precarious state of mind, no idea whether some seemingly innocent comment or question would be enough to set the girl off again.

Lauren left the bathroom, the bedroom. Walked down the hallway, the rooms she passed all empty and quiet, as though the tumult that had occurred such a short while before had never happened. She wandered lost for a time, backtracked, then finally stumbled upon the outlet to the stairs that led to the fourth-floor guest wing. She reached the first landing before she realized that she gripped the railing with her injured hand.

She wriggled her fingers, then rotated her wrist, found the pain had eased to a dull ache and the gashes had stopped bleeding. Even the swelling had gone down.

Lauren relived the light pressure of Kaster's hand, the way he traced along bone and around each wound. A caring touch, at odds with his attitude, the man he seemed to be.

Full of surprises. She took hold of the railing again and headed up the stairs to her suite.

LAUREN SHOWERED, AS much to wash away memories of the last several hours as the dirt and sweat. She recalled dinner the previous evening, when Sam had announced her aversion to the open-air shower. Stood still as the water rained down, and tried not to think about how quickly it could all go to hell.

She decided that the odds of any group dinner were slight given the circumstances, so she dressed in shorts and a faded UW T-shirt and wandered downstairs to the bar to look for Jenny. Walked in to find Peter and Stef huddled at one of the small tables, and was about to turn tail when Peter beckoned to her. *Damn.* She stopped by the bar, debated straight vodka, but settled for wine.

"We just left Nyssa." Peter scooted aside so Lauren could pull up a chair. "Andrew's going to stay with her until she goes to sleep."

"Did she say what happened?" Lauren caught a look pass between the pair, one of those glances that spoke volumes in a language an observer couldn't begin to understand.

"This isn't the first time she's injured herself, unfortunately." Peter stared into his drink. "But what happened today touched her deeply. Or perhaps 'rattled' describes it better. She talked of nothing but you all during her examination. Andrew had to shush her repeatedly."

Lauren finished her wine, then beckoned to the bartender for a refill. "You'd think anyone who worked here would be used to seeing unusual things."

"Well, there's unusual and then there's . . . what you did." Stef toyed with a tea ball steeping in a small china pot. "Virginia never told us of your ability to transmigrate."

"She wouldn't have put it in the Gideon report." Lauren looked through the window at the world outside, where dusk had fallen and all was quiet and one could nurse a drink and try to come to terms with a hellish day instead of arguing about proper magic reporting procedures. "It's developed over the last few months."

"There is this amazing invention called the telephone." Stef poured her tea, then added sugar. She stirred for some time, then set the spoon aside and clasped her hands as though to say grace. "I know you feel that this is nothing but bureaucratic rigmarole, but we must be kept informed about the level of talent of all the Children. It's a suspicious, reactionary world in which we live. Rumors spread like wildfire and no matter how mad they sound, they'll be believed. The next thing you know, someone's being interviewed by one of those two-bit paranormal shows. Those silly tabloids. Then people start asking questions. Digging for information. We don't need those kinds of surprises."

Lauren held back all the comments that sprang to mind, snide or otherwise, and instead tried to figure out why Stef chose this time to be civil. *Maybe because we've all been through enough today.* Somehow, she couldn't bring herself to believe that. "I have been through something like what you describe.

I managed to keep my mouth shut, as did everyone else in Gideon who survived."

"For now." Stef turned to look out the window. "But the times, they are a-changin'."

They sat in silence. Then Peter cleared his throat. "I told Stef about your method of mending the breach in the warding. And who you saw. I'm trying to convince her that we're going to need to go back there soon, perhaps as early as tomorrow. We need to inspect the wards that are there, strengthen them if necessary."

Stef shook her head. "The fact that all Lauren saw remained within the bounds of Jericho tells me that the wards are still working."

"What about what I saw at the bottom of the garden?" Lauren watched Stef's hands. The woman was a cuticle-picker, the skin around her thumbnails showing red and raw. "What about the fact that we've all seen Fernanda everywhere?"

"Everywhere but here, in this house." Stef noticed where Lauren looked and folded her hands in her lap to hide the damage. "As long as the house is protected, then Nyssa has safe haven. A place where she can find peace."

"How can you say that when she just tried to kill herself?" Lauren turned to Peter, who, if not an ally, at least seemed willing to listen. "Carmody was upset about the ward's destruction. He wanted to replace it immediately. I asked him what had happened there. He wouldn't tell me."

"Something is going on there, Stef, and it's starting to bleed over." Peter leaned close to Stef while pointing to Lauren. "How do you explain her seeing Fernanda?"

"She did live in this house for five years. It is more than likely that she visited Jericho at some point." Stef slipped off her owlish glasses and rubbed her eyes. Without the rounds of black plastic, her face looked very small. "A place can retain memories of all that has occurred within its boundaries. Those occurrences do not necessarily have to have been bad. They don't always have to portend awful things."

"That makes no sense. If there's no danger, why was the place warded to begin with?" Lauren felt the warmth of the wine, saw that she had already drained her second glass. *Take it easy.* "I spent part of today in the library with Jenny Porter. She dug up a boatload of information about the Carmody companies, and about Jericho, up until the late sixties. After that, nothing about Jericho. It's as though it ceased to exist." She glanced at Peter, who polished off his drink and now rolled the empty glass back and forth between his hands. Another nervous habit, like Stef's nail picking. *So much nervousness.* "I didn't just see Fernanda today. I saw the construction of a newer facility, and the people who worked there. Their clothing looked like late sixties or early seventies, the time where any mention of Jericho stops."

Stef shook her head. "What you saw made no sense. Heavy equipment. Cranes and trucks. You don't need those to build simple wooden structures like those that are there now."

"My old job involved the management of lab construction projects." Lauren thought back to those days, a seeming lifetime ago. "They may have built things underground."

Peter perked up. His hands stilled. "Why do that?"

"One reason? Stability. Some lab equipment, like electron

microscopes, function best in a vibration-free environment. That's often more readily achieved by setting them up below-ground." Lauren replayed the scene in her head. All those people going into those tiny cabins, but no one coming out. "Simpler explanation? If it's underground, you can't see it." She stood. "If you'll excuse me—I need to get some air." And she needed to be alone, so she could think.

The evening still held on to the heat and humidity of the day. Lauren felt the moisture settle on her skin as she crossed the patio and leaned on the railing. Forest sounds reached her. A flicker overhead as a bat or bird took wing. The odd grunt, and the sense of being watched by things she couldn't see.

Then came the sound of the French doors opening and clos-ing. Light footsteps.

"I know what you're thinking. I'm every over-officious man-ager you've ever known rolled into one. Consumed by minutiae. Blind to the big picture." Stef moved in beside Lauren. She had donned a light wrap in spite of the warmth and pulled it more tightly around her. "I don't know what Andrew and Gene told you about why you were asked here. I thought I knew, but after what happened today, I'm not so sure." She looked out at the woods. "I've always thought of Andrew as the son I never had. But he's also his father's son, and Steven was . . . calculating. I suppose men like them need to be. It's one of the qualities that make them what they are." She smiled, a small, sad curve of lip. "Given how I've treated you, I doubt you'll be favorably inclined toward anything I say now. But I'm going to tell you anyway. Whatever Andrew has offered you, whatever he has promised you, he will expect something in return and it will not be cheap."

Lauren held back a laugh. *And you think I work for them and you're trying to drive a wedge.* The Carmody men weren't the only ones with a knack for deviousness. "He wants me to talk to Nyssa."

"Is that what he told you?" Stef placed her hands on the railing. In the settling dark, her sore fingertips looked as though they had been dipped in blood. "Whatever else you are, what you did today was exceptional. We all realize that. More importantly, Andrew realizes that." She touched Lauren's arm. "You must take care."

Brava. "Believe it or not, I have gathered that." Lauren edged away as discreetly as possible. A strange sensation, Stef's touch. Like paper crumpling to ash.

"Good. See that you remember it." Stef massaged her forehead. "And I shall now bid an early good night, and pray to the Lady that tomorrow is better." She trudged toward the house, as bent as a woman decades older. "It can't get worse." Before she reached the door, however, Peter opened it, his look grim and a fresh drink in hand.

"You better get in here." He ushered Stef inside, then waited for Lauren.

They entered to find Carmody, Kaster, and Jenny waiting for them. Both men looked somber, while Jenny appeared shaken.

"I'm afraid the news isn't good." Carmody walked to the center of the room, and stood with arms folded. He had yet to change clothes, and his hair hung lank and straggly. "Sam's dead."

CHAPTER 17

Carmody waited until everyone settled before continuing. "She succumbed about an hour ago. They seem inclined to call her death accidental, but due to the circumstances, there will be an autopsy. Depending on the findings, there may be an inquest. If there is, there's a good possibility we'll be questioned."

"Will Heath be coming back?" Stef's voice came quiet.

"Not tonight." Carmody lowered to the edge of the couch and worked his hands through his hair. "He collapsed after he received the news. They're going to keep him at the hospital overnight. The earliest he could possibly return is tomorrow, assuming he'll want to. I will contact him in the morning if possible and find out what his plans are."

Stef stood and walked to the windowed wall, pressed her hand to the glass. "I don't know why they would need the inquest. It was an accident. Avoidable, yes, but still."

Jenny went behind the bar and grabbed a bottle of beer from the refrigerator. "Heath said that she used to eat things in her shop to see what they'd do. It drove him crazy, but apparently she felt she was protected in some way, that nothing she ate would hurt her." She took a sip, and winced. "Why did I open this—I hate beer." She dumped the rest into the sink, then filled a glass with water from the tap and took a seat at the counter.

Lauren sensed motion at the entry. Nyssa, slipping inside, then moving along the far wall like a shadow and taking a seat in the darkened corner.

"Did anything else happen during your hike?" Peter stood and walked to the window to stand next to Stef. "Anything, however trivial it seemed at the time?"

Lauren shook her head. "Like I told you. We walked. She wanted to see Jericho. The ward made of bird bones upset her. As we examined it, some flies that had been hiding in the ward attacked us. That's how she got bitten. When we tried to get rid of them, that's how the ward got scattered."

"It was just a tragic accident." Stef still stood with her hand on the glass, as though she wanted to push her way out.

"Sam was poisoned?"

Carmody shot to his feet. "Honey, you shouldn't be here."

"I'm fine." Nyssa emerged from the dark. She wore blue and white striped pajama bottoms that ballooned around her thin frame. A black Sleater-Kinney T-shirt. Sneakers without laces served as slippers.

"We'll be discussing things that aren't very pleasant."

"And that's different from the rest of my life how?" Nyssa held up one bandaged forearm. "I got off easy this time. Didn't even need stitches. But the last time, when I had to go to the real hospital, one of the nurses told me that if I didn't shape up, you would do to me what you did to Mom."

The only sound that followed was a sharp gasp from Stef. Then came silence, as all eyes fixed on Carmody. He remained standing, statue-still, face a blank, all traces of the happy-go-lucky surfer boy a distant memory.

Then he spoke, in a voice so quiet. "What was her name?"

"It was a guy, Dad." Nyssa bypassed the chair that Kaster had dragged over for her, instead sitting on the couch next to Lauren. "People say things like that to me all the time. They have for years. So maybe we're past having to worry about Nyssa Carmody's tender sensibilities, especially now that people are dying and everything."

Carmody watched his daughter for a few moments. Then he walked to the bar and fixed himself a drink. Ice. Whiskey. Knocked back half, then stared down at the glass. "Sam ate something she shouldn't have. In the woods." He finished the rest, set the glass in the sink, then extracted a can of soda from the bar refrigerator and split the contents into two tumblers. Carried them back to the seating area, handed one to Nyssa, then returned to his place on the couch.

Nyssa mouthed a *thank you*. Sipped, then traced a circle in the condensation that had formed on the outside of the glass. "She always brought me little things from her store. This time it was incense. We would talk about whatever. She was nice."

Quiet reigned as the fact of Sam's death settled over them. Then Carmody checked his watch and stood up. "I don't know if anyone's hungry. I'll have something set up in the dining room." He tugged at his grimy shirt and frowned. "I need a shower." He shot a look at his daughter, followed by a slight nod at Lauren. "Give them a half hour or so. The usual schedule's gone off the rails today." Then he walked out, his the heavy step of a man twenty years older.

"Stef? I think we need a break." Peter took the woman's elbow and steered her out of the bar, nodding to Lauren and the rest along the way. For her part, Stef seemed dazed. She leaned on Peter so that he put his arm around her to keep her steady and slowed his step to match hers.

"I'll just—" Jenny slid off her seat and waved to Lauren. "Later."

Kaster waited until they had all departed and he heard the *ding* of the elevator. "Well." He sat forward, elbows on knees, and gazed upon Nyssa with a look that held a tenderness that Carmody's never had for all his obvious concern. "How are you doing?"

"How many times do I have to say it? I'm fine." Nyssa glared into her glass. Then she smirked. "Where are your girlfriends? I haven't seen them since this morning."

Kaster ran a hand down the front of his shirt. Drummed his fingers on his knee. "They departed after breakfast."

"For what? Eight a.m. classes?" Nyssa made a "rah-rah" motion with one hand. "Cheerleading practice?"

Kaster started to speak. Then he hung his head, blew out a breath, and stood. "I should follow my lord and master's example." He nodded to Lauren. "If you will excuse me."

Lauren waited until he was out of range. "He really was worried about you."

"I know." Nyssa sighed. "I like him. I do. But sometimes he acts more like my dad than my dad does, and I just can't."

Silence followed. Nyssa seemed content to sit quietly, but Lauren felt her usual restlessness. She got up and went to the bar. Debated wine and settled for soda. Felt Nyssa's eyes follow her as she returned to the couch. "You like Sleater-Kinney?" She pointed to the T-shirt.

Nyssa shook her head. "It was my mom's. I found it in the laundry room years ago. Dad had all her things cleared out after she disappeared. This was the only thing they missed." She drummed her fingers on her thigh. "I heard Pete say you cut yourself today." She took hold of Lauren's left arm and turned it to expose the gash. Then she held out her own—the muted room light washed over the whitened crisscrosses that the bandage didn't cover. "Does it help you? It helped me for a while, but then it stopped."

Lauren fingered her wound, which had closed and scabbed over. It didn't even hurt anymore. *Kaster's magic touch.* "I only do it when I need blood. I tried to repair a ward over in Jericho. It was the only thing I could think of to do."

"You've done it before?"

"It worked before, back home. A ward to keep the demons away."

Nyssa's voice lightened. "Can you ward people?"

Lauren's eyes stung. She blinked back the tears before they fell. "I wish." She scolded herself. Told herself once again that this girl's problems were none of her business. That there were people in Gideon who had survived so much worse. "There are protective spells." Yet she kept talking, and wished that she knew the words to make one teenager's pain go away. "Charms. But I don't know a lot. Apparently I'm not the world's best student."

Nyssa smiled. "Can everyone back where you're from walk through walls?"

"No. That's my superpower." Lauren flexed her left hand. "Although I didn't do such a great job today."

"My dad said you just needed more practice. He was pretty impressed."

Was he? Lauren recalled Stef's warning, then set it aside for later pondering. "Did he ask you about the blood on the mirror?"

Nyssa hesitated. She took her time finishing her soda, then got up and took a coaster from a nearby table before setting down her glass. "He just figured I did it for reasons, like always. Poor little rich girl. Spoiled little bitch girl. Don't wannabe witch girl."

Lauren waited until Nyssa had returned to her seat. "You said, *'Leave me alone.'*"

Nyssa flinched. Her breathing quickened. "That's really creepy, you know that?" She pulled on the hem of the T-shirt. "It—" She rocked back and forth. "It was my mom. In the mirror. I saw my mom."

Lauren stood. "Nyssa, do me a favor. I know you love her—"

"Past tense. She's dead."

"Yeah, okay, but please take that shirt off."

"There's nothing wrong with it."

"Please." Lauren pulled the girl to her feet. "We have to get rid of the shirt. Then you have got to tell your father." Her fingers brushed the black cloth, and she felt chill sliminess, like the wall of a cave. "Did she say anything?"

"She said it's time." Nyssa took her hand and squeezed. "I'm fifteen, and I'm a grown woman now, and it's time for me to go to her."

"WHY DIDN'T YOU tell me this before?" Carmody stood in the middle of the room, hair dripping, a towel draped over his shoulders and hastily donned shirt and shorts sticking to his damp skin. "Like, years ago, when you found the damned thing."

Nyssa stood in front of him, arms folded and shoulders hunched, the T-shirt replaced with one of his button-downs. "Are you mad?"

Carmody paced a tight circle. "I'm not—" He stopped. "Anything to do with your mother, I have to know immediately. We've been through this."

Lauren stood in the doorway and fought the sense that she was trespassing. Nyssa had led her into the private wing and a sitting room just off Carmody's bedroom, a place of weighty but worn furnishings, the air touched with the man's sandalwood scent. Old rugs on the floor, older paintings on the walls. A room designed for comfort, a refuge from the world. *Not anymore.*

Kaster bumped into her as he entered, waved a hurried apology. "I've disposed of the shirt." He looked as though he had been dragged out of the shower as well, wrapped in a bathrobe, hair damp and face half-shaven. "Nothing left but ash, which has been dispersed." He walked across the room and sat on the edge of a couch, and used the sleeve of his robe to wipe traces of shaving cream from his face.

"I've had it for years. I've worn it lots of times." Nyssa sniffled, wiped away angry tears. "If it was such a big deal, why didn't it bother me before?"

"I don't know." Carmody took the towel from his shoulders and scrubbed it through his hair. "Why the hell did you keep it in the first place?"

"Because—" Nyssa pressed her hands to her mouth, then slowly lowered them. "Because it was hers. Because you got rid of everything the day after she disappeared and everything she ever gave me was gone and then one day I go down to the laundry room and there it is." She fielded her father's surprised look with a quiet laugh and soft voice. "You think I don't remember? That I had toys and clothes and books and all of a sudden they were all gone? All her pictures that hung on the wall. Even the magazines with her photos."

"You know why I had to do that."

"You did it because you hated her."

"Nyssa." Carmody closed his eyes, then turned away.

The sound of approaching footsteps drew Lauren's attention. She stepped out of the way just as Stef rushed in, Peter at her heels.

"It's not possible." Stef lowered to the arm of a nearby lounge chair. "That she could have broken through. It isn't."

"I'm not lying." Nyssa joined Kaster on the couch. "She looked like she did in all the photos. Young and gorgeous. And she said it was time for me to join her." Kaster placed a hand on her shoulder, and she took hold of it and squeezed. "The T-shirt let her in, didn't it? This is my fault."

Stef rose, holding out her hand so Peter could help her. "I will strengthen the wards immediately."

"Nyssa and I are going to get something to eat." Kaster pulled the girl off the couch and maneuvered her toward the door.

"I'm not hungry now." Nyssa tried to shake off his grip, with no success. "I want to stay with Lauren."

"It won't do you any good to get sick." Lauren glanced at Kaster and received a quick wink. "We all have to be at our best now."

"That sounds like something out of a really bad movie." Nyssa looked from Lauren to Kaster as though she had figured out their tag-team ploy. Then she yawned and rubbed her eyes. "What are you going to do?"

"I'm going to go to the bar and have a very big glass of wine."

"That sounds good." Nyssa looked back at Kaster, who shook his head. "I guess not."

"I'll get you fed and then you'll get some sleep." Kaster took hold of the girl's shoulders and steered her out of the room. "I have a feeling tomorrow is going to be a busy day."

"You're going to finish shaving first, aren't you? Because you look really weird."

Lauren leaned against the doorway and listened to the two bicker their way down the hall.

"I thought you were going to get some wine." Carmody stood in the entry to his bedroom and regarded her with the drawn, tired gaze of a man who just wanted to be alone.

Not yet. Sorry. "Is there anything in your father's office about Jericho?"

"There's information in the library."

"Nothing later than the early seventies. Which was the era of the clothing I saw."

"Yeah. Pete told me what you thought you saw."

"What sort of research went on there?"

"Research? It's a deserted camp. Housing for workers."

"I saw people in lab coats walking into the buildings." Lauren tried to piece things together, make connections, even though her head ached and she felt like she was trying to nail smoke to the wall. "Did it have anything to do with the Carmody Foundation?"

"The foundation funds legitimate scientific research, charitable endeavors, and many other things." Carmody ran the towel over his hair one last time, then flung it over his shoulder. "You weren't brought here for this."

"But it matters."

"No, it really doesn't. Just take care of my daughter." Carmody headed for the bedroom, then stopped. "The night my wife vanished." He kept his back to Lauren and rested one hand on the doorjamb. "I knew she would come back here for Nyssa. I phoned ahead, told the guards to detain her and not let her into the house. When I arrived, I was told that she had come back to the mountain. We found her car parked along the road leading up here. But she had not tried to enter. She went somewhere out there"—he waved toward the bedroom windows, the woods beyond—"and vanished. Maybe she thought she could sneak back in after I left, and something happened to her. Maybe she fell and injured herself and couldn't call anyone for help. The list of possibilities is damn near endless, but the end result is the same. She's still out there, trying to get back in. It used to be safe here, but she found a crack. Stef and Pete will seal it, and we'll go from there."

"I saw her in Jericho." Lauren recalled Fernanda's angry

expression. Was it fury over being discovered, or because she had seen her husband? "That's where she went. Why?"

Carmody sighed. "Jericho's in the woods. That's where she is."

"She was inside the ward."

"And the ward is broken. It needs to be repaired. We will repair it."

"The ward is part of a ring. It's not impervious anymore, but it's still strong. A run-of-the-mill entity wouldn't be able to cross it." Lauren struggled for the words, the best way to explain. "Was Fernanda a witch?"

"No."

"I can't help you unless you level with me."

"And if I want your help, I'll ask. Which I have. Take care of Nyssa. She needs somebody now."

"She has you, and she has Gene."

"And she has you." Carmody's voice rose. "When you're in my house, you do what you're told."

"Or you'll do what? Fire me? Given how things are going, that sounds pretty good. Do I have time to pack my bags, or will you send my stuff along?"

"Lauren." Carmody knocked his forehead against the jamb. "You are proving to be a real pain in the ass, you know that?" He stood quiet. Then he patted the pockets of his shorts. "Wait." He went into the bedroom, and emerged a few moments later holding an ID card strung at the end of a lanyard. "This should save me a call from security that you've tripped an alarm."

Lauren followed Carmody out of the room and down the

hall to the elevator. They rode in stiff silence, eyes on the floor indicator.

Second floor. Lauren wished she had brought her phone, even though she knew that there wasn't a chance in hell that Carmody would allow her to photograph anything. She trailed after him down a wide corridor carpeted in institutional greige and lined with more framed photographs of Carmody facilities, then stood to one side as he pressed the card to a scanner located in the wall next to a set of double doors. A beep followed, after which Carmody flipped up a small plate set at eye level and leaned forward. Faint green light moved over his face. After a few seconds, another beep sounded. Lock mechanisms clicked.

"Here." Carmody pushed the doors open with a flourish, like a real estate agent showing off a grand property. "The sanctum sanctorum."

Lauren stepped past him into the office of the late Steven Carmody. She hadn't thought about what to expect, but neither priceless antiques nor intimidating ultramodern would have surprised her.

Instead she found herself in a cramped, boxy room that looked like every teaching assistant office she had ever known. A battered metal desk stood in the middle, coupled with an old swivel chair of silver-painted metal and cracked green vinyl that rested at an angle, as though whoever sat there had gotten up, soon to return. Both were set atop an area rug in an eye-watering black-and-white checkerboard pattern, stained and frayed by use and age. Metal bookcases lined one wall, while the one opposite was filled by a framed map of the world, the United States, and several South American countries studded with red and white thumbtacks, the sites of Carmody facilities circa whenever. Only the view from the windowed fourth wall made a lie of the rest, looking out as it did over the garden, the mountain.

Lauren walked to the desk, a model of Spartan neatness upon which rested a large paper blotter with fake leather corners and a pen holder made from a tin can stripped of its label.

She picked up one of the pens. An old ballpoint, the Carmody logo long since worn away. *Carmody wasn't kidding when he called this place a shrine.* She opened the top drawer, which held nothing but some paper clips and a tire pressure gauge.

"See?" Carmody walked over to the map. "It's just an office." He pulled out one of the thumbtacks, then pushed it back in. "Dad had the furniture brought here from the old Portland headquarters. That was his desk and chair from his first job. He started in the proverbial mailroom."

Of the family company. Lauren kept that observation to herself and walked to one of the bookcases. The shelves contained a scatter of green plastic binders, the odd paper file folder shoved in between. She pulled out a folder and opened it, and caught a sheaf of black-and-white photographs just before they tumbled to the floor. As she leafed through them, she heard Carmody approach.

"These documents may seem innocuous." He drew alongside and reached for the photos, then pulled his hand away, reluctant to share for all he wished to seem the opposite. "But they can only be viewed by someone at or above senior executive level, so I would appreciate if you told no one I let you in here. I don't need Legal crabbing at me on top of everything else."

Lauren pulled out a photo of a twenty-something Steven Carmody, the mailroom a distant memory, standing around a table with an army general and other assorted suits. Jackets had been doffed and sleeves rolled up as far as late sixties business protocol allowed in what was obviously a tableau of work in progress. In one corner stood a pole bearing a U.S. flag, while the wall behind the men held a blackboard covered with equations. "Your father worked for the government?"

Carmody nodded. "We've always garnered our share of contracts. The electronics divisions, mostly, at least at the time that picture was taken. Vietnam. The Cold War bubbling away in the background. It was a busy time."

"Is that why those history books were in the other library?"

"History books?"

"Histories of intelligence organizations. OSS. CIA. In the other library." Lauren leafed through the other photos, all the while concentrating on whatever sense of the former occupant she could draw from the room. "Just seemed like odd things to have in a company library."

"Unlike the grimoires and pseudepigrapha?" Carmody shrugged. "My father liked history."

Lauren continued her examination of the photos, but after a few minutes, she was compelled to admit that the office held no magical memory. *Wiped clean. Like fingerprints from a firearm.* She shoved the file folder back in its slot, then perused a binder filled with blueprints of a sixty-year-old fertilizer plant as the realization settled that Carmody would never have allowed her through the door if there had been anything in the office worth seeing. She pushed the binder back in place with enough force to send the rest toppling over. The vibration shook the case, and something tumbled off the shelf above, bounced off her head, and fell onto the rug.

Lauren picked it up. She thought it a river rock at first—black, oval shaped. But then she saw the slight widening that formed a base, the eyes and claws inscribed in what proved to be dried clay. "This is like the forest figurines in the garden. Your mother made it?"

Carmody took it from her and turned it upside down. "It's hers. She signed everything on the bottom." He pointed to a tiny script *c* stamped into the lower edge of the base, then handed the figure back.

Lauren returned it to the shelf, then wiped her hand on her shorts. She felt nothing when she touched the piece, but the appearance alone was enough to give her the creeps. "I guess I'm surprised he kept it here, given that—"

"Given that she left him?" Carmody sniffed. "He missed her. At least, he said he did." He reached up and set the figure farther back from the shelf's edge. "We don't seem to have much luck when it comes to marriage."

"You both only gave it one shot."

"Once was enough." Carmody stared at the little clay oval for a few moments, then went to stand by the open doors.

Lauren flipped through files containing information about plants in Colorado and office space in Lima, Peru. Stuck the last folder back into its slot, then walked to the middle of the room and scuffed her flip-flop through the rug.

"Satisfied?" Carmody didn't quite manage to keep the *I told you so* out of his voice. "I suppose I should be grateful that you didn't just walk through the walls."

Lauren held up her left hand. Even though the bruises had already begun to yellow, it still looked nasty. "It's not that simple."

"If it were, think of what you could do." Carmody waved for her to step out into the hall. "I don't mean to seem rude, but there are other things I need to attend to."

Lauren trudged out, hands in pockets. She heard Carmody close the doors and reset the locks, and didn't slow down when he hurried to catch her.

"I'm curious. What did you think was in there? What did you expect to find?" He held up a hand in front of her, forcing her to stop. "If I felt there was any chance that the answers we needed were in that room, don't you think I'd have torn it down to the studs months ago?"

Lauren met his eyes, so different now that he had stopped trying to charm her. Washed-out blue, bloodshot, the skin beneath darkened and pouchy. "I suppose."

"I don't know what you saw in Jericho, or what you thought you saw. I'm trying to play straight with you, but there are limits. You're not entitled to know my business dealings, or details about my personal life."

"They matter."

"I disagree." Carmody stuck a finger in Lauren's face, then retracted it when she took a step back. "Nyssa may tell you things she says she remembers, but she was only five years old when Fernanda disappeared. Much of what she claims to recall consists of years of overheard rumor combined with wishful thinking." He turned his hand over so it was open, pleading. "She's powerful, more powerful than I will ever be, and it affects the way her mind works. The way she sees the world. She needs to be around someone like you, who's dealt with the jolts and setbacks. That's what I need from you. Now, are we on the same page?"

Not even in the same library. Lauren remained silent until Carmody swore under his breath and left her in the middle of the hall. She knew he lied. She had to think of a way to prove it.

CHAPTER 18

L auren first thought to hide out in her suite and consider what to do next, but hunger drove her downstairs to the dining room. Given the hour and the hell that the day had been, she didn't expect to encounter anyone, so she was surprised to find Jenny seated alone at a table by the window. Lauren stopped at the buffet and collected cold salmon and salad, then joined her.

"I thought I was going to pass out up there. Then I remembered, no dinner last night and a cup of yogurt for breakfast." Jenny looked a little less gray than she had in Nyssa's bedroom, but her voice sounded scratchy and her eyes were red, as though she had been crying.

Lauren watched her pick at her food. "Are you all right?"

"Yeah, I'm rockin' it, can't you tell?"

"It's just that in Nyssa's room, you looked pretty shaken."

"Well, we had just come back from shipping a deathly ill guest to the hospital only to find the daughter of the house threatening suicide, which you prevented by walking through a wall." Jenny paused to sip the sparkling water she had opted for in place of anything alcoholic. "Call me overly sensitive."

"I'm sorry. I didn't mean—"

"I don't know what you're used to back in Gideon, but out here, that all adds up to a really rough day."

Lauren stabbed a piece of salmon with her fork. "I didn't walk through a wall. I just passed my hand through it."

"You're right, that's totally different. What was I thinking?"

They ate in peevish silence. As soon as Jenny finished, she got up without a word and departed, leaving Lauren to stare at her plate and wish she had given in to her initial impulse to stay in her room.

Then she saw Jenny walk out onto the deck and lean with her elbows on the railing and her head in her hands, and went out after her, first detouring to the bar to collect a bottle of wine, this time complete with glasses.

When Jenny heard Lauren approach, she straightened, then hurriedly wiped her eyes with her shirtsleeve.

Lauren filled both glasses and set one on the railing. A truce.

Jenny stared at it for a time before sighing and picking it up. A sip first, followed by most of the glass. Then she stared out over the garden, a single tear spilling down her cheek.

"Seven months ago this week, I drove to my grandmother's house to pick her up to take her to church. It was Saturday night, when all the flower ladies set up for services the next morning. I knocked on her front door, and went in, as always. Called out to her. She always had a snack set out for me, fresh coffee and some of whatever she had baked that day. That Saturday, it was lemon squares. Three of them, set out on a plate on the kitchen table. Napkin and fork beside the plate. She hadn't brewed the coffee yet. She always waited until I walked in the door." Jenny's voice cracked, and she drank a little more before continuing. "'Coffee has to be fresh,' she always said. 'Fresh coffee for my fresh little girl.'"

Lauren braced her hands on the railing. She knew what was coming. But her job now wasn't to jump to the end of the story; it was to listen.

"I called out again, and when I didn't hear anything, I thought maybe she had gone out to the backyard to get her laundry. Even though we bought her a dryer years before, she still had to hang her laundry outside. But I looked, and the lines were empty." Jenny traced a finger around the rim of her glass. "So I walked through the house, calling. I started feeling a little scared then, that maybe she had fallen and hurt herself, perhaps was unconscious. I went to her bedroom last of all. The door was open, and she would have closed it even if she were having problems because that's how she was. Even though she lived alone. I looked in and saw this haze of steam coming out of the bathroom. Like fog. I walked across that bedroom—it took hours, it seemed like. Days. I found her in the tub, in her dress and hat. Shoes still on her feet. She had run the water hot—the mirrors were dripping and I almost fell, the tile was so slippery. She had—" Jenny mimed cutting her wrists, first one, then the other. "She must have done it just before I arrived."

Lauren touched her arm. "Words don't help, I know. But I am so sorry."

Jenny nodded absently. "We thought maybe she was sick and hadn't told us. But her doctor said no. The usual complaints, but

JERICHO

nothing out of the ordinary. Nothing to explain why she would do what she did." She turned to Lauren, eyes wide. "You can smell blood, you know? I did that day—the bathroom reeked of it. And I could smell it today, running down the hallway to that girl's room. I didn't have to see. I knew what she did."

Silence came as a relief. Lauren refilled Jenny's glass, then her own. She spotted movement down in the garden. Stef and Peter, moving from level to level, recasting the wards. In the distance, the mad yipping of coyotes erupted. Hadn't she once read that those were sounds of greeting, of the pack becoming reacquainted at the end of the day?

Her mind drifted. Then the sound of the approaching helicopter shattered the quiet. It swooped low over the house, then circled back toward the helipad and touched down.

Jenny leaned out over the railing, craning her neck one way, then the other, as she tried to see the new arrival through the trees. Then she stilled. "I thought he wasn't coming back until tomorrow."

Lauren joined Jenny in time to see Heath hiking toward the house. He wore fresh clothes, jeans and a light sweater, and had traded Sam's handbag for a cross-body messenger bag.

"This can't be good." Jenny shook her head.

"Maybe he came to get his things."

"Carmody could have shipped them to him. He'd have had them first thing tomorrow morning."

They headed back inside the house and reached the main living room to find Heath and Carmody in heated discussion while Kaster paced nearby.

"You said I had the chopper at my disposal." Heath looked

more the worse for wear up close. He needed a shave and eight hours' sleep, and looked ready to throw a punch at whoever had the nerve to suggest it.

Carmody nodded. He had switched out shorts for jeans but still wore the same shirt. He looked just as rumpled as his unanticipated guest, but with him it was a feature, not a bug. "Yes, I did. I just didn't expect to see you here until tomorrow at the earliest."

"What's the problem? No time to get your stories straight?"

"Careful what you say, Heath." Kaster's voice came quiet and his tone remained calm, almost light. You needed to look into his eyes to see the ice, the promise of the avalanche to come.

Apparently, Heath did. He stepped back from Carmody, then spun on his heel, wobbly as a top losing momentum.

Carmody grabbed him as he stumbled. "Perhaps you should have stayed in the hospital for one night."

Heath shook off his hand. "I signed myself out. Nothing they could do for me. Nothing anyone can do for me." He looked one way, then the other, when he realized that Lauren and the rest had filtered in. He squinted at Lauren, then pointed. "She spent the day with you."

Lauren felt all eyes move to her. Glanced toward the stairs in time to see a shadow flicker beneath. Nyssa the spy, at her post. "She spent two hours with me."

"Everybody said that fungus doesn't work that fast. That mushrooms don't work that fast. You gave her something, didn't you? You killed my Sam!"

"Why would I do that? I didn't even know her."

"Sacrifice." Heath mimed stabbing someone. "An offering

to that—that bitch you worship." He moved toward her, fist still raised as though he held a weapon. "I knew you didn't belong here. The rest of us are educated. Accomplished. You're nothing but a trumped-up business with no sense or talent or grace—"

"That's enough, Heath." Carmody came up behind him, took hold of his wrist, and brought it down. "You're finished here."

"Finished? I haven't even gotten started."

"Go upstairs to your room. Get some rest."

Heath stilled. Then his face crumpled. "My girl. My gorgeous girl." He wept, shoulders shaking and his sobs echoing off the glass.

Carmody motioned to Peter. They grabbed Heath under his arms and led him to the elevator. "We'll take it from here." He looked back, face flushed with a blend of exertion and embarrassment, his gaze settling on Lauren until he entered the elevator and the doors closed.

"Well, that was . . . unfortunate." For the first time, Kaster appeared unsettled. He stood in the middle of the floor, his hand to his mouth, eyes fixed on nothing. Then he looked at Lauren, and the air of imperturbability returned. "You'd think some people would know when to call it a day, wouldn't you, Mistress?" He bowed his head, then turned and headed across the room toward the entry to the house's private wing.

Lauren watched him leave. A beat later, she caught another movement in the shadows as Nyssa exited her observation post. Then she heard footsteps from behind and turned to find Stef regarding her coolly.

"We've reset the wards." Her voice, the way she held herself, offered challenge, but whether it was to invading entities or to Lauren wasn't entirely clear. "Nothing can enter this house now unless we give it leave."

"Too bad the same thing doesn't apply to people." Jenny looked down at her empty wineglass, then out toward the deck. "If you don't mind, I sort of want to be alone right now." She hesitated, then gave Lauren a quick hug. "Thanks." She nodded to Stef before departing.

"Do you have a minute?" Stef's smile held an edge, as though refusal wasn't an option.

As my Mistress commands. Lauren followed Stef into the bar and sat at a table in the corner while the woman got herself a glass of water, then settled into her chair.

"This has been a time for you, hasn't it? Quite an introduction to the Council." Stef paused to sip, then set the glass on the table and turned it one way, then the other. "We've weakened so over the years, become scattered by migration and circumstance. Both the Council and our guardian settlements. We've lost track of who we are. Our purpose. We need an injection of something positive. Life. Hope."

"Cash." Lauren looked out toward the woods, and wondered what walked the trails as the darkness closed in.

"As you say." Stef smiled. "The type of financial assistance that you believe Gideon requires is outside the Council's current purview, of course. It would mean an entire layer of administration and expertise that we do not currently possess. And of course there's Andrew to convince."

"Of course." Lauren felt as though she had just been dropped in the middle of a foreign-language film without subtitles. *Just smile and nod.* If she could discover why Stef had decided to be so nice, maybe she could also learn why she had been so abrasive in the first place.

"The Carmody Foundation has provided support for the Council for some time, as you know. It's unfortunate that matters have taken the turn that they have. It pains me deeply." Stef pressed a hand to her heart. "A good word from you could, I believe, help smooth things over."

"Quid pro quo." Lauren nodded. "Which I might be quite happy to do if I knew what exactly what I was quid pro quoing for."

"You have an annoying habit of playing coy."

"And you and everyone else in this house have done nothing but blow smoke since I arrived. Why exactly do you believe I was invited here?"

"Officially? To help Nyssa."

"How about unofficially?"

"We both know the answer to that, now, don't we?"

Lauren sat back, and let her business brain churn for the first time in months. *Something financial.* "I would rather you explained it to me."

Stef's mood flipped, the anger returned. "You are so like your father. Arrogant. So certain yours is the only way. When I approached him in Seattle to return to the host, he ordered me out of his sight."

"You knew my father?" The revelation threw Lauren at first, but she soon recovered as Peter's words returned to her. *It's a small world we inhabit.* "He was trying to protect me."

"And yet, here you are." Stef closed her eyes. "How fortunate for us all."

Lauren backtracked. Smiled. "I appreciate the offer to help Gideon, I honestly do. But the assistance you're offering benefits the town. What about me?"

"I'm afraid I don't understand. What do you want?"

"Some questions answered."

"I'm not sure I can help you."

"I think you can. You've known the Carmody family for how long?" Lauren waited until Stef gave her the barest of nods. "I wondered about Andrew's father. I know he supervised work for the government before he took control of the company, and I wondered what it consisted of."

"You should ask Andrew." Stef sniffed. "Though I expect he would decline to answer, therefore so must I."

"So the wards around Jericho—"

"Are for Fernanda only."

That was well rehearsed. Lauren wondered if Carmody and Stef had already compared notes. "Elliott Rickard."

Stef's hard shell softened slightly. "My Lady, I haven't heard that name in ages."

"Was he a medical doctor?"

"He never treated patients. He preferred the research bench."

"What was his specialty?"

"Clinical psychology." Stef's brow knit. "I believe behavior modification was an interest. Ways to treat anxiety." She quieted, her hands massaging the arms of her chair. "If you have no more questions, I shall retire for the evening." She struggled to her feet. "Peter and I meet with Andrew tomorrow morning at ten. I look forward to hearing of your fulfillment of your part of the bargain, at which point we will fulfill ours."

Lauren watched Stef shuffle out of the bar. *We've only been here a day and a half.* Yet the difference between the woman whom Lauren had met at the Carmody airport and the one with whom she had just spoken was profound. *She's really not well.*

She watched the doorway of the bar for a while. Then she got up and went behind the counter and searched for pen and paper. Normally she typed notes on her phone, but sometimes it helped to actually write down the words.

Especially when you don't know what in hell is going on. She grabbed a soda out of the refrigerator, returned to her chair, and set to work.

Steven Carmody. A wealthy man whose family had a vein of magic running through it. Lauren had grown used to the presence of the nether talents in her life over a short period of time. What would it mean for a family like the Carmodys to possess that sort of power over generations? How would they use it? Abuse it?

Elliott Rickard. Steven Carmody's good friend. *Behavior modification.* Lauren thought back to the toy car, the depths of discord and pain it had contained. She hadn't seen Rickard's face among the shades she had seen at Jericho, but she had seen the photo taken there with Carmody. *And his toddler son, Andy.*

"And this has what to do with Fernanda?" Possibly nothing. All families had multiple issues, and given the Carmody wealth and reach, theirs would be whoppers.

The Council. Carmody apparently provided them support. Judging from Stef's clumsy bribery attempt, something had happened to jeopardize that. *I call shenanigans.* Why did it always boil down to money?

"So deep in thought."

Lauren flinched so hard she almost dropped the pen. She looked up and saw Kaster standing at the counter, watching her. His bathrobe had given way to jeans and a mossy green pullover, and he had finally finished shaving.

"I didn't mean to startle you." He held up a plastic bag. "I came down for some ice."

"There isn't any in the family wing?"

"The icemaker in the refrigerator is broken." Kaster went behind the counter, flipped up the lid of the ice chest, and commenced scooping. "The repairman will be here in the morning. Should I notify you when he arrives?"

"Everybody here hates questions, but they all want answers." Lauren folded her notes and tucked them in her pocket. "How's Nyssa?"

"Asleep, finally." Kaster hunted through cupboards until he found an ice bucket. He dropped the filled bag inside, shut the lid, then tucked it under his arm. "She picked my brain about you. Wanted to know everything I could tell her. I'm afraid I embellished a bit, just to make her laugh. If she asks you tomorrow about the miniature horse and the White House visit, feel free to deny everything."

"Golly. An actual joke?" Lauren looked outside, and spotted Jenny curled up on a lounge chair at the far end of the deck, either asleep or passed out. "This isn't a happy place, is it?"

Kaster set the bucket on a nearby table, then sat in the chair Stef had vacated. "No less so than most places."

Lauren shook her head. "I don't think it ever was. Happy." She played with the pen, clicking it open, then closed. "When a place goes bad, the way Gideon went bad, it starts small. But then it feeds on itself, grows fat. Strong."

Kaster eyed his watch. "Is it that time of night already?"

"Time for what?"

"Philosophical ruminations."

"This never was a good place. Was that why Steven Carmody built the house here? Did he think he could work whatever lived here to his advantage?" Lauren looked Kaster in the eye until the humorous light flickered. "I've seen that before, you know. It didn't end well."

"He built the house here because it's a beautiful location."

"The Coast Range is jam-packed with beautiful locations." Lauren stopped to breathe. Her mind raced. She felt lightheaded, as though she'd had too much to drink. "Everything here—it's all zeroing in on Nyssa, like she's a lightning rod. You all claim to care about her so much, but you're standing back and letting it eat her alive."

"I beg to differ." Kaster looked toward the entry, then leaned forward and lowered his voice. "If we felt that way, you wouldn't be here."

"I'm still not sure why I am here. I'm supposed to be helping her, but I'm not allowed to ask how this place came to be or why she is the way she is. Unless you get to the source, she'll never recover, and that will never happen until you stop treating her like a simple wild teenager."

"You think we don't know that?"

"I think you know it. You just don't want to do what needs

to be done. You have to address what's attacking her. You have to dig it out, root and branch, and grind it to fine powder, and I am sensing a reluctance to do that." Lauren stood. "When bad things happen in a thin place, when they keep happening, who knows what connections are made, what is awakened, if given that much pain to feed on? A steady diet, like an IV drip, supplemented with the occasional massive influx. Eventually it grows too big to contain. Too big to control. It breaks free."

Kaster sat back. Sighed. "I'm so glad you came down here. I haven't heard a good ramble about the nature of good and evil in ages."

"I am serious." Lauren walked to the bar and set the pen on the counter. "I should've turned you down."

"I'm glad you didn't."

Lauren started to leave, then walked back to the sitting area. Kaster watched her with an intensity that she knew should have alarmed her, but whatever feelings he inspired at that moment, fear wasn't one of them. "What are you?" She held up her left hand, then wiggled her fingers.

Kaster shrugged. "A simple witch like you."

"Not so simple."

"That makes two of us, then, doesn't it?" Kaster looked out over the deck. When his gaze settled on Jenny, he frowned. "It disturbs me to see those I like in pain."

"So you like me?"

"Oh, yes." A thin smile, weary and a little surprised.

Lauren lowered to the edge of the chair opposite. "I think you know what's happening here. Why don't you stop it?"

Kaster took the ice bucket from the table and lifted it onto his lap, raised and lowered the lid, ran his hands over the sides. "We all have our roles to play. Mine is quite well defined, and I step out of character at my peril."

"Do blond twins and big black cars mean that much to you?"

Kaster's hands slowed. Stopped. "Whatever you choose to believe, I like you. I do. But this is a very different place than Gideon, with different rules, and if you run afoul of them, I cannot help you."

"I'll keep that in mind." Lauren stood and headed once again for the door, then stopped and looked back over her shoulder. "Embezzlement?"

Kaster's brow furrowed. "I beg your pardon?"

"Just trying to read between the lines of a conversation I had with Stef Warburg. What's going on between the Council and the Carmody Foundation?"

"You're wasted in Gideon." The light returned to Kaster's eyes. "Money has disappeared from accounts, yes."

"How much?"

"Enough."

"Stef thinks I was brought in as some sort of sniffer dog. I'm supposed to put in a good word so you call off the hounds."

"In exchange for?"

"Financial support for Gideon."

Kaster sat quiet for a few moments. Then he stood. "It wouldn't matter what you said. You don't take what belongs to a Carmody." He walked past Lauren and out the door, bearing the ice bucket in both hands as though he carried an offering, or a saint's head on a plate.

CHAPTER 19

H eath Jameson lay in bed and stared at the ceiling. Glanced at the clock yet again, even though he knew that only a few minutes had passed since the last time he checked and that time always moved more slowly when you needed to wait. He had done this before, this waiting for the right time. He knew the drill.

He hated having to embarrass himself in front of people he had known for years—Stef, Pete. But he needed to get back to this house and finish what he started. Any thought he might have given to waiting vanished when he remembered the bills that waited for him at his house, at the gallery.

It took longer than Heath thought, but the house eventually quieted. Porter, the lawyer, had been the last to retire. He had watched from his window as she stumbled in from the deck off the bar, wine bottle in hand. Funny. He never figured her for a drunk. Under different circumstances he might have felt sorry for her. Now he just needed her out of the way.

Just a little longer. He continued to study the ceiling. Wood tongue-in-groove, it was, peaked and beamed and just about every other damn thing you could imagine. He counted the number of boards on one side, then the other, took their square root, divided them by three. Played with numbers over and over until—

Now. The little voice in his head alerted him, and it had never been wrong. He eased out of bed, got dressed, tried to forget how humiliating it had been to pretend to be so loaded that he couldn't undress himself. The look on Carmody's face . . .

I'll make it right. He could pay back what he borrowed from the Council. Except that "borrowed" wasn't the legal term for what he had done. No, he had no choice but to brazen it out. *Stef knows.* He could tell by the way she looked at him. *And Carmody.* That was the only explanation for Mullin. The fixer of Gideon, come to fix the Council. *They've backed me in a corner.* If they had just left things be, given him time, he would have taken care of it. Now he had no choice but to keep juggling time bombs and hope that he could pull together enough cash to get the hell out of town.

He hefted the messenger bag, slung it over his shoulder. That had been the worst part, letting Pete slip it off over his head and toss it on a chair. Not that the objects inside were that heavy, and he had taken care to pad them well and secure them at the bottom of the bag. But accidents happened, and the sight of one of his carefully manufactured fakes rolling across the floor would have brought the evening to a rather nasty close.

He gathered up his shoes and crept out of the room in his socks. Stairs instead of elevator, then through the cavern of a living room to the bar, and from there to the side door that the smokers on Carmody's staff had disabled so that they could sneak out and grab a few quick drags as the need arose. He smiled as he slipped through the door, the wrecked lock indicator light shining red as though it worked just fine. Nothing rendered a security system to crap more than a desperate smoker in need of a fix.

He walked out onto the patio, paused a few moments in the shadows to scan the garden for signs of guards out on patrol. No motion lighting to worry about—the glare would have burned through all the damned glass and awakened the whole house, so Carmody in his good host's wisdom had decided to go without.

Heath moved quickly, across the patio and down the steps to his first target, the bronze hare. He knelt before it, then looked up at the house. He couldn't see anyone in the windows, but if they stood back far enough in the shadows, they would be well enough hidden that he wouldn't have been able to. *Security cameras. Sensors.* He hadn't seen any during his previous passes through the garden, and more important, he hadn't sensed any. No one gave him any credit for his witch sense, even those who should have known better.

He told himself it wasn't stealing. Not even close. He was protecting the pieces from further exposure to the elements, securing them homes with collectors who knew how to care for delicate works of antiquity. Besides, the bastard Carmody owed him. Yes, what happened to Sam was an accident, and if anyone seemed bound and determined to end her life as a Death by Misadventure, it was her. But still. *Call it restitution.* Payment for pain and suffering.

Heath glanced up at the windows again, then quickly extracted the fake hare from his bag. Damn Harris for wanting this particular piece—it was the only one located in full view of the house, which made it the most difficult one to substitute. But the woman was his best customer. He needed to keep her happy.

He remained still as the seconds ticked by, poised on the brink of action yet unable to make the next move. Then he leaned forward, weight on his left hand, his body blocking the view of the palmed figurine in his right. Bent close to the hare, as if for closer examination.

Finally, with one smooth motion, he pushed it off its pedestal with his right hand and set the fake in place, then picked up the real hare and tucked it in his bag as he straightened up. Spent a few more moments pretending to brush away dirt and study the nearby fauna. Then he stood and continued down to the next level.

One down, three to go. Heath's heart hammered in excitement, anticipation, a delayed case of nerves. *This is going to work.* Just fill up the bag and return to the house, then leave first thing in the morning with his host's relieved blessing. *This is going to work.*

He didn't bother to kneel in front of the pottery boar. At this point, he was well and truly hidden from view of the house, so no mucking about was necessary. Instead he simply took the fake out of his bag, removed it from its cloth wrapping, made the switch, then wrapped the real piece and stashed it.

Two down, two to go—

Heath's gut clenched as the crunch of footsteps sounded

from behind a planter. He dropped the bag behind a rosebush and lowered to the nearest bench. Slumped forward, his head in his hands, and cobbled together his tale of woe. He couldn't sleep—his gorgeous girl—it was all too much—he had to walk—

"There's my monkey."

Heath slowly raised his head.

"I've been looking all over for you."

"Sam?" Heath closed his eyes, opened them, rubbed them. Blinked again. She stood before him, hair shimmering in the moonlight, wearing the same clothes she had that morning. The clothes that the hospital had bundled into a paper bag and handed off like so much Chinese takeout, that he had stashed in the trunk of his car because he couldn't bear to look at them. "How can you be here?"

"I never left, silly." Sam bent forward, hands on her knees, as if she was talking to a child or a small dog.

"You're in Portland. In the hospital." Heath rose slowly, then stepped around the bench so that it stood between them. "In the morgue."

Sam smiled. "Nonsense. I'm right here."

"I'm dreaming." Heath backed up as Sam drew closer. "I'm still in bed. I'll wake up any second now, and there I'll be." He closed his eyes.

Counted to three.

Opened them, and sighed in relief.

He still stood in the garden walkway. But at least Sam had vanished.

"Guess again, silly."

Heath's heart stuttered. He turned his whole body at once, like a doll on a pedestal, and found Sam standing behind him. She had positioned herself a few steps above him, so she could block him if he tried to get around her and flee back to the house.

I need to tell them—I should just scream—

"No, you shouldn't, Heath." Sam shook her head. "Because they'll all come running down here and you know sure as hell that with your luck someone will find that bag you hid behind the rosebush."

"What bag?"

"Oh, honey, we're way past that stage where you lie and I believe you because the truth hurts too much."

Heath felt his face heat. "I don't know what you're talking about."

"Yes, you do." Sam descended one step. Another.

Then before Heath could back away, she stood in front of him. He felt her fingers close over his, as cold as if she had just pulled something out of the freezer. The moonlight hit her full in the face, revealing whitened skin and bluish lips. Clouded eyes. *She's dead. I kissed her goodbye.*

"So kiss me hello." Sam stood on tiptoe, parted her lips.

Heath shook off her hold and once more circled around the bench. Then he sniffed the air and winced. "Do you smell that?"

"Smell what?"

"Like something crawled under the deck and died." He looked again toward the house, all the darkened windows, no faces in any of them. Didn't anyone suffer from insomnia anymore? Were they really all sleeping, dead to the world?

Don't think dead. He glanced down the steps that led to the bottom of the garden. *I could run down there, then circle around and run back up the mountain to the house.* But the steps vanished into darkness that grew closer as he watched, consumed one step, then another, like a rising tide.

"Time to go, Heath." Sam smiled, but even though she had stopped speaking, her cheeks continued to move.

Heath swallowed hard. "Why is your skin moving?"

"Because I'm talking."

"No. That's not it." He flashed back to a summer's day like this one. A hike through the woods, he and his brother. They had come upon a dead fox, except that at first they thought it lived because it seemed to be moving, even though it made no attempt to get up as they drew near.

Then they looked closer, and realized that it wasn't the fox that moved.

Fifty years gone by, yet Heath never forgot. The stench of rot. The buzzing, which filled his ears and rattled his brain and vibrated along his bones. He had poked the fox with a stick, and the flies and maggots responded by moving one way, then the other, making it look as though muscle rippled beneath the dull pelt.

How a single fly emerged from the fox's mouth and flew at them, driving them away.

"Heath? It's time."

"*Stay away from me.*" Heath looked toward the house, waited for somebody, anybody, to turn on a light, step outside.

"Oh, Heath. You never could learn to just give up." Sam parted her lips, and something large and black emerged, crawling out of the corner of her mouth and down to the point of her chin.

Then it took to the air, straight at Heath's head. He slapped at it, but it darted past his hand—he lost track of it until he felt the stabbing pain burn on the side of his neck.

"*Ow.* That sonofa—" Heath doubled over as heat like an acid burn laced around his neck, up the back of his skull and down his spine. *Dying—I'm dying.* His heart slowed, then picked up speed, faster and faster until all he felt was one long beat.

Then it ended. He had fallen to his hands and knees at some point, and he struggled to his feet, brushed grime from his trousers. His head felt clearer now. Or maybe *different* was the better word.

"Are you ready?" Sam took his hand again and pulled him toward the steps.

Heath looked up at the house, saw faces in some of the windows, figures looking down at them from the roof. Quite a few faces—he hadn't realized that there were that many people there. *No, not people.* The faces were all wrong. The bodies. They reminded him of Celia's statues, the same squat silhouettes. "Who are they?"

"They were here first." Sam led him down the path that wound around the house to the backyard. "They've been waiting a long time."

"Does Carmody know they're here?"

"He will."

Soon they left the house behind. Heath squinted into the gloom. He could barely see more than a few feet in front of him. Even Sam seemed to blend with the dark. "Sam, something isn't right." His tongue felt thick, as though the dentist had given him a shot.

"Don't worry, sweetie." Sam smiled back at him. "It'll be better soon."

They veered off the path and cut across the sloping lawn. At first Heath thought they were headed for the helipad, but Sam stopped him short, then stood on tiptoe and whispered in his ear. "Just wait."

Heath caught a whiff of Sam's breath. It had smelled horrible before, but now it reminded him of soil, fresh, warm, teeming with life. Cleansing rot, the great equalizer. It broke everyone in the end, king and commoner, and made them all one.

I'm a poet. The thought made him smile. Then he heard a rumble, the grind of metal on metal. Looked toward the house, and stared as the small train emerged from the darkness.

"Isn't this nice?" Sam bobbed up and down on the balls of her feet, and stepped into the first car as soon as the train stopped.

Heath hesitated. "No one's driving this thing, Sam."

"It'll be fine, monkey."

"But how can it move if there's no one to hit all the buttons?" He waited for Sam to answer, but she just looked up at him with those weird eyes until he gave up and got in the car and sat next to her. "I don't know how this can work if—" Before he could finish, the train lurched forward, then slowly settled into a steady chug.

Heath tried to figure out where they were, and which direction they were headed. Tried to recall the trail that Carmody had driven down earlier that day. But the darkness ate everything—all he could see were vague shapes on either side, which might have been trees or rocks, or concrete abutments on the freeway for all he could tell. The only indications of forward motion were the gentle rumble of the train and the sensation of the breeze through his hair.

Time passed. Every so often he sensed that someone sat behind him, that they rested their hand on his shoulder. But each time he turned around, there was no one there.

Heath started to check his watch, then remembered that Carmody had removed it back at the house. He squinted into the gloom and tried to recall whether he had seen any sign of the railroad tracks near the trails. As far as he could remember, just enough had been laid for the little train to take visitors to the house from the helipad. If that were true, then why in hell was this trip taking so long?

If it wasn't, then where in the hell were they headed?

"Is this track going around the mountain?" Heath looked at Sam, then shrugged. Her face had that focused look she used to get when she listened to music. She always felt that she could detect sounds on recordings that no one else could hear. "Who are you listening to, baby?"

"The children." Still with the smile, only this time Sam placed her hand on his knee.

He yawned, rubbed his eyes. When he opened them, he stared. He had seen Jericho only once, when Carmody had parked the Rover at the top of the hill, but he would have bet what little money remained in his bank account that the circle of wooden structures he looked at now was the same place. Only—

"The driver told us that we couldn't ride this from the house to Jericho. He said that the track at the house and the one here were different widths."

"Shows you what he knew." Sam stepped out of the car, then held out her hand. "Let's go."

"Where?" Heath gripped her hand, and flinched at the sensation of chill, damp slickness. "Your hand's gotten cold, baby." He looked back over his shoulder at the train, but it had already gone. Thought he heard rustlings in the grass, sounds of whispering and chalked them up to small animals, and the night breeze.

Sam led him to the largest building and knocked on the door. Still bouncing, still smiling. The last time she had acted this mysterious, she had led him to the upstairs room of their favorite restaurant for what turned out to be a surprise birthday party. Heath had pretended to have a good time for her sake, but truth was, he hated surprises.

He heard footsteps from inside the building. The click of a lock. Then the door opened.

"Ah, Mr. Jameson. We've been expecting you." A middle-aged man in a lab coat waved him inside. "Please, come in."

Heath tried to put the brakes on as Sam got behind him and pushed. "What the hell is going on?"

"Not to worry, Mr. Jameson." The man picked up a clipboard from a nearby desk. "We just need to run a few preliminary tests before entering you into the program." He pointed to the chair in the middle of the room, a vinyl-covered recliner that resembled something from a dentist's office. "Have a seat."

"I don't want to have a seat. I want to know what's going on?" Yet a beat later he found himself seated, the chair tilted back so his feet were elevated and Sam bent over his legs, buckling restraints around his ankles.

"I—" Heath tried to raise his hand, realized that the wrist restraints had already been tightened.

"You have been selected for a very special program, Mr. Jameson." The man in the lab coat stood opposite him. He still held the clipboard in one hand, and with the other he shook a fountain pen as though trying to get the ink to flow. A name had been picked out in black thread over his right breast pocket. *Dr. E. Rickard.*

"Program?" Heath tried to attract Sam's attention, but she had gone to stand against the far wall.

"A program of discovery. Of self-realization." Rickard continued to make notes, his pen scratching across the paper. "What if I told you that there was another world that existed alongside the one in which you lived for fifty-seven years? A world of knowledge that, once joined with yours, will allow humanity to attain heretofore unimaginable depths."

Through the fog that had settled in his brain, Heath detected the mismatch, the words that didn't fit. "You mean heights, don't you?"

"A common error." Rickard took hold of Heath's wrist. "You have never seen the signs of this new world. A witch of your poor powers could never know its existence without taking certain measures. But others have. We follow in the footsteps of giants, Mr. Jameson. Men who had the foresight to act when others cowered, who saw when others remained blind." He pressed two fingers to the pulse point. "Just making sure." After a few moments, he smiled. "Zero beats per minute. Excellent."

"Bullshit." Heath tried to move his hands, but the restraints held him fast. "I'm alive."

Rickard chuckled, a weird, wet sound. He started writing again, then shook his head and held out the pen to Sam. "More ink, please."

"Yes, Dr. Rickard." Sam walked to Heath's side. "This won't hurt a bit, monkey." She pressed the pen to the crook of his arm and pulled back the little lever one used to draw ink into the cartridge.

Heath flinched as he felt a needle-like prick, the warm weirdness of blood being drawn. He looked down at his arm, watched Sam manipulate the pen, pressing the nib more deeply into the crook, turning it one way, then the other, as the cartridge filled with silvery-black. "That doesn't look right."

"It's perfect." Every so often, Sam flicked the cartridge with her finger. "Have to get rid of the bubbles," she said by way of explanation. Then it was finished—she withdrew the nib and handed the refilled pen to Rickard.

Heath looked at his arm, saw no sign of a needle entry, no bead of blood, and the realization settled that this was no dream. He had gone down the rabbit hole, and he would never, ever be able to climb back out.

As he watched, the walls took on a different aspect, plain white giving way to grey, then to black that pulsed and vibrated. Buzzing filled his head. The room darkened. He could no longer see Sam. Rickard, meanwhile, was visible only as a vague shadow against the far wall.

"What do you fear most, Mr. Jameson?" Shadow Rickard had taken the refilled pen from Sam, and now added more notes, the sound of the nib moving across the paper like the scratch of claws on glass. "Wait, I see we already have something here. We can go ahead and get started."

"What? I never said—" Heath stopped, then coughed as something thick and cold filled his throat. The smooth vinyl on which he sat changed, grew rough, chilly. His restraints vanished, but even so, he still couldn't move. Yet he sensed motion around him, rustling noises. Heard birds, so faint. Felt a ruffling sensation, like a soft breeze.

"Loss of control, isn't it, Mr. Jameson? Dependent on others for mercy you know they will not show?" Another damp laugh. "How unexpectedly reflective. I wouldn't have thought it of you."

Heath felt movement inside him, deep in his gut, his limbs, his brain. Things that didn't belong there, destroying what he had been and taking over what remained. Using it. Letting it be used.

All his nightmares returned at once. All those fears of the dark, the cold, how it felt to be . . .

"Eww—what is that?"

. . . alone . . .

"Touch it, Heath. Touch it."

. . . forgotten . . .

"Poke it—see what happens."

. . . taken apart . . .

"I can see inside it."

. . . exposed for all to see.

Now it was his turn to be the fox.

CHAPTER 20

Lauren rose with the sun, showered, and dressed. The morning promised the same heat and high humidity as the day before and the day before that. Not a great day for a hike.

Yes, she had to go back to Jericho, to search for answers that Carmody and the others refused to give her. They would go nuts when they found she had gone, and she had no doubt they would come after her. Maybe by then she would have learned something useful.

She would have preferred light clothing, but couldn't risk it because of the flies. That meant long pants made from ripstop fabric. A long-sleeve shirt of the same material. Her boots. She tied a bandanna around her neck and stuffed several more into the day pack some previous occupant had left in a dresser drawer. Dug through her toiletry bag and suitcase for anything else that might come in handy—nail scissors, emery boards, a hotel room sewing kit. Finally, she added the toy car, because it held something of Jericho in its cast metal body.

She stepped out onto the balcony, looked overhead at the sunrise sky, robin's-egg blue tinged with gold and coral, and wondered if she would ever see it again. *I need to stop this.* Virginia called it *Gideon fatalism,* that ever-present undercurrent of unease, the realization that one wrong step at the wrong time could mire you in some in-between place from which you would never escape.

Lauren watched the sky lighten, until the other colors vanished and only eye-watering blue remained. Listened to the birds sing until they were overwhelmed by the now-familiar thumping sounds of Carmody's approaching chopper.

A few minutes later, she heard the soft beat of running footsteps coming from the hallway, and went to see what the commotion was about. She opened the door and walked out and barely missed colliding with Peter, clad in running gear.

"Have you seen Heath?" Peter continued to jog in place. Sweat coated his skin, soaked through his Corbin College T-shirt—this trip had apparently been a detour from his morning workout. "The chopper's out there waiting for him, and no one can find him."

"I assume he's not in his room."

"You assume correctly. All his stuff is still there, though."

"Bed been slept in?"

"Yes, but only because Andrew and I undressed him and wrestled him into it last night." Peter shook his head. "Add that to the list of things I will never be able to unsee." He resumed his jog down the hall. "Tell him if you see him, okay? They can't wait for him forever." Then he clumped down the stairs and across the living room in the direction of the bar. "Hey, have you seen Heath?"

Lauren walked to the railing and looked out over the living room. Early morning quiet eventually reasserted itself, the only sounds the distant clatter of dishes and, from outside, the giant insect buzz of a lawn mower. She ambled downstairs and cut through the dining room to the outdoors, picking up a cup of coffee and a handful of granola along the way. Walked along the patio, and watched bees and butterflies flit here and there. Stood at the top of the steps that led down to the garden, and wondered where Heath Jameson had gone.

She tossed the last bits of granola into her mouth, wiped her hand on her pants, then plucked a handful of leaves from an elder tree and stuck them in her pocket. Started down to the next level of the garden, then doubled back and grabbed another handful of leaves. *Demons hate the smell.* She told herself that would be all the protection required.

Then she spotted several members of Carmody's house security team wandering through the lower levels of the garden. Except *wandering* didn't describe the way they poked through the shrubbery, checked under benches, kept in constant touch via walkie-talkie.

Then one of the guards dug behind a rosebush and pulled out a large leather cross-body bag, the metal fastenings shining softly in the daylight.

"That's the bag Heath had with him when he arrived last night." Peter drew up beside Lauren. "What the hell is it doing out here?"

As they watched, the guard opened the flap and rooted through the contents. Freed a wallet, a small notebook, a phone, and a liquor flask.

Then she pulled out a small, cloth-wrapped bundle. Unwound it and revealed a pottery boar.

Peter's jaw dropped. "Why, that—"

"—SONOFABITCH." CARMODY STOOD hands on hips and glared at the collection that the security chief had laid out on a dining room table. He wore his usual denim ensemble, had switched out clogs for sandals, and had tied a bandanna around his forehead to keep his hair out of his eyes. He had been in his office when Peter collected him—a wireless earpiece still glistened in one ear.

Lauren looked toward the dining room entry and spotted Nyssa just as she backed out of view. Then she straightened the boar pulled from Heath's bag, which was set at the end of the table opposite the one that another guard had removed from the outdoor niche. They had arranged the other pieces the same way, the ones found in the bag on one end, the ones found in the niches on the other. The bronze hare, a small deer, and a fist-size pot.

"Can you tell which ones are yours?" Peter pointed to one grouping of figures, then the other. "They look identical to me."

Carmody picked up the pottery boar that had been found in Heath's bag and turned it over. Examined it for a few moments, then grumped under his breath and pulled a pair of rimless reading glasses from his shirt pocket and maneuvered them on. Resumed his study, and pointed to something just inside a rear leg.

Lauren leaned close and sighted down where he pointed,

and saw a minuscule mark inscribed in the clay. It appeared to be a letter *c*, but it was backward, and oddly shaped.

כ

"That's the ID mark." Carmody pointed it out to Peter and Jenny, while Stef paced nearby. "All the old pieces have it. They were a gift to my grandfather Elias, but there's no record of who gave them to him."

Peter wrote in the air with his finger. "It looks like the Hebrew letter *kaf.*" He tilted his head. "Could be Aramaic, too. The line is so thickly drawn, I really can't tell."

Carmody shrugged. "I doubt it could tell us anything about the giver at this late date." He set the boar back down on the table.

"They were a gift from a grateful investor."

They all turned as Kaster entered. He again proved the most formally dressed person in the room in his pale blue cashmere pullover and gray slacks, soft black loafers scuffing softly against the hardwood floor. "They were given to him around the time he started to make a name for himself." He joined Carmody at the table.

Carmody frowned. "You never mentioned it before."

"It never came up. No one ever had the stones to attempt to steal them before." Kaster picked up the marked boar, turned it over and studied it for a moment, then set it down. Then he picked through the other pieces, switched the pots and deer, then backed away from the table when he finished.

"Are you sure you sorted them properly?" Peter picked up the deer that Kaster had designated the fake and turned it over.

"You didn't even look at them." His brow arched as he examined the piece. "Well, you nailed this one." He returned it to its place with the rest of the fakes.

"I have spent my life in this house." Kaster pointed to the flower-scaped expanse. "I helped design that garden. I know these pieces like I know myself."

Jenny took out her phone and started photographing the pieces. "It's not my business, but given the value of these things, they should be better secured." She poked the genuine pot with one finger, then motioned for Kaster to turn it over so she could record the identifying mark. "Your insurance company could deny reimbursement if they proved negligence."

Carmody huffed. "Well, call me old-fashioned, but I don't automatically assume that my guests are planning to steal from me."

"What about your employees?"

"Only if they planned to flee to the Antarctic because they'd never find a job worth a damn anywhere else." Carmody yanked off his bandanna and worked a hand through his hair. "Speaking of which, has anyone seen Jameson since last night?"

Jenny continued her recording with the irritated air of one who considered herself the sole adult in the room. "You have security cameras out there, right? Please tell me you at least have those."

"We have CCTV." Carmody must have sensed everyone's surprise. "It's in the interest of safety. Someone could fall down the mountainside while exploring one of the lower levels, and no one in the house would ever know. It has happened. Just last summer—" Before he could finish, one of the security guards appeared in the entry.

"Sir?" The woman fidgeted, hands in and out of pockets, then tugging at the gear hanging on her belt. "You need to see this."

They hustled en masse to the elevator and rode down to the garage, then crowded into the small security office as the guard ran the video from the previous night. It proved to contain the bulk of the guards' search and discovery of Heath's bag, which flitted by in lightning-quick reverse. Then came the darkening sky as morning altered to dawn and then to nighttime.

"I was out on the deck until just after midnight. I confess I slept for most of that time, but I didn't see anyone when I came back in." Jenny stood by the guard's shoulder, twirling her finger for her to continue rewinding. "Stop now." She pointed to a figure standing at the top of the steps. It was possibly male, face and figure obscured by the dark. "That could be Jameson, but I can't tell. Shouldn't motion lighting have come on?"

Carmody shook his head. "No lighting." He met Jenny's pained sigh with one of his own. "Not when I have guests. Because of the windows. Every time a skunk waddled into a beam, it would wake up the entire house."

"Maybe he stashed that bag there earlier, after we left him." Peter shrugged. "He ran scared. Thought someone saw him. He bolted."

"Without his wallet and his phone?" Lauren recalled her first days in Gideon, when Blaine's malign influence had been sufficient to disrupt any signal. How lost she had felt without her phone. "Unless he planned to come back."

"Is anybody else going to look at the actual video?" Jenny

motioned for the guard to reverse, then to freeze the image. "What's that?"

They all bent close, and saw . . . something . . . moving down the levels, drifting like smoke around shrubs and planters.

"A shadow." Stef waved a dismissive hand. "Just a shadow. Probably made by an animal. That's what scared Heath off."

"There's nothing that shows Heath was even there." Kaster paced the small office, then perched on the edge of a table.

"The question is, where is he now?" Carmody nodded to the guards, who filed out of the office.

Stef closed the door after them. "He was a practitioner. We tend to forget that. He likely obscured himself in some way. I am sure we'll find the appropriate spell-casting materials among his things." She walked over to Carmody, placed her hand on his arm. "Besides, you have your figures in hand. What's the point in pursuing this any further?"

"I think we both know the answer to that, Stef." Carmody eased out of the woman's hold, then turned away. "Why didn't you tell me that he was in financial trouble?"

Stef glared at Lauren, then took a deep breath. "I'm sure I don't know what—"

"Please, Stef. Anyone with eyes could see that business at his gallery had tanked. He hadn't sold a piece of any significance in months."

Stef's face darkened. "You checked up on him."

"Credit checks are run on all employees once a year. Research is performed when needed."

"We of the Council are not your employees."

"You are if I haul your freight." Carmody kicked at a plastic trash can and sent it tumbling across the room. "Speaking of which, the discrepancies in the Council accounts. Almost three-quarters of a million appears to have walked. Something else you neglected to tell me."

"Yet you uncovered it all the same." Stef smiled sadly. "And here you said that you didn't expect guests to steal from you."

"I'm not a sucker and I pay attention, facts that those closest to me always seem to forget."

Lauren watched Carmody pace, and wondered how much of his rage was real and how much was an act. "You set Heath up, didn't you?"

"You should know." Peter caught her eye and arched his brow.

"I know what you thought I was doing here. I finally figured it out last night, when"—Lauren glanced at Stef, caught the flash of fear in her eyes—"when I had a chance to sit in the bar and think. I wasn't invited here to investigate anything. Believe me, or don't, but it's the truth." She saw Peter shake his head, and wondered if he and Stef would ever believe anything she told them.

"Well, I'm the nonmagical civilian in this crowd, and all I can say is whatever that shadow thing was, it was no animal." With that Jenny left the office, followed closely by Kaster, who walked with his head down, seemingly lost in thought.

"I'll have my people notify the sheriff and a few of the places along the main road. Tell them to keep an eye out for Heath. Without his wallet and phone, I doubt he gets very far." Carmody hesitated before finally placing a hand on Stef's shoulder. "You really shouldn't keep things from me, however you think

I'll react. If we can't work as a team after all we've been through together, what's the point of continuing?"

Stef nodded, eventually. Wiped her eyes. Silence and nerves settled, and they filed out. Peter and Stef went first, the looks they gave Lauren indicating that her protestations had fallen on deaf ears.

Lauren tried to follow but found her way to the door blocked by Carmody. When she tried to skirt him, he grabbed her by the elbow and held her back until the others had boarded the elevator.

"Anything you want to tell me?" Carmody let her go, his hand hanging in the air for a moment before he shoved it in his pocket. "I caught that hesitation as you explained your brainstorm in the bar."

"Ask Gene—I told him."

"I want to hear it from you."

"Do you ever lose track of which side you're pitting against the other?"

"No." Carmody waited, finally smiling as time passed and it became obvious that he would get no answer. He stood back, looked Lauren up and down. "Going somewhere?"

Lauren quickly assessed all the cover stories that sprang to mind. *Pick one, dammit. Now.* "I just wanted to explore the grounds."

"The hiking boots are overkill, don't you think?" Carmody started walking, but instead of heading toward the elevator, he strode in the opposite direction, through the garage and out into the backyard. There he stopped, pulled his bandanna out of his pocket, and tied it back around his head.

Lauren lagged behind, unsure whether he expected her to follow or if he wished to be alone. She had just about decided to duck back inside the garage when he beckoned her.

"I can't stop thinking about how you put your hand through that wall. *What if she could get her whole body through*, I wondered. *Think how useful she would prove to be.*" His blue gaze fixed her with earnest intensity. "I would love to pursue it, but I won't. Not without your permission."

"Pursue it how?"

"You're kidding, right? You are a pearl of great price."

"And you want to string me up and wear me around your neck?"

"Our circle is small and word will get around. It always does. I would simply appreciate the chance to counter any offers you might receive. I'm a bastard to work for, but I will make you rich. There are worse fates."

Lauren walked farther out on the lawn, then turned back toward the house so that she could see the garden. "You didn't have to let Heath return here. But you knew about his problems and that he planned something, and you wanted to catch him at it." She pointed toward the woods. "He could be anywhere out there. I don't think he'll ever be found."

"Some people go through their entire lives with targets painted on their backs. Who am I to get in their way?" Carmody made as if to say more, then instead raised a hand in farewell and headed back toward the house. But after a few strides, he stopped and turned back to Lauren. "Nyssa likes you. She seems happier than I've seen her in months." A ghost of a smile. Then he vanished into the maw of the garage. "Enjoy your walk."

CHAPTER 21

Lauren followed the path across the backyard that led into the woods. She passed the empty helipad on the way. If Heath ever worked up the nerve to return, he would have to wait until tomorrow to fly back to Portland.

Assuming he's still alive. Which she didn't. At this point, anyone who walked into the Carmody woods alone risked never coming out.

So what am I doing here? Lauren wiped her face with her sleeve. *My job.* Like a doctor dropped into a disease-ridden town. *Stop the infection before it spreads.* Even if she risked dying of it herself. *The fixer of Gideon.* Jesus, who in hell had given her that nickname? *Thanks a bunch.*

The heat intensified and the air felt hot-shower thick. Lauren unzipped the vents in her clothing and tied a fresh bandanna around her forehead to keep the sweat from running into her eyes. She didn't see many animals along the path—a few jays, a squirrel with a bent tail—and thought of Gideon's crows, which followed her everywhere, their caws announcing her passage like a personal pack of town criers. *I miss you, you little bastards.* She hadn't seen any since her arrival, and wondered if whatever inhabited the mountain had driven them away, if that were a sign that the Lady had abandoned this place.

Every so often, she slapped away a fly identical to the ones that had flown out of the toy car. She had coated herself with bug spray as soon as she entered the depths of the woods, but even that failed to dissuade the creatures completely. They buzzed around her head and past her ears, swooped from on high like miniature dive bombers, tormented her in every way short of biting.

Lauren checked her hands. The wounds from the first attack had healed completely, not a scab or welt to be seen. *Maybe the bites really aren't that bad.* Maybe something else had caused the blackened welt on Sam's hand.

Or maybe it's only a matter of time. She shoved her hands in her pockets and kept walking.

THE SUN SHONE high in the sky by the time Lauren rounded the bend that overlooked Jericho. She walked past the tire tracks that marked the site of the previous day's search. Hiked to the top of the rise, looked down over the settlement, and froze.

"I wondered when you were going to get here. I thought you got lost or something." Nyssa stood leaning against the old gate. She wore cutoffs and a white tank top, clothes more suited for an afternoon by the pool than a hike through the deep woods. Her only concession to the conditions proved to be her hiking boots, which reached mid-calf and looked heavy enough to smash rocks. "There's a shortcut. It's kinda over-grown now, and you have to do some climbing, but you can still get through. I would have told you about it, but you didn't ask anybody for help, so . . ." She shrugged, looked around in feigned innocence, then pushed away from the gate and circled around it toward the settlement. "Coming?"

Lauren pointed back toward the house. "Go home. If I'm not back by sundown, tell your father where I've gone."

"No." Nyssa stopped. She had already stripped off her ban-dages. The cuts she had made showed ruby bright against her white skin. "What were you going to do?"

"I don't know. That's why you have to go back. I don't know what I'm going to find, or what I'll have to do to protect myself, and if I don't know how to protect myself, how can I protect you?"

"But you said I was strong. I can protect myself."

"You don't know what to do."

"So maybe I'm like you. I'll figure it out as I go along."

"Go back, Nyssa."

"So you're just going to go down there, walk in, search through all the buildings?"

"Pretty much, yeah."

"You're an idiot. You're, like, the first one that dies in all the movies."

"You're not wrong." Lauren pressed a hand to her forehead—the heat had given her a pounding headache. "This is what I do. I wing it. I feel my way, and sometimes I screw up. That's why you can't come with me." She tried to think of something that would persuade Nyssa to leave. "I saw your mother here yesterday."

Nyssa nodded slowly. "She liked it here. She used to bring me here when I was little."

Lauren blew out a long breath, even as she realized that she shouldn't have been surprised. *Alone on this mountain for weeks at a time.* Fernanda must have explored every nook and cranny out of sheer boredom. *And who knows what she found.*

"During the day we'd run through the buildings. Play tag. Pretend that the big building was our house." Nyssa toyed with the busted gate latch. "But we came here at night a few times. Mom called them our 'camping trips.' She brought blankets, a picnic basket. We slept out in the middle there." She pointed to the central expanse of grass. "Counted the stars. Sang." She quieted, then sniffed, and brushed away a tear. "People say all kinds of things about her, and maybe some of them were true. But not all of them."

"Did your father know?"

"No." Nyssa kept her eyes fixed straight ahead. "Grandfather did, though."

Lauren walked to the gate and placed her hands on the top railing near the place Elliott Rickard had stood. "Were your mother and your grandfather close?"

"For a while. Grandfather was sick by then, and Mom used to spend time with him. I'd see her pushing his wheelchair on the patio. Then they'd just talk."

"What about?"

"No idea." Nyssa's lip curled. "I know what people thought, though. I heard Heath say it once, a few years later. That even

JERICHO

though he was so sick that he couldn't even walk, Grandfather
was my real father. I ran crying to Dad because I didn't have
Mom anymore and Grandfather was dead by then. I didn't want
both my parents to be . . . not around." She kicked at the fence
post. "So Dad and Gene sat down with me and Gene took out
a paper calendar and the two of them very carefully explained
about how and when Mommy met Daddy and then they
counted days and months and showed me that Dad really was
my Dad." She managed a smile. "It's funny now, thinking back.
Dad's face was so red. He was, like, glowing."

"He must have been furious. You wouldn't think that he'd
invite Heath here after that. He doesn't strike me as the forgiv-
ing type."

Nyssa shrugged. "Heath was stealing from him. Bringing
him out here and exposing him in front of his closest friends is
Andrew Carmody all the way through." She looked at Lauren
with eyes dulled by memory, the events of the last few days.
"People think I can't figure things like that out. That I don't
remember anything. They don't know me at all. Not even
Dad." She gave the gate latch one last yank. "I haven't been here
since Mom disappeared."

Carmody's last words to her rattled through Lauren's head.
Enjoy your walk. "Your father knew I was coming here. I'm the
fixer."

"This isn't your problem to fix." Nyssa headed down the
slope, then stopped and waited by the guard shack.

Lauren extended her hands as she walked toward the shack,
feeling for any breach in the warding, the ripples in the dark
space that she had sensed the previous day. Felt nothing even

after she entered, and wondered whether it was because her blood ward had worked so well, or because whatever inhabited Jericho had fooled her. *It's a trap.* The thought settled like an earworm in her brain, replayed over and over. *And I'm leading a child right into it.* She walked the perimeter of the small space, in search of anything that had changed since the previous day. "Do you feel anything? Any increase in the buzzing? Change in temperature?"

Nyssa held out her hands as Lauren had done. Turned one way, then the other, like a horror show mummy emerging from its crypt. "I don't feel anything different." She pointed to the line of brown spatter that dotted the floorboards from one end of the shack to the other. "Is that your blood?"

Lauren nodded. "Yeah." She let Nyssa take hold of her cut arm and examine the wound. "It just itches a little. It's healing."

"You heal fast, like me." Nyssa held out her arms. Up close, her wounds looked like cat scratches rather than deep gashes. "Gene wrapped them as soon as he got hold of me. He said that helped."

"Uh-huh." Lauren kept her thoughts about Gene Kaster and his healing touch to herself. *Poor witch like me, my ass.* "I don't see anything different here." She beckoned to Nyssa, and together they left the shack.

They walked down the hill in tandem, then split up, each taking one side of the settlement. They searched around the buildings, checked windows, opened doors, and peeked inside.

"Nothing looks weird." Nyssa swung a door back and forth, its hinges squeaking like small animals in distress. "But I don't know what I'm supposed to be looking for."

"If you see any piles of bones, let me know. But don't touch anything." Lauren checked the last of the small structures on her side, then closed the door. "They'd be against one of the walls. And they'd be small, maybe only a handful. Possibly with some feathers surrounding them in a ring."

"That's so gross. And mean. Poor little birds."

"That's what Sam thought, too." Lauren walked to the middle of the open yard and studied the largest structure. "When I saw your mother, I also saw people going in and out of all the buildings. But here, more went in than came out." She took one of the elder sprigs out of her pack, crumpled it, and rubbed it on her clothes. "Here." She gave another to Nyssa.

Nyssa grimaced as she crumpled the leaves and rubbed them over her skin, her clothes, leaving trails of green stains behind. "This smells horrible."

"To demons, it smells worse."

"What are they? Demons. Do they all come from Hell?"

"I think Stef or Peter could answer that question better than I can." Lauren rubbed the leaves between her palms until they formed a damp, stinky mass, which she distributed among all her pockets. "The one we fought in Gideon had been human once. I guess you could say he went all the way over to the dark side." She wiped her hands on the seat of her pants, and wondered whether the litter-box stink would ever wash out. "I think the term defines actions and behavior more than the type of *being* something is. But I've never met an official Bible-type demon, though I have heard they exist." She felt a hard mass pressing against her leg. Stuck a finger in the side pocket of her pants, and hooked out the toy car.

Nyssa hurried over to her. "Where did you get that?"

"At the bottom of the garden. There used to be a pond there."

Nyssa nodded. "I remember. It wasn't there long. Dad didn't like it." She took hold of the car. "Grandfather gave me this. He liked giving me boy toys because he knew it irritated Mom." She held it in her cupped hands, like a baby bird. "Can I keep it?"

Wing-it decision the first. Lauren took the car back, squeezed it, felt nothing. *It's empty.* All magic spent. "Okay." She gave it back to Nyssa. "But let me know if it starts acting weird."

"Like if it gets hot or something?"

"Or if anything comes out of it."

"Okay."

They circled the building first, searching for signs of warding or anything else that looked out of place. Lauren rooted through the grasses and weeds with her hands, while Nyssa rummaged a length of broken board and used it to poke around. They worked in opposite directions and met in front of the door.

"Ready to go inside?" Lauren studied the knob before she put her hand on it. "This looks newer." She gave it a push as she twisted it, expecting to find it locked. But it turned freely and slipped out of her grip as the door opened. The panel swung back before she could stop it, and banged against the inside wall with a sound like a gunshot.

"Smooth move." Nyssa stepped inside.

"Whatever's here already knows about us." Lauren followed her. "Did anything ever happen here that you can recall?" The space felt as dead as the rest of the settlement, the air still and stale.

Nyssa shook her head. "No. It was always just the two of us."

She stopped, then bent low and clapped her hands over her ears. "Can you hear that?"

"Hear what?"

"Nothing." Nyssa straightened. "It's so quiet." She headed to the far end of the room and crouched in the corner. "There's bits of black plastic here. Like someone smashed up something hard."

Lauren walked along the windowless wall, saw the trails of black on the floor. A few larger pieces, but bits, mostly, along with powder. "I'm seeing the same thing."

"Is it a ward, too?"

"No. I think it's just junk that the wind blew in." Lauren caught sight of something in the shadowed corner. "There's something here." Flashes of white as she drew closer. "It's another bone pile. It looks bigger than the other one." She held up her hand as Nyssa came closer. "Maybe a larger bird."

"Who set them? Stef?" Nyssa started to reach for the bones. "I'm going to have to have a talk with her. How do you protect a place if you have to kill things to do it?"

Lauren grabbed the girl's wrist. "Don't touch it. Don't think about it and don't touch it. It needs to stay in place." *For all the good it's doing.* She maneuvered Nyssa out to the middle of the floor, felt the flex and creak beneath her feet. Stopped, and studied the boards, saw the squarish outline, the slight difference in the color of the wood. "Look down at the floor here. What do you see?"

Nyssa looked where Lauren pointed. She started to shake her head, then stopped, stepped back, and paced back and forth. "No way."

Lauren dug through her pack. "Did you bring any tools?"

Nyssa patted the pockets of her cutoffs. "No."

Lauren pulled out a nail file. "This might be enough." She lay flat on her stomach and sighted along the floor, looking for any deviation from perfectly flat.

"Just jam it in here." Nyssa pointed to the hair-thin space that ran down the middle of one of the boards.

"If this is what I think it is, there should be a handle somewhere."

"Maybe it's operated below the floor—only someone down there can open it." Nyssa walked to the entry and hunted around the jamb. "Or maybe there's a hidden panel here." She probed between boards with her fingers.

"I've got it." Lauren inserted the tip of the file into what looked like a tiny lip obscured by the tongue-and-groove joint, and twisted. A section of the floor whispered upward, the hinges and workings silent despite their age and the rust and grime that coated them.

And in the opening, just visible through the darkness, metal steps, the open-tread type used in factories and fire escapes. Dust dulled the silver surfaces, while spiderwebs that were disturbed when the door opened fluttered like torn flags with the movement of the air.

"Are you kidding me?" Nyssa crept toward the edge of the opening. "Was this always here?"

"No. Your grandfather had it built in the late sixties." Lauren stuck the file back in her pack, then hunted for a flashlight. "Underground labs, invisible from the air. He must have been worried that someone would find out what he was doing."

"Did my mother know about this?" For the first time, Nyssa's voice held a hint of Carmody ice.

Oh hell yes. Lauren forced a noncommittal shrug. "I don't know."

"But you think she found out stuff from Grandfather." Nyssa paced around the opening. "I'll go first."

"You don't have to."

"No, but I will." Nyssa took the flashlight from Lauren and descended the steps.

"I BET THERE'S an elevator in one of the other buildings." Lauren followed after Nyssa, struggling for balance as the soles of her hiking boots caught on the toothy tread. "No way I'd want to climb down this thing every day in a skirt and high heels."

"Maybe no women worked here."

"I saw them. Unless they were limited to aboveground offices off-site, which I confess wouldn't surprise me given the time period."

The flight of stairs proved short, reaching down only a single level belowground. Lauren felt hard flooring beneath her feet— the flashlight beam revealed bare concrete, thick rubberized baseboards, a cement block wall painted chalky mint green.

Then a sizzling, popping sound filled the air, and overhead lighting sputtered to life.

"Wow." Nyssa gaped.

Lauren stared at the lights, and wondered what powered them. *A generator, triggered by the door?* But what powered a forty-five-year-old generator? Any petroleum-based fuel would have degraded. Batteries would have gone dead. *Solar cells were invented in the fifties.* But assuming Steven Carmody had opted for such an exotic technology, the arrays of solar plates would still need to be in place outside. *There aren't any.* Her heart beat just a little faster. *We're someplace else now.* Dorothy and Toto had kissed Kansas goodbye.

Narrow corridors lined with observation windows and solid-looking doors radiated from the area around the staircase like the spokes of a wheel. They seemed to stretch on for hundreds of feet, and ended in darkness.

Nyssa grimaced. "Do you smell something rotten?"

Lauren sniffed. "It smells like the fungus that Sam ate."

"She put something that stank like this in her *mouth*?" Nyssa made retching noises, then turned off the flashlight and handed it back to Lauren. "So which way do we go?"

"Let's see what this sign says." Lauren walked partway down the nearest corridor until she came to a large, old-fashioned black menu board complete with stick-on white letters. "There's X-Ray. Psychology." She hesitated. "Interrogation."

"Was this a hospital?" Nyssa came up behind her and read the sign over her shoulder.

"I've never been in a hospital that had an interrogation room." Lauren scanned the other items on the board, which proved to be numbers separated from proper names with hyphens. *Offices.* She hunted for any names she recognized. Found only one.

0023–Dr. E. Rickard

Lauren looked down each corridor in turn. The fact of the smell bothered her. Where did it come from? She walked down the corridor toward the first observation window, and trailed her hand along the wall. She pressed her hand to the cold, painted surface but felt nothing.

Then she stood before the window. On the other side was some type of examination room. A chair stood in the middle, a recliner like you'd see in a dental office. But there were restraints on the arms, the footrests. A strap dangled from the curved headrest, and the ends of a seat belt dangled over the sides.

"Once you sit in that chair, you're in it for good." She stepped back from the wall. Rubbed her fingers together, then looked down at her hands. Something thick and shiny, like ointment, coated her fingertips. She sniffed it. "Nyssa? Pull a bandanna out of my pack."

Nyssa dug one out of a side pocket and handed it to her. "What happened?"

"I touched something." Lauren wiped her fingers, then sniffed them again. "It smells a little like the fungus that Sam ate. Maybe more sweet."

"I'm sure that makes a difference." Nyssa stamped her booted feet, the thump echoing along the corridor. "Is it growing down here? Yuck."

"Don't make so much noise."

"You said that whatever's here already knows we're here. I want to see it."

"Careful what you wish for." Lauren felt around the window. Then she found it. A small patch of jelly-like material the size of a child's hand, located beneath the lower edge of the window frame. The rest of the wall was clean. *A patch of mold?* She had never seen colorless mold before. She looked up at the ceiling, which consisted of the same acoustic tile she had seen in classrooms and offices all her life. Darker than usual in places, from dirt or the green kind of mold. She gave her fingers a final wipe, then folded the bandanna so that the mess was on the inside, and tucked it into her pack's outer pocket. "I'm going to check inside."

"It's just a room." Nyssa put a hand to the glass. "Isn't it?"

"Wait here. Keep an eye out for anything." Lauren turned the knob and pushed open the door, then checked the other side. *No knob.* Anyone who worked in here would have had to depend on an observer to let them out if whoever sat in the chair got loose, became violent. She spotted a wheeled cart set against the wall, pulled it over, and used it to block open the door.

The exam chair looked old and tarnished, the surfaces coated with a thin layer of dust. Lauren brushed off the footrest then pressed her hand to the upholstery. She hoped for leather, but it proved to be vinyl—the chill, grimy surface crackled under the pressure of her touch, but gave up no secrets.

She walked around the room. Opened the drawers of a metal table set against the far wall, found nothing but a roll of ancient gauze, a few paper clips, a scalpel. When she touched the cotton gauze, the air hazed for a few moments, but soon cleared. She stuck it in her pack anyway, along with the scalpel.

She found a trash can next to the table and checked the contents. A crumpled piece of paper, blank but for a line of inked X's that might have been doodles, or part of an evaluation. Some wadded tissues. A small block of wood, the size and thickness of two fingers.

Lauren picked up the wood and examined it closely. It was light-colored, like birch or white oak, and sanded smooth.

"Are you almost done?" Nyssa pushed the cart out of the way and blocked the door open with her body. "I think I hear something."

"I thought you wanted to meet it."

"Maybe I changed my mind."

"Almost done." Lauren held the wood up to the light, turned it over, angled it one way, then the other. Picked out the depressions that formed semicircles on each side, the telltale scrapes and ridging of tooth marks. Closed her hand around it, pressed her fingertips to the marks, and felt—

—blood in her mouth and stabs like wasps stinging and the fear and so much pain.

Then a scream, which rattled her like the concussive force of an explosion.

Lauren dropped the wood, staggered, fell against the exam chair, and slid down to the floor as the room spun and acid rose in her throat.

Nyssa started toward her, then stopped so she could keep the door from closing. "Are you all right?"

"Yeah." Lauren pulled herself to her feet. "We need to get out of here." She picked up the wood block with two fingers and stuffed it in her pack.

"About time." Nyssa waved Lauren back through the door, then pulled it closed. "What happened to you? I thought you fainted."

"I almost did." Lauren felt a strange pressure in her sinuses, the trickle of something out of her nose. Touched it, then stared at her blood-smeared fingers.

"Your nose is bleeding."

"I know."

They rounded the corner and headed for the stairway, and stopped.

The stairs had vanished, and someone blocked their way.

"Hello?" The man cocked his head. He wore a lab coat over business clothes and carried a clipboard. Middle-aged or a little older, his face lined and dark hair streaked with gray.

Lauren studied the man. *He looks like he did in the photo.* And then there was the smell. "Dr. Elliott Rickard?"

"Yes." Rickard looked down at the name sewn on his pocket, then back at Lauren. "Do I know you?" He looked her up and down. "You are not on my list." He then directed his attention to Nyssa. "But you are. She's been waiting for you. You can go to her now." He looked back at Lauren and frowned. "I don't know what to do with you."

"She comes with me." Nyssa took hold of Lauren's hand. "She's my friend."

Rickard shook his head. "She was most adamant. She wants you all to herself." He took a step toward Lauren and reached out his hand.

"Stay away." Lauren took out the scalpel.

"Now, Miss—" He studied his clipboard again, and flipped to a different page. "If you could just sign in here and we can start to process—"

"I'm not signing anything." Lauren waved for Nyssa to stay behind her. "You worked for Steven Carmody. You tested people. Psychological evaluation. Why?"

"Steven?" Rickard's brow furrowed. "He's not here."

"You tested them." Lauren pulled the wood block out of her pack's side pocket. "And some of them failed."

Rickard stared at the block, and something about his eyes changed. They darkened. Clouded. "It's sad, when they fail."

Lauren took a step closer, ignored Nyssa's frantic poking. "Did Heath Jameson fail?"

"Yes." Rickard nodded. "He needed to be sent back."

"You let him go?"

"We sent him back. For retraining."

"He's not making any sense." Nyssa whispered into Lauren's ear. "Can't we just go?"

Lauren waved her quiet. "Where did you send him?"

Rickard straightened, his eyes clearing as he fixed on something behind Lauren. "You'll soon see."

Lauren turned, dreading what she'd find.

Nyssa gasped.

Fernanda Carmody walked down the corridor toward them, big as life and more beautiful than any photograph. She wore the same dress that she had when Lauren had seen her the previous day, a sleeveless rose-tan mini a few shades lighter than her skin. On her feet she wore flat-soled sandals fashioned from spaghetti-thin straps of bronze leather. Her black waist-length hair hung loose, and any makeup had been applied so skillfully as to be invisible. Frozen in time, she looked more like Nyssa's older sister than her mother. A face that could launch a thousand ships, or break a man into a thousand pieces.

"Darling." A mellifluous voice, touched by an accent. "You've finally come to me."

"Mom. Mommy." Nyssa's voice shook. "You're dead."

Fernanda smiled. "Never." She held out her hand. "You know I am not. You've seen me often enough."

"I've never seen you."

Fernanda tsked. "Now that's a lie you know it's a lie you shouldn't lie, darling." The words flowed together in something like a song, hypnotic and soothing.

Oh, you got good. Lauren sensed the woman's power. It touched her skin like chill air, needling along her fingers and up her arms.

"You understand, don't you, Lauren? That a girl should be with her mother?" Fernanda shrugged, then gestured toward Nyssa, her hand floating in the air with a ballerina's grace. "What good has her father done her? What good did your father do you? Fathers are men, after all, and men lie, and when you face them with their lies, they kill you."

"My father didn't kill me." Lauren waited for Fernanda to reply, but the woman—the ghost—the demon—only had eyes for her daughter.

"You see only part of the world, darling. You must come with me to see the rest of it. The best part."

"She means that you have to die, Nyssa." Lauren jostled the girl, who seemed transfixed.

Fernanda shot Lauren a hate-filled look, then turned back to her daughter. "Do you remember when I brought you here, darling? All those years ago?" Her voice had taken on an edge that she struggled to control. She spoke more slowly, and forced a smile. "I pulled you in your wagon. We sang songs, and ate chocolate, and spent nights beneath the stars." She took one step forward, another, slow and collected as a cat on the prowl.

"You loved it here, because it was home. You are home now, with all those who love you."

"Dad loves me, Mom." Nyssa had pinched the skin of her forearm between two fingers and twisted it white.

She's struggling to not succumb. Lauren took hold of the girl's hand and squeezed it, and fielded another angry look from Fernanda. But this time the witch added pain to the mix, broken glass scrapings that made Lauren feel as though someone ran a knife between skin and muscle and peeled peeled peeled.

"Your father doesn't know the meaning of love. I learned that too late." Fernanda drew a small square in the air. "He knows power, and control, and cruelty." Her eyes glistened. "I sense your pain, angel. I know what you suffer because I suffered it as well. But there is a life beyond yours. An amazing life filled with magic and beauty." She glanced at Lauren. "Yes, and power, too. Your new friend can tell you of the power." With that, she twitched her hand.

Lauren caught herself to keep from stumbling as the pain ceased, like a bulb switching off. Then, a few seconds later, it flared, held her in its fiery grip for a few more tripping heartbeats before dying once again. She met Fernanda's eye, saw both the smile and the warning it contained. That this was only a taste. That she could subject Lauren to tortures that were so much worse.

"I don't want to die, Mom." Nyssa gave Lauren's hand a light shake, then released it, as if she knew that any show of affection between them angered her mother.

"It doesn't hurt." Fernanda eyed Lauren sidelong. "Ask your friend. She died once, and yet here she is. It is an interlude only, like walking through a door. And after that, we can be together forever." She pointed to Rickard. "I passed all his tests. And you are my daughter, so you will, too."

"If I go with you, what happens to Lauren?" Nyssa crossed her arms, injected her native stubbornness into her voice. "You'd let her go, right?"

Lauren heard footsteps coming up from behind, and turned to find Rickard standing behind her, clipboard in hand.

When their eyes met, he smiled.

"Of course she can leave." Fernanda made a shooing motion in Lauren's direction. "She can do what she wants in the world that has your father in it. But you and I will have a different world, an unimaginable world, filled with wonder."

"Did you learn about that world from Grandfather?" Nyssa's breathing had turned rapid, shallow. "People are dying, Mom. Disappearing. It's not a good world."

"But I came here first and I'm your mother. I made it safe for you." Fernanda held out her hand. "Leave her. Come to me."

Nyssa stared at her mother for a few long moments. Then she turned to Lauren. "What do we do?"

"*Run.*" Lauren swung the scalpel at Rickard as he tried to grab her, slashed through his lab coat sleeve and whatever lay beneath. Silvery fluid that stank like the fungus sprayed from the wound, and he howled, the sound echoing down the corridors.

Lauren ran behind Nyssa, scalpel at the ready in case Rickard followed. She looked back and found Fernanda chasing them instead.

No, "chasing" was the wrong word. She didn't run, no. She

didn't have to. She walked, lips moving in silent spellcast, her eyes fixed on Lauren.

Lauren braced. It didn't help. The pain hit like barbed fire under her skin and she staggered, then dropped to one knee.

"No. You can't do that now." Nyssa grabbed Lauren under her arm and dragged her to her feet, then pulled her along.

"It's your mother. She can make me hurt, and I can't block it." Lauren pushed the girl down the corridor. "Run. Look for an exit. There had to be more than one way out of here."

"I'm not leaving you." Nyssa stopped in the middle of the corridor nexus, where the stairway should have been. "What happened to the steps? Did they move them?"

Lauren passed her hand through the air around the spot where the stairs should have been. "They're still here. We just can't see them."

"They can do that?" Nyssa looked past Lauren. "We need to run. Now."

"You're being silly, Nyssa." Fernanda's rich laugh followed them.

Lauren looked back to find Fernanda only a few strides behind. Rickard shambled beside her, cradling his arm, the front of his lab coat smeared with stinking gray slime.

"Come on." Nyssa grabbed Lauren by her shirt and dragged her down the corridor they had explored before, past the menu board and toward the examination room.

"We'll be trapped in there." Lauren tried to stop Nyssa from entering the room, but another wave of pain washed through her. Stars flashed and faded before her eyes, and every step rattled along her spine and sent muscles cramping.

"We can break through the ceiling tiles and find a vent to crawl through." Nyssa pushed Lauren into the room, then slammed the door shut and dragged the metal table in front of it.

"That only happens in the movies." Lauren fell to the floor, pushed herself against the wall so she could sit up. *We're screwed if we stay here.* She tried to work into a crouch so that she could stand, but her muscles seized and she slumped back down.

Nyssa pushed everything movable in front of the door—the rolling cart, a couple of smaller chairs. "I'm going to tell Dad, if we ever get out of here. That she brought me here. That we slept here." Then she hurried to Lauren, sat on the floor, and scooted next to her. "Do you think something happened to me when we did that? Is that what got into my head?"

"I don't know." Lauren strained for any sound of Fernanda's approach, tried to prepare for what she knew to be coming. *Take the worst flu ever, and quadruple it. Then double it.* And just when she reached the point where she could bear it no longer, Fernanda would push her until she passed out. *And where will I wake up?* Assuming she did. *I'm just extra baggage.* Something for Rickard to test.

It's sad, when they fail.

"What is that noise?" Nyssa got up and walked to the window. "It's like buzzing." She pressed close to the window so she could see down the corridor. "Oh. Oh no." She backpedaled, stumbled, and fell, then dug her heels into the floor and pushed backward until she rammed against the wall next to Lauren.

Lauren listened. A buzzing sound, yes, but with weird harmonics, the rise and fall of crowd noise.

Then she saw the shadows. They began as a darkening of the corridor walls, the ceiling. Then they streamed out into the air, the flies of the forest, tumbled clouds of black and gray that swirled into tighter shapes that took form and mass and grew arms and legs. Crawled along the walls and ceiling and across the window, their clawlike hands scratching against the glass, squeaks like marker on whiteboard.

Faces—they pressed them against the window. Noseless. Jagged-tooth mouths round as octopus suckers. Bulging black eyes. Rugose bodies of dark green, skin like moss that flaked and smeared the glass.

"Can you see them?" Nyssa covered her face with her hands, stared at the window through her fingers. "Please tell me you see them, too."

"I see them, too." Lauren hugged the girl close, rocked her like a baby as she trembled.

"'We are the forest. We are the darkness that hides. We are the children of the howl and the cry. The makers of fear. Spawn of shadow and the longing for hell.'" Nyssa's voice came rushed and hoarse. "Grandfather wrote that. He told me and Mom that we would foster the children. He said we were special, and that someday the world would be ours. How can I remember that now? I forgot it for so long but now it's like it's burned into my brain. Like this place made me remember. I told him that I didn't want that world, but he said I'd change my mind." She shook her head. "I haven't changed my mind."

Lauren watched the creatures continue to mill, like bees crawling through their hive or flies massing on a corpse. "Those are the forest people, like the figures in the garden."

"They're the children. They're my children."

"They're nobody's children."

The buzzing lowered, the creatures stilled. Then some of them moved apart, leaving an open space. A shift of light and dark, and Fernanda appeared. She pressed close to the glass, hands on either side of her face, like a child staring at sweets through the candy store window.

Her eyes met Lauren's, and she smiled.

Nyssa buried her face in Lauren's shoulder. "We're going to die."

"Like hell we are." Lauren forced herself to move, pushed through every shuddering wave, every cramp. She worked her hand into her pack, dug out the wooden block. Squeezed it, massaged it, felt where it had been, how it had been used. Sensed the remnants of the person who had been strapped into the vinyl-covered chair and subjected to who the hell knew what while a hallway full of Elliott Rickards watched through the glass and took notes on their clipboards.

"All the pain you felt," she said to the shade of whoever had suffered and probably died with that piece of wood clenched in their mouth, "let me give it back." She slipped the block between her teeth, fitted them into the impressions that poor bastard had left behind, and willed the wood to release its memory. Tasted nothing but the dusty dryness, felt nothing but the polished smoothness.

Then the block warmed and grew damp and she tasted saliva and coffee, the coffee that they had drugged and then came the vomit though he had tried to hold back, so ashamed, the pain the hurt and then the metal taste of blood and the salty sting of tears—

—rattling through her teeth and along her jaw like the dentist's needle jammed too deep. Down her neck and into her chest, where it formed a white-hot ball that wound tighter and tighter then pushed out through her hands, her eyes and ears and nose and mouth every part of her back arching as she cried out and gave voice to the last scream of a dying mind.

"**LAUREN!**"

Shaking shaking shaking.

"Lauren!"

Lauren opened her eyes.

"They're gone. They're gone. You have to get up. We have to go." Nyssa grabbed her under the arms and sat her up. "You—I don't know what you did. You screamed and it was like you had a seizure and out in the hall it all went swirly black and blew apart, like they all went to pieces." She dug into Lauren's pack, pulled out a wad of tissues, and pressed them to Lauren's face. "We have to go now."

Lauren told hold of the tissues. She tasted blood, her nose felt stuffed full of cotton, and every bone and muscle ached. "Go."

"Yeah, we have to." Nyssa pulled Lauren to her feet and pushed her into the exam chair. Then she rushed around the room, grabbing objects and flinging them at the window. The trash can. A surgical tray.

Finally, she hefted the metal table and slammed it repeatedly against the glass. One hairline crack formed. Another.

Lauren wondered if she could manipulate dark space, push through the window and drag Nyssa after her. But the atmosphere of the room was a tumult, her thoughts, a jumble. "Aim for the lower corner." She pulled the tissues away from her face and stared at the blood. Tossed the wadded mess aside, stood, and shuffled to Nyssa's side. "Use it like a pick-ax." She took hold of the other end of the table, and helped the girl bash the point of the leg at the window again and again.

No luck, at first—the pane was thick, shatter-resistant. Lauren felt the blood trickle from her nose, fought the urge to vomit as nausea gripped her with a cold, clammy hand. Heard Nyssa's panicked whimpers.

Then, at last, chips of glass sprayed. Tiny ones first. Then a hand-sized shard broke away and clattered to the floor outside.

"That's enough." Nyssa dropped her end of the table and snaked her arm through the jagged hole, wincing as sharp edges scraped her skin. "I can't—yes I can—I've got it."

Lauren pushed the table aside and staggered to the door, waited until she heard the knob turn. Then she wedged her fingers into the narrow gap between the panel and the jamb while Nyssa pushed just enough. Felt her fingernails bend and snap as she pried and levered and finally pulled the door open.

"Now." Nyssa took Lauren's hand and dragged her into the corridor.

Lauren tried to put one foot in front of the other. Stumbled once, then again.

"The stairs are back." Nyssa ran up to the top of the flight and pushed up the hatch. "Come on." She scrambled through the opening to the floor above, then lay on her stomach and held out her hand.

Lauren mounted the steps, then struggled to keep her footing as Nyssa pulled her through. But as she fought to stay upright, she sensed something else in the air. She sniffed. "Do you smell something?"

"I don't know how you can smell anything." Nyssa touched Lauren's face, and winced. "We have to go now." She took hold of Lauren's hand, and together they walked out the door.

Then they stopped, and stared at the darkness that surrounded them. Stagnant air that stank of ponds on summer days, damp cellar corners, and left a thin sheen of oil behind as it drifted over skin.

Nyssa coughed, covered her nose with her hand. "Where are we?"

"I don't know." Lauren squinted into the murk, caught sight of shapes moving toward them. "We need to go back inside."

"I am not going back in there."

"We have to." Lauren dragged Nyssa back into the building and pulled the door closed just as several somethings bumped against it. Faces pressed against the windows, then seemed to melt against the glass, mouths drawn out in perpetual screams.

Then came sounds from overhead, the rapid patter of small, running feet.

"They're on the roof." Lauren backed into the center of the room.

"There's no place they can get in, though, right?" Nyssa pointed. "There's no chimney or anything. They can't come down like Santa Claus." She laughed, a bark of nerves and fear. "Some really fucked-up Santa." She clapped a hand over her mouth.

"If they get in, leave me. Run to them. They won't hurt you."

"What will they do to you?"

Lauren swallowed, tasted the metal of the blood that ran down the back of her throat. "Don't worry about me."

"I'm not leaving you."

Lauren backed closer to the wall, then stopped as the sounds overhead changed from footsteps to hard pounding.

Nyssa looked up at the ceiling. "I guess they don't need a chimney."

Lauren followed her line of sight, saw the first cracks form in the boards, then radiate along the lengths like ice shattering. Dust and cobwebs fluttered down.

Then the weakened boards creaked like trees in the wind, and bowed under the weight of whatever it was that stood on them. As the first splinters fell, Lauren extracted herself from Nyssa's grip and turned to the wall. Pressing her hands to the rough boards, she struggled to concentrate as the banging sounded louder and louder.

Sounds filled the space, battered the very air. Shattering glass. The crash of a broken-down door. Buzzing so loud that it rattled down her spine.

Lauren focused on her hands, and where she wanted to go. *Home . . . home . . .* Gideon. Seattle. A hole in the ground. *Home.* Her fingers seeped through the wood to the first knuckle, then stopped as something pushed back.

Flies settled on her neck and face, biting again and again.

You knew this would happen one day.

Shadows. She felt them wash over her like frigid water.

You knew this is how it would end.

Their gabbling whispers filled her ears, promises of pain that they yearned to keep.

Nyssa wrapped her arms around her and screamed, a sound that shook like a cry in a gale.

Then came silence.

Lauren slumped forward, felt arms wrap around her, lift her, carry her. A light frisson as fingers brushed over her face.

"You're safe now, Mistress."

She pressed her face against softness, breathed in, tasted sweetness in the air, caught the barest scent of spice.

Passed out.

CHAPTER 22

Lauren drifted in and out, awakened every so often by jostling and the sounds of argument.

"—told you never to go there—"

"—have a right to know—"

A figure in scrubs peppered her with questions. *How many fingers? Who's the president? What's your name?* She mumbled answers, felt herself being undressed, examined, tucked into bed.

Dreams. She sat on the outcropping overlooking the mountains as behind her, someone spoke. She didn't recognize the voice. Felt she knew the speaker, yet couldn't recall his name. The same words, over and over.

It wasn't supposed to be like this.

She opened her eyes to find Gene Kaster standing over her, the collar of an emerald-green pajama shirt poking out from beneath his bathrobe.

"What happened?" Lauren tried to sit up, then sagged back against her pillows when the room rocked. "Is this dead?"

Kaster bent close. "What?"

"Am I dead?" Lauren grabbed the front of the man's robe. "Where's Nyssa?"

"She's fine, she's fine, you're fine, everyone's fine." Kaster pried her fingers loose, then patted her hand and set it on her lap. "Sit. Quiet."

Lauren listened, heard nothing but the sigh of ventilation, the electronic tick of the nightstand clock. No screams. No howls or crash of shattered wood and glass. "This isn't hell?"

"Not last I checked." Kaster pointed to the clock. "It's just after midnight. You've been out like the proverbial light for about ten hours." He took a step back, then lowered into an armchair that had been drawn up next to the bed. "We've been taking turns keeping an eye on you. I drew graveyard shift."

Lauren looked around the small room, which possessed the distinct look and smell of a hospital. "Did you evac me to Portland?"

"No, you're still on the mountain. This is the house clinic."

Lauren nodded as reality started to seep back in. Memory. "What did you do?"

"Such a luxury, having one's own clinic on site. Nothing is too good for the guests of the house." Kaster reached into the pocket of his robe and removed a silver flask. "Not to mention that when one has accidentally OD'd or gotten a personal appliance inserted too deeply in the wrong orifice, it's a relief to know that help is just an elevator's ride away, and that the information will never be recorded in one's official medical history." He picked up a glass that rested on a stand by his chair, splashed some of the flask's contents into it, then held it out to Lauren. "Age-old remedy."

Lauren took the glass, sipped what proved to be whiskey, then winced and pressed her hand to her mouth.

"Nothing broken." Kaster stood, then walked into the adjoining bathroom. "But you did bite down rather hard on the inside of your cheek. You may need to eat soft food for the next few days."

"My whole face hurts."

"As well it might." Kaster emerged holding a hand mirror. "Don't be too alarmed. As I said, nothing's broken. Just bruised."

Lauren took hold of the mirror, then tilted it and moved it slowly sideways, so she could examine a little of her face at a time. Puffy cheek. *Check.* Split lip. *Check.* Then came the black eye, the swollen nose. *Another black eye.* The gash across her chin. "As Virginia would say, 'oh my Lady.'"

"The concern, of course, is that the injuries may not stop at your face. No signs of any internal bleeding so far, but you will be staying here through the day, at least." Kaster sat back in his chair, elbows on armrests, and tented his fingers. "Nyssa told me what you did with the wood block. People have died attempting that sort of spell, you know. Anytime one serves as a conduit, one takes a great risk of, well, shorting out." He regarded her over his manicured fingertips. "Nyssa said you suffered a seizure, and as you did, various creatures, and I am quoting now, 'blew up'?"

"That would include Fernanda, I guess." Lauren finished the whiskey, set the glass on the end table. "I don't know if she exploded. I had—passed out by then."

"I assume this is the item in question?" Kaster again reached into the pocket of his robe. "It was in your pocket when we brought you in." He set the wooden block on the edge of the bed.

Lauren stared at it for a time before picking it up. "I found it in one of the examination rooms. It had been placed in somebody's mouth to keep them from screaming. Possibly to keep them from swallowing their tongue if they seized. It was in his mouth when he died."

"He?"

"I sensed a man." Lauren set the block on the end table, then looked back at Kaster to find him studying her, chin resting on his fist. "What was that place?"

Kaster drummed his fingers on the arm of his chair. A slow, steady beat. "I am betting that you already know a good deal."

"I think I know the what and who. You'll have to help me with the how and why." Lauren waited, but Kaster simply watched her. *So it's Twenty Questions. Fine.* "Was the government involved?"

Kaster's hand stilled. "Steven tried to obtain their support. Given some of the research they had financed in the past, what he proposed wasn't that much of a stretch." He smiled. "Or perhaps it was. For whatever reason, they drew a line."

"The CIA?"

"And a few more acronyms that no one has ever heard of."

"So he financed it privately via the Foundation." Lauren rubbed the back of her neck, felt the small, raised bumps of the fly bites. They felt warm. Itched a bit. She wondered what they looked like, if any of them had turned black. "Did Heath know?"

"I don't believe so, if only because if he had, his next step would've been blackmail, and I would've heard about it."

"What about Stef and Peter?"

"You should ask them." Kaster massaged his forehead as though a headache had come to call. "Steven . . . his vision was so different from Andrew's. He wanted to expand knowledge, however ruthless his methods. Andrew? He needs to win. I think you would have an easier time convincing the father of the error of his ways than the son."

"*You* think?"

"Based on what my father told me about Steven." Kaster kept his eyes fixed on some point above Lauren's head.

Lauren debated waving to snag his attention, but her shoulders ached too much. "I know why. It always boils down to money and power, doesn't it? Control of others by any means possible. Fear. Greed. As for how? Families in Gideon made deals with demons. Most didn't live long enough to see the payout. For the few that did, the price turned out to be greater than they ever expected to pay." She fell silent until Kaster finally looked at her, the space between them heavy with things unsaid. "How did you get us out of there? What did you do?"

Kaster pointed up toward the ceiling. "We're just below the bar. There are five very shaken people up there."

"Will you please not change the fucking subject?"

"Language."

"It was you." Lauren lay back against the pillows. "I tried to get us out of the room, and I had gotten my fingers into the wall but then something stopped me." She fell silent, breathed slowly to quiet her pounding heart.

"You need to settle down." Kaster leaned forward and took hold of her hand.

"I thought that was it. I knew Nyssa would be as okay as possible given the circumstances, but they had no use for me. Except as a research subject." Lauren started to pull her hand away, then decided that she really didn't want to. "How did you do it?"

"Why are you so sure it was me?"

Lauren roughened her voice. "*'You're safe now, Mistress.'*"

Kaster's face reddened. He let her go. "I prefer to think that we worked as a team. I couldn't have sensed just anyone over that distance, especially through all that warding and interference. You partially burrowed out, and I partially burrowed in, and we met in the middle. Then I dragged you out the other side."

"Where did we end up?"

"My bedroom." Kaster glanced back at the door, then lowered his voice. "Everyone else believes that you accomplished this feat on your own. I would greatly appreciate it if you played along. I emerged from my dressing room to the sight of the pair of you tumbling out of thin air onto my carpet. Imagine my surprise. That's been my story. Please stick to it."

"Why? What you did was amazing. Take credit for it." Lauren felt her own face heat. She reached around and fluffed her pillows to hide the fact, and gasped as a pulled muscle went *zing*.

"A compliment from you. Praise indeed." Kaster bowed his head. "That will have to suffice. I can't admit my part in this."

"Why not?"

"For someone who woke up mere minutes ago thinking she had died and gone to hell, you ask a lot of questions."

"The last witch, the only witch I ever met who I think could've pulled off what you did was over two hundred years old."

"I read your Mistress Waycross's report. Technically, he was much younger. He'd been dormant for a while."

"You've changed the subject again."

"If it helps at all, think of me as a satisfied investor. A silent partner. A helping hand."

"It doesn't."

Kaster stood again, this time walking to a table by the door. "Could you please accept that I have my reasons, and move on?" He lifted the cover off a dish. "Nyssa prepared you a tray. I hope you like tuna salad."

"I'm starved. Why am I starved?" Lauren sat up slowly as Kaster set the tray on a wheeled bed table and rolled it over. "Nyssa was amazing, by the way."

"She said the same about you." Kaster plucked a grape from a dish of fruit and popped it in his mouth. "She seems different, since you've been here. The knife edges have blunted. I hesitate to use the word 'happy' for fear of jinxing, but we've all noticed the change." He lifted another cover and his face lit. "There's strawberry ice cream."

"No thanks."

"Homemade. Mount Hood strawberries."

Lauren shook her head. "I need protein." She tried taking a bite of the sandwich, but it proved too thick for her sore jaw to deal with, so she used a fork to pry out the filling, which she carefully inserted between her teeth.

"Ice cream has protein." Kaster held out the bowl to her. When she shook her head again, he sighed, then picked the dessert spoon off the table, sat down, and dug in.

Lauren polished off the sandwich filling, then started on

the bread, which she broke into small pieces. "Did he kill her?"

Kaster paused, his spoon halfway to his mouth. "Is that what Fernanda told you?"

"She accused him of everything but."

"Then you should ask him yourself."

"The subject has come up. He says he didn't."

"But you don't believe him?"

"He has it in him."

"Don't we all? Don't you?"

"This isn't a philosophical rumination. What happened between them is still feeding whatever lives in Jericho." Lauren dispatched the bread and chose a banana from the fruit bowl. "And whatever it is, it's getting stronger. Something has to be done."

Kaster finished his ice cream and set the dish on the tray. "You need to rest." He stood, then dragged the chair back to its place against the wall. "I will inform the others that you're as ever you were." He smiled, but the expression wavered when he met her eye. "You look better now than when you first arrived. Good as new in no time." Another quick bow of the head. Then he walked to the door, put his hand on the light switch. "On or off?"

"On." Lauren raised the knife she was using to slice the banana. "I'm still—" But before she could finish, he had already gone.

CHAPTER 23

Lauren tossed and turned. The windowless clinic room felt cold and closed in, and she debated returning to her suite to see if she could fall asleep there. She had made up her mind to try to get up when she heard muffled footsteps in the hallway. They paused in front of her door, and she waited for the night nurse to stick his head in and check whether she slept or if she needed anything, which he had already done three times thus far. As the only patient in the five-bed clinic, she had been the focus of everyone's attention since her arrival.

But after a few moments' delay, the footsteps resumed in the direction of the nurses station. *Stop—start—stop*. Then a quickening, as though whoever it was broke into a run.

The sound brought Lauren to her feet before she realized it. Rib muscles seized, then relaxed just enough to allow her to breathe without pain. She crept to the door, cracked it open, stuck out her head, and looked in both directions. Saw no one.

Then she heard soft beeps, followed by the slip of a door

being very carefully opened. She scuttled down the hall and rounded the corner in time to see one of the doors just on the verge of closing. She ran, caught it just before it clicked shut, told herself that she was about to surprise the hell out of the night nurse, and threw it wide anyway.

Nyssa stood before the drug cabinet, one hand on the door handle. She stared wild-eyed at Lauren, then blinked and backed away. "You're supposed to be asleep." She wore a man's white T-shirt, red boxer shorts. Her sleep-mussed hair hung in her eyes.

"Yes, this is me, asleep." Lauren stepped inside the room and closed the door behind her. "What are you doing?"

"Nothing." Nyssa shrugged. "I've been coughing—that air did something to me. I was looking for something for it."

"Go see the nurse. He'll find you something."

"I don't want to bother him."

"Trust me, he wants to be bothered. He's bored to—" Lauren almost said *death,* decided not to tempt fate. "He's very bored."

"Fine. I'll go see him now." Nyssa started for the door, one hand where Lauren could see it, the other hidden by the folds of her shirt.

"What are you hiding behind your back?" Lauren side-stepped into Nyssa's path.

"Nothing."

Lauren held out her hand. "Give it to me."

"I don't have anything."

"Now."

Nyssa's eyes dulled. She started to speak, then shook her head, and held out her hand.

Lauren took the bottle of tablets. Her eyes stung when she read the label. "Digitalis. You were going to take these? Do you know what this would do to you?"

"Yes." Nyssa wedged into the corner. "It would kill me."

"You were brilliant today. You kept your head. You helped save us—"

"You saved us."

"You got us out of the basement when I could barely walk." Lauren shook the tablets, which rattled like dice in a cup. "Why?"

Nyssa wiped away a tear. Then she slapped the side of her head. "They're back. The noises. The voices muttering. I mean, they've been there for most of my life, like this drip-drip sound, but they've been getting worse for, like, a year now. Dad sent me for hearing tests and I had brain scans and psych evaluations and there were times when I wanted it to be cancer or something because then at least there'd be a reason and maybe they could make it stop."

Lauren leaned against the door frame. Her own voices had quieted soon after her arrival, and she had taken it as a sign, but she also appreciated the peace. Gideon nerves—she had them bad, and she knew that the day she left this place, they would return. "It's something you can learn to live with."

"You don't know what they say to me. The things they tell me to do." Nyssa pointed to the wall, the woods beyond. "Except today it was quiet. I was terrified, and we were in that room and all those things were crawling all over the place and I thought we were going to die. But I could hear everything so clearly. The things breathing and the sound of their claws on the glass. I mean, I never want to see it ever again and I think I'll have nightmares every time I close my eyes but in my head, it was quiet." She rubbed her arms, ran a finger along one of the slashes. "Dead is quiet, too. If it's a choice between this or nothing, I'd rather have nothing."

Lauren pressed a hand to her aching ribs and sat on the edge of a stack of plastic carriers. "We can work together to help you deal with this."

"I have worked with Stef, and Pete, and every other member of the Council. Dad even flew in a hypnotist from France." Nyssa walked to Lauren and touched her cheek. "I know you're trying. Everyone tries so hard, and I keep letting them down."

"That's not—"

"But this is me and I have to deal with it my way." Nyssa sniffled, then walked to another cabinet and dug through the shelves until she found a box of tissues. "I'm older than I look. In here." She tapped the side of her head, this time more lightly. "They saw it in the MRI. I have the brain of a thirty-year-old. Better judgment, that's supposed to mean. Not as inclined to take risks."

"So what—"

"So that means that the decisions I'm making now aren't just me being dramatic or overreacting. I've thought this through. I know what's best for me. I know how I want to live, and how I don't want to live." She wiped her nose, her eyes. "I know you'll tell my dad, and he'll have me monitored more closely, for a while. And as soon as they let their guard down, as soon as they get bored. I'll be able to do what I have to." She opened the door, stuck out her head and checked in either direction, and left.

Lauren remained seated, the bottle of tablets in hand, long after the motion sensor turned off the lights and left her in the dark. Then the sound of voices roused her. She opened the door of the drug room just as Carmody walked past with the night nurse. Before they could say anything, she handed the bottle of tablets to Carmody.

The nurse paled. "We change the entry codes for that room and the cabinet daily and we do not write them down."

Lauren held up her hand. "She has ways of finding things out that you don't know about." With that, she took hold of Carmody's sleeve and led him down the hall until she felt sure the nurse couldn't overhear.

"How did you find her?" Carmody looked down at her wide-eyed, rocked from one foot to the other.

"I just happened to be up. Couldn't sleep." Lauren paced. "She didn't hear the voices in Jericho. That's why she tried. She wanted the quiet back."

Carmody examined the bottle of tablets, sucked his teeth when he saw what they were. "But she's been so good these past few days."

"I've heard that from other people. If I'm responsible, fine, but I'm a bandage, not a cure." Lauren started back to her room, then turned again to Carmody. "Jericho. Close it down. I don't know what the hell you're waiting for. Burn it to the ground and sow salt." Before she could say more, a noise froze the words in her throat. Faint insect hum, like a swarm of persistent mosquitoes.

Or flies.

"Do you hear that?" Carmody spun on his heel, scanned from one end of the hall to the other. "I don't see anything."

Then metallic *pings* mixed in with the humming, which grew louder and louder.

Lauren looked up toward the ceiling. "The air ducts."

"Oh, shit." Carmody shouted to the nurse. "*Get out. Now.*" Then he hurried to a nearby wall panel and mashed buttons. A siren sounded first, followed by a canned message ordering everyone to evacuate immediately.

Lauren grabbed a lab coat off a hook by the nurses' station and pulled it on over her pajamas. Then she took off after Carmody. Except for her ribs, she felt okay. She could run if she had to. Fight, if she had to.

She used the stairs to get to the first floor and found the others standing outside on the patio. Stef and Peter huddled with Carmody in urgent conversation while Nyssa stood to one side with her hands over her ears and Jenny paced.

"They're up on the roof checking stuff now." Jenny stopped and gave Lauren a quick hug, then resumed fidgeting. "It's the middle of the night, so no one can see anything."

"We heard them, though." Lauren backed up to see if she could spot the staffers. "Are they wearing protective gear?"

"The guy from the grounds crew is wearing a beekeeper's getup. And Stef sprayed the other guys with some stuff that she called repellent." Jenny pressed her hands to her face, stretching her skin so tight it looked like a mask. "I was so wiped that I slept through the house alarm. Pete had to go back inside and bang on my door." She finally stopped pacing, and jogged Lauren with her elbow. "How you doin'?"

"Okay. I think I look worse than I feel." Lauren pressed a finger to one of her shiners to see if she could gauge the swelling,

ALEX GORDON

"You look fine." Jenny shrugged. "Of course, it is dark."

"Thanks." Lauren managed a smile. But that faded when she caught sight of the men on the roof. They stood gathered around an intake vent, a shiny aluminum construction that was usually hidden behind wooden screening.

"This is one of those times when I wish I hadn't quit smoking." Jenny held up two fingers in a V and pressed them to her mouth. "Maybe they just need to drop a bug bomb down there."

"Here's hoping." Lauren took a deep breath, then exhaled slowly. She breathed in once more and felt her gut clench. "Do you smell that?"

"What?" Jenny sniffed, then screwed up her face. "Did something die up there?"

The workmen backed away from the vent. A knocking sound followed, echoing through the trees.

Then the flies came, spewing out of the opening like a geyser from a hydrant. The workmen tried to scramble to the ladder, but the swarm wrapped around them like a blanket and swept them off the roof to the ground four floors below.

Nyssa screamed.

More groundskeepers pelted around the back of the house, bearing water hoses, fire extinguishers, and brooms, and ran to the fallen men. But the flies rose and gave chase, driving them back into the garage. Then, instead of returning to their victims, they swept around the house, landing on the windowed walls, the glass roof, until they coated the entire structure in a shining, thrumming, twitching layer.

As this was going on, Lauren and the other guests fled the patio and into the garden. Carmody, meanwhile, had returned to the house, emerging soon with the head of his security team. They stood arguing on the patio about next steps to take and who to call.

"This is incredible." Peter stood behind Stef, his hands on her shoulders. "How the hell could Andrew let it go this far?"

Lauren watched Stef start to speak, then shake her head, as though she couldn't think of a defense, either. Then Jenny jostled her elbow and pointed at the house.

"They've stopping buzzing. Moving. Everything."

Lauren listened. Heard . . . something, barely audible, like the softest tone in a hearing test. She ran back onto the patio, and headed for the far end, ignored the shouts of the others and Carmody's call to *get the hell back to the garden.*

Then everyone fell silent and headed in the same direction. They all stopped at the railing that overlooked the rear yard, the forest beyond, then raised their hands to shield their eyes from the glare as the outdoor lighting blazed on.

Lauren saw the shadows flicker down the trail, waited for what cast them to become visible. They appeared as soon as the light touched them, the little barrel bodies, scores and scores of them, toddling like children in Halloween costumes.

Nyssa had moved in behind Lauren and grabbed her hand. "She's come to get me."

"We won't let that happen." Lauren turned just as Carmody and Kaster drew near. The men stopped and stared, Carmody's face paling while Kaster just closed his eyes.

Then the creatures stopped, and parted like a shallow, black sea.

"Look at all of you." Fernanda Carmody emerged from the darkness of the wood and walked down the path the creatures had made. "Such long faces. Isn't my husband entertaining you?" The little bodies broke ranks and milled around her, tugging at her dress, pulling at her hands. "Bad husband. But then we all knew that, didn't we, Andy? He hates that, you know. He thinks it a child's name." Her expression hardened. Even from a distance, you could tell. "A little name for a little man."

Jenny stood with a hand over her mouth. "What are those things?"

"The children of the forest." Nyssa pushed closer to Lauren. "The children of the howl and the cry."

"Are we supposed to be afraid of them?" Peter looked around, as if trying to assure himself that everyone else could see what he saw. "They're so small."

"So are the flies." Lauren put her arm around Nyssa's shoulders. "We saw them combine to make bigger beings, creatures, then melt away and vanish when they had to."

"The flies are everything." Kaster stepped away from Carmody and walked to the railing. "They can become whatever they need to be."

Lauren watched the man. He seemed as concerned as the rest of them, which was worrisome given his usual detachment.

"Stay the hell away from me." Nyssa muttered. "Go back where you belong."

"I can hear you, darling." Fernanda's voice took on an edge. "I can see you, too. Your life here is over. It's time for you to come home with your mother."

"I'm not going anywhere with you." Nyssa forced some strength into her voice. "You killed people."

"Not kill, darling. Change. It's your father who kills."

Lauren felt Nyssa tremble, the sweat that coated her palm. "She's staying here, Fernanda. Go back to Jericho."

"Oh, it's you. The noble one. The interfering one." Fernanda shook off the creatures' hands and pushed through them until she stood in front of them, alone. "I know how to hurt her, Nyssa. You know I do. Come with me like a good daughter, or I will hurt her again."

Nyssa pressed her face to Lauren's shoulder. "What do I do?"

"Just stay right where you are." Lauren elbowed Peter. "If anything happens to me, hold on to her." She braced for the first hit, felt it as a tingle that started at the base of her neck and radiated down.

Peter leaned in. "What's going to happen—" He glanced at Lauren's face. "Okay, hang on." He took her hand, then grabbed Stef's. "Let's spread this around a little. She can't hit all of us at the same time."

"Don't be too sure." Lauren felt the man's hand tighten hard enough to hurt, heard him gasp.

"Okay, maybe she—can." Peter gritted his teeth. "Stef, I'm going to let go of you."

"Don't you dare," the woman snapped.

"Your heart—"

"—can take it." Stef gripped the railing with her free hand, her knuckles whitening.

Then Jenny stepped in beside the woman, and placed her hand over hers.

"I am the queen of the flies. Feel my sting." Fernanda laughed. "You will all feel much worse if you don't return my daughter to me."

"Gene?" That from Peter. "If you have any suggestions, this might be a good time to make them."

"I'll try to talk to her, face-to-face." Kaster started toward the doors that led back into the house.

Lauren leaned against Nyssa as the first wave of pain dissipated. She wondered why Carmody had remained silent and let the rest of them take the brunt of Fernanda's attack. She turned and searched the patio for him, but couldn't see him.

Then she heard Peter swear.

"Oh, shit." The man staggered to the railing. *"Andrew, get back here."*

Lauren limped after him, reaching the railing in time to see Carmody stride across the lawn toward Fernanda.

"Damn you, leave Nyssa alone!" Carmody held something in his hand, an herb bundle or some sort of charm. "It's between you and me, Nan. Take it out on me." As he drew near, he raised his hand and made ready to throw.

"As you wish, Andy." Fernanda twitched her hand. "Children, protect your mother."

The creatures moved as one, like a wave rising and crashing down, swarming over Carmody like bees over an invader of the hive. He wheeled and tried to run back toward the house, but the weight of them dragged him down to the ground. He cried out, but his voice muffled as they buried him, vibrating bodies emitting a high-tension wire crackle and hiss that served as a call to the others. They streamed in from the house and piled on, a milling, pulsing mass.

A blood-covered hand pushed through the bodies, then vanished beneath.

"Andrew." Kaster vaulted over the railing to the ground below. It was a drop of more than a story, but he landed feetfirst and ran toward the swarm on legs that should have been broken or at least damaged. But no, he ran, like a young man who had spent his life running.

Then he shouted. Words. Orders. At least Lauren assumed they were orders made of words because they were short sounds strung together and when Kaster uttered them, the creatures tumbled out of the pile as if they had been doused with gasoline and lit afire, screeching and shuddering and waving their arms. Struggling to cover their ear-holes with hands that didn't quite reach.

After Kaster grabbed the few creatures that remained atop Carmody and flung them across the yard, he knelt beside the man, lifted his head onto his lap, and rocked back and forth. As he did, more sounds emerged, a singsong chant that drew the creatures back. But they kept their distance this time, encircling Kaster and his fallen friend, and standing, silent and still.

"Is he . . . talking to them, or to Carmody?" Jenny stood with her hands pressed to the sides of her face. "What's he saying?"

"I—can't understand it." Stef tugged Peter's sleeve. "Peter, have you ever heard anything like it before?"

"No." Peter shook his head. "They're listening to him like they did to Fernanda. But they're afraid."

Lauren watched Kaster wipe blood from Carmody's face, then bend close and kiss his forehead. Then he lifted the man in his arms, carried him as easily as he would have a child. "He's headed to the garage." She hurried after Peter, who had already vanished into the dark of the dining room.

They arrived at the garage in time to watch Kaster gently place Carmody atop a stretcher. A pair of the house paramedics then got to work, while the rest ran outside to see to the fallen workmen.

Lauren looked past Kaster to the stretcher and stared in sick disbelief. Carmody's face had swelled into an unrecognizable mass of lumps and open sores, his distended body straining against clothes rendered a wet mess by his blood and other fluids.

"Dad?" Nyssa drew alongside. "Daddy?" She reached out to touch the man's hair, but one of the paramedics steered her away, then helped the other insert a breathing tube.

Kaster muttered under his breath and pressed a hand to Carmody's forehead. Then he backed away from the stretcher and headed toward the entry to the outside.

"She's dangerous," Lauren called after him.

"I know what she is." Kaster stepped into the illuminated darkness and stopped a few paces away from Fernanda, who stood on the paved pathway. She looked more like the figure that Lauren had encountered in the Abernathy College corridor, older, disheveled, her dress and skin dirt-smeared and her hair a tangled mass shot though with leaves and twigs. A true mother of the forest.

"Hello, Gene." Her voice held a mocking lilt. "My husband's protector. You take such good care of your little boy." She looked past him into the garage. When her gaze fell on Carmody's stretcher, she smiled. When it moved to Nyssa, her eyes alternately softened with need, then narrowed with greed.

Then her gaze moved to Lauren, and settled like snow.

Lauren felt the chill, the hatred that formed it. Hoped that if she stayed in the shadows, Fernanda wouldn't be able to tell that she had landed a blow.

But of course she could tell. Another smile, this one more feral, anticipating the bloodshed to come.

"This won't end well, Fernanda." Kaster's voice sounded as it never had. Stilted, the accents on the wrong syllables. "You have one last chance. Return to the dark you love so well, and stay there. Leave the living be."

"So gallant. Such a defender. A defender of killers." Fernanda put her hands around her neck. "He killed me. My wonderful husband. You all know it's true. Do you hear me, Nyssa? Your father followed me into the woods that last night. He killed me and left me to rot on the ground like a piece of garbage." She tried to draw closer to the place where her daughter stood, but Kaster moved to block her. "Nyssa? Is that who you want to live with? The man who killed your mother?" She reached out to the girl.

Lauren glanced back at Carmody's stretcher, and found the paramedics struggling to keep their patient still. Only when Nyssa forced herself past them and took his hand did he slow. He said something to her, his voice muffled by swelling, as she nodded and wiped her eyes.

Lauren turned back to Fernanda. At first she thought a fly had landed on the outside of Fernanda's wrist. *No, not a fly*. A round, black dome of shiny skin that reminded her of the welt on Sam's hand.

She pressed a hand to the back of her neck, felt the raised bumps of her own fly bites. Vowed to check them as soon as she had the chance even as she feared what she might see.

"Leave." Kaster raised a hand, sketched a sigil in the air. "Now."

"You tell my husband. It doesn't end here."

"I said, leave."

Fernanda bared her teeth and hissed at him. Then she turned and headed back up the path toward the forest trail, her charges hurrying after. Soon they vanished into the shadow, leaving behind only their smell and the bodies of their dead, which had already begun to decompose, skin peeling and crumpling and fluids leaving smoking blotches in the grass.

"She won't quit, Gene." Peter went to stand behind Kaster. "She's got time on her side. And numbers."

Kaster watched until the last creature had gone. "I bought us some of her time."

"To do what?" Lauren pressed a hand to her ribs. As diluted as Fernanda's assault had been, it had still been strong enough to aggravate earlier injuries.

Kaster looked toward Nyssa. "She wants her daughter. But she's as reckless in this life as she was in her old one. She can be had." When the paramedics pushed the stretcher toward the elevator, he trotted after it, collecting Nyssa along the way.

CHAPTER 24

W e have to go out there." Peter paced the hallway outside the treatment room into which Carmody had been taken. "We can't delay."

"She'll be waiting. We know she won't be alone." Lauren dragged a chair out of an adjoining room and sat down. "The night's their time. The wind dies, and everything is quiet. The gaps in dark space get bigger, and they walk through. That's why most hauntings happen at night. Why we have night-mares. Why we're scared of the dark." She shrugged, gasped as her shoulder complained. "That's my theory, anyway."

Peter crouched next to her. "Maybe the night can be our time, too. Have you ever thought of that? This dark space of yours flows both ways, right?"

"Like I said, the night's their time. They live in it. They're used to it. It's their daylight. We need a solid plan, and it has to be bulletproof, because we won't get a second chance. They want us to blunder in now. They're counting on it."

"You're afraid." Peter sounded disappointed.

"Yes, I am." Lauren shivered in memory. "Been there. Lost people. Mopped up blood with the T-shirt."

"Then we should leave." Stef emerged from the shadows. "If it's as bad as you say, then let us pack up and go. Let them have the mountain."

"You're kidding, right? You know we can't do that." Lauren saw Stef reach out a hand to steady herself. Stood and offered her the chair, and received a sharp head shake in reply.

"She's right, Stef. This mess needs cleaning up." Peter turned to Lauren. "I've been trying to think whose children they are. Fernanda called herself 'queen of the flies.' As incredible as it sounds, that can only mean . . ." His voice trailed off.

Lauren could almost see the names and references and ancient texts unfurling in the man's memory. "Spit it out, Professor."

Peter frowned, brow furrowing, as though he could not accept what he needed to say. "Beelzebub. The Lord of the Flies."

Lauren thought for a moment. "Beelzebabies."

Peter closed his eyes. "Not now, Lauren."

"I'm not trying to be funny."

"Good, because you're not." Stef shook her head, then left them and entered the treatment room.

Lauren and Peter remained outside, peeking through the door every so often at the bed on which Carmody lay.

Peter answered Lauren's unspoken question. "He's conscious. Stef's poultice should draw out the venom."

"Should?"

"We're winging it here. I've never seen anything like this. She hasn't, either."

"Maybe we should have evac'd him to Portland with the other men."

"We wanted to. He said no. He was afraid Fernanda would send her flies to bring down the chopper." Peter leaned against the jamb and massaged his hip, an aching remnant of Fernanda's assault. "Besides, it's not that kind of venom. Any of the usual treatments would prove useless."

Lauren inhaled slowly. Exhaled. "Do me a favor." She turned. "Check the back of my neck."

"What am I looking for?"

"A raised black welt." Lauren held her breath as the seconds passed.

"I just see little red bumps, like mosquito bites." Peter whistled through his teeth. "We saw a black welt on Sam's hand. Do you think it indicates something?"

"I saw one on Fernanda's hand as well." Lauren adjusted her pajama top. "I think it could be a sign of . . . the only word I can think of is 'infection.'"

Peter brushed past her. "Then we should check Andrew."

They entered to find Carmody trying to sit up while Nyssa struggled to push him down and Stef shuffled back and forth with a steaming bowl filled with something that smelled like boiled pinecones.

The patient looked much improved. Carmody's facial swelling had reduced to the point that Lauren could see his eyes—he looked as though he had survived one hell of a bar fight rather than an assault by otherworldly creatures. Stef and Nyssa had stripped off his ruined clothing and draped a sheet so that he was covered from waist to thighs, his bare chest and legs left exposed. It would have made for quite the picture if he didn't resemble a badly wrapped mummy with an extreme case of eczema.

"He wants me to bring him his phone and his tablet. Like he's going to try to work now." Nyssa swatted Carmody with the cloth she had been using to soak his wounds.

"I just want—them here in case we need to—call for backup." Carmody's voice emerged gravelly, and he had to pause several times to clear his throat. "Do you have anybody—in the area?" He cast a long look at Peter. "Do you have anybody—anywhere? I can send a plane for them. The chopper. Anything you require."

Peter nodded toward Stef. "We can pull together some names." He caught Lauren's eye and jerked his chin toward Carmody, then took out his phone and went to sit at the doctor's desk. He motioned for Stef to join him, and together they got to work.

Lauren circled Carmody's bed and studied his exposed skin. "How do you feel?"

"Lousy. Which is a helluva lot better than I felt—an hour ago." He shuddered. "I think I'm going to have nightmares for the rest of my life." He pointed to his face, then to Lauren. "We're a matched set."

"No, I think you win this one." Lauren bent close to a suspicious looking wound on Carmody's arm. Felt the pressure of a stare, and looked up to find him eyeing her.

"What are you doing?" He leaned away from her, then looked down at the spot she had been trying to assess.

Lauren poked the injury, which turned out to be a scab. "Checking." She told him about the black welts. "The venom works fast, I think. Sam disappeared an hour or so after we returned from Jericho." She glanced at the wall clock. "So I would say that if you're infected, you should be feeling it about now."

Carmody stilled for a few moments, then shook his head. "Fernanda wouldn't want me yet. She'd wait until the end, after she had gotten hold of Nyssa and destroyed everyone and everything else I cared about." He swung his legs back and forth, like a little kid sitting at the edge of a pool. "If you're not infected, she must not want you yet, either."

"I think she just wants me dead."

"It's not true. What she said. None of it."

Lauren nodded. She tried to think of the diplomatic thing to say, and decided that at this point, tact was a luxury they couldn't afford. "Bottom line? It will always be your word against hers. Do I think she hates you enough that she would lie? Yes. Do I think it possible that you killed her and managed to justify it to yourself, or call it an accident? Yes." She felt his stare like the rake of nails down the side of her face. "I don't mean to sound brutal, but you two deserved one another."

Carmody scanned the room until he spotted Nyssa, safely out of earshot on the opposite side. "Don't hold back, Lauren." He started to say more, then just shook his head. Lay back and closed his eyes, the round sucker wounds, cuts, and scratches on his neck and chest angry red in the fluorescent lighting.

Lauren watched his breathing slow as he fell asleep. Then she left the room and walked down the hall and around the corner to where Jenny sat leafing through a large book bound in worn burgundy leather.

"Did you know that there are fifteen different types of charms you can make from rose thorns?" She looked up at Lauren, then pointed to the book. "Magic for beginners, or whatever you call it." She closed the cover. "I found it in the library. Thing's so old, it doesn't even have a title."

"Academic interest, or are you planning on giving it a go?"

"I don't know. Doesn't seem to have done any of you much good, has it?"

Lauren shrugged. Given the events of the last few days, it was a fair point. "It isn't all horrible."

"Not exactly a ringing endorsement."

"Maybe ask the same question in a few days." *Assuming we're all still alive.*

"Those other books aren't there anymore." Jenny rubbed her eyes, then yawned. "The ones about the CIA and those other agencies. Somebody cleaned house."

Lauren tried to stifle her own yawn, then gave in to it. "Did I ever mention those?" She wiped her eyes with her lab coat sleeve. "I don't think I ever mentioned those."

"I noticed them the other day. I see things, too, you know."

"I never said you didn't." Lauren studied the woman, who looked as exhausted as she felt. "You don't have to stay here, you realize that? You're a civilian. This isn't your fight."

"Yes, it is." Jenny set the grimoire on the floor. She had left her hair loose, a gold-tipped halo of brown curls, skin beneath her eyes purpled from lack of sleep. "I'm in this as much as you." She paused. "Elliott Rickard was my grandfather."

"I—okay. Wow." Lauren lowered to the floor beside her. "But he vanished in 1978. You couldn't have known him."

Jenny inhaled a shaky breath. "Momma told me about him. She said he was intense. When a project caught fire, he wouldn't come home for days at a time. My grandmother told her that the story of him going missing at the picnic never rang true, because he was neck-deep in a project. He would never have stepped away for even a moment to do some social thing."

"Did your grandmother know what he was working on?"

"If she did, she never told my mother." Jenny shook her head. "I didn't believe Nyssa when she told us what had happened there, in that room underground. What you found. What you did. I thought she was just being a drama queen like always." She finally looked at Lauren, and winced. "Then I walked into the treatment room and saw your face as they were working on it, and I almost lost it." She stopped, swallowed hard. "How could he do that to people? How could he subject them to such awful things?"

"I'm guessing they were volunteers." At least, that was what Lauren hoped. "Maybe he convinced himself that they knew what they were getting into. That whatever they went through was for the good of humanity, or their country."

Jenny shook her head. "It wasn't government backed. Anything after the early seventies was privately funded by Carmody. They were doing it for the money, for power, to discover things that they could sell to the highest bidder. There was nothing noble, or pure, or—" She pulled a tissue from her pocket, but it was too late. Her eyes filled, and she didn't bother to catch the tears as they fell. After a time, she cleared her throat and wiped her eyes. "What are you going to do?"

"For now, I'm just going to walk around. Keeps the nerves at bay." Lauren stood, stuffed her hands in her pockets, and wandered up and down halls until she came to the elevator. Rode to the first floor, and went to the bar. Found Gene Kaster sitting at the counter, a tumbler of whiskey in hand and the bottle at his elbow, lost in thought.

Lauren tiptoed behind him. "A retreat, you said. Relax with other witches, you said."

Kaster jerked upright, then spun around on his stool. "I'm sorry." He tried to smile, but it didn't last. "I didn't want this to happen."

"Who would?" Lauren boosted onto the seat next to him. "That was some spell you pulled out of your back pocket. It didn't just drive those creatures away, it killed a few." She reached over the bar and grabbed a can of seltzer from a tray of mixers, then plucked a glass from the overhead rack. "Makes me wonder whether you couldn't have done something earlier, before any of this happened."

Kaster pushed a plastic cup filled with ice down the bar toward her. "I told you before. I am limited as to what I can do."

"By whom?" Lauren poured, added ice, waved off Kaster's offer of the scotch bottle. "Your boss? I don't believe he would object to a little assistance at the moment."

"Andrew knows what I can and can't do." Kaster set his elbows on the bar, fixed his eyes straight ahead. "He accepts the terms. He sticks by them. He's a good man of business."

"Is that what this is? Business?" Lauren waited. "What are

you?" She held out her left hand, the bruises already faded. "You healed this. I think you've been healing Nyssa's self-inflicted injuries for years. Fernanda called you her husband's protector. I'm surprised you haven't healed him."

Kaster swirled his glass. "Who said I didn't?"

"Stef's poultice—" Lauren replayed the scene in her head, the way Kaster held Carmody, brushed his hand over the man's face. Then she reached out and placed her hand over his.

Kaster eyed her sidelong, then eased his hand away. "I could, you know. Let you get the full sense of me. But I'm afraid it would kill you, and I wouldn't want that on my conscience."

"So you have one. Coulda fooled me."

"You have stumbled into something so much bigger than you can imagine."

"I didn't stumble anywhere. I was invited, by you."

"By Andrew." Kaster paused to drink. "I was merely the messenger."

"I don't think there's anything mere about you."

"I'll take that as a compliment."

"I didn't mean it as one." Lauren dug an ice chip out of her glass and slipped it into her mouth and crunched it. The chill felt good against her sore cheek. "Are you human?"

"As human as you." Kaster refilled. No ice, this time. "As human as I need to be."

"Why can't you stop this?"

"Because whatever the outcome, it is, essentially, a family matter." For the first time, Kaster showed something like anger, his cheeks reddening, nostrils flaring. "People make decisions. Those decisions affect people they love, people they hate, people they don't even know. They make their choices, and they pay, or others pay. They see the fallout. They live with the consequences. How else do they learn?"

Lauren checked the wall clock. "Isn't it a little too late?"

"For what?"

"A ramble about the nature of good and evil. I think I know which is which now. Thanks for that." She slid off her seat. "I need to go. Pete and Stef are calling other Council members. Looks like I'll finally get to meet some of them."

Kaster glanced at her, then quickly away. "How is Stef?"

"Wobbly. Worried. She wanted to leave, which surprised me."

"She's scared."

"We all are."

"You're worried about what's to come. She's worried about what's been done. Or not done."

Lauren stilled. "She set wards."

"Yes. She did. They aren't working very well, are they?"

Lauren pondered. Then she closed her eyes. "Shit."

Kaster raised his glass in a toast. "I'm surprised you didn't figure it out sooner, given your personal experience."

"I didn't—you knew this, too?" Lauren thumped the side of her head with her fist. "Damn you. Does Peter know?"

"What do you think?" Kaster polished off his drink, then poured another. "It's been a day of discovery, has it not?"

"Yes." Lauren stared at the man—the whatever the hell he was—but he refused to meet her eye. "Yes, it has." She swore under her breath and hurried out of the bar.

LAUREN RETURNED TO the clinic to find Stef seated in the hall outside the treatment room, dozing. The woman opened her eyes and straightened as soon as she saw her.

"Lauren." Her appraisal held less antagonism than usual. "Gene had given us to believe you sustained some serious damage, but you look quite well. A bit battered, but that would be expected."

Lauren lowered cross-legged to the floor in front of the woman's chair. "How long?"

Stef managed a puzzled half smile. "I'm sorry?"

"How long do you have to live?" Lauren kept her voice low. "Forgive my directness, but we don't have time. You're dying. That's why your wards are failing, even after you strengthen them."

"We are fighting an enemy of incomparable strength." Stef leaned forward until her face was only inches away. "How dare you suggest that I am not making every effort to contain it."

"I didn't say that." Lauren studied the lines of Stef's face, noted the yellowish tinge of her skin and the whites of her eyes. "My dad probably sacrificed at least twenty years of his life squelching my powers. He thought he was helping me, and that he could fight my battles for me. Except that he couldn't because what he fought had time on its side. It could afford to wait." Tears sprang, as they did every so often when she thought of her father, and she wiped her eyes with her sleeve. "Does Pete know?"

Stef made as if to argue. Then she slumped, as though someone had pricked her and let out a little bit of air, and shook her head.

"You have to tell him. Now." Lauren started to reach out, hesitated, then placed her hand over Stef's and felt the same papery brittleness that she had the first time she touched her. *I should have known then.* "I'm sorry. I am so sorry. But this isn't about you anymore."

Stef looked past Lauren into some middle distance. "As long as I cast the wards, Andrew would support the Council."

"Did he know your condition?" Lauren gave Stef's hand a slight shake. "Stef?" But the woman continued to stare at nothing, eyes dull with secrets kept for far too long.

CHAPTER 25

hey set to work, eyes on the clock or on the view afforded by the clinic's narrow window, the sun's relentless journey west. Carmody called down plats of the mountain and aerial views of Jericho, so that they could map the location of the existing wards and plan the placement of the new ones. After a while, Kaster joined them. He nodded to Lauren, then focused on the old maps, marking the location of wards that Stef remembered.

The first helicopter arrived later in the morning, disgorging a half-dozen Council members weighed down by equipment bags. Despite Lauren's fears that they would be unable to handle the seat-of-the-pants rigors of fieldwork, they quickly split off into pairs and set about preassigned tasks. Several of them approached her and introduced themselves. All were middle-aged, dressed in various stages of rumpled, the men balding, most all bespectacled. It struck her how she had yet to meet any Child of Endor who resembled the stereotypical witch, and she felt a surge of affection for the whole ragtag gaggle. *I wish*

I could've known you better. She fought the urge to say that to every one of them. She didn't want to scare them. Or herself.

"So while we're constructing this ring of wards, what is Fernanda going to be doing?" Stef poured tea from her cup into her saucer, and blew across it. "As soon as she senses us, she will know what we plan, and she will attack us the same way she did Andrew and Lauren." She raised the saucer in a toast to no one, and drank.

Peter had bucked the trend of the house and requested a beer, and now sipped it slowly, as though he feared it might be his last. Every so often, he would reach out to Stef and touch her hand, his expression the quiet daze of someone for whom the bad news had yet to sink in. "If Gene's concoction can hold off the Beelzebabies"—he rolled his eyes at Lauren—"we should be able to set the wards in place and scram before she comes after us herself. It isn't going to take that long."

"What are you using?" Lauren forced a last mouthful of ham sandwich through a jaw still stiff from the previous day's business.

"A concentrate of elder that we developed at the Council laboratories. Also, rosemary, myrrh, and attar of roses." Stef tugged at her blouse, to which the scents of the warding materials still clung, and held back a sneeze. "It is quite the eye-watering combination."

Lauren sniffed the air. Coughed. "So she'll smell it before it's completely in place." She heard murmurs, and looked to find Jenny and Nyssa seated against the far wall, bent over Jenny's magic book, pointing out the old pen-and-ink drawings of the plants that Stef had named.

"Could we spray it from the helicopter?" Nyssa lifted her head from the book long enough to mime holding up a spray can and spritzing the room.

"I wish we could. But it isn't just the ward, it's the witch who puts it in place. Otherwise, anyone could ward a location." Peter avoided Stef's stricken gaze as he drank the last of the beer in a few gulps, then stared forlornly at the empty glass. "Unfortunately, ours is still a tactile practice."

"If I might say something, just as a point of information." Kaster walked to the clinic coffeemaker and filled a glass beaker with hours-old coffee, the biting smell of which fought the pungent aromas of the warding concoction to a draw. "Fernanda has the support of the children's father, and he is stronger than all of us together. I believe she held back last night because Nyssa was present and she didn't want to scare her. This time, she won't be so kind."

"You call what she did holding back?" Carmody looked down at his arms, which had improved in appearance but still looked as though golf balls had been implanted beneath the splotched skin.

"The research performed at Jericho opened a passage to the netherworld and access to the powers contained there. But passages work in both directions, and what has lived in the dark since the dawn of time now wants out." Kaster glanced at Lauren, then away. "I kept trying to tell you, Andrew, but you never listened. You really have no idea what your father unleashed, do you?"

Carmody's chin came up. "And you encouraged him."

"I counseled Steven in the direction he would have gone any-

ALEX GORDON

way. I urged caution. Unfortunately, delving into the unknown didn't scare him."

"Neither did other people's pain." That from Jenny, who kept her eyes fixed on her book.

Lauren took the ibuprofen bottle that Carmody handed her and shook out a couple of tablets. *Four hours of pain relief.* She wondered where they would all be in four hours.

"We still need to decide who pronounces the ward." Peter stared down at the piece of notebook paper on which he had written the spell. "It's complicated and tricky, so we need some-one who has the experience to administer magic of this mag-nitude."

"I will." Kaster shrugged off Peter's look of surprise. "You said it yourself, Peter. It isn't just the ward, it's the witch who puts it in place. No one here is stronger than I am."

"Are you sure about this, Gene?" Carmody sounded skeptical.

"Of course not." Kaster smiled, and for a moment the air of the confident roué reasserted itself. Then it faded. "I believe we've all learned enough from this exercise in hubris. It needs to end." He looked again at Lauren, this time holding her gaze until she broke away.

"We need a decoy." She spoke without thinking, then real-ized that even if she had been able to plan for weeks, she would have come to the same conclusion. "Someone to distract Fer-nanda and keep her inside the perimeter of Jericho long enough to close it." She took note of the head shakes, heard Nyssa's muttered "No oh no," and waved it all away.

"Who else are you going to send?" She pointed to Stef. "You—have a heart condition." She nodded toward Peter.

"And you two are in love anyway, so risking one or the other of you wouldn't be right." She fielded embarrassed glances from the pair, then nodded toward Carmody. "You have Nyssa to take care of, we need Gene to pronounce the ward, and none of the other Council members knows enough about what to expect." She gave the tablets a last look, then tossed them in her mouth. Chased them with water, and wished it was something stronger. "So it's me. I've done something like this before. I've gone over, and come back. I have the best shot at surviving this." She shifted in her chair, felt the twinges and aches, and hoped the ibuprofen kicked in before they left for Jericho. "Besides, Fernanda hates me so much that she won't miss the opportunity to let me have it with both barrels. I'm the perfect distraction."

Stef tapped a staccato beat on the ward map with her pencil. "But how will you be able to overpower her? She controls those . . . *things*, and then there's the pain. Peter and I felt just a fraction, and we could barely tolerate it."

Lauren pretended that this was a regular project meeting and she needed to explain how she planned to deal with a balky vendor. It was one of the little lies that kept her sane that she had started to employ at times like these. "If she suffered any physical or psychological trauma over there, or here, while she lived, I may be able to release the memory from her body. I have to get close enough to touch her, which won't be any fun. But she already believes I'm no threat, so maybe I can get her to let her guard down."

"She never spoke of any childhood accidents or dire events." Carmody shifted in his seat as all eyes focused on him. "The pain I inflicted upon her was emotional. I don't believe that applies to this particular situation."

Stef pressed a hand to her lower abdomen. "She did go through childbirth."

"That's good. That might work." Lauren sensed the looks of discomfort from the others. Even Kaster looked queasy. "What is that saying about politics? That it ain't beanbag? It ain't got nothin' on witchcraft."

TIMING. IN ORDER to provide the optimum amount of coverage, Peter determined that they needed twenty minutes to set the wards. Lauren would have to go in first, find Fernanda, and do what she could to distract her.

"Then we'll come in behind you." Peter sat hunched over his phone, inputting the map with the designated points, the spell they would utter.

Lauren cleared all the personal information from her phone. Photos. Her contacts. She wasn't sure how up-to-date the other side was when it came to tech, but in case of capture, or if she just lost the thing, she didn't want any of the demon horde getting hold of images of Katie or her other friends, or anyone back in Gideon. "Don't send any of that information to me. They may be able to figure out what's going on without any help, but why make it easy?"

"We're coming for you after we've finished." Peter pushed his phone aside, folded his hands, and leaned forward so he could speak without the others overhearing.

"Once you set the circle, you can't breach it. That's what got us into this mess in the first place."

"We'll close it on the way out."

"Too risky." Lauren stood, bent close to his ear. "I'll take care of myself." She caught his gaze, and smiled. "I'll be fine." She left before he could argue, before he could see what she knew must have shown in her eyes. That chilly light of fear, and the knowledge that she probably wouldn't get out of this alive.

She left the clinic and headed toward the elevator, on the way to her room to shower, change clothes, prepare for the fight ahead. She heard the footsteps behind her but didn't turn around. She sensed sandalwood, even though she couldn't smell it. She knew who followed.

"Are you sure that this is the only way?"

Lauren turned to find Carmody standing in the doorway. He had found the strength to shower and change clothes, but he still looked wobbly. It would take all the strength he had to complete his part of the circle. "I think you know the answer to that."

"I should be the one to go in there. She's my wife."

"Nyssa needs you."

"She needs you, too." Carmody shuffled forward. "I should feel jealous, the way she's taken to you. But all I feel is a sense of relief that she finally found someone she can talk to. Someone who understands her."

"If something happens to me . . . put out feelers. I'm sure I'm not the only one like me out there." Lauren turned away. "We have to get ready."

CHAPTER 26

The sculpture garden was at its best in the late afternoon sun, as the first dusky shadows darkened leaves to green velvet and the roses, hydrangeas, and other flowers revealed their deepest colors. Lauren wandered down the steps, soaked it all in, breathed in the sweet air. Tried to squelch the thought that it was for the last time.

T minus fifteen minutes and counting.

Kaster stepped out from behind a dogwood tree and fell in beside her. He wore jeans and a black T-shirt. Hiking boots. He carried the same day pack as everyone but Lauren, filled with herbs and oils and a small ewer for pouring the final blend. "Are you really so eager to die? You could take one of Andrew's cars and be in Portland in two hours. They would assume you had gone off somewhere private to make peace with your Lady. They wouldn't even know you'd left until you were safely away."

Lauren thought to argue, then decided there was no point.

They walked in silence, pausing to sniff flowers or examine one of the statues, each acting as though the other wasn't there. Lauren tried to ignore the first of the creature figures that they came to, but it drew her eye no matter how she tried to look away. *We are the forest.* She wondered how many would be waiting for her in Jericho. "What changed your mind? About getting involved?"

Kaster shifted the branches of a rosebush so that they hid the thing from view. "I've been here too long."

"How long?" Lauren waited. "Please? Consider it a last request."

Kaster stood quiet. Then he walked around the corner, and returned holding one of the Etruscan pieces, the deer that Heath had tried to steal. He fussed over it, brushing off dirt and scraping away a fleck of mud with his fingernail. Then he turned the piece over and pointed to the identifying mark carved into the clay.

ב

"That's your mark? You made that? With your own hand?" Lauren recalled the statue's placard. *700–600 B.C.*

Kaster nodded, eventually. Then he carried the statue back to its niche and set it down.

"Those photographs in the vestibule showing your father, your great-great however the hell many, they're all you?" Lauren waited for Kaster to answer, but he concentrated on the flowers instead, sniffing them one by one. "While we were hashing out the plan, you slipped. You said you counseled Steven Carmody. You wouldn't have been old enough. Except that you were, apparently." She felt a cool finger of evening air, another indication of time counting down, and her heart tripped. "According to the Book of Endor, the Lady roamed the world gathering followers for two thousand years. Did you know her?"

Kaster had started to walk back up to the house. He stopped, then looked back at her. "I knew her."

"But you didn't follow her?"

"Once." Kaster shrugged. "All families have disagreements. Some are more divisive than others."

"So there are other witches like you?" Lauren waited for Kaster to nod. "They're the ones you answer to." Another nod. "Will you get in trouble for helping Carmody?"

"Not as much as you." Kaster checked his watch, then looked up at the sky, the gathering evening clouds. "We need to go."

THEY ALL MET in the garage. The plan was for Lauren to leave first in one of the Jeeps, and for everyone else to follow in a trio of Rovers. Carmody had set up the most stripped-down of bars on the tailgate of one of the Rovers—bottles of whiskey and water, a soda for Nyssa, glasses. One of the Council members offered a blessing, then everyone gathered to toast their mission.

Everyone, that is, except for Kaster. He remained outside, pacing back and forth like an animal in a cage.

"Could he possibly be nervous?" Peter leaned against the tailgate. "I've known him for almost fifteen years, and I don't believe I've ever seen him on edge like this." He drank, and continued to watch Kaster over the top of his glass.

"Did you know?" Lauren took a sip of her watered whiskey, then set it aside. "Who he was? What he is?"

"Every so often, he would say something that made me won-der." Peter frowned. "We'll talk. After all this is behind us." He raised his glass, toasting the confidence that there would be a tomorrow, and that they would still be alive to see it.

Lauren looked around the garage, which was deserted but for their small group.

"Andrew sent the staff away." Stef drew alongside Peter and linked her arm through his. She had dressed in more casual clothing, khakis and a gingham shirt, and had tucked her hair beneath a brimmed hat. "He told them that there was some sort of infestation in the woods, that it was the cause of his condition."

"I never thought he'd be up and about this quickly." Peter nodded in Carmody's direction. "Looks like your poultice did the trick, Stef."

Lauren looked outside, where Kaster still paced, and bit her tongue. Felt her edginess grow. Took her pack from her shoul-der and opened it, and checked to make sure she had all the things she thought she might need. There would be no second chances, no do-overs.

It tugged at the back of her mind, the sense that she had for-gotten something. Then she remembered. She hurried through the garage and the myriad doorways, the twists and turns, to the clinic. Returning to her room, she swore loudly when she saw it had been cleaned, the bed stripped and the tables cleared. She checked the trash can next to the bed and found it empty. She crossed her fingers and checked the bathroom can, a blackened bronze cylinder with a flip-up lid that reminded her uncomfortably of the Beelzebabies, and felt a stab of relief when she found the wooden block amid the discarded cleaning rags.

She dug it out, then rooted through the shelf filled with clean linens until she found a washcloth, which she used to wrap it. Then she tucked it into her pack, her own little piece of hell.

She returned to the garage to find that not all of Carmody's staff had vacated the premises. Carmody stood by a black Suburban surrounded by three large men wearing serious expressions and varying degrees of business casual. They talked in low tones for several minutes. Then Carmody beckoned to Nyssa, who had been hovering around Stef and Peter and asking questions about everything, her nervousness expressing itself in nonstop talking and a relentless urge to move.

"You're flying to London tonight. You'll stay with your grandmother until this is over." Carmody nodded to the men, who positioned themselves behind Nyssa so that one of them would be able to block her no matter which direction she tried to bolt.

"No. I can help. I know things now." Nyssa pointed to Lauren. "She told me all sorts of stuff. Please."

"It's too dangerous."

"It's me she wants, Dad. If I'm not here, she won't hang around. She'll break through whatever you try to put up to stop her and go looking for me. You can't hide me." She paced a tight circle, then stopped and turned to Lauren. "Tell him."

Lauren looked around to find that everyone else had found something to do elsewhere. She couldn't blame them for fleeing. This was going to be an ugly scene no matter how it played out. "Can I talk to Nyssa alone, please?"

Carmody shook his head. "There's no time. Besides, she's my daughter."

"Yes, she is—that's why I'm asking you."

Carmody nodded, eventually. "One minute." He waved off the men, who retreated to the far side of the garage.

Nyssa swooped on Lauren as soon as they stepped outside. "You have to tell him that you need me, and that I can stay."

Lauren looked out toward the woods. Every breath she took smelled clean. She saw birds and squirrels and heard the whisper of leaves in the breeze and it all looked so normal. So safe. "He's doing it for your own good."

"Oh, please."

"What we're trying to do—it's dangerous. It's no place for you."

"It's no place for you, either." Nyssa's hands had taken on a life of their own, pulling at her clothes, her hair. "I've heard what they're all saying when they think I'm not listening. They're scared for you. They don't think you're going to—" She wiped her face as the tears fell. "And it's me she wants. She'll know I'm not around here and she will take it out on you and how am I supposed to live knowing that?"

"It's our responsibility. Me. Your father. Peter and Stef. Kaster. We're the grown-ups. We were supposed to know better. We were supposed to keep you safe. There are some things that you shouldn't have to face now and this is definitely one of them."

"No. No." Nyssa shook her head so hard that her neck crackled. "Everything I've learned from you, it's like, I had to open my eyes and see what was in front of them, and accept what I could do. So you teach me that, but then it's like, forget it. You don't give me credit for knowing what's in front of my eyes."

ALEX GORDON

"I give you credit for knowing a lot. But I'll be damned if I'll let you pay the price for any of this."

"You're wrong. You're wrong and you're stupid and you're the one who's going to pay the price for all of it."

"Better me than you." Lauren stood aside as the men came and herded Nyssa to the Suburban. She closed her ears to the cries and accusations because they cut to the heart and because some of them were true. *Maybe I taught you a lot. Maybe I taught you too much. But there are limits.* The sins of this father, this grandfather, would not be visited upon a child.

Carmody was waiting for her when she reentered the garage. "Thank you."

Lauren nodded as she watched the Suburban pull away. Saw the face in the rear window, hands pressed to the glass. Knew that Carmody had made the best decision possible under the circumstances, and that it still might not matter.

CHAPTER 27

They departed soon after in their four-vehicle caravan, Lauren leading the way in the Jeep. Peter had offered to ride shotgun with her so she wouldn't have to make the journey alone, but she turned him down. She was in no mood to attempt small talk or discuss strategy, and even the pressure of the man's silence would have been too much to bear.

She parked in the designated spot, a quarter-mile away from Jericho. She got out and started down the trail toward the settlement, and kept walking even when she heard the other vehicles rumble up from behind.

When she heard the yelling, however, she stopped.

"Don't tell me that." Carmody's voice boomed out every time someone opened a door of his vehicle. "You find her and you hold on to her and you do not let her out of your sight." He pounded the steering wheel with the flat of his hand. "No, what I want to know is how three grown men lost a fifteen-year-old girl in the middle of a half-empty—"

"Somebody tell him to keep his voice down." Lauren walked up behind Peter. "What happened?"

"Need you ask?" Peter sported the narrow-eyed glower of a man with an incipient migraine. "Nyssa escaped her handlers."

"Is she on her way back here?"

"Do you have any doubt?"

"We will be finished by the time she gets here." Stef stood with clasped hands, looking like a little old gardener at prayer. "She's on foot, after all." The woman looked up at Lauren, then reached out and squeezed her arm. "Lady keep you."

"Thank you. You, too." Lauren swallowed hard. Wasn't it funny, how one single, quiet gesture could shake you to your core when all manner of madness went right over your head?

The shouting finally ended. Carmody exited the Rover, his face red, his movements quick and compact, anger overwhelming whatever aches he still felt from the previous night's assault. "Let's go." He headed up the trail. "Gene—stay with me. Pete, Stef—lead the others." His eyes met Lauren's, and he slowed. "Your turn."

Lauren nodded. "See you in a few minutes." She broke into a trot and passed him, her chest tightening as she looked up the trail and spotted the bend that overlooked Jericho. Felt a tingle along her spine, and turned back to find Kaster standing in the tall grass, watching her. He raised his right hand and twitched his fingers, a gesture or sigil that she hoped like hell was the ancient equivalent of *good luck*.

THE MUTED LIGHT of dusk had settled over Jericho by the time Lauren arrived at the gate. She sniffed the air, wondered if it was her imagination or if she indeed smelled the barest hint of elder.

It's starting. She dug the wooden block out of her pack, unwrapped it, gripped it tightly for a moment, then shoved it in her pocket. *Whatever happens, let it be quick.* She headed down the slope and wondered if anything watched her from the other doorways and windows. *She knows I'm coming.* Of course she did. *Mother of the forest.*

Lauren stopped and stood in the middle of the grassy central yard and did a slow 360, just to make sure. *All eyes on me.* Never mind the smell, or the sounds of those other witches in the weeds. *I'm the one you want, Fernanda.*

The door of the main building opened as easily as it had before, as though operated by some invisible attendant. She rummaged through her kit for a screwdriver, then knelt on the floor and hunted for the telltale ridge that marked the doorway to the lower level. Probed and prodded until she found the catch, shoved the screwdriver home—

—and froze when she heard the front door open, the soft creak of footsteps on old wood plank.

I didn't think she'd meet me in the open. Lauren stood, raised her hands in the air like a thief caught red-handed. She turned slowly toward the door, then stopped when she saw Jenny standing in the entry.

Jenny held her day pack the same way she had held her book of magic, before her like a shield, a defense against the madness that surrounded her. She sidled into the room, closed the door behind her. "So this is where the big bad wolf lives."

Lauren struggled to keep her voice down. "How the hell did you get here?"

"I hid in the back of your Jeep. There was a blanket back there. I covered up."

"Okay. So what the hell are you doing here?"

"There's something I have to do."

"What?"

"Never mind, just—"

"Dammit, Jen." Lauren slipped the screwdriver out of the seam and let the panel close. "Is this about your grandfather?"

"Just leave me be, okay? This has nothing to do with you."

"Did it ever occur to you that you could be screwing the rest of us right into the ground?"

"I'm just adding to the chaos. They won't know who to attack first."

"So they'll just wipe out all of us."

"Let me do this, Lauren. Leave me alone and let me do it. I don't need a hand-holder. I'm not Nyssa, okay?"

Lauren took a closer look at Jenny's day pack, and the bundle of what appeared to be twigs sticking out of the top. "What did you do?"

"There are fifteen spells that use rose thorns. I found the one I needed."

Lauren looked the woman in the eye and held her gaze until she realized that Jenny would rather drop dead on the spot than look away first. "I just wish you'd have told me." She knelt back on the floor, jammed the screwdriver back into place, and popped the latch.

"You'd have tried to talk me out of it." Jenny hurried to the other side of the portal as it raised, and helped lock it into place. "I don't know what the hell I'm doing. I just know that I have to do it."

Lauren managed a smile. "That's the answer to the first question on the test."

"Is it?"

"So far, you're passing with flying colors. We'll make a witch out of you yet."

"I can't wait." Jenny set her foot on the top step, then looked up at Lauren. "Who goes first?"

"I think I better." Lauren took a deep breath, then headed down.

The lights fizzled on as soon as Lauren set her foot on the floor. Jenny followed hard on her heels, then stopped and looked around.

"Do you think there are ghosts here? Of all the people who died?"

"I don't think it worked that way for them." Lauren sniffed the stale air, on the alert for the first hint of rot. "I think maybe they were sent somewhere humans don't usually go, or—"

"Or?"

"Or nothing survived the testing."

They headed down the long corridor that Lauren had walked with Nyssa the previous day. Jenny stopped in front of the menu board, then stood on tiptoe and pressed a finger to her grandfather's name before moving on. The examination room seemed just as bleak, just as still, the tumbled furniture and dried smears on the window glass the only signs that something out of the ordinary had occurred.

"I'd like to find his office." Jenny checked the room numbers as they continued down the corridor. "Just to see what it looked like."

Lauren pulled out her phone, checked the time. Ten minutes gone. She would have expected Fernanda to meet her by now. "I have to keep going."

"I get it. I understand." Jenny started to walk in the opposite direction. Then she stopped. "Lauren?"

Lauren turned.

Elliot Rickard looked a little worse for wear than he had the previous day. His lab coat was still spattered with whatever had dripped after Lauren had slashed him, while his injured arm hung limply at his side.

"It's you." He frowned at her, then glanced at his clipboard. "Someone is waiting for you. She will call for you shortly." He turned his attention to Jenny. "You're not on—the—list." His eyes narrowed, then widened. "I know—your face. I know—" He took a step forward. Another. "Linda?"

"No, that was Gramma." Jenny's voice shook. "I'm Lizzybet's daughter."

"Lizzybet?" Rickard nodded. "That's my daughter's name. Elizabeth. Her little cousin couldn't pronounce it properly when he was little, and it became her nickname."

"I'm her daughter, Jennifer." Jenny's voice steadied, grew chill. "I'm your granddaughter."

Rickard blinked as through dazed. "How is my Linda?"

"She—" Jenny stopped. Breathed. "She's gone. Earlier this year." She walked to the thing that had once been a man until he let another man take it all away. "You did it, didn't you? You reached her somehow through the mirror and she saw you and you were the last thing she ever wanted to see. So she killed herself so she wouldn't see you anymore." She paused, wiped her eyes with the back of her hand. "She knew, didn't she? She found out what you did. What you were."

Rickard looked down at his clipboard. At the floor. "I haven't seen her in so long."

"Did she know?"

"I want to see her."

"Did she know?"

"Jen?" Lauren whispered, and hoped that Jenny heard. "Sometimes you never learn the truth." Maybe the woman heard her. Or maybe she was so angry that the answer didn't matter anymore.

"Grampa?" Jenny pulled her pack around so that she could reach the zipper. "You have to stop this. This isn't right. You're hurting people."

Rickard drew up straight. "But we have to learn, dear girl. Learning is important. Building the pathway. Opening the door."

"You can't open this door. No one learns like this. They just hurt, and then they die, and it's wrong."

"Knowledge is important. We have to learn all we can—" Rickard stopped, shook his head. "I want to see Linda."

"I can take you to the place where you can see her." Jenny slipped the twig bundle out of her pack. "Hold on to this, Grampa." She held out the bundle of thorns, which she'd wrapped in a rag so that she could hold them easily. "Take hold of it, and I'll take you to see Gramma."

Rickard shook his head. "I don't understand—"

"Just do as I say." Jenny smiled. "Please."

The tainted remains of the man named Elliott Rickard hesitated. Then he reached out and took hold of the thorns.

"And now I'll sing the song you two always loved. From *Twelfth Night*, remember, the song that Gramma made up to go with the words?" Jenny sang, the quiver returned to her voice. "*O Mistress mine, where are you roaming? O stay and hear, your true-love's waiting, that can sing both high and low; trip no further, pretty sweeting, journeys end in lovers' meeting, every wise man's daughter doth know.*"

As she sang, Rickard rocked to and fro, a strange rumble emerging from his throat that Lauren realized was him trying to sing along. It rose in pitch and volume to a humming that vibrated in her head and set her teeth on edge.

As Rickard continued to hum, Jenny shook off his hand from the bundle of thorns. "This journey's over, Grampa. No more meeting." Then she raised the bundle, brought them down like a dagger, and stabbed him in the ribs.

Rickard screamed as his chest stove in and the gray mess that animated him spewed forth, splashing across Jenny, the walls, the floor. He collapsed to his knees, stared up at Jenny with eyes gone round with shock and fear. Then he slumped forward and crumpled like a wad of paper set afire, his skin blackening and his body curling in on itself, until nothing remained but a pile of greasy ash from which streamed a thin line of noxious smoke.

Jenny stumbled against the far wall and vomited, then made frantic swipes at her face and arms, trying to wipe off Rickard's effluent. Lauren rooted a rag out of her pack, then hurried over to her.

"Will this kill me? Will this hurt me?" Jenny grabbed the rag and wiped her mouth, her eyes. "It smells so bad—am I going to die?"

"Just don't swallow it." Lauren dug out a bottle of water and handed it to her. "Rinse and spit."

Jenny flushed out her mouth, then used the rest of the water to wash her face. "Is it in my hair?"

"Yes. Just wipe it as best you can." Lauren looked up and down the corridor. Fernanda must have heard Rickard's howl, but so far there was no sign of her or any of her little charges. *Maybe she doesn't give a damn about Rickard*. Or maybe she had seen through their ploy and had already attacked Carmody and the others.

"This stuff burns." Jenny rolled up her sleeves so that places where the gray mess had soaked through wouldn't touch her skin.

Lauren examined Rickard's remains, which had started to solidify, or clot, or whatever the proper term was. "That wasn't a nice spell, was it?"

Jenny concentrated on wiping away the mess. "It did what it had to."

"Did it?" Lauren sniffed the air, but it was still so ripe with the stink of Rickard's decay that she couldn't have smelled one of the forest creatures if it stood right in front of her. "You need to get out now."

Jenny kicked the sodden, filthy rag down the corridor. "I'll stay with you."

"No. You need to get out."

"Why?"

"Weren't you listening back at the house? Because they're

going to enclose Jericho in wards so strong that nothing can get in or out."

"So what the hell are you doing here?"

Lauren lowered her voice. "I'm going to distract Fernanda so that they can set the wards. Now get out of here."

"But then you—you're committing suicide. Why?"

"I'll manage."

"How? No—"

"Get out now." Lauren grabbed Jenny by the elbow and steered her down the corridor toward the steps. "Get out to the trail and look for them. Stay with them. Whatever happens here, don't come back."

"It's not right." Jenny struggled in Lauren's grip, tried to break away. "You don't have to die for me."

"I'm not doing it for you or for anyone else here." Lauren pushed Jenny halfway up the staircase, then climbed after her and herded her the rest of the way. "I'm doing it because this place needs to burn." She prodded Jenny through the opening onto the floor above, then ducked out of her way when she tried to grab her and pull her along.

Jenny glared through the opening. "Damn you."

"Get in line." Lauren stayed out of reach as Jenny struggled to her feet, waited until she saw the woman bolt out the door, then backed down the stairway. Sensed movement out of the corner of her eye.

Turned, and found one of the Beelzebabies standing at the mouth of the corridor.

CHAPTER 28

*B*eelzebaby. Too cute, that name, too harmless-sounding for this thing that looked up at her now. Its bulbous black eyes lacked lids—the edges of the orbs had darkened to light tan and looked dried and cracked, like an old piece of cheese. The mossy substance that covered its body seemed to have a life of its own, color altering between light and dark as it emitted a thrumming sound. Like bees in a hive.

The thing tottered toward Lauren, and she backed up until she bumped into the staircase. She stopped, turned, and found another creature standing at the mouth of the next corridor, blocking her retreat.

What will they do if I run? Visions of Carmody vanishing beneath a pulsing mass of the things replayed in her head. *And Kaster isn't here to save me.* She sidestepped around the staircase, pressed one hand to the wall, and felt . . . vibration, as though a generator or other machinery lay behind it. *It's powering the lights.* Did it also keep the place warm, ventilated? Did it keep these things alive?

Was there a way to turn it off? She ran her hands over the surface, which felt rough to the touch even though it appeared smooth to the eye.

"Have you brought my daughter to me?"

Lauren looked back over her shoulder, and saw Fernanda Carmody standing next to the first creature. Her hand rested atop its head, ruffling the spiky black tuft of whatever grew there. She appeared older now than she had at the house, even older than she would have looked if she still lived. Hair streaked with gray as well as tangled with leaves and twigs, skin blotched and lined, eyes sunken. Her dress had darkened to brown with filth and damp, and clung to her bony frame.

"No." Lauren paused to swallow as the smell hit her, poured into her nose and down her throat thick as liquid. No clean forest scents, no, this was charnel rot, the stink of graves. "I've come here to make sure that you don't get your hands on her."

"Ah." Fernanda smiled, showing teeth as brown as her dress. "Do you love my husband, Lauren?"

Lauren shook her head. "No."

"That much we have in common." Fernanda chuckled, a wet sound like a loose cough. "Did he hire you to do this?"

"No. I wanted to help."

"So you are doing this without pay." Fernanda bent close to the creature's ear hole. "See how blessed my husband is, that he can find people like her to clean up his messes. To die for him."

"This isn't about him. It isn't about whatever happened between you. This is about Nyssa." Lauren gestured around. "It's about this place."

"What about this place?"

"It needs to burn."

"You came here to destroy my home?" Fernanda's gaze settled on the blackened puddle. "Is that Elliott?"

"Yes." Lauren reached into her pocket and pulled out the wooden block. "That's what will happen to you."

"You think so?" Fernanda shrugged. "He was just a worker. We have many workers." She turned back to Lauren. "But there is only one mother. Only one queen."

"And as the queen goes, so goes the hive." Lauren covered the distance to Fernanda in three steps, grabbed hold of her, and pushed her against the wall.

Fernanda fought Lauren's hold, raked her nails along her arms, tore the cloth of her shirt, and left stinging trails in her skin. Kicked and punched. Grabbed handfuls of her hair, and pulled.

Lauren's leg burned. She looked down to find one of the creatures wrapped around her calf, mouth pressed to her knee. Another tottered to her other leg, grabbed and held on and bit and chewed and the heat moved under her skin, into her veins, coursed upward toward her heart. She focused on that agony, held it close, and sent it into the piece of wood that she held.

Fernanda howled. Her cries brought more creatures—they skittered across the floor and crawled along the walls and ceiling, climbed over their siblings and up Lauren's body, rode her back and squeezed her neck with mossy arms, scratched with claws like needles along her face. Reached for her eyes.

More pain, like fire where her heart had been. Lauren sent it into the block. Every slash, every stab and drop of blood. Shook off one creature that held on to her arm, elbowed another.

Then one of the creatures on her back toppled off. The shift in weight freed her arms. She pushed forward, shoved the block between Fernanda's teeth, and commanded all the agony and fear that it contained to come forth. The corridor darkened, the lights fizzing and flickering.

Fernanda screamed again and again.

Then Lauren joined her as the pain looped between them, the anguish building with every circuit from one to the other.

Then came the bolt of light, the screams of the tortured dead.

Recoil. It hurled Lauren against the wall, sent the creatures that had attacked her tumbling like dice in all directions. Some scurried along the floor, the walls, and ceiling, stopped, toppled, twitched, and grew still. Others fell to the floor shuddering, legs kicking, the humming noise they emitted rising and falling in tone and pitch.

Lauren pushed herself into a sitting position. Her pants legs were torn, piebald with blood. One leg felt numb—she tried to bend it, and the muscles shuddered with cramp.

Then she looked down at her hand. It rested on the floor, the floor that felt soft and cold and damp. She pushed her fingers through the concrete, dug into it, brought up dirt and root and small stones.

"You will never leave here." Fernanda slumped against the opposite wall. Her dress had torn and blood black as pitch dripped from cuts on her face, her arms, and legs. "So much work to be done. So much testing. And the ones who will work on you—they are not as nice as Elliott was. And I will watch and I will laugh and every scream will be music to me." She pushed to her feet.

Lauren braced with her good leg and stood, leaned against the wall for support. *Not much longer.* Kaster and the others should have been able to set the wards by now. *Or they're dead.* And if that proved the case? *Go down fighting.* "I can do this all day."

"But what will you do tomorrow, and the next day, and the next?" Fernanda wiped whatever flowed from her mouth with the back of her hand and staggered toward Lauren, her remaining charges massing behind her. "You think if you keep fighting, you will die, but I won't let you. Their father won't let you. You will live until the sun burns to a cinder and your body will feed us all and your pain will be like wine—" She sprang.

Childbirth. Lauren kept her hands low, gripped Fernanda by the hips even as the woman reached for her face. *Memory of pain, come forth.*

Fernanda's hands slid down Lauren's cheeks to her shoulders as her back stiffened and her hips bucked and something milky flowed from her eyes. She staggered back again, then fell to one knee as around her, the walls rippled and darkened and roots poked through and worms emerged and fell writhing to the floor.

She doesn't breathe. Lauren listened for any sound of gasping or struggle, but Fernanda simply pressed against the wall, then rose to her feet. *If she doesn't breathe she's already dead and you can't kill what's already dead.* Her thoughts ran together in a single stream and she knew that the creatures' venom had started to slow her, poison her, kill her.

Fernanda started toward her again. Then she stopped.

Lauren heard the sound of footsteps coming down the staircase. Knew who it was before she turned to look and even if she couldn't have guessed, the expression of triumph on Fernanda's face would have told her.

Still, she turned, and she looked.

Nyssa stared down at her, eyes widening as she took in the blood and other damage. "I told you that you should've let me do this."

"Darling." Fernanda held out her hand. "You've come to me."

Nyssa's hand tightened on the railing. "I really don't want to."

"Of course you do." Fernanda laughed, a sound not quite human. "You always used to say that. The first word you ever said was 'no.'"

"Nyssa?" Lauren tried to stand, staggered, gripped one of the stairs, and worked upright. "This place isn't what it looks like. It's a warren. It's a pit. It's dirt and cold and damp. It's not a place for you. You'll die here."

Nyssa descended the last step. "I'm broken. You know I am. I told you. If I stay in this world, I'll always be like this. Over in her world, I'm not. Over there, it's quiet and I can think, and if I can think, I can fight. Can't you understand that?"

"Of course I can." Lauren tried to nod, but stopped when the stars flashed before her eyes. "But you can learn to cope here, too. I could teach you."

"Darling?" Fernanda's voice bit. "Why are you talking to her? You should be talking to me."

"Shut up!" Nyssa's voice sounded muffled, deadened by the dirt that surrounded them. "I'm talking to my friend and you can just shut up." She turned back to Lauren. "No, you wouldn't be able to teach me anything because you came here knowing you weren't coming back." She touched Lauren's hand. "It's the one thing I can do to help. I've never been able to help anyone ever. But I can do this one thing that no one else can. All the awfulness my family did, I can make right." Her eyes brimmed. "Please."

"I don't know what you'll find over there." Lauren's voice cracked.

"It has to be better than what I've got here."

"Not necessarily."

"Can you let me be the judge of that?"

"This isn't a trial run. You go with her and you will become something else and you may not like what that is."

"I've been that person my whole life." Nyssa looked at Lauren with eyes infinitely old, infinitely kind. "Let me go." Without waiting for an answer, she turned to the thing that had been her mother. "You brought me here when I was little and you gave me to them. I don't want to go to your world, but I don't have a choice, do I? You broke me for this one."

"You belong with me, not with the men who would destroy us both." For the first time, Fernanda seemed shaken, subdued. Human. "I talked with your grandfather so much. He told me about this place. About what happened here. Your father knew, and he didn't care. I knew, and I cared. I did what was best for you, darling."

"Sure you did." The fear, the shakiness, fell away from Nyssa like a shed skin. She looked back again at Lauren. "Tell Dad I'm sorry. Tell him I know he tried." She took one step toward her mother, then another, as the creatures crowded around her and stroked her and thrummed. "You don't want me here because you love me—"

"Yes, I do, darling, so much—"

"—but because you hate him. There's a difference." Nyssa gestured toward Lauren. "Do you remember how she stopped you?"

"She never stopped me, Nyssa."

"She took all the pain in a block of wood and put it on you, pain you didn't even have anything to do with." Nyssa held up her hand. "What about the hurt you did make? What about everything that's happened to me? Every overdose. Every nightmare. Every second of the never-ending hell inside my head. What would happen if I gave it all back to you?"

Fernanda took a step back. "Darling—"

Nyssa sprang forward. She stood taller than Fernanda and possessed the strength of the living, the drive and desperation and anger. She pushed the thing that had been her mother back, pummeled her with her fists, down the corridor until they fell into the spreading dark. The creatures leapt about, back and forth, unsure whether to attack because this female was of mother and therefore was mother. Mother attacking mother.

Lauren felt it all through the floor, the walls. The air rippled, eddies forming and fading, as the lights flared, then flashed off. Pitch dark now, but for the thin light through the hole in the ceiling. A doorway no longer, but a hole carved from dirt and strung with roots and the remains of dead things.

She looked down the corridor, squinted into the dark. Detected movement of some sort, along the floor, the walls and ceiling. Rippling, buzzing, getting closer.

You better run, Lauren. Nyssa's voice, rattling through her brain. *Now.*

Lauren felt the ground beneath her feet shudder as a scream rent the thick, stinking air. The cry of an animal in pain as limbs shattered and tore away. The cry of a woman who finally got what she asked for, and realized too late what that meant.

The air boiled.

Lauren struggled up the rusted, filthy staircase. Dragged herself out of the hole, then shambled through the building and out into the night on legs gone stiff and numb. She could hear them from behind, the creatures that still lived, felt their confusion and their rage and their fear.

No mother. Need mother.

Find mother.

Lauren stumbled and fell. She looked back and saw the flames lick and tumble out of the building, burning creatures spewing forth like sparks, smoke billowing. She tried to get up, but this time her legs refused to obey. The numbness had moved past her waist. She fought to pull air into her lungs and lost the battle.

She lay her head in the cool grass. Closed her eyes. Waited for the fire.

Mistress?

Lauren stirred as the voice filled her head.

Can you hear me? Please say you can hear me.

She tried to move her jaw to speak, but the words wouldn't come. So she thought them instead. *I can hear you.* As soon as they formed and faded, she felt herself floating, drifting, twisting through the air, as though she were a kite being reeled in. *Did it work? The ward?*

Of course it did. A sensation of injury, surprise. *I am quite good, you know.*

Lauren knew when she passed through the ward, like a rake of static over her face, her arms. Flexed her toes as the numbness subsided and feeling returned to her legs, the pained tingling of awakening nerves.

A favor, Mistress? If someone should ask about me, tell them you didn't see me here. A beat of silence. *Better yet, tell them you never saw me at all.* Then came a blare of sound—shouts and cries, the pound of running feet.

Rocks poked Lauren though her shirt. She opened her eyes, raised her head, squinted into the gloom, and saw Jenny run off the trail and pelt down the slope toward her.

"We need to get out of here." Jenny grabbed a fistful of Lauren's shirt and dragged her to her feet as behind them, buildings exploded and flames raced toward them.

They met others along the way—Stef, and Peter and other members of the Council—and ran toward the vehicles. Then Peter slid to a stop.

"Stef?" He whirled around. "Where—?" He cried *"No"* and sprinted back down the trail.

Lauren looked over her shoulder to find Stef collapsed and Peter kneeling at her side. She shook out of Jenny's grip, left her swearing, and hobbled back up the trail

"Leave me." Stef worked into a sitting position. "I can slow the fire down."

"*No.*" Peter tried to pull her to her feet. "I'll carry you. I'll carry you."

"You'll carry a corpse. To what purpose? Let me do what I can here, now." Stef pressed a hand over her heart, then touched his face. Raised her voice as the fire roared ever closer. "We all pay for our sins in the end." Her gaze moved to Lauren. "I'm sorry." She pulled away from Peter and turned to face the flames just as they licked out and caught her, held her and consumed her. Then they flashed and faded and shuddered back, black smoke billowing, as though they had been doused by a deluge.

Lauren pulled Peter along, and together they barreled down the trail and into the waiting Jeep. Before they could settle into the seats, Jenny hit the gas and sped down the trail as behind them evergreens exploded, the force sending fireballs shooting through the air like bombs.

Lauren held on to the seat with both hands as the Jeep bumped and jostled and exhaustion struck like a punch in the gut. She slumped forward, heard Jenny shout. Felt arms wrap around from behind.

Then came Peter's voice in her ear, telling her to hang on. It started strong, but then faded to a whisper and finally to nothing as the darkness claimed her.

LAUREN OPENED HER eyes, then squinched them shut as light stabbed, drew tears, made her sneeze. She waited a few moments, then tried again.

She still sat in the front passenger seat of the Jeep. Jenny and Peter had buckled her in, covered her with a striped beach towel in lieu of a blanket, and left a bottle of water and a candy bar on her lap along with a note.

Decided to let you sleep—we're inside the diner. Jen.

Noise gradually seeped in. Voices. The roar of engines and the *whap-whap* of helicopters. Lauren uncapped the water and took a long swig, then looked around. *Parking lot. Truck stop.* Pickups and fire engines. Network news vans.

And, in the distance, a burning mountain, smoke boiling upward like the belch from a volcano.

She undid her seat belt and slid out of the Jeep, then held on and waited for her legs to adjust. The right one still felt numb. Hand-size patches of dried blood stained her pants, her shirt was torn, and she smelled as though she had been dragged through a pile of burning garbage.

She looked toward the diner and saw someone wave at her through the window. Jen, holding up a cup of coffee and motioning for her to join them.

Lauren pointed to her shirt, then held her nose. Rummaged for the candy bar, unwrapped it, and dispatched it with a few bites. Tried not to think about the past night, or how it had ended.

As she continued to watch the organized uproar, a white stretch limousine drifted into the adjacent space. The windows of the passenger section had been tinted black, making it impossible to see whether anyone sat inside.

Then one of the rear windows lowered.

"Excuse us." A young man stuck his head out. "We are looking for someone. We fear that he was on the mountain." His voice lilted, the accents on the wrong syllables. Whatever his first language had been, it wasn't English. "Eugene Kas—" He frowned, blinked. "Kaster." A broad smile revealed perfect white teeth. "Have you seen him?"

Lauren looked past the man to the person who sat next to him. A woman. An intimidating blonde, tall and expensively dressed in a black business suit.

"Excuse us." The young man waved in Lauren's face. "Have you seen him? Was he on the mountain?"

Lauren smiled. "I haven't seen him." Not for several hours, anyway.

"But he was on the mountain?"

"He may have been. There were so many people there. A conference at the Carmody compound." Lauren shrugged. "I'm sorry." She bent as low as she could, and looked past the man to the blonde. "Do you have a photograph? I'm not even sure if I know who he is."

The woman stared back, jewel-green eyes as unblinking as a snake's. She placed a hand on the man's shoulder and he settled back in his seat. The window whispered closed and the limousine drove off.

Lauren watched it turn back onto the road and vanish around a bend. *Heads up, Gene.* She wondered where he was now, and if he would be able to run far enough, hide well enough.

Then she looked around the parking lot, in search of the last person in the world she ever wanted to see.

She found Carmody seated on the tailgate of a battered pickup, his pack and a half-empty water bottle by his side. She waited for him to look at her, then realized that he never would. "It finally hit me, why you never called in the Council before to shut Jericho down. You wanted the knowledge that was trapped there. But you couldn't tap into it as long as Fernanda was up there waiting for you, and you couldn't shut her down without breaking the connection and losing it all. What were you going to do with it? Sell it to the feds? Personal use?"

Carmody took a bandanna from his pocket, and wiped sweat and grime from his face. "My daughter's up there now, burning, isn't she?"

Lauren hesitated. However much she disliked this man, she didn't want to break the news to him. "She wanted me to tell you that she's sorry. She knows you tried, but—"

"It was supposed to be you." Carmody's voice shook. "She's supposed to be alive now, not you. You are supposed to be up there." He jerked his chin toward the flaming mountain. "That was the plan."

Lauren shivered despite the heat.

"I read the Gideon report. You were ready to die, to save people you barely knew. Strangers. You would've died, if Connie Petersbury hadn't saved you. You take the bullets—that's your nature." Carmody flexed his hand, made a fist. "You were supposed to take hers."

Lauren racked her brain for a response, but what do you say to someone who just informed you that they planned your death? She turned, and started back to the Jeep.

"This doesn't end here."

Lauren looked back over her shoulder in time to see Carmody slide off the tailgate and disappear into the crowd.

ALEX GORDON

366

CHAPTER 29

The fire burned for three days, destroying Jericho, the Carmody compound, laying waste to the mountain. Experts couldn't determine why the flames didn't spread despite the dry conditions and the prevailing winds. Luck, they said.

Magic.

CHAPTER 30

Portland, Oregon
Three Weeks Later

Lauren paused on the sidewalk in front of the midcentury building and leaned against a lamppost to catch her breath. She had spent a week in the hospital after the fire. Peter snuck in poultices made according to Stef's recipe while the doctors consulted botanists and entomologists and tried to figure out what in hell had caused her injuries. When she felt strong enough, she signed herself out, leaving them none the wiser. Some truths you just had to keep to yourself.

She took the stone stairs one slow step at a time, hampered by a residual limp that waxed and waned with her energy levels. The building was a four-story space that had served as a start-up incubator during the dot-com boom and still bore a stylized atom etched in the glass over the entry door.

"We should get rid of it, I guess." Peter met Lauren in the lobby, which was lined with glass-walled meeting rooms and centered with a polished maple reception desk. "But I like the incongruity." He led her into the first of the building's two small elevators, which bore old-fashioned dial floor indicators. "Stef did, too."

"You mean, science versus what we do?" Lauren felt a jolt of irritation. "I'd like to think there's a link in there somewhere."

"When you find it, let some of my former colleagues know." Peter hit the button for the basement floor, and offered the weak smile of a man who had received a few too many wizard hats for Christmas.

"Are you going to be able to keep this place without Carmody's assistance?" Lauren held on to the handrail as the car jostled downward.

"I think so." Peter leaned against the polished metal wall. "We're looking into alternate income streams."

"Such as?"

"You would be surprised at who's been contacting us since word got out that we're no longer affiliated with Andrew. That man has more enemies than he realizes."

The car rattled to a stop, and they stepped out into a narrow, door-lined corridor made bright by two parallel tracks of fluorescent bulbs. The chalky green walls reminded Lauren of the Jericho site, and she fought the feeling that if she turned around, she would see one of the forest children standing there, watching her. She forced herself to look back over her shoulder, confirmed that nothing was there, wondered if the time would ever come when she would stop looking. "You really keep your office down here?"

"I like it." Peter pulled out a set of keys from his pocket. "It's quiet, and lack of windows means fewer distractions." He stopped in front of an unmarked steel door, unlocked it, then stood still with his hand on the knob. "I decided that I could do with a little less scenery for a while." He stared down at the floor for a moment, then opened the door.

Lauren followed him inside what proved to be a large, well-furnished space complete with a small library and a separate meeting room equipped for videoconferencing.

"I tried to schedule for a little later in the day, but she was insistent. I guess time and horses wait for no Mistress of Gideon." Peter led Lauren into the room, then went about setting things up.

"Can you give me a hint what you're thinking?" Lauren rolled a chair in front of the video screen, then grabbed a cup of coffee from the carafe on the side table.

"No, I'm going to be mean and keep things close to my vest for a bit longer." Peter booted up the system, then punched in a phone number.

Lauren sat in her chair, coffee in hand, and watched the screen change from white to blue standby.

Then the display lightened, and a familiar face flickered into view.

"Well, look at that." Virginia sat at the desk in her tiny office, her gray cap of waves and light blue shirt bright against the wood-paneled wall, the plank shelves. "I can see you like I'm looking through a window." She fiddled with a sheet of paper. "Brittany set this thing up, wrote out the directions telling me which keys to press and which to leave be. Glad somebody here understands this stuff." She studied the sheet for a moment, then set it aside.

"How do you like your present, Mistress?" Peter stepped out of range of the camera long enough to grin at Lauren.

"Back when I was a girl, if you wanted someone to write you a letter, you gave them a box of stationery, which is pretty much what this thing is, only it's easier to erase your mistakes, and that's all I'm going to say about that, Peter Augustin." Virginia tucked an errant curl behind her ear. "At least with paper and pen, it doesn't matter what your hair looks like." Her blue gaze settled on Lauren. "Morning."

"Mistress." Lauren bobbed her head.

"You look . . ." Virginia stopped, then chewed her lower lip for a few moments. "I read Peter's report. So, the Carmody family was guided by some ancient witch. Peter thinks other rich families have sponsors, too. Teaching them magic we don't know. Shepherding them through life." She arched a brow. "All that stuff I've been reading in the newspaper makes sense now."

Lauren laughed. "It does explain a lot, doesn't it?" She straightened her left leg, which still ached from the beating she took from Fernanda. "There's so much going on that we never knew."

"Well." Virginia sat stiffly, clasped hands resting atop her desk, like a schoolgirl at attention. "You can tell me all about it when you get back." She looked to the side. "Is she coming back, Peter?"

Peter stepped back within range of the camera. "I've seen her in action."

Virginia nodded. "As have I."

"So I won't waste time with any preamble. We all know that events of the last seven months have caught us flat-footed. We're looking at situations we never realized existed, and we're woefully unprepared. We need to expand our operations, and intensify our search for talented individuals who we can bring into the fold." Peter paced back and forth. His hand motions made it appear as though he were trying to thread a needle, which probably wasn't far from the truth. "I believe that while Gideon is important, it is currently in good hands." He bowed toward Virginia. "Although, if a dire situation ever again presents itself, I hope we will not have to learn about it on the evening news."

Virginia's jaw worked before she finally answered. "Understood."

"The Council is going to take a more active role in overseeing our outposts. I've learned the hard way that simply sending out forms and hoping for the best is a waste of time and paper."

Virginia sat back and folded her arms, her eyes narrowing.

"But we're also going to follow some of Lauren's recommendations with respect to your host. Support, financial and educational. Not much to start with, but we have plans to expand. We cannot let the town die."

"That sounds promising." Virginia caught Lauren's eyes, and winked.

Peter stopped in front of the screen. "I want Lauren to stay in Portland for the foreseeable future. She's shown that she can handle difficult situations and thinks well on her feet. One of our plans is to assemble a quick-response team to address situations like those that came up in Jericho and Gideon. I would like her to lead that team." He turned to Lauren. "Are you good with that?"

Lauren had to replay Peter's words in her head a few times before they finally sank in. "I have a job?"

"You have a big job." Peter's smile wavered. He cocked his head. "Do you want it?"

"Yes." Lauren nodded. "Yes, of course." She caught the relief in Peter's eyes, but also the disappointment in Virginia's. Damn videoconferencing, anyway.

"Well, glad that's settled." Someone knocked on the outer office door, and Peter gave Lauren one last look before leaving to answer it.

Virginia leaned forward and lowered her voice. "Are you all right?"

Lauren started to nod, even as nightmare images passed before her mind's eye unbidden, as they had since she fled the mountain. "Can I call you later?"

"Of course you can." Virginia picked up her instruction sheet, then folded it and shoved it under her keyboard. "But not on this thing. A real phone." She tilted her head in the direction that Peter had gone. "Is this what you want?"

"For now. Are you okay with it?"

"My life is here. What else am I going to do?"

"We're so enthusiastic."

"It's a terrible honor. Sometimes it hurts. Other times, it's the only thing that makes you feel like your life is worth a damn." Virginia made as if to say more, then checked the small clock on her desk. "I have to go. Zeke's bringing in a load of hay."

"Give him my best."

"You'll be fine."

"I know."

"Rocky won't be happy, though. He's been saving his nickels."

"Tell him to hang on to them. I'll visit as soon as I can."

"I have to go now."

"Yes, Mistress." Lauren waited for Virginia's screen to darken. Then she disconnected, turned to leave, and found Peter standing in the doorway.

"Should I have told you first? I don't want you to feel sandbagged. You can still refuse if you want to."

"No. I want the job." Lauren rubbed her hands together, tried to find the right words. "I'm sorry about Stef. I never said."

"You don't have to." Peter slumped against the jamb. "She thought she was doing the right thing. And she loved Andrew. What hurts is that she realized at the end how he used her. I will never forgive him for that." He looked to the ceiling, his roughened breathing a sign of his struggle to keep it together. "I figured it out. Nyssa's problems began around the time Stef received her diagnosis. That was when the wards started crumbling. It was all downhill after that."

Lauren tried to shut out the image of Stef's face vanishing in the flames, but knew that she would carry it with her for the rest of her days. "She was so brave, and I never got the chance to tell her."

"I think the time would have come when you would have." Peter put his arm around her shoulders, gave her a shake. "We few, we battling, argumentative few." He quieted, then pulled away. "I have another surprise for you. There's someone here who wants to see you."

CHAPTER 31

Lauren rounded the corner, followed by Peter. Through one set of double doors, then another, each hung with elder and hawthorn and spattered with something dark and pungent.

The room they entered looked as though artistically talented five-year-olds had been turned loose with a packet of crayons, every flat surface covered from baseboard to ceiling with arrows, curves, words in languages Lauren didn't recognize. Even the observation window had been papered over and inscribed. "Hebrew?" She pointed to one string of letters she thought appeared familiar.

"Aramaic." Peter pointed to other words in turn. "Also Sanskrit. Latin. Anglo-Saxon." He sighed. "Every obscuring ward and barrier we could think of, and a few we made up as we went." He shook his head. "He's afraid. I've never seen him like this. You have no idea how unsettling it is." He walked across the room to a whiteboard, ever the instructor, and plucked a marker from a tray. "He said they all chose names associated with fallen angels. His is Kasdeya. 'The Chaldean.' " He brushed an elder leaf over the surface of the board, then drew a series of Hebrew letters.

כסידיא

"The fascinating thing is that this is the variation of his name that he used for some time, Kasyade, a derivation that supposedly means 'covered hand' or 'hidden power,' which is obviously wrong. I told him that whoever suggested it did not understand consonant shift between Hebrew and Aramaic, and he said he understood consonant shifts quite well, thank you." He capped the marker, then stood back and folded his arms. "He admitted that he actually worked an incorrect derivation of his name into the research because he preferred it. 'Hidden power.' Damned appropriate, don't you think?" He turned to Lauren, eyes bright as a kid's at Christmas.

"You are such a word nerd." Lauren drew alongside him, and pointed to the "כ."

Peter nodded. "The Etruscan figures from the garden. He witnessed their making, and inscribed them with his own hands." He looked toward the observation window. "I'm boggled every time I look at him. He's so incredibly old." He sighed, shook his head, unlocked the door, and opened it. Then he stood aside, and beckoned for Lauren to go in.

Lauren hesitated. "I asked you before if you knew. You said we'd talk later. Is this later enough?"

"I don't have much to add. Stef and I had always wondered about him. We tried researching him, but of course all our leads fizzled. And now you say there's a whole passel of them out there." Peter shrugged. "We've got our work cut out for us."

LAUREN FELT THE wards as she passed through them, like walking against a strong current, or a stiff wind.

The witch she had known as Gene Kaster sat at a bare wooden table garlanded with elder boughs. His chair was wooden also, straight-backed and just as heavily laden. His clothing lacked the elegance that had marked him to that point. Baggy khakis. A white T-shirt. Sneakers.

He looked up when Lauren entered, and it was obvious that the warding interfered with his ability to control his appearance. She walked in front of him, back and forth, and watched as he altered, like one of those holographic photos that changed depending on the angle of view. Old man. Middle-aged. Young. A boy. A girl. A woman. A crone. So many aspects, like the facets of a cut gemstone. "You look tired. Are you all right?"

Kaster's neck muscles bulged as he tried to shrug. "All this protection does weigh me down. But Peter says it's for my own good. The magical equivalent of soaping the windows so no one can see in."

Lauren dragged a chair over to the other side of the table, shedding leaves along the way. She sat down. "I feel like I'm visiting you in jail."

"You are. For all it's a jail of my own choosing."

"How long will you stay?"

"Until I feel it's safe to leave." Kaster's brow knit. "It may be a while this time."

"You've interfered before." Lauren smiled. "Why am I not surprised?"

Kaster hung his head in mock shame. Then he looked at Lauren through his lashes. "Congratulations on the new job."

"Pete told you?"

"We traded intel. I made him tell me all about your job. In exchange, I showed him how to set up the videoconferencing system."

They both laughed, perhaps for too long. Because it felt good, for a change. And because it saved them having to talk about other things for a little while.

But that while passed quickly. Lauren picked up a loose elder leaf from the table and tore it into pieces. "Given your powers, none of this had to happen."

Kaster nodded. "It didn't have to, no. Steven could have decided not to build on the mountain. I advised him not to. He could have never formed his partnership with Elliott Rickard. I advised against that, too. Andrew could have torn the place down after his father died. He and I discussed it, but he always had an excuse to leave it be. Every step of the way, someone could have said 'no more.'" He sighed. "But you don't. Of all the people I've counseled through the millennia, I can count on one hand the ones who knew when to quit. It's what you are. Greedy children terrified of missing out on cake. But we love you, so we give you what you ask for. We counsel you like adults instead of leading you by the nose like caged animals. Treating you like pets. Then we hope that eventually the lessons will sink in. But they never do."

"That's a definition of insanity, you know. Doing the same thing over and over, expecting a different result."

"This insanity has its advantages."

They sat in silence for a time. Then Lauren shifted in her seat. "I still don't know if I did the right thing."

Kaster arched his brow. "Welcome to my world."

"There's a difference between a fifteen-year-old girl and a forty-year-old man."

"Not as much as you think." Kaster rocked his hand back and forth. "At least, not from my perspective."

Lauren nodded. She checked her watch, and stood. "I have to go. I have an appointment."

Kaster struck the table with his fist in mock anger. "Break it."

"I can't. I'm looking at apartments downtown. They go fast. If I see one I like, I need to apply for it immediately."

"You're staying in Portland?" Kaster's smile faded. "Be careful of Andrew. He played you every step of the way, and in the end, you still ensured the one thing he feared most. He doesn't like to lose." His voice grew hushed. "I see her, when I close my eyes."

Lauren nodded, eventually. "So do I."

More silence. Then Kaster drummed his fingers along the table's edge. "Will I see you again? I fear I'll have to leave sooner rather than later. I'm causing poor Peter no end of trouble as it is." He glanced at the papered-over window and whispered. "Besides, there's nothing to do except answer his questions. His never-ending questions."

"No blond twins to relieve the monotony."

"Oh, Mistress Mullin. I would much rather debate the nature

of good and evil with you for days on end." His eyes glittered. "May I see you again?"

"It might be risky." Lauren thought back to the cars she had seen parked near hers outside her friend Nance's house, the people she had passed on the street that morning. "I think your friends are watching me."

Kaster wrinkled his nose. "They'll take me back eventually. I'm the one who keeps them from getting bored."

Lauren smiled, even as she recalled the icy blonde who looked as though she would have preferred a little boredom. "I really have to go." She walked to the door, and raised her hand to knock for Peter to open it.

"I could read your thoughts."

She looked back at the lonely looking man seated at the leaf-strewn table.

"That day I plucked you and Nyssa from Jericho. I heard your voice as though you spoke in my ear. 'Home . . . home.' The stronger it grew, the easier it became for me to reach you. You prayed for home and that brought you to me. What do you think that could mean?"

Lauren met that sad blue gaze. Minutes passed. Then she knocked on the door and left without replying. Perhaps because she didn't know the answer.

Or perhaps because she did.

SHE TOOK HER time walking back to her car, pausing every so often to gaze into store windows. Every so often, something claimed her attention, a flicker of brightness that seemed to come from inside the glass. It could have been someone, a stranger, watching her from the depths of the shop. Or it could have been an image of a young woman no longer a stranger. Once of this world, but now a traveler in other, unfamiliar places, passing through for a moment to say *hello . . . I'm all right . . . I'm better now.*

You did the right thing.

Lauren stopped in front of one window, and waited. This time she picked out a flash of pale hair. But by the time she pressed her face to the pane to get a closer look, the figure had vanished, leaving her staring at herself.

ACKNOWLEDGMENTS

Thanks to Alis Rasmussen and Dr. Robert Littman, Professor and Chair of Classics at the University of Hawai'i at Mánoa, for their assistance with Hebrew and details from the Book of Enoch. Big thanks to best beta reader David Godwin. Thanks to my agent, Jennifer Jackson of DMLA, and my editor, Kelly O'Connor. Thanks also to Pamela Spengler-Jaffe, Caroline Perny, and the rest of the great team at Harper Voyager.

ABOUT THE AUTHOR

Alex Gordon resides in the Midwest. When she isn't working, she enjoys watching sports and old movies, running, and playing with her dogs. She dreams of someday adding the Pacific Northwest to the list of regions where she has lived. She is the author of *Gideon*.